Desired Haven

Evelyn M. Richardson

DESIRED HAVEN

Peoples Book Club

CHICAGO

AUTHOR'S NOTE

I wish to acknowledge my indebtedness: to *Crowell's History of Barrington Township* for facts; to Ellen Fulton for constructive criticism; to my family for help and understanding; and to my fishermen friends for patience in answering questions. All characters in this book are entirely fictitious, and any resemblance to any living person is purely coincidental.

This is a special edition, published exclusively for the members of PEOPLES BOOK CLUB, Box 6570A, Chicago 80, Illinois. It was originally published by Macrae Smith Company.

Manufactured in the United States of America

TO MOTHER

Foreword

THIS STORY IS LAID ON THE SHORES OF AN IRREGULAR NOVA SCOTIAN bight whose waters share the surge and recoil of Fundy's turbulence and the Atlantic's profounder currents. Southerly storms sweep the bay unbroken, but three sides are guarded by mainland hills, a wooded headland and a broken string of islands.

The largest and outermost of these islands is roughly circular, a mile or so in diameter; it humps its back against the southerlies and thrusts a shoulder out as breakwater for the snug anchorage in its lee. From this small deep harbor a passage leads into a large cove, too shallow and inaccessible for any but its own craft. Boisterous winds find and whip the gray-green waters, but when the winds sleep, islets bejewel the damascened surface; shore spruces lean above the full tide's lifted mirror.

The faces of islands and mainland are alike freckled with the residue of a glacial cap: rocks of all shapes and sizes, from huge flat-sided boulders that loom like fish sheds out of the prevalent fog, down to polished pebbles that fit a boy's throwing hand. Along the low shoreline sea-scoured folds of bedrock thrust into the tide.

The people have some of the shore's granite in their faces—the strength and often the rigidity—but it is a granite fretted by storms and tides into a beauty of its own. Bedrock and salt water make a rightful setting for these men and women who, almost without exception, trace their ancestry back through the Plymouth Pilgrims to the English of the North Sea ports and to the Vikings.

Before the *Mayflower's* famous voyage, the French had known this region which endured as an Acadian seigniory for more than a century of alternating French and British ownership, while between the scattered fur-posts and fishing hamlets Micmac canoes slipped among the fringing islands and up the brown rivers as they had done before the white man's coming.

The Acadians had been scattered in exile and their lands offered to New England settlers when in 1761 a handful of Cape Cod families arrived to build new lives near the teeming fisheries. They

7

had crossed the open sea in their own small vessels, cabins crowded with seasick women and children, holds and decks packed with chattels and livestock. None had wealth but few came empty-handed; and of greater value than any cargo, they brought to this new land strength and skill, a mighty faith and a mind to work.

At Barrington, snug behind Cape Sable Island, they weathered the early difficult years. A newly planted settlement of less tenacious stock might well have been uprooted when the storms of the Revolution were so soon added to the pioneer privations and the pull of blood and memories; but this clung to the rocky shore until the skies had cleared. Then it sprang to work—in fields and woodland, in shipyards and upon the wide water. Young and restless spirits began a movement away from the parent center: a few, with red mud sullying the good salt water in their veins, made farms along the rivers or from the primeval forest behind the preempted shore lots; but most moved to adjacent capes and harbors so that they and their sons were soon thrusting their blunt-bowed fishing boats into the sea and spreading their catches to dry at every inlet along the southwestern coast.

Some of this highly independent breed chose the added isolation and greater proximity to the fishing grounds offered by the islands, and not until the railways' rigid steel and puffing engines replaced the flowing wakes and quiet sails of the coastal packets did mainland attractions drain life from the isles. Today the outer harbors, where sailing vessels clustered, lie empty. The grandsons of the wind-ships' crews are skilled and courageous seamen, but in their motored craft they return each night to sheltered wharves.

The past does not die, however. It lives on in today's seamanship and in tales passed down through the generations. To some of us it speaks from abandoned island homes and decaying wharves. Stories heard from lips long stilled clamor to be shared.

I have attempted to draw only an imaginary harbor and settlement. Resemblances to the shore I know and love have crept in against my will and remain, if they do so, only from my lack of skill in erasing them. Incidents, breathlessly absorbed in my childhood, have found their way into the story, but I have long forgotten exact details and these I have twisted to suit my purpose. Characters and names are, of course, completely fictitious.

8

Desired Haven

Chapter 1

IN THE GAMBREL-ROOFED HOUSE ON GRANNIE'S HEAD, MERCY NICKerson stood before the kitchen's southern window. The waning December sunlight misted her coifed braids palely, bronzed her heavy lashes, and gilded the folds of her russet linsey-woolsey. Under the coarse unflattering fabric her tall young form was round and strong, but her head drooped wearily as she pressed her brow against a small, cold pane and her fingers gripped the thin sash with near despair. Her gray eyes were darkened by anxiety, and her lips, though retaining the curves of remembered smiles, were firmly closed upon fear. Prince's Cove boasted prettier girls than Captain Sam's Mercy, whose face was neither plump nor dimpled, and whose mouth was judged too wide, but at a village gathering many turned from prettiness to watch her slow, sweet smile.

Her gaze skimmed the sloping field and stopped at the rocky outer shore where a woman, head-down into the wind that whipped and whirled her tattered hems, struggled towards a spray-drenched shanty.

In the draining light Nabby Nolan's gray shack looked its most disreputable. Ma was right in declaring it an eyesore and a disgrace to the Nickerson lot. And for all Pa didn't hold with the Cove's fear of witches, Mercy remembered that when he had sailed away she had breathed easier because neither Nabby Nolan nor her eldritch mother had been on the foreshore. Mercy shrank inwardly from Nabby, who glared spitefully and would never return a civil greeting; yet now her heart went out to the solitary figure that reminded her somehow of a wing-broken gull—earthbound and forgotten by its own, but fiercely defiant.

11

Though I suppose if you've no one to love but a grouty old mother, you don't have the worry and fear for your menfolk heavy on you, Mercy conceded with a sigh.

Nabby's flapping skirts and billowing shawl bent into a gust and disappeared around the corner of her bleak home, while Mercy's eyes slipped over its sagging roof to search the long, irregular bay beyond.

Forming the bay's western side, Pilot Point jutted, low and straight, into the cobalt water, its trees notching the paler sky like black saw teeth. The Point's tip lay three miles away so that the heavy surf breaking there appeared only as white yarn mending the long reef-slits in the sea's crumpled fabric. On the bay's eastern shore, hilly Ryder's Island was white-ringed, and so was Narrah Isle, but the twisting channel separating it from Grannie's Head darkened peacefully as it broadened into Prince's Cove.

From the opposite window Mercy could have overlooked the Cove (for Grannie's Head rose between it and the bay), but nothing was moving on its sheltered waters and nothing, she admitted sadly, on the sea before her. No village craft had put out today, and what homeward-bound vessel could have weathered last night's gale?

From dark till dawn huge seas had trampled up the bay and flung themselves against Grannie's Head, shaking its very bedrock and sending a shudder through the stout timbers of the Nickerson home. Above the billows' thunder the wind had screamed and torn at roofs and chimneys, or in squalls whipped Mercy's window with sheets of rain till every sash bubbled and the monotonous drip from a leak marked the storm's momentary lulls.

At daybreak the gale, weary of the ocean's subservience to its southerly lashing, had struck suddenly from the north, buffeting the house anew as it passed over the shore, where broken seas and broken rocks contended, and on out to challenge the proudly cresting breakers. By midafternoon the surges, flattened to half their morning height, were dragging against the ebb's pull and the wind's push to dissolve in harmless suds among the gutted ledges.

Now towards sundown, sea and wind had called a truce; the billows sank back exhausted; the wind lowered its shrieking rage to a fretful whine; and, though it had taken no part in the day's struggles, the dropping sun looked wasted and worn.

Mercy, too, was wearied by her own warring hopes and fears and by the outer turmoil, though she had lived all her seventeen years here where sea and earth perpetually grappled, where at a whim the wind threw its power against one or the other—and all three lay in wait for passing ships.

Each sunset for weeks she had strained to catch a glimpse of sails; always the bay had worn this emptiness and indifference. Had the *Didamia* been hove down by giant seas or chewed to splinters on some lee shore? Had the hurricanes or pirates of southern waters claimed her?

Two months had passed since that sparkling October morning when the thirty-ton schooner had slipped out the mouth of Prince's Cove, Havana-bound with her full cargo of dried fish. She had been a pretty sight as the crew worked her through the channel. Pa as master and builder had had reason to be proud, for she had been fashioned from hackmatack, spruce and oak off the Cove's woodlots.

From the front steps Mercy had watched her father and brothers moving about the decks. At sixteen, despite their smooth faces and the golden curls under their woolen caps, the twins were men grown, but there'd been no mistaking their slender suppleness as the mainsail swung clear. Long Tom Doty and Obie Knowles, who completed the crew, had worked in the Nickerson boatyard from the day the *Didamia's* keel was laid until the last block was rove, and had taken their pay in vessel shares according to custom. Long Tom's hooked nose, 'twas said, could smell out weather still abrewing and (Mercy had smiled to herself), if Tom was close-mouthed, Little Obie, the cook, would offset him.

Clear of the land, the crew had set the square topsail for the long free run down the bay and, with all her new canvas taut, the *Didamia* had given herself to the racing ebb and leaned to the

13

lee foam. Then Mercy had seen her father's tall figure swing loosely about and stand looking back at his home, the lone house on the headland just cleared.

Surely he had seen the three white splashes against the gray porch where his wife and daughters spread their aprons cornerwise to the wind. Ma's pride in the new schooner bearing her name had known no bounds, but it hadn't been the *Didamia* scudding down the bay that had held her there in the cold morning breeze; her husband's every voyage had been sped by the farewell flutterings of her snowy apron.

Dreaded Cape Sable had crouched, a thin line of the sea's rim. Mercy had pictured it, its silver dunes curling like a wind-blown mane and, purple against the jade of underwater sand, its ledges waiting like unsheathed claws for the entrails of any ship wind and sea might harry within reach. The *Didamia* had had nothing to fear in that fair weather, but the womenfolk had watched until she was hull down beyond the Cape. Those who sailed her would have been thinking (even as those who watched her snowy canvas fade into the empty blue) how many ships cleared the bay to enter it never again.

I mustn't cry, Mercy told herself severely. *I mustn't let Ma think I've give up hope.*

Damie, a small neat figure at her firelit spinning wheel, watched her daughter's silhouette. *Ah, how she favors her pa*, she thought with a tug at her sore heart. *The twins, too, and Charles, they all take after Sam. Only Bethiah's like my people.* And though the Cove considered Sam "a homely man till ye git to know him" Damie would have been well content if every one of her children had resembled the big, yellow-haired husband she adored.

She asked no questions now as Mercy turned from the window since the girl's silence rendered them needless.

I never expected aught else, she assured herself, but her hand trembled as it relaxed from the tenseness of waiting. If the *Didamia* had gone down she was left with nary one of her four men. The dull ache for Charles, her first-born, missing now for two

14

long years, mingled with the new and sharper pain for Sam and the twins. But in Damie's code idleness was the unforgivable sin and her busy hands at the spindle denied what her fearful heart might moan in the gathering twilight.

From habit she spoke sharply, "Now Mercy, don't just stand there, gawkin'. High time that Bethiah was a-gettin' home with them cows. I do declare she's the pokiest mortal!" The wheel whirred and Damie's black eyes snapped in the firelight. "Though the little hussy's fast enough to go a-rarin' and a-tearin' over fences, strippin' the clothes from her back."

Her daughter reflected wearily, *Poor 'Thiah! She'll not hear the end of that torn petticoat for many a day. Why can't Ma copy Pa's patient ways?* Then in a rush of pity and understanding, *But 'tis hard for her, with no sign of the* Didamia *after so long.*

Aloud she exonerated her sister, "Like enough with the wind this way the cows are in the woods and that would keep 'Thiah. I'll go call her."

She went quietly through the big kitchen—so terribly empty without the talk and clutter of menfolk—while the firelight reddened the scoured softwood floors and the ceiled walls, lustred the plates racked on the dresser, danced on the eastern windows where the twilight's quicksilver turned the panes to mirrors.

The back entry held a wooden washbowl and mug of soft soap on a split-log bench, a full water bucket and extra towels hung hopefully upon the peg, for Damie held that men were great ones to splash and splutter and leave more dirt and water on the towel than in the washbowl.

The damp chill of the entry, which got no sun during the short winter days, struck deep after the kitchen's warmth, and when Mercy stepped out on the back stoop the air, though still mild, smelt plain of cold not far off.

Prince's Cove, settled by five families, now boasted more than thirty homes. To Mercy, looking across the quivering water, the village houses along its shore, actually widely separated and placed to overlook the channel mouth, appeared to cluster about Meet-

15

inghouse Hill. The small unpainted cottages looked weatherworn but as stubbornly set as the gray boulders about them. Behind their narrow clearings the forest stretched black and primeval, for the Cove men turned inland only for firewood and for timbers to carry them seaward.

Standing on the stoop, Mercy could feel at her back the abiding strength of the Nickerson house, alone on its headland and old by local measure, for it had been the first frame house this side of Barrington. More than fifty years had passed since it replaced Grandfather Prince's log cabin.

For a few moments she daydreamed, picturing the shoreline of those olden days when virgin hardwood had met high water, except where waving marsh grass fringed the tidal estuaries. No houses nor fish stores had stood among the rocks, no small boats had ridden at jone-poles, no vessels at anchor, when Prince Nickerson and his bride came to the Cove. And the tale of their coming was one Mercy loved.

On a May day in 1783 young Prince Nickerson had straightened his long back and lifted his blue eyes from the potato patch to such a sight as was never before or after viewed from a Barrington hillside. The cloud of canvas on the southern skyline rapidly became British men-of-war and lofty transports carrying the first Loyalists to found Shelburne town. Rapt by the noble ships, Prince had given no thought to their unfortunate passengers. He could not know that one press of sails wafted Abigail McLarren, the girl who would be his wife before another potato-planting time.

A few weeks later, easing his goosewinged skiff westerly before a savage summer storm, Prince had tacked into a small cove, almost hidden by a narrow island and an overlapping mainland point. His keel might well have been the first to cleave the water of the twisting inlet. He had landed on the wooded headland to wait out the gale and found himself dreaming of a house placed to overlook the outer bay on the one side and the snug cove on the other. Before he set his homeward course he had picked the

16

spot where he would build, *when the time comes,* he had told himself, *for me to pick a wife and make a home.*

That time had soon come. The very next spring Abigail had named the headland. As she and Prince approached it in their sloop, while the newly erected log cabin was still hidden in the trees ahead and Barrington's familiar shores were far astern, the tumbled boulders of the foreshore had momentarily aligned themselves into a bold but benign profile. "Look, Prince," she had said, shyly touching her husband-since-the-morning, "See the granite head smiling to welcome us."

So they called the hitherto nameless capelet "Granite Head," but to the families who soon settled the cove's inner shore, "Grannie's Head" had a homelier ring, and Abigail's Narrow Isle, across the channel from her cabin, became "Narrah." But the shallow basin was never anything but Prince's Cove, in honor of the first-comer who proved the settlement's mainstay and who bore a name* handed down through generations to tie (with however fraying a thread) this new shore to the homeland.

Abigail, who had been helped to bed by a sleepy maid after New York's Tory balls, and whose heaviest task had been the making of her father's posset, learned to cook and scrub; to plant and hoe, since Prince must be on the fishing grounds from daylight to dark; to shear and wash and spin wool from their sheep; to milk the cow and churn the butter; to bring her children into the world with only a neighbor's clumsy help; to nurse them through their illnesses, far from a doctor; to follow a tiny coffin to the corner field, so soon set apart as the family burning ground.

At first the other women, suspicious of all outside the close-knit Barrington families, were distant from Prince's Loyalist wife by more than the mile-long shore path between them; but Abigail developed an unexpected skill as nurse and midwife, and her spare figure sculling Prince's dory to the landing place of a stricken family became the Cove's conception of a ministering angel. A conception that had endured, for old voices softened

*Thomas Prince or Prence was an early Plymouth Colony governor.

17

when they told Mercy, "You'm like yer Grammie Abigail. Ye sh'd be proud to walk in her footsteps." And Mercy was.

Forty years ago Sam, the youngest of Abigail's brood, had been born in the house on Grannie's Head. He loved every silvered shingle of it, and he had passed that love of home on to his children, though only Mercy felt with him the tug of the past upon the present. She shrugged it off and came back to the anxieties of the ending day.

From across the Cove the windows in Captain Ephie Doane's kitchen ell contentedly flashed back the pale sunset. They might well be content—the Doane brig rode safe at anchor—but Mercy knew other hearts were as heavy as her own after a day of fruitless watching.

The barn lay between her and the open trees of the pasture, but she hopefully raised her clear young voice, "Be—thi—ah! 'Thi—i—iah!" As if in echo, across the darkening water drifted other high voices calling other loiterers home to supper in firelit kitchens.

Bethiah answered gaily and soon appeared, alder switch in hand, behind the two plodding cows. At twelve Bethiah was dark and quick like her mother, but her twinkling eyes and the pert tilt of her nose were none of Damie, while her mouth's one-sided quirk was Captain Sam's all over again.

Her giggling and flightiness caught the bitter edge of Damie's tongue though Sam was wont to say, "Now, now, wife; she's naught but a child." Damie would sniff and remind him *she* had been out to work at twelve, but her scoldings were mostly a sop to her driving conscience.

Mercy waited, hugging herself against the increasing chill, until Bethiah had stanchioned her charges and tossed hay into the mangers. Finally the younger sister ran up the steps and slipped her hand into Mercy's.

"Ma mad?" she asked carelessly. Her mother's tirades slid off Bethiah like the proverbial water off a duck, and indeed Damie

18

had ground for her reiterated complaint that none of her family paid her words any heed; her chidings had become a background noise, ever present like the surf's roar or the tide's lapping, so that only a real storm or a deep calm roused them to awareness.

"Not so very mad, 'Thiah. Only worried," Mercy reassured her fondly. Then hand in hand they turned to scan the bay.

Suddenly Mercy's grip tightened, her eyes sought Bethiah's and saw there the reflection of her own incredulous joy. Together they looked again, and *yes!* Catching the sunset on her scanty canvas, a vessel was rounding Pilot Point into the bay.

Bethiah, hood dangling, skirts billowing and black braids straight out with her going, tore through the entry and into the kitchen with Mercy close behind. Face aglow, the child tugged at her mother's arm. "Ma! Oh Ma! The *Didamia!* Rounding Pilot Point from the west'rd. Come *see!* Quick, afore the light goes."

Damie could not stop the first rush of joy from flooding her face and crumbling the harsh lines of worry and fear, but not for the world would she have her daughters guess her emotion. Besides, she warned herself out of a lifelong distrust of good news, the girls might be mistaken.

She had straightened her face and was herself again before she replied crisply, *"See!* A great lot I'd see this time o' day. Like enough 'taint yer pa after all. The's other vessels in the world besides the *Didamia,* milady. It don't pay to go countin' yer chickens . . ."

"Ma-aw!" Bethiah almost wailed her impatience with her mother's pessimism and her trite sayings. "You know very well the's no other vessel due in the Cove. It's almost *bound* t'be the *Didamia* with Pa and the twins."

She ran to the window for another look.

"Tsch." Damie put her wheel aside. "If tis yer pa, he'll be like to die o' shame at havin' a wild Injun fer a dorter." She pretended not to hear Bethiah's giggle against the pane.

"Mercy, you git them sea ducks Mr. N'miah sent us. You know how yer pa and the twins relish a good duck stew; 'twont take

19

but a minit t' get the feathers off and the innards out, whilst I go to the pork barrel." Damie bustled about preparing to welcome home her men. "With the wind dyin' out an' all, they'll be a good spell a-beatin up the bay."

Tasks were not lacking to pass the time of waiting; the cows must be milked and bedded and the milk strained into the skimming-bowls; the woodbox filled; the birch broom applied again to the spotless floor; the goosewing put to service among the hearthstones; potatoes, onions and turnips added to the ducks simmering in the iron pot. Then Damie decided the womenfolks would eat and be free to serve the men their supper.

Mercy moved with a miraculously lightened heart as she set out the cornmeal porridge and the jug of rich milk, the Barbados molasses, the riz-bread and the butter, and laid the pewter spoons and horn-handled knives next the earthenware plates. Though Damie had her china set in the parlor cupboard, she would as soon have tossed them among the shore rocks as set them out for family use.

When the meal was ready, Damie shamed herself into eating, lest the girls think her unseemingly moved, and she commanded the impatient Bethiah to finish her plate of porridge though that young lady swore she was bound to puke at the next mouthful.

Mercy, too, lost her appetite to excitement and happiness. How blessed to know that Pa and the twins were almost home, bringing stories and gifts from strange ports and a feeling of completion before the winter. But for the first time her woman's heart, awaking from childhood's sleep, sensed that her joy lacked something which her mother's held; realized that father and brothers returning were not the same as husband or lover. . . . Longing and unfulfilment stirred faintly.

I'll be having my own man back from a voyage, all in good time, she scolded herself while her gray eyes softened behind their thick lashes and her lips curved. She dreamed vaguely of this one or that among the Cove's young men, but none satisfactorily filled the role of husband welcomed home. Then Little Obie popped into her mind—unbidden, though the *Didamia's* fat young cook

was an avowed suitor. His sheep's eyes and high-pitched mono-
logues on Little Obie were a source of shared fun between Mercy
and her father, in spite of Damie's insistence that Obie was honest
and good-living, and many a girl went through the woods to pick
up a crooked stick at the last, and she for one didn't know as it
paid to be too choosey—and Sam needn't sit there grinnin' fit to
split his face!

Memories of Little Obie's full-moon countenance wearing what
he considered a lovelorn expression quenched Mercy's brief flame
of unrest. As she rose to clear the table she was humming happily
and she soon broke into an old song in which Bethiah joined with
interpretive gestures whenever her mother's back was turned.

> There was an old man came over the sea,
> Ah-hmm, ah-ha, but I'll not have him.

The dishrag waved defiantly as Bethiah's tilted nose and down-
drawn mouth registered violent repudiation of the old man's suit,
while Mercy's clear voice held controlled laughter,

> Came over the sea, a-courtin' me
> With his crinsome, cransome,
> Flourishsome, handsome,
> Billy Mo-dicks, Mo-die, Mo-dee.

The song went through its many verses with accompanying
flourishes and shrieks of laughter from Bethiah.

"You'm workin' up a gale, sure as you'm alivin'," warned
Damie, to whom merriment—like a fine day—must be a weather-
breeder. Then she remembered that gales had lost their worst
terror, now the *Didamia* was in. She recalled that Sam liked to
hear the girls singing about their work and often joined them
with his deep hum. Their young voices blended sweetly, and
Damie, completely tone deaf, told herself smugly, *Thank goodness they can carry a tune. Not like some ye hear.*

Meanwhile she kept the fire leaping since Sam and the twins
would watch for the glimmering windows of home. As plain as if

she heard him she knew how Sam would say, "I smelled duck stew as soon as ever I rounded Pilot Point," and she would sniff and reply, "Most like! I never heard my cookin' smelled *that* bad!" But she didn't know if she'd ever want Sam to stop codding her like he did.

The dishes dried, Bethiah hovered near the window and called to the others as the *Didamia,* on her short tacks up the bay, first showed and then hid the light on her foremast.

Other eyes must have caught the glint of sails at sunset for as the schooner neared, lanterns and flares wavered from the Nickerson wharf, on the inner side of Grannie's Head, and Ephie Doane's shrill old quaver rose to Mercy's ears as she stepped out to empty the dishwater. The men of the village were gathered to welcome the *Didamia.*

Before the schooner reached the Cove's entrance the moon rose, full and clear, behind the trees of Narrah, pouring molten silver into the cupped anchorage and turning the shoreline to ebony. The two girls threw on their shawls then and stepped out upon the back stoop. The air was dry and sweet-sharp from off the land; and all her life after, whenever Mercy caught that tang of a still winter night, she was back again beside Bethiah on the stoop, watching the silver path across the Cove, the wharf spiles white and black with moonlight and shadow, the small boats nudging out into the glory, the flares' red flames almost quenched in the moon's lustrous flood.

Then the *Didamia,* on her final tack, passed the shoulder of Narrah, slipped through the channel, catching the moonblaze on her sails, and whispered through the silvered water to her anchorage. Mercy stood unmoving, bound with a million threads of beauty and happiness.

A few words of command, an anchor's splash, the harsh rustle of canvas, a rattling of mast-hoops, come clearly from the vessel as the crew went about snugging down. The girls returned to the grateful warmth of the kitchen while all the house gathered itself in a tender expectancy.

After many minutes had shamelessly outstayed their welcome, voices sounded along the winding path from the wharf and from across the fields as the crew and their friends dispersed. Bethiah could contain herself no longer. With skirts and black braids again flying, she left the kitchen door wide open behind her, though Damie clicked disapprovingly as she stirred the stew. Mercy paused to light candles, one for the window overlooking the path, one for the entry bench; then she followed Bethiah out onto the stoop and the firelight flowed after her.

Halfway up the path were the twins, casting identical shadows across the moonlit field. Mercy failed to note the small figure between them, because almost at the foot of the stoop was her tall, broad-shouldered father and Little Obie, dumpy as ever in his sea coat. She looked no farther, for between them was a stranger, plainly in need of their supporting arms. Not quite so tall as her father, he topped Little Obie handsomely and, though he wore sea clothes, he was obviously no seaman.

In a momentary flare from the fire Mercy saw his pale face lift towards where she stood. She made a half-step forward and put out her hands in a compassionate gesture. Unaccountably her heart sang to her, "Already you welcome your man from the sea." And she did not stop to chide it, "This is a stranger!"

She saw him drop her father's arm, gather himself upright and take a firm step before he stumbled. Captain Sam's strong arm caught him.

"Steady as ye go, son," he said gently and helped the young man up the narrow steps.

Chapter 2

MEN POURED THROUGH THE DOORWAY AND FLOODED THE KITCHEN with the clumping of sea boots, the surge of talk and laughter;

with the strong forecastle smells of bilge and spray-soaked woolens; with the happiness of homecoming.

Captain Sam saw the stranger comfortably stretched upon the couch before he drew first his tiny wife into one arm and his daughters into the other and held them all close and treasured for a moment.

Not until he had released her did Damie notice the small boy with enormous black eyes. He was almost lost in one of Sam's sea coats, though he had worked a hand through each huge cuff and was clinging with fingers like bird claws to the twin on either side. "My soul and buddy!" she gasped at sight of this second stranger, but she turned first to her own boys.

Prince's Cove might long ago have given up the struggle to distinguish between them, but Damie needed no second glance to tell her which was Isaac and which Levi. She reached up to kiss their smooth, salt cheeks as shyly as if these tall youths were no kin at all instead of her own flesh and blood.

Little Obie had stepped in to share the welcome home and to note Damie's surprise at having two strangers landed upon her. He now attempted a few ingratiating remarks, but finding Mercy completely absorbed in the others, he said his "good nights" to hearty if absent-minded "Come ag'ins" and let himself out the back entry. Stumbling through the rocky pastures towards his own home nearer the village, he ruminated, *Don't it beat all how things come in bunches! A man could spin quite a yarn about this trip!*

His face fell as he realized he couldn't spread his story before morning, when other versions would be abroad. He pondered morosely his mother's long tongue and the deafness that served her so conveniently. *Fer wunst, Ma'll have to listen to my tell. Leastwise,* he conceded, *fer a little while.*

Back in the Nickerson kitchen Sam spoke gravely, with a gesture towards the couch, "I've brought you an extra man to do for, wife." Then for her ear alone, "It might be our Charles, this very night, in need of . . ."

Damie cried out in pain, "Oh, do hush now, Sam. As though you needed to remind me!" Then, "But where did ye find him? Has the' been a wrack? Oh, Sam, I might 'a' knowed from yer face. He's nigh drowned, that's what—and us standin' here ajawin'."

"Now, Damie," Sam soothed her. "No need to make a touse. He'll be all right. But we got to the Ragged Ledges noan too soon."

He told her how off the Cape they had fought out the gale, how shortly after dawn the *Didamia* was plunging and rolling through the ugly cross-seas, her sails close-reefed, her decks awash. A smur on the horizon ahead meant the hills behind Prince's Cove and each man was watching for well-known rips and breaking shoals.

"My feet were fairly itching for Grannie's Head rocks under my boots," Captain Sam confessed.

So near home his weary eyes had relaxed their long vigilance against sea and sky and the ship's boat to leeward might well have been passed unnoticed; but as the *Didamia* lifted to a sea, Levi had hurried aft.

"Pa," he said, "I though I caught sight of something, 'bout two p'ints off the leeward bow there. A plank, most like. But it could be a boat, low in the water."

So Captain Sam had swung the *Didamia* down on the flotsam, had come up into the wind and lain flogging and slatting while the down-haul boat had fought its slow way to the bit of wreckage and back. Then a young man had been lifted aboard—more dead than alive.

In the after-cabin, Captain Sam had finally succeeded in forcing some rum between his clenched teeth; then by rubbing and rolling had started the blood through the fine young limbs, corpselike and cold. Little Obie had slithered between galley fire and cabin with hot bricks and warm blankets and, before the *Didamia* rounded Pilot Point into the bay, the young man had shown signs of returning consciousness.

25

"I'm afraid his ship was lost off the Gannets last night," the captain concluded soberly. "If so, few escaped. Long Tom says there were no other bodies in the lifeboat."

"But this *boy*, Sam, poor pinnikin' mite, ain't he off the wrack, too?" Damie's face showed the confusion into which so many puzzles had thrown her.

Her husband dropped a big hand on the child's untidy head. "This is Philip Cadell and I cal'ate he's our boy now. Let me tell you, pinnikin' or not, he saved the *Didamia* and every man jack aboard."

Damie could only gape in bewilderment and a rising suspicion that she was being codded.

"From pirates," Sam added carelessly, but couldn't keep his crooked grin from breaking out.

"Pirates! That baby! Now, Sam'l Nickerson, I *know* you'm a-yarnin'." Damie flounced away. "Ye'd best get washed up fer supper, the lot o' ye. Time enough for such spinnin'-off after ye've et." She turned to her son, "And Levi, you take that coat off the poor child. He's wore out with the weight of it."

The seafarers found accustomed seats and the first happy confusion subsided. As Mercy set the table once more, she found her attention pulled again and again to the stranger lying in a semi-stupor. She noted the short nose, the finely molded lips, pinched and blue though they were, each contour of face unbelievably handsome to her young eyes, in spite of its startling pallor against black hair and sideburns. But when the stranger stirred and opened his eyes, she was quick to avert her own.

"Ah-h-h-h," he breathed, and the knotted ropes beneath him squeaked as he turned another portion of his sea-chilled body to the fire's tingling bliss. The bare walls of a strange room reeled and dipped so that he gladly closed his eyes again and drifted away from them.

Mercy longed to have him waken, to share the room's warm love as well as its fire. Suddenly (while she stood rooted at the table's edge) she imagined herself gathering that curly black head

26

to her bosom, pressing her cheek to that unshaven one, and knew a sweep of tenderness mixed with a wilder flame, sweet and fierce beyond enduring. It died as swiftly as it had risen, but amazed and shaken that this, and more, lay in the unfathomed depths of her womanhood, Mercy fumbled with the milk jug and kept her blazing face downcast lest it betray her to any casual glance. What would Ma think!

But her mother, like a quick blackbird, was darting back and forth between the fire (where the stew emitted a tantalizing fragrance whenever she lifted the kettle cover) and the scrubbed center table. The neat black wings of her hair lay as smooth and tight as water and a determined hand could plaster them, and she tilted her head birdwise first on one side and then on the other as her bright eyes went from husband to sons and back. She would have thought shame of herself had she guessed how much showed in her face.

When the stranger next stirred, Damie flew to him and laid an experienced hand upon his forehead. "Stay jest as ye be. You'm only *beginnin'* t' thaw out."

She returned to the fire, removed the pot cover, and sniffed. "Done! Now, Bethiah, you fetch the chair from the bedroom; Mercy, you set them plates t' git pipin'."

Just as she had known he would, Sam declared, "I smelled something peculiar the minute we rounded the Point. I said to myself, 'Damie's got one o' them horrible stews of hers over the fire.'"

But though Damie tossed her head, she found to her surprise that she couldn't force the planned retort past the lump in her throat. So, instead, she gave the stranger a long considering look and decided, "He can have some bread sopped in gravy; he'll feel perkier after a bite t' eat."

The young man bore out Damie's theory that life held few ills that "a bite t' eat" could not alleviate, for he obviously responded to the bread and gravy, though he turned from the mug of tea with its generous 'lasses sweetening.

27

"Where am I?" he asked as he settled back upon the couch. Damie laughed when Grannie's Head and Prince's Cove proved foreign names to him. But his query gave her freedom to ask, "And where do *you* hail from? What might your name be?"

Every face turned to his as he answered, "I'm Dan Redmond, ma'am, from Dublin city bound for my uncle's home in Boston. Tell me," he demanded piteously of Captain Sam, as memory loosened his tongue, "what word, sir, of the *Morning Star?*" He pulled himself upward with a distraught look.

"Nothing new," Captain Sam soothed him. "By daybreak boats from all along will be out searching. Word will spread that judging from where I picked you up, a ship has struck on the Gannets."

"The Gannets! Yes, that's what a sailor cried when we struck, 'God be merciful! We've hit the Gannets!' As if the very name held doom."

Mercy thought she had never heard so charming a voice, though her Prince's Cove ears found its accents strange. She could have gone on listening forever, but Damie tugged the pillow into position and pushed her guest back upon it. "You'm to talk no more now, Mr. Redmond. Wait till yer strength comes back."

She turned her attention to the boy called Philip. When his tousled head had nodded over his supper Mercy had gone up the back stairs and prepared the trundle bed. Now, at his mother's bidding, Isaac set the child upon his feet. "Say 'Good night, all,' Philip, and I'll show ye to bed."

The boy shook the sleep from his eyes and walked slowly to where Damie sat. He bowed politely, then picked up her work-roughened hand and, to the family's astonishment, carried it to his lips before she could snatch it away. As he straightened, the boy's eyes sought Damie's, pleading for she knew not what; and she, bound by the ingrown shyness of years, couldn't take this young 'un in her arms before everyone. But perhaps her face again betrayed more than she guessed, for the child seemed satisfied. He slipped his hand confidingly into Isaac's big palm and

28

sent Levi the first smile the womenfolk had seen on his pointed, dark face. It was sweet rather than merry and above it his eyes kept their haunting pathos as he repeated Isaac's "Good night, all."

Nobody spoke as the boy's light steps echoed Isaac's heavier tread up the stairs, but Mercy noted that her mother folded her apron corner over the kissed hand and sat gazing into the fire until the dishes were put away and the family gathered close to hear the story of the voyage.

Chapter 3

"YOU REMEMBER," CAPTAIN SAM BEGAN, "WE HAD FAIR WEATHER AT the start. Three days out we ran into a rough, but the *Didamia* waded through it like a boy through a mud puddle. The rest of the voyage we never reefed a sail. Everything was smooth sailing in Havana, too; we sold our fish at once and loaded with sugar and molasses for Baltimore. On the last day I'd settled my business ashore and was anxious to get back aboard where all was ready to move out on the afternoon ebb."

He paused and explained, "You know, many a man's been knifed for sticking his oar in where it wasn't wanted, so that away from home I most generally look the other way from any fracas and tell myself there's no accounting for foreigners."

In no port would Captain Sam consider himself the foreigner.

"Well, hurrying along I turned a corner quick into the black shadow of a warehouse and almost stumbled over a child. At first there was only a little white face and then my eyes made out that a greasy-looking man had a boy by the arm and was twisting it cruel. It was a pitifully thin arm, but although he'd gone so pale, the child wasn't letting out a whimper. Somehow, right then and there, I forgot all about my rule for looking the other way—and what the Scripture says about being slow to wrath."

Captain Sam's eyes were made for their customary blue twinkle and his homely mouth fashioned for its humorous lopsided grin, but in his remembered anger his eyes were ice-hard and his mouth a clamped white slit.

"Before I knowed what I was doing I'd grabbed the man by the shoulder and spun him about. I cal'ate I looked mad—I did if what I was feeling *showed!* Anyway he dropped the boy's arm and began to chatter an amazing string.

"'Don't ye wave your stinking hands under *my* nose, nor spit your jabbering at *me,*' I gritted out, giving him a heave and the toe of my boot. He was scuttering for cover before he landed, almost."

"The boy hadn't taken his eyes off me," Sam went on. "You never saw such eyes! So I asked him, 'Well, bub, what's *your* name? And what's your parents thinking of, to leave a little sprit like you at loose ends?'

"To myself I said, 'A little Spaniard, most like, and won't understand ary word I utter.' But I hoped my voice might show him I meant kindly.

"I was taken aback when he replied plain and clear, 'I'm Felipe Cadell; my father and mother are dead, so they don't know I'm at loose ends.' His voice had an English sound like you hear in Halifax and it quivered a bit when he spoke of his ma and pa.

"'I run errands for seamen off the ships,' he said, proud-like. 'I earn my living that way.'

"Then he told me the big boys and wicked men often took his coins from him, and that the specimen just kicked was fond of threatening to slit the young 'un's throat and toss him to the fishes."

Damie could only moan and shake her head at that.

"'Well,' I said, 'you must have *someone* to turn to.' But he said no. No one since his mother had died of fever in the spring.

"Then he made me a rusty little bow and turned away as if he didn't want to bother me with his troubles, but not as if he had

30

anywhere special to go. The boy's ten but he looked no more than half Bethiah's age, and I couldn't bear to see his weary little droop and his forlorn way of walking. I recalled the twins and Charles —why, at that age they scarcely ever walked, but went skipping and running the day long! Fearing the bully I'd kicked might be waiting to take his spite out on the child, I couldn't go and leave him; yet I knowed the crew must be getting impatient for me to show up.

"So I called after him, 'Just a minute, son. If you've nobody, like you say, how about signing on as cabin boy this trip?' Of course, I no more needed a cabin boy than I needed tail feathers!

"The poor little fellah swung about and looked at me with those big eyes of his. He said, '*Si senor*—yes, sir. Thank you,' polite as could be; then burst into sobs fit to tear your heartstrings. So I picked him up—'bout the heft of a herring scale—and hurried along to where the small boat was waiting.

"Once aboard the *Didamia* I pushed the child into the galley and told Obie, 'Here's a nubbins for you. Fill him up and treat him good.'

"Well, I'd no sooner got aft when I heard a hail and said to myself, 'More foreigners,' thinking, of course, someone'd come after the boy. I was half glad, half sorry.

"The two men in the stern-sheets of the harbor-boat 'longside were foreigners right enough, heavy-featured, dark-complected— Spanish West Indians, I judged—and they had a battered sea chest at their feet.

"Both grinned and nodded like monkeys and while one stood up to speak me the great earrings of the seated man swung and glittered in the sun. I didn't take to either one.

"They declared they'd missed the vessel they'd engaged passage on and they must get to Baltimore. I wasn't anxious to have 'em though they flashed gold coins to show they could pay well, but they wouldn't take 'no' and I *could* swing two hammocks in the locker aft. They told me how bee-oo-tiful the *Didamia* was, and all that guff, so finally I said, 'Come aboard.'

"I couldn't pay much heed to 'em, we were getting under

31

weigh; but at the head of the after-companion the talker turned to ask if any aboard spoke Spanish. Thinking they wanted some o' their own to gab with, I told 'em, no, we were all Nova Scotians. They grinned some more and went below."

Captain Sam's blue eyes were looking inward upon a remembered scene. His audience waited.

"We cleared the harbor just before the sunset gun boomed out from Morro Castle." The captain turned to his older daughter, knowing her love of beauty. "I wish I had words, Mercy, for how sudden and bright the sunsets flame out and are gone in those latitudes. This one poured over the old castle like flung paint, ran down its rocks and spread over the harbor, crimson, violet, orange, any color you could name. Unnatural-like but beautiful beyond telling."

Mercy failed to visualize more glory than a summer sunset washing across the bay.

Her father went on, "Everything promised well for the return voyage, but that night under the huge stars a breath of forewarning came to me, plain as the night breeze on my cheek, and I shivered though the air was milk warm."

His audience stirred at mention of a premonition. The twins smiled, knowing all the story, but they listened as intently as Bethiah.

"Yet Long Tom didn't sniff a coming storm; the boy proved a good sailor and hearing him laugh with the twins, I'd feel glad I'd brought him aboard. Sometimes I feared Little Obie would swamp him with talk, but in spite of all his questioning all the cook could find out was that the child's father had been Spanish and his mother English. Probably we'll never know more; but I think Little Obie's right in vowing the boy comes of good stock. It's plain he's no wharf rat."

Damie nodded emphatic agreement. "For my part, I mistrust he's *highborn,* so polite and old-fashioned and all."

"Now 'Felipe' was no name for Prince's Cove tongues to curl around," her husband continued, "but 'Philip' suited everybody

32

fine. Little Obie prides himself he's as smart with needle and palm as he is with his galley-gear, and he coaxed and tormented us all until he got duds he could cut down for the boy. Meanwhile, the passengers proved little trouble though Long Tom claimed it gave him the shivers to look up quick and find their beady black eyes fixed on him sharp and spiteful-like; and it didn't make him feel a mite better when they flashed their toothy grins. He declared honest men would be more sober-faced with strangers.

" 'Them heathenish Spanish names,' Little Obie snorted, and called the strangers Yappy and Earrings. They didn't make of Philip though he often hung around them, and they had little to say to us. But they talked plenty to each other—leastways Earrings mostly listened and nodded, his big loops swinging, while Yappy did the talking.

"Little Obie used to tell me, 'I can't see, Cap'n, why he don't wear his tongue down to the stump! Sech outlandish gibberish, too! But I don't s'pose a man can help the talk he's been brung up to and the' seems no great harm in either of 'em.' But Obie sung a different tune after a bit.

"Off Cape Hatteras Tom took t' sniffing and muttering, and sure enough, we were soon fighting gales and headwinds, snatching sleep when we could. Then one afternoon, after the weather had seemed to moderate, I routed all hands out before a squall. They were scampering to shorten sail when Philip flew like a streak out of the after-companion way. He grabbed my sleeve, where I stood at the wheel, his face as white and his eyes as big as the time I first saw him. He began to sputter about pirates and I thought the child had taken leave of his senses.

" 'Captain,' he said over and over, 'they're getting their swords and pistols to kill you and take the schooner!' All the time he was half-crying because he couldn't make me understand that our precious passengers were figgering to heave me overboard, then have the crew at their mercy. And at first I *couldn't* credit it. Then I could. Several things came clear to me. I swung the

33

Didamia off before the wind, yelled for Isaac, and made for the after-companion way, snatching a belaying pin as I went.

"Soon Yappy stuck his head up, knife in mouth and pistol in hand. (A pretty sight!) He never knew what hit him. I hove him towards Isaac whilst I jumped square on Earrings and we went sprawling to the bottom of the steps, with me on top.

" 'Twas all over in a hurry and no harm done." He turned his hand to the firelight so that a white scar showed at the thumb's base. "The only wound of the whole fracas." He grinned. "And cut by an earring at that."

Then he sobered, "But their chest was crammed with cutlasses and such. 'Twas plain they'd planned to arm any who preferred a new captain to drowning, and to turn my *Didamia* into a pirate ship. I remembered then—when it was nigh being too late—that as they came aboard in Havana they wouldn't let Long Tom help them below and that the chest had seemed to drag heavy between them.

"Just as well we had them roped up when they learned how Philip had been their undoing—a little boy who always spoke English but who knew Spanish fully as well, and who'd soon caught enough of their talk to make him suspicious. That afternoon he'd crept down and listened at their door though he must have realized they'd make short work of him if they caught him.

"I often ponder on what would have happened if I hadn't befriended the boy." Captain Sam turned to his wife, "You see, Damie, why I say Philip Cadell is our boy, to do for so long as he needs our care."

Damie nodded. Bethiah, crying bitterly now that the story was happily ended, threw her arms about the embarrassed twins and kissed them wetly. Mercy reproached herself for paying so little attention to Philip. Without him there would have been no *Didamia* wafting her crew safe home through the moonblaze. Why, without him there'd have been no *Didamia* to pick up a stranger near the Ragged Ledges. Plainly he had been a chosen instrument of the Lord!

Her father was rounding off his story, for—to top all—when he'd gone ashore in Baltimore to swear out his protest of the attempted piracy, he'd found a warm welcome awaiting both men, and a reward of five hundred dollars posted for Yappy. Philip was more than ever the pet of the crew, and a full share of the reward money was voted into Captain Sam's care for the boy.

Having reloaded with flour for Barrington, the *Didamia's* crew left Baltimore in high spirits, only slightly dampened by Little Obie's never-ending tales of how he had suspicioned the strangers from the instant he had clapped eyes on them. "I could tell by the cut o' their jibs," he'd declare while Philip gazed in bewilderment; for fear of Little Obie's ridicule, the boy had hidden his own mistrust of the passengers.

"And what's more," the cook proclaimed over and over, so as to impress on the others his words of wisdom, "don't never put no faith in a man that has a lot t' say. Fer my part I never trusted Yappy for one minit."

The family laughed at Captain Sam's reproduction of Obie's chatter. Then Mercy brought her mind back from the storms and pirates to the firelit kitchen and the stranger. She saw his eyes open as stools and chairs were pushed back for the evening's final rite.

Captain Sam bent to light a candle at the dying fire, then placed it before him on the table as Damie reached the heavy Bible down from its corner shelf. The head of the house would consecrate the safe completion of another voyage.

All knew what tonight's reading would be and the well-worn Book opened under the knotted hand as if it shared the family's awareness. The father's slow voice took on depth and timbre to give full beauty to the words.

The walls drew near and the flickering fire steadied while the words rose and fell in sweeping cadences like those of the ocean. Long afterward Mercy was to know that the stranger listened with her, though he was still lifting and dropping on giant waves, so that some words were lost to him in the troughs though others

35

came to him clear and full as he was carried along on the crests.

> They that go down to the sea in ships, that do business in
>   great waters;
> These see the works of the Lord, and his wonders in the deep.
> For he commandeth, and raiseth the stormy wind,
> Which lifteth up the waves thereof.
> They mount up to the heaven,
> They go down again to the depths:
> Their soul is melted because of trouble.
> They reel to and fro, and stagger like a drunken man,
> And are at their wit's end.
> Then they cry unto the Lord in their trouble,
> And he bringeth them out of their distresses.
> He maketh the storm a calm,
> So that the waves thereof are still.
> Then are they glad because they be quiet;
> So he bringeth them unto their desired haven.

Captain Sam bowed his head. "Let us give thanks unto the Lord," he said, and every heart was humble.

When the Bible had been lifted back to its place, Damie turned briskly to her older daughter. "Do now, Mercy, see to the twins' beddin' whilst your pa and me help the poor young man."

Then as the house quieted Damie stepped into the warm kitchen-bedroom, her room and Sam's all these years, but now given over to their guest. She lifted the candle end from the bed-side chair and, shading it with her hand, gazed down upon the white face, relaxed in sleep. A nice-looking young man. About Charles' age, she thought with a stab of pain.

If the sea had tossed this youth into her life in recompense for her own boy, it was a sad bargain.

"I'll have noan of it," she whispered harshly in repudiation, so that the young man stirred in the feather bed's depths and spoke, "Mercy. A gentle name. A gentle maiden. . . . A . . . A desired haven."

He said no more and Damie tiptoed out. "Talkin' in his sleep," she breathed to herself, "and what he said don't make sense. But strange he should be usin' Mercy's name."

Chapter 4

THREE MORNINGS LATER DAN REDMOND OPENED HIS EYES TO FIND the sluggard winter sun already risen. As he drowsily identified the subdued voices and household stirrings outside his door, memory struck him awake with the horrors of the *Morning Star's* destruction. He closed his eyes to summon the calming recollections of a moonlit anchorage and a rocky path ending before an open doorway. Then Mercy Nickerson was there against his lids, her hair a golden halo, her slender figure and welcoming hands outlined in firelight. Was it only a few nights ago he had striven to reach her and known as in a dream, *Here is warmth and plenty after cold and empty years?*

To just such memories he had awakened each morning on Grannie's Head, and just as now the picture of Mercy waiting had brought him out upon the cold floor.

Mercy's day really began when Mr. Redmond appeared in the kitchen and gave them "good morning." Plainly youth and a sturdy constitution had completely repaired the ravages of shipwreck, for he looked alert and refreshed.

His water-damaged clothes had proved beyond Damie's utmost efforts at reclamation, but the mixture of homespun garments lent by the Nickerson men could not hide his slender, well-knit figure; his hair curled glossily; his eyes, deep-set and so dark a blue as to be almost black, had lost the shock and pain that at first marked them; his lips were no longer blue but warmly red and smiling. So handsome. With a sigh Mercy wished her face were not so thin, her hands so red from the scrub-water.

The guest was soon seated before a bowl of porridge and milk, while the sunlight slanted across the table, the fire danced and the kettle on the hob sang softly of menfolk home at last.

"Never before did I properly appreciate dishes that didn't jump about the table and a level floor under my feet." Dan's laugh asked his listeners to share his new valuation of stability. "Indeed, Mrs. Nickerson, your kindnesses have given this room the feel of home for me. I can't find words to tell you how grateful I am."

Obviously touched, Damie replied deprecatingly, "La! 'tis nawthin'. In a place where the menfolk follow the water, who wouldn't do what they could fer any shipwracked soul?"

Mercy had started to speak, but she let her mother's words suffice. As she moved about her work Dan's eyes followed her. Though tendrils, escaping from the heavy braids, caught and held the sunlight, her hair was a paler yellow than the red-gold it had first appeared and he knew a pang of disappointment. Her wide gray eyes under their bronze lashes seldom glanced his way.

And why should they? he asked himself wryly. *A sorry sight I must be in these garments.* Yet Mercy's apparent lack of interest piqued him, since Dan Redmond's handsome face and fine figure had found favor in the eyes of other maidens, while as for clothes, Mercy's own would have brought condescending smiles from his feminine acquaintances.

He couldn't know that a dozen times a day Mercy flushed, remembering that at first sight her heart had claimed this stranger whose speech and bearing showed him to be a gentleman, above the likes of Mercy Nickerson. She had determined that no one should guess how foolish and mistaken a heart could be, but she would have wept to know that Mr. Redmond thought her cold.

Others in the family need show no constraint. Bethiah greeted the guest merrily as she came in red-cheeked from feeding the hens, and Damie's voice was warm as she told how Sam and the twins had breakfasted two hours before and gone to the wharf, "With Philip trailin' like a dory on behind. Seems he can't let them out of his sight."

Her husband entered on the heels of those words. "Good morning, Mr. Redmond. No, don't get up! Make your breakfast, man, such as it is!

"I was wondering if you'd like to come with the twins and me to Barrington. There's no telling if this fair wind will hold, and information about the *Morning Star* should be laid with Lloyd's agent there. You could leave a letter for the first Boston-bound vessel so your folks won't worry." He glanced at the young man's face. "But maybe you don't feel up to another voyage so soon."

Dan knew the older man would understand should he hesitate to face the sea that had mauled him, but a glance out the window showed perfect sailing weather.

"Indeed, I feel completely myself again, thanks to you and your good wife." He bowed to Damie, then assured the captain, "I'd like to go along." Miss Mercy should not think him a coward.

Damie called the twins to join their father in a snatched "mug-up" while Bethiah fetched Dan heavy socks and mittens from the yarn-barrel's plentiful supply.

Descending the path to the sloop beside the wharf, Dan gulped deep of the exhilarating air, which flowed down, crisp and pure, from the northland. Reflections of stubby wharves and tilting fish sheds wavered across the Cove's crystal saucer to mingle with those of sloops and pinks riding at anchor. From a dory steering a most erratic course the shouts of small boys and the splash of clumsy oars rang joyously. The rough coast, having failed to destroy the stranger, seemed bent on charming him—and likely to succeed.

Once she had cleared the twisting channel the sloop, belying her clumsy appearance, stretched merrily down the bay.

Captain Nickerson at the tiller, and the twins braced against the weather-side, each wrapped himself in his own deliberations as in his salt-encrusted coat and sat wordless. Dan was never to know the twins well, for the high, slender yards of full-rigged ships had entangled their hearts and they were to leave home a few days later for a three-skysail-yarder out of Saint John; a ship that would carry them to adventure and a step towards that deck each would some day walk as master. They seldom spoke, even in the home, for they understood each other without words and felt little need of other communications.

Dan himself was preoccupied with his changed circumstances. Ryder's Island, passed well alee, was merely part of the unknown shoreline slipping by.

At Barrington Captain Sam led the way to Mr. Robertson's office at the head of a busy wharf and here, to the sober-faced Lloyd's agent who had recorded the final chapter in the stories of many ships, Dan made his statement.

Twenty-eight days out from Dublin the Boston packet, *Morning Star,* held the last of the Nova Scotian coast abeam and the passengers were growing excited and impatient as the end of a slow crossing neared. Suddenly a fog-breeze smothered down upon the clipper and by early nightfall had whipped itself into a gale with volleying rain-squalls. The *Morning Star* fought in vain for sea-room to clear the sunken coast with its furious tides.

To the agent's probing questions Dan could state there had been no panic among passengers, no failure by master or crew as they struggled with mounting desperation to avert their doom.

As a feeble dawn lightened her murky pall, the packet struck. No faintest shadow of land loomed through the fog and Dan could see nothing but boiling surf. He repeated the sailor's despairing cry, "God be merciful! We've hit the Gannets!" Captain Sam interposed the opinion that from his reckoning of wind and tide the ship must have been in that vicinity.

The master of the *Morning Star* had ordered the ship lightened in hopes of refloating her, and the able-bodied men among the passengers worked with the crew, but the flood tide brought mounting seas that swung the doomed ship broadside, lifting and dropping her on her beam-ends in a cruel play. The starboard boats were smashed, or useless, the fore and main masts with their rigging soon went overside in a crazy battering tangle. In the cold fog and lashing rain the passengers clung about the jagged mast-stumps or to the mizzen rigging, seeking vain shelter from the snatching seas that breached the helpless ship at every send, while the fanged reef gnawed the new timber and spat forth bright splinters to bite still deeper.

Dan had been one of six men and women who succeeded in gaining a larboard boat in the wreck's lee. Beside the second mate he was desperately fending the tossed craft from destruction against the ship's side, while a woman and child were being lowered from the deck.

He apologized for his lack of coherence in explaining what happened next. "Sir, the following moments were those of a nightmare that piles horror upon horror in a flash, yet suspends one immobile and helpless for an eternity. My memories are still confused."

A tremendous comber, raking in at an angle, snapped the painter, whirled the boat with its fright-frozen passengers past the bow of the wreck, flipped it over and roared off into the fog.

Dan did not see the fate of those he had worked to save. He knew nothing but black water and bursting lungs and a struggle to reach air, until he found himself again on the surface and sucked against the capsized boat. There was no sign of the *Morning Star*. He gained the keel and clung there for a time while tearing seas flung the boat through the reef's boiling crosscurrents and into deeper water. Here a monster surge swept him clear. He was too spent to struggle, until from the crest of the succeeding billow he glimpsed the boat—again righted.

He had no memory of how he reached it or got aboard, nor how long he lay retching and stupified as seas carried the boat crazily along, before he roused enough to loop the painter's end about his body and the forward thwart. He then lay insensible of individual seas or the passage of time, in a purgatory of cold and battering water.

As Captain Nickerson explained, had Dan been able to lift his head he could have seen nothing of the agonized clipper or of his shipmates, for already the tide must have carried him away from the Gannets' outer reef and its foul accomplishments, although the seas still pounded the boat and its unconscious passenger as if bent upon obliterating the last stubborn traces of the *Morning Star*.

Mr. Robertson questioned Captain Nickerson further as to the time and set of tides, then, placing his pen in its sandwell, pushed his chair back from the desk. He informed the others gravely that boats searching the waters between Cape Sable and Yarmouth had found no trace of survivors, that Mr. Redmond must be presumed the only soul left alive out of seventy passengers and a crew of twenty-six; and that the empty boat, left by the *Didamia* to Cape Sable's tides, the only wreckage now apt to be sighted of the *Morning Star*. He would so notify her owners in Boston.

Seeing Dan was white-faced and shaken after his recital, Captain Sam leaned across and patted him reassuringly on the knee. "It's not for *us* to say who will be spared and who taken, Mr. Redmond. You played a man's part at the time; and you've told your story like a man now when it had to be told and there was no one else to do it. You can do no more than thank the good Lord for saving you." Mr. Robertson nodded grave assent to this.

Rising, he urged them to accompany him home for dinner, but the wind, bearing out Captain Sam's opinion of its instability, was already blowing off the sea. They hastened to clear the harbor, but the sun was low by the time the sloop, beating towards home, tacked offshore and Dan saw to leeward the second love of his life.

There lay a shore laced with foam and behind it on hillsides still faintly green, a few silver-gray cottages enclosed by windswept trees or low stone walls—and a misty light over all. Dan's heart, still boyish and more homesick than he cared to admit, leaped at a sight so like some he had known as a child.

Touching Captain Nickerson on the arm, he pointed. "What's that land, Captain?"

"That's Ryder's Island."

Near the western tip a steep-roofed cottage ran up a whipping pennon of supper-smoke while from under sharp eaves like questioning eyebrows, two A-windows gazed at the sloop.

The shores approached and receded as the boat tacked; rocky spits and shallow coves licked by white water dropped out of sight as others took their place. The hills' gentle rondures arched and flattened.

Dan thought, *Oh, the lovely little island. Like old Ireland itself. If it were mine I'd name it New Erin,* and always after he called it so to himself.

Chapter 5

DAN REDMOND LEANED HIS CROSSED ARMS ON THE POLE FENCE, RESTing one aching foot after the other on the lowest bar. Here a footpath turned from the main road through a narrow V-gate, meandered down a rocky pasture to planks across a swampy bottom and climbed slowly to the Nickerson house, aloof on its headland.

Today Dan had passed many such solitary homes, turning their backs to the execrable roads and watching the bays and harbors where even neighborly calls were made in a boat.

Looking across the lifeless fields, Dan reminded himself that in the Old Country spring was caressing the awakened land. The almanac proclaimed late March and denied this Nova Scotian winter that still held the matted tan grass about the field rocks and moaned through the broken reeds and sodden sedges along the Cove's marshy inner shore. Only a winter sun in setting could so brass the cloud edges above it and the crests of the sullen chop beneath. He shivered. Winter's own spite was thrusting those ice-spears across the roadside puddle at his feet and probing his heavy sea jacket to find the very marrow of his bones.

True the morning had held promise of spring and the miles to Barrington had seemed no distance. Along the lonely stretches of shorepath or rutted "short cuts" he had whistled and twirled his heavy stick, with the sun warm on his face. The few folks met along the way had given him "good day" and turned to stare after him, so that he'd felt pleasantly conscious of making an impression and had carried his head high.

The expected letter from his uncle had awaited him at Barrington. There everyone he met, assuming he was anxious to be on his way, had taken pains to inform him that the Wilsons' *Fancy Free* would be sailing for Boston inside the week.

On the return walk he had scarcely left the last Barrington houses behind when the sun and his spirits alike came under a cloud. The air had turned coldly raw and the miles had dragged in spite of his preoccupation with the letter in his pocket and the problems it raised.

As requested, Uncle Jonathan had forwarded money from Dan's deposit in a Boston bank. He urged his nephew to come to him with the least possible delay. He had heard stories of "Nova Scarcity" and he wrote worriedly lest Dan's "Health be undermined by scant Rations, if not Want and Hunger."

Dan had smiled, remembering Damie's bountiful meals. Nevertheless, the sensible thing would have been to engage passage on the *Fancy Free,* for he had accepted the Nickerson hospitality far too long.

When he left for Boston he would miss the home on Grannie's Head and the kindly Cove folks; but he did not deny the truth to himself—he could say, "God bless you," and be gone with no more than passing regrets, but for Mercy Nickerson.

Mercy's smile, her clear gray gaze and the flowing movements of her slender body held him. He knew with all his quickening manhood how that pliant strength would melt to tenderness in his arms, how that pale head would feel above his heart; yet he had no more than touched her hand.

44

In Dublin his dreams had sometimes included a wife whose dowry could help him on his way; but this shore brought different dreams; if Mercy lacked the money and accomplishments of young ladies he had known, she had a true gentleness that aroused all the best in Dan.

Should he follow his uncle's advice and ask Mercy to wait until he could return to claim her? Should he work out his own destiny here where the sea had flung him? Thoughts of the island, New Erin, and Mercy persistently intertwined. Would she go there with him? If Mercy Nickerson loved a man, she would follow him to the ends of the earth, he knew. Better, she would walk beside him, sharing and easing his burdens.

Ah, that was the crux—if she loved a man.

His memory rewarded him with Mercy's welcoming gesture to him, a stranger from the sea. Hadn't she shared, that night, his feeling of a search ended? She had shown pity and distress when he told of his plight after the *Morning Star's* destruction, and rejoiced at his miraculous escape. *But,* he admitted now, *any shipwrecked seaman would have touched her tender heart.*

He recalled his first mention of Molly to the Nickerson family, about the evening fireplace when a rising wind had tightened their circle to close the gaps left by the seafaring twins.

The firelight had flowed down Captain Nickerson's lean cheek and flickered along his knife as he fashioned a butter print for his little wife; it had softened Damie's features where she bent over her mending so that Dan could see the young Damie who had won Sam's heart. In the shadows Mercy had sat knitting, for she was never idle—a piece of work flew by magic to her hand the instant she was seated. Bethiah had been applying herself to a long gray stocking; Philip, prone at the captain's feet, had soberly lost himself in the wonder of colored flames.

The relaxed friendliness had moved Dan to speech. "Captain Nickerson, I'm interested in the island we passed returning from Barrington. Ryder's you called it. I often stand here on Grannie's

45

Head and look across at it; though less rugged it reminds me of a Galway shore I knew. It must be a charming spot in summer."

"So it is," the captain had agreed. "Pretty as any hereabouts. A few years ago there were nine families on it, but now they've moved off to the main, all but old Zenos, and he's waiting to sell his stock."

"Why should they leave?"

Damie had had a tart answer to that. "They *claim* 'tis because the firewood's all used up. Though I've a mind if Zenos Ryder had his strength again he'd find a way to make out. But he's old and crippled with rheumatics. The young people are different, looking fer the easy way and scairt t' death of a little work, same as on the main here."

Her thimble had clicked the needle while Bethiah had squirmed knowing herself to be an example of degeneracy, but Captain Sam's mouth had taken the upward quirk that marked his reception of Damie's tirades.

"Times change," he'd remarked soothingly, if tritely, "and seven greedy fireplaces have surely stripped the island of wood, so that, as the Ryders say, it's easier to bring their families off to the main than 'twould be to boat fuel to the island.

"But not long ago Ryder's was a thriving fishing settlement. The island's a mile nigher the grounds than what the Cove is, and better yet, the tides don't bother there; no finding your boat high and dry on the flats just when ye want her. An excellent harbor right in your backyard, you might say."

When the captain had paused and squinted along his whittling Dan had hesitantly suggested, "Suppose a man, young and strong, with a few thousand pounds, say, wanted to go there. Couldn't the island be farmed? Stocked with sheep and cattle? Would there be no way to get fuel for one family?"

"Oh, yes! to the west'rd wood can be bought cheap by the vessel-load, and a schooner brings Sydney coal to Barrington— it could be boated from there. As to farming Ryder's . . ."

Captain Sam's eyes had narrowed, but if he'd suspected Dan's young man might be anything but suppositional he had given so sign. Dropping his hands loosely between his spread legs he had leaned towards the fire in his favorite attitude for considering a question.

"I wouldn't like to say offhand. A stranger there would have a pile to learn about winds and tides. And everybody don't take to island life; say what ye like, it's lonesome when there's but one or two families and sometimes cut off by storms or ice. A man living there couldn't *always* count on neighbors in sickness or trouble, like we can here on the main.

"Another thing," he had continued positively, "island life's not for a bachelor; in such places a man needs a good wife to keep him on an even keel."

Dan had asked himself, *Did Mercy stir in the shadows where her needles catch and knit the firelight with the white yarn?*

"You make it sound desolate, Captain," he had replied ruefully. "Yet, as we sailed past, it seemed to have—well, almost a cozy look."

"Cozy enough in its way. Zenos brought up a big family there and lived content. You can't ask more of any place. Still, I don't know about making a living from sheep and cattle. Around here, 'most everybody raises their own and there'd be no market nigher than Boston or Halifax."

He had laughed then at his own pronouncements and swept them into the fire with an opening gesture of his big hands. "But listen to me talk! As if *I'd* be a judge of such matters! Noan of us hereabouts knows a great deal about farming; seems like we have to be on the water." He had straightened and resumed his whittling. Dan had sensed there was more to come.

"Now if 'twas me going there," the captain had resumed, "a young man with a tidy fortune, like you mention, and a mind to work, I'd set up to supply the vessels that put into Ryder's harbor from the fishing grounds. Vessels from Boston, Providence, Marblehead and Gloucester, all the New England ports, as well as from our own coast. I'd lay in a stock of salt and sea duffle:

sail duck, cordage, nets and lines, provisions—anything a vessel might run shy of, or lose in a storm."

Dan had not fancied this plan; it smacked too much of his father's mercantile business upon which he had so recently turned his back. He had been picturing himself a country gentleman, riding about his New Erin farm like his English cousins; forgetting the island's resemblance, not to the lush Surrey acres, but to the stony fields of Galway.

"Perhaps I'd not make a farmer," he had conceded, "and what would Molly say after all my fine talk of a Boston house if I brought her to an island she's never heard of?"

Sudden silence had stopped Damie's poised needle, and held the shaving suspended from Sam's knife, while Mercy had searched intently for a dropped stitch. But Philip, with a child's obliviousness to adult undercurrents, had drawn his absorbed eyes from the fire and lifted his head. "Is Molly your wife or your little girl, Mr. Redmond?"

Dan had laughed rather too heartily. "Wife! Come now, Philip! I've no wife, nor betrothed, either. Molly's my sister, and I promised to send for her as soon as I got settled."

He had tried then to make them see Molly's sweet face and gentle ways. "Not much bigger than you, Bethiah, but older than Miss Mercy. She's all I have in the world, for my mother died when she was born. My father was never the same to me after, and now, God rest his soul, he is gone too. I'm sure you would all show Molly kindness, since you've been so good to me, and she is so loving and lovable."

He'd glanced at Mercy then, but her eyes had been upon her knitting and her needles were again flying with their customary smoothness.

Now, shifting his weight from one road-bruised foot to the other and hunching closer against the increasingly bitter wind, Dan asked himself, *Would her fingers have faltered if I'd told Philip, "Molly is my wife"?*

The winter evenings had brought further discussions to which

48

Mercy listened without ever venturing any comment. Too, she had persisted in seeing nothing but courtesy in all Dan's efforts to break through her reserve. As that evening when she had stood gazing across the sunset harbor to the house on Ryder's point, and Dan had joined her at the window. He had asked, "What do *you* think, Miss Mercy, of Ryder's Island? It isn't far from your home here, is it?"

She had replied sweetly, "It always looks nigher before an easterly."

Dan had tried again. "Do you believe it would be too lonely a place for a woman to live?"

"I don't imagine most women would try to live there alone, but no doubt one could if she had to," she replied perversely.

"I didn't mean alone, exactly. I meant a married woman. Could she be satisfied in such a spot—without neighbors? If she were with her husband . . . If she loved him . . . If they were all the world to each other? . . ."

"Oh, like enough it wouldn't seem lonesome to a woman who was fond of her husband." Mercy had heard of such sentimental creatures, her demure tone had implied.

Dan had wished he could see her eyes—wasn't there a hint of teasing in her voice?

But she'd been serious enough when she had faced him. "It would be a thousand times better than seein' your man sail away, not knowin' if he would ever come back."

Before he could say more she had smiled an excuse. "I must be seein' to supper."

Had some Cove youth taken her heart with him on a long voyage? He had heard no mention of such a one. Dan had refused to face another possible barrier between them; time enough when he knew she loved him.

Of late Dan believed Mercy modeled her speech upon his, dropping colloquialisms. Did she wish to gain his approval or was she naturally bound to absorb the gentlest and the best?

49

When she flinched at her mother's trenchant phrases Dan longed to take her in his arms and in a glow of condescension comfort her, "Never mind, mavourneen, I see through the hard words to the kind heart, and through your father's homely ways to the gentleman he is. Such things don't hide their true worth any more than your plain gown hides your loveliness."

Then he would dream how, fast-locked in his arms, that loveliness would flow straight to his heart; he pictured Mercy dressed in satins and silks of his choosing—more beautiful because she wore the tokens of his love. But he had never put any of these fancies into words for Mercy.

All the way from Barrington he had turned these matters over and over in his mind, but while the road ruts froze under his boots, his plans had refused to crystallize before he had reached the Nickerson back-bars. Here his feet stayed as if they refused to budge until he had come to a decision.

His eyes searched for some outward sign to break his irresolution.

Above Narrah the bare tops of New Erin hills showed bleak and uninviting, but Zenos Ryder's empty house and abandoned wharf seemed, as always, to beckon him. Nearer, the Nickerson boatshop and wharf blended with the darkening shore, but above them the house and sloping-roofed barn loomed against the wind-tattered clouds.

The main portion of the dwelling stood cold and unwelcoming, its windows black squares, its front door impregnable. The big central chimney rose unstained, so few fires the "company rooms" had known in all their years. The warmth and life of the home stayed in the kitchen ell, where now a fitful gleam told of wood recently added to the red coals where supper simmered. He pictured the room and its occupants—the firelight would be tangling in Mercy's braids as she bent above the hearth and lying in the soft hollow under her throat.

In Heaven's name, why was he standing here half-frozen when all the warmth in the world awaited him yonder?

50

Chapter 6

WHEN DAN STRODE INTO THE KITCHEN MERCY STRAIGHTENED FROM the fire and her eyes flew to his. He read in them an answer to all the questions of the road; but when he let his joy show in his face she turned shyly away.

He was satisfied. *She's waiting for me to tell her I shan't be going to Boston. She knows I love her and is glad.*

In the blinding ecstasy of this he did not notice the extra figure at the fireside until a nasal voice brought out, "Been a-usin' Shank's Mare consid'able fer a fine gentleman, ain't ye?" And there was Little Obie, his eyes sharp behind their colorless lashes, his thick lips ready to smack over other people's affairs.

Suspicious that this lout might have read the look between himself and Mercy, Dan answered short and sharp and saw Mercy turn in astonishment.

From that moment forward, Mercy believed, she had never put in such a miserable evening and, coming after the rapture that had blazed between her and Dan, its frustrations seemed all the harder to bear. A fog of misunderstanding settled over the kitchen, dulling everything and shutting each person off in a groping world by himself.

The day had been bad enough, dragging unendurably because she had begun to watch the road long before Dan could have reached Barrington, let alone return. At twilight a man's boot scraping on the back-entry mat had set her heart pounding, but the door had opened not to Dan but to Little Obie's red face thrust coyly into the room and his perennial, "Ary person t'hum?" with the cackle that followed such flights of humor.

Why couldn't he stay away, just for once?" Mercy asked herself rebelliously.

51

True, at home he had only his old mother who, in Prince's Cove terms, was "losing her faculties," and since he had installed a hired girl to cope with her whims, he felt free to visit cozier kitchens. Pa allowed that Little Obie babbled everything he heard or guessed, not to cause trouble—but from sheer inability to keep his hatches battened down. Mercy considered that her mother and other matrons abetted his gossiping, for though each was recurrently astounded when her own betrayed secrets came back to her, each welcomed Obie to the family fireside and drank in stories of her neighbors' frailties and misfortunes.

Since Dan's coming Mercy had felt a rising intolerance for the fat cook's silly jokes and long-winded yarns about nothing, but Obie was not noted for his thin skin and her coolness left him quite unruffled. Now he hung his coat and cap upon the entry pegs and Mercy's heart sank when he stood his well-swathed fiddle in the corner, for this meant he'd come for supper and the evening.

I wish I had a bit more of Ma's outspoken tongue right this minute! I'd sent him off on a different tack before Dan—Mr. Redmond—gets back. But there! she sighed, *I'm too soft-hearted to hurt even Little Obie.* And at the humbling conjecture that to Dan Redmond her love might be as unwelcome as she found Obie's attentions, she was filled with pity and unhappy tolerance.

She set the table distraitly while the visitor drew a stool to the fire and, blinking against its blaze, drew out his plug of tobacco. Obie's thick lips were perpetually cracked by summer's sun or winter's wind, and as he chewed he habitually ran the brown juice over them with his tongue; now he punctuated his remarks with fierce, dark squirts that sizzled in the fire and threatened Mercy's stomach. She went limp with relief when her father brought the clean smell of worked wood from the boatshop with him and engaged Little Obie in talk of the *Didamia's* spring voyage.

That left her free to dream over the past winter when Mr. Redmond had brought a new world to Grannie's Head with his stories of Dublin and London, even of Paris. He carried that world with him in his manners and speech and always it set him apart, though he had thrown himself wholeheartedly into each humble family task. He'd gone before daylight into the woods to take the other end of Pa's crosscut and in the bitter winter twilight plodded home behind the piled sleds and slow oxen.

On moonlight nights he and Pa had gone gunning on the ledges and returned half-frozen, but with ducks slung proudly on their gun barrels. Yet Dan Redmond only pretended to be a Cove man; when he taught Philip and Bethiah their lessons or referred to the servants at home, to his school, to Dublin balls and theatres—to a life she could scarcely guess at—Mercy felt her heart sink into her boots.

When he was absent her own home seemed strangely poor and empty. She stole to the pantry window that commanded a view of the main road beyond the pasture. Still no sign of a tall, swift-striding figure. She asked herself, *How will I bear the lonesomeness if he leaves for good and all? Will I go about the rest of my days listening for his footsteps?* Her young despair assured her it would be so.

When at last Dan appeared in the kitchen she knew swift and sure the day had brought a decision—a happy decision—that concerned her. For a heart-stopping moment the eyes of man and maid clung and spoke to each other.

Mercy saw Dan start at Little Obie's rude query and snicker; and when his eyes met hers again they had changed. They asked hotly, *Why is this man here when I want you to myself?*

Mercy turned away, her own eyes dulled. *Can't he see it's no wish of mine that brings Little Obie? If he loved me truly he would know.*

So fragile, so short-lived are the few moments of perfect communion even with those most loved.

To Damie's inquiries Dan replied briefly if politely. Yes, he had completed his business in Barrington and Mr. Robertson sent his compliments; and no thank you, he was not too fatigued; and yes, it was growing much colder.

Reluctantly Damie had to forgo further questioning in front

of Little Obie, whose ears were standing out like stuns'ls in the hopes of catching a breath of news that would speed him along the shore paths.

Obie accepted with alacrity the invitation to draw up his chair and share supper; crunchy pork scraps over johnnycake, stewed West Indian tamarinds whose acid struck through the sweetening and clotted cream to pucker the mouth and set the juices running. No lack of conviviality on Obie's part made the meal such an awkward one. Bethiah soon sat sulky and silent under his teasing while Mercy played with her food and looked on the verge of tears. Damie became short-tempered at the obvious but incomprehensible constraint and snapped at Bethiah and Philip; Sam alone seemed unaware of tension but, as he was never one for talk at table, he was no help.

Once Dan, looking at the cook's bulk overflowing his chair, inquired coldly, "May I ask why you're called *Little* Obie, Mr. Knowles?"

"Why, yes, I cal'ate ye can ask. No harm in askin'. Fur as that goes, the's no harm in answerin'. He! He!

"One vessel I sailed on when I was a young sprit carried a mate by name of Obediah Knowles. From down to the east'rd he was. No relation o' mine—fur as I know, that is. 'Thout it might be through my great-uncle Eben, my Grampy Jeremiah's brother; he married down that way, one o' the Snow girls, old whats-his-name's dorter, him that wedded the Doane . . ."

He appealed to Damie and Mercy sighed as her mother stirred briskly, ready to voyage through the tortuous waters of local relationships; but Sam wrecked that by muttering impatiently, "Get under weigh, there, Obie; get under weigh."

"As I was *a-sayin'*," Little Obie resumed after a hurt glance, "the' was another Obie Knowles on this vessel and two men with the same name's apt t' be a mite confusin' on board ship. He was a tall man, well over six foot, so fust thing I knowed they'd took t' callin' him Big Obie and me Little Obie. I never heard who thought it up," he concluded admiringly.

54

"Smart man, whoever 'twas," Captain Sam commented dryly, over a buttered slice of johnnycake. "Likely took all one watch figgering it out."

"Well, I d'know as t' that, now. I wasn't nigh onto as heavy them days as I be now and anyways I was a different build from him. My size never did run t' height," he said complacently.

"I understand, Mr. Knowles, thank you," Dan cut in with an air of vast indifference and again the conversation languished.

Things were no better when they gathered about the fire later. Even Obie sensed that for this audience his yarns and jokes lacked appeal. Not that he didn't try. But he had a card up his sleeve— a fiddle in the corner—which he triumphantly produced.

His quick ear and the tunes picked up in strange ports were a source of commendation both aboard the vessel and at "gatherings" ashore; for though the consciences of this Pilgrim breed knew dancing to be the devil's own coil, their unregenerate feet tapped brisk time to a jig or reel.

Little Obie played as in a trance, fiddle across knee, eyes fixed, mouth agape, sore lips and cud of tobacco alike forgotten; fleshy hand clutching the bow determinedly and a heavy boot marking the time. Prince's Cove was right, Obie had music right in him— the notes were round and sweet, the time true.

The tension dissolved; Philip remembered the same tunes in the *Didamia's* forecastle and the crew's kindness to a frightened boy; Bethiah forgave Obie's silly teasing and tapped out the beat; while almost in spite of themselves Mercy's needles took on the quick rhythm. Only Mr. Redmond, they noticed, folded his arms stiffly across his chest and kept his frown.

Mercy feared he had no ear for music, but when Little Obie paused to wipe his forehead and put the wad in his cheek to use again, she was surprised to see Dan lean forward and pick up the violin. "May I?" he asked Obie formally, and ran his slender hand caressingly along the smooth wood.

Little Obie beamed. He'd showed this high-toned stranger, he guessed. "That fiddle's worth lookin' at, I want ye t' know. I paid four American dollars fer it, at a secondhand shop in Boston."

Dan did not appear impressed by this. With a faraway look he tucked the violin tenderly under his chin, stretched his long legs in front of him, and bowed the strings lightly but searchingly until they gave out a melody with a lilt and a sob in it. No one stirred as he went on to other airs, losing himself in them and filling the kitchen with such music as none of his listeners had ever heard.

He stopped lingeringly and turned to Little Obie. "You have an excellent violin there, Mr. Knowles. Indeed, it's sweeter than the one I lost on the *Morning Star* and I took great pride in that."

"Land sakes, Mr. Redmond," Damie interjected, knotting her thread and sending her needle flying to catch the minutes lost under the music's spell. "You never told us you was a fiddler."

"I had some musical training at school," Dan replied stiffly. "My teacher thought I had talent, but my father at that time wanted me to learn his business and so my music was put aside." The boy's bitter disappointment colored the man's voice.

He turned to Obie then, and said pointedly, "But I still feel it a desecration to *misuse* a fine instrument like this."

Little Obie was cut to the heart. He rose with unexpected dignity, rewrapped his fiddle in its long woolen muffler and with a quiet "Good night, all," closed the entry door softly behind him.

Mercy, who had been wishing him gone, now wanted to cry at his going. "Noan of us thanked Obie for his music," she said timidly and Captain Sam nodded, his face closed.

Dan laughed scornfully to hide his discomfiture. "Music, Miss Mercy? The man has no knowledge or training whatever."

Now it was one thing for Mercy or Bethiah to poke a bit of fun at Little Obie, but another for this outsider to assume such a contemptuous tone. Mercy flushed angrily but before she could speak Damie broke in sharply, "Come, come, now, time we was all a-gettin' to bed. Bethiah and Philip, off with ye now! Up all night and lie abed all mornin'!"

She rose and smoothed her apron with finality. "Mercy, I want ye t' start a sponge before ye go, for I'm that sleepy I'd fall in the flour bar'l sure. Good night, Mr. Redmond; come, Sam," and she had cleared the kitchen before Mercy could remind her that they had baked off bread only that afternoon.

Since Dan had the kitchen-bedroom, the captain and his wife were relegated to the chilly garret, and as Sam hurriedly shed his outer garments he complained, "Dan shouldn't have criticized his playing, but I do wish Obie'd stay to home more—not that I mind him running in and all, but I *was* looking forward to talking to Dan. I wonder if he's decided when to leave for Boston."

Damie's tone was as positive as the jerk with which she tied her nightcap strings. "Boston! He'll not leave for Boston! He's a-goin' t' buy Ryder's, and I fer one sh'll be glad t' see him settled there."

"Yes, we'd all miss him if he left." But Sam's voice held reservations. "A fine young chap in many ways. There's only one thing, Damie; I don't consider an island ary place for a single man. As I've told Dan, a wife . . ."

"Oh, you great goose, Sam'll Nickerson! Do stop yer jawin' and say yer prayers so's we can git t' bed. If ye can't see what's under yer very nose 'n' eyes!"

But to Sam's indignant, "What in time's under my nose and eyes, *now?*" she deigned no more than an exaggerated sniff.

When her prayers were over she flounced down into her side of the feather bed, declaring, "Jealous, that's what," and chuckled happily. But Damie could be terribly aggravating by times and Sam refused to rise to that bait. Besides, he was not so blind as his wife thought.

They lay silent for some time and when he spoke it was gently. "Wife," he asked, "do you know what church Irishmen most generally belong to?"

"Church?" Damie's voice tried for impatience but Sam felt her stiffen. "Church, I never give it a thought . . ." Then in triumph, "Why, Mr. Redmond goes to the Baptist Meetin'house with us."

"Yes, twice last winter he rowed with us to prayer meeting at

57

the Cove. Did he testify? Did he say a word about it afterwards? I don't forget that when I stripped him there in the *Didamia's* cabin, he wore round his neck a little golden crucifix."

Though he knew his words were blows to shatter Damie's dreams he made himself continue evenly, "I'm every bit as fond of Dan Redmond as you or—or as anybody could be. But I hoped he'd engaged passage for Boston. Damie, any Irish I ever saw were Papists." There! It was out.

Damie could not speak. Papists were nothing but a name to her, yet a name holding the bitter intolerance of generations. Unthinkable that Dan Redmond, that likable, upstanding young man, should be one of them.

Her distress was palpable through the darkness and the feather tick's folds. Sam reached out and drew her into his arms. "There, little wife. I never meant to say aught about it, for a man's religion is his own and no business of ours. And perhaps we're mistaken in thinking—whatever it is you're thinking. Go to sleep now, Damie. No use for us to fret; we must put it in the Lord's hand, if—if things turn out that way."

For all his refusal to put a name to his fears, Sam was worried, Damie could tell. She lay awake and, with the threads of a mother's love and pride and the patient needle of hope, mended the torn fabric in her dreams for Mercy. Dan would come to see the error of his ways, she was sure, and all would yet turn out well. She closed her eyes and prayed again—mightily.

Meanwhile, in the kitchen the constraint thickened while Mercy busied herself with flour and yeast. Dan, now stiff and weary from his long walk, scowled silently into the fire, ashamed at having taken out his resentment upon an inferior. Somehow he had not expected his words to cut so deep, though he had barbed them purposely and, remembering Little Obie's hurt face, he wished them back.

A wave of homesickness aroused by the old tunes, of longing for Molly and his own land washed over him. How had he ever felt so close to these strangers on Grannie's Head? What had made him believe he wanted to share the life of this tall, pale girl? Where was his elation born of the meeting of their eyes? Wasn't her silence an acknowledgment that she, too, sensed the lack of understanding between them?

He lashed out at her from his hurt and bewilderment, "I beg your forgiveness, Miss Mercy, if I've offended a suitor."

As Mercy's only reply was a choked sigh, he went on, "Perhaps a favored suitor. But I hardly expected him to show resentment of my simple music." *Lord, what a fool I sound,* he thought, but he heard his voice continuing with heavy sarcasm, "Of course, I realize I am not in a class with Mr. Knowles."

Dan had never seen Mercy anything but shyly serene. Indeed, she completely lacked Damie's quick and shallow temper, but to his amazement she turned upon him now with flashing eyes and a face alive with scorn. Scorn!

"It fits you poorly, milord, to poke fun at Obie Knowles and his fiddling. Could you do better, think you, if you'd had no kind teacher but had larnt what you could by listening and watching in smoky fo'c's'ls and water-front taverns? Could your fingers find such lovely music if instead of a book and a pen they had held oars and cod lines since you were twelve, been cold and wet and swoll with salt-water boils before they'd got their growth even? Obie's no older 'n you, Mr. Redmond, but he's been making his living from the water for a dozen years.

"I shouldn't have to remind *you,*" she continued, "that for all his tongue he has a kind heart. Who helped Pa bring you back to life when the sea had almost claimed you?

"You've shown all too plainly this night that you consider the likes of us beneath you. But you've shown me more—that a gentleman can lack real kindness, for all his fine ways. I've put up with Little Obie a sight longer than ever you'll have to—*you'll* be off to Boston now that spring's broke—and I've thought sometimes I couldn't bear his yarns another minute. But I couldn't see him hurt like he was tonight without despising the one who'd hurt him."

She brushed the hair back from her brow with the back of a floury hand and finished what she had to say, "I think, too, Mr. Redmond, that you forget yourself. We've noan of your fine manners here in the Cove, but in another man's home we wouldn't pick at his friends."

Dan stood stricken and sick with shame for his behavior as seen with those clear gray eyes and detailed by an aroused Mercy, surprisingly articulate and unbelievably beautiful with her golden head defiantly erect.

He couldn't see how the candlelight swam in orange circles through the tears in her lashes nor could he know how heart-breakingly dear was his profile against the fire's red glow.

Suddenly her anger deserted Mercy and she crumpled, putting flour-whitened hands over her eyes. Her voice was pitiful. "Oh, I've always fancied you so noble, so kind. I felt you understood that Little Obie cannot help what he is. That Ma cannot. Nor me. That you . . . liked us, in spite of our being different from them you'd always knowed. It's . . . It's not Little Obie, really . . . it's that *you* are not what I thought."

Dan did not answer or move. He had lost Mercy by his own conceit and selfishness. He, who had pictured himself stooping, was plainly unworthy. He had no choice now but Boston. A hateful empty place it would prove, too; how had he ever thought it held anything for him?

Almost as if she had followed his self-communing, Mercy asked in her customary gentle tones, "When do you think to sail, Mr. Redmond? I hope . . . I wish you . . ." It was no use, her voice had dried up completely.

She lifted her hurt and piteous eyes to his and Dan found himself beside her, telling her hoarsely in an agony of self-flagellation of his selfish and jealous disposition; found his arms about her young softness, her head upon his breast and his voice murmuring broken endearments; and, best of all, found—just as in his dreams—Mercy's sweetness flowing into his heart and washing away the miserable doubts and misunderstandings;

60

found her cheek wet with tears, her mouth warm and quivering under his own as he told her that *nothing* could drive him to Boston; that he was going to buy New Erin and go there—with her as his wife.

Chapter 7

A MAY MORNING LAID MAGIC UPON PRINCE'S COVE AND THE ENCIR-cling shores, but at the Nickerson landing place Captain Sam paid it no heed. He flipped the last scoopful of water up the dory's inclined side and out before letting the boat fall back on its flat bottom. He fitted the tholepins more carefully into place, pressed a thwart down tighter and gave the plug an extra thump. Then when he could no longer delay, he nodded to Dan and with him ran the dory down the gravel-embedded poles.

Dan stepped aboard and proudly took the oars while Captain Sam turned to the weeded rock where Mercy stood gazing with parting's sharpened appreciation at the familiar shore. He took her into his arms and held her close. "The Lord keep you, little daughter, and bless you in your new life."

As he lifted her onto the stern thwart he added in a heartier tone, "We'll all be on for a visit, soon as you get settled." He splashed through the shallows to shake his son-in-law's hand. "Don't forget to call on me, Dan, if ever I can help."

Then, moving to the stern, he gave the dory the final shove that set it free from Grannie's Head and started the young couple towards their new home. He turned and, without a backward glance, strode across the pebbled beach and up the path to the gray house, but he walked as if his sight might not be too clear.

After an early farewell kiss Bethiah and Philip had hurried to a vantage point on the outer shore, but Damie stepped out on the back stoop to flutter her apron briefly. *How dear and good they all are!* Mercy thought, *How I shall miss them. My own family.* Not until she was leaving for her new life had she realized how great was the love that had bound them all together in the old, how sure and strong the tie between her parents. The best of Damie went out to her husband and this was as it should be. Dan would always come first with her, Mercy knew.

Yet it wasn't easy to be leaving her old home, and the gray house was brooding sorrowfully over her departure. She looked back again to the little upper window marking her bedroom, her girlhood refuge. Dan had seemed, these last nights, almost an intruder there; but girlhood had been left behind her when she had set sail on her marriage trip and tonight she and her husband would sleep in their own home.

Decisively Mercy turned her eyes forward. She tucked up the skirt of her old linsey-woolsey and placed the scoop under her cobbled shoes, for a wash would soon form in the dory bottom in spite of her father's thorough bailing. She smiled tenderly at his solicitude. *As if I hadn't slopped around boats all my life, or a little water would hurt me!* She settled herself upon the thwart.

Dan was already swinging the dory around the wharf end where clusters of gray periwinkles and knots of forlorn seaweed clung, bereft of the tide. He was heading out the twisting channel between the rocks with their skirts of sea tangle swinging with every pull and push of the eddies.

There were Bethiah and Philip balanced on the outermost rock of Grannie's Head. Oh dear! 'Thiah would catch it if she slipped and got wet! When the dory drew opposite Dan pulled close with great splashes that sent Bethiah scrambling and shrieking in delicious if pretended terror, while Philip's big eyes glowed in laughing admiration. Then the children, perched like awkward gulls on the slippery rock, waved the dory along, shouting good-bys that echoed across the channel from the boulders of Narrah's end.

Mercy must point out to Dan the granite profile smiling upon the departing lovers as it had welcomed an approaching couple

62

two generations ago, and tell him how Grandma Abigail had named the headland.

Mercy's thrifty common sense had prompted her to wear the old dress and sturdy footgear, but love and the desire to look comely in her bridegroom's eyes had chosen the soft, wide-fringed shawl and the new bonnet that tied with a blue bow. What she saw in Dan's face proved she had chosen wisely.

Though the sun had long been up, the morning breeze still slept and beyond the channel the harbor lay wide-eyed but motionless, assuaged by the night's embrace. Thus she sometimes lay of a morning, beatified in mind and body, and unstirring lest movement shatter perfection. At such memories and Dan's ardent glance she felt the hot color sweep up to her bonnet, and turned her head. High time, she scolded herself, that her heart stopped such flighty hammering, for she'd been a married woman all of a fortnight.

To teach it decorum she kept her gaze fixed upon the distant sloops and dories fishing the Ragged Rip, black specks floating between sea and sky; or she looked beyond Dan's shoulder to the house on New Erin with its two A-windows watching the harbor approach.

Exquisite beauty lay all about—in the arched translucence above, upon the shimmering water, in the crystal depths below the boat. There soft brown string weeds and wide kelp blades streamed gently to and fro, disclosing glimpses of fronded mosses, red and green, purple and yellow. Black cunners darted among the upper branches; sculpins moved lazily at the roots, their hideous jaws opening and closing, their fanning tails raising a flurry of sediment. A matronly hermit crab crossed a bare stretch of sand between one rock and another, its claw tips appearing and disappearing like feet beneath full skirts. *Off to the neighbor's to borrow something for dinner,* Mercy pretended, and lifted her smiling face to share the conceit with Dan.

He did not wait for her words. Instead he told her, "I'm remembering another morning when you sat so straight and proud on a thwart and looked just as kissable as you do now." His dancing eyes held hers. "But then you sat beside me with your hand in mine. I think I'll . . ." and he moved as if to draw in his oars.

"No, now, Dan! Please! You must keep rowing. We'd drift aground. Or someone might see you!" Mercy looked around at the empty waters and put out her hands imploringly.

"See me kissing my wife! Shocking! Never mind, my shy little one, I was only teasing; I'm every bit as anxious to reach New Erin as you are. But *do* you remember, too?"

Her heart leaped at his tone as it would have beneath his forestalled kisses. As if she would *ever* forgot!

Everything had worked out so happily for her, after a time when Dan's religion had been an obstacle to their marriage. Dragging with heavy lids and leaden heart about the house, she used to ask herself, *What can it matter that two persons find God through different churches?* But it had looked as if Dan would be leaving for Boston after all. Then he and Pa had talked long before the fire one night and in the morning Pa had put her hand in Dan's and given his consent.

The Reverend Mr. Allbright had been due in Prince's Cove for his annual May meetings, and then Uncle John Chetwynd of Halifax (he that was married to Ma's sister Griselle) had ordered a vessel-load of pickled fish and Pa had suggested that the young couple come along on the *Didamia* for a marriage trip.

So one fine morning the parlor door had been thrown open to relatives and neighbors, the curtains pulled aside to let in the bright day, and there Mercy Nickerson of Grannie's Head had been given in marriage to Daniel Redmond of Dublin.

That afternoon they had set sail for Halifax on a voyage that proved a rapturous dream from the time the *Didamia* had weighed anchor in the quiet Cove until she had dropped it under the hills of Halifax where the tangle of masts and rigging had been like a stand of winter hardwood. With his daughter and son-in-law on the stern thwart Pa had worked the small boat through the harbor traffic to a wharf's slimy steps. In the bustle

64

and clatter of Water Street she had clung desperately to Dan while Pa had gone to find Uncle John.

From his dank office above the harbor-lop Uncle John had immediately summoned a carriage and taken them to his stone mansion across from Government House. As they drove through the streets Mercy had seen no man, not even the officers in their brilliant uniforms, to compare with Dan in his new blue coat, tight fawn trousers and the travelers cloak he wore with such an air. No other sideburns had shone so blackly, no other linen had gleamed so like snow, as those of the husband beside her.

Aunt Grizzie's hair was frizzed and her eyes an undecided brown, but she was small and dark like Ma. Dan had won her the instant he bowed over her veined hand, for she set great store by fine manners. Although her acquired English accent *had* seemed a bit "put-on" after Ma's bluntness, she'd been good and kind, assuring Mercy (who'd needed assurance) that the new bonnet and cape were vastly becoming and that Dan could well be proud of his bride.

Uncle John had pale piercing eyes under brows like bursting haymows and a dry laugh that might be a cough. Or was it a cough that might have been a dry laugh? He had been polite to the newlyweds in a preoccupied way, but he couldn't hear enough news of the Cove—of the people and the vessels he had known as a boy.

Alone with Mercy that night, Dan had admitted, "When your father spoke of John Chetwynd being 'well-off' I didn't imagine such a sumptuous home as this. I find it hard to picture him a barefoot boy of the Cove."

She had tossed her head and answered with a laugh, "Oh, Prince's Cove boys and girls can be smart when they've a mind to." Then more soberly, "From the old folks' tell, Pa's mother had a finer home than this before the war drove the loyal ones out of New York and 'most everything was lost. But she married a fisherman and went to a log cabin on Grannie's Head. What you *have* don't matter so much, Dan."

In their big bed, Dan had whispered through her loosened

hair, "I'll build us a big house, Mercy mavourneen; not in Halifax but on our island. I'll give you servants like your aunt has, and fine dresses. Our children will be little lords and ladies of New Erin."

Mercy's happiness had overflowed in tears for her new husband to kiss away. "That will be marvelous, Dan," but she had been thinking as her breath caught, not of the big house or the fine clothes, but of the children, hers and Dan's.

Now here they were on their way to New Erin at last, and all the rapturous memories of their marriage trip were in her smile as she answered Dan's question, "I'll never forget, my dearest."

The dory passed over a shallow ledge where the rockweed burred along the bottom and caught the dipping oars, and then it was on the deepening water of the half-mile-wide harbor between Narrow and Ryder's islands.

Pa had trimmed the dory nicely, Mercy and her round-topped trunk in the stern balancing the supplies in the bow; but the ebb was running strong and forcing Dan to straighten his course repeatedly. Mercy herself could handle a dory—many's the time she had rowed across the Cove on an errand—but it was not a woman's place to give orders, especially in a boat. And Dan was so proud to be rowing her to their new home! So she let him alter his course after each glance over his shoulder and never mentioned how much easier 'twould be to keep the dory on a mark astern.

It's a blessing a crooked wake disappears so quick. Any Cove man that came across ours would surely have a good laugh, she speculated ruefully. But what did it matter? Dan sat straight and tall, his dark eyes adoring hers, his hands slender and white upon the oars. *He's splendid, aristocratic-looking,* she told herself, *in his soft leather boots, his fine serge, his white shirt. And oh! how I love him. If I wanted a rower, Little Obie would have done.*

Even Dan's wavering course soon brought them into the landing cove on New Erin's inner shore. On one hand rose the island's two hills, Nigh and Further. On the other the point

66

jutted out into the bay, its greensward a flowered carpet; at places the red clay bank rose eight to ten feet above sea level; at others the green carpet had slipped and rested in a fold upon the pebbled beach.

Pa judged the cleared point of Ryder's held five or six acres, but it looked smaller to Mercy; for while Grannie's Head had the mainland at its back, this stood alone between bay and harbor.

Under the point's shoulder stood the usual fish store and a short wharf whose crooked spiles sprawled, slimy and weeded, above the ebb-bared silt. It could never have been much of a wharf, Mercy decided, and was now badly in need of repairs. The broad-beamed sloop lying against the wharf must be the one Zenos Ryder had sold Dan, the trim skiff pulled above high-water mark must belong to the hired man, Mercy judged. With the dory Pa had lent them, Ryder's—no, New Erin—already boasted quite a fleet.

Mercy had never set foot on the island and at close range it lost the familiar outlines seen from the Grannie's Head. *All the more exciting,* she told herself.

She gazed at the house, a hundred yards from the shore, and at the low barn and outbuildings which detracted nothing from its lonely appearance. From the back chimney a fan of smoke spread against the sky, but the front windows were blank, the door shut tight. The weathered home looked smaller than Mercy had expected—and more forlorn.

Never you mind, she assured its drooping lines as Dan hastened his strokes towards the landing, *you'll not be lonely much longer. Once I'm out of this dory! You're going to be my house, mine and Dan's.*

A man in a shapeless jersey and heavy pants thrust into the inevitable sea boots rounded the corner of the house and made his way towards them with the roll of one who had taken more steps afloat than ashore.

"That must be Kiah Atwood," Mercy said, though she had never seen him before.

She smiled remembering Little Obie's comment on learning that Kiah had promised to settle the young couple on the island. "Kiah's a good enough man," the fat cook had allowed judiciously. "Leastways as fur as ever I heared." Then peering up at his captain he had demanded, "But say, you, don't he look like somebuddy's whittled him out fer a tholepin?"

Pa had replied somewhat testily, "Well, we can't all be thick and short enough for dory-plugs, Obie."

Now Mercy thought, *But Little Obie was right for once. Somebody surely whittled Kiah out for a tholepin!*

She was to learn the surprising strength of those long, sloping shoulders, the infinite endurance of that lanky figure. But even when Kiah had long been the Redmonds' mainstay, she was to wonder how so much kindness and downright goodness could hide behind so unprepossessing a front. Ears jutted from his long thin face like jug handles, and under the straight, sandy hair his red-brown eyes appeared not much larger nor darker than their surrounding freckles. Something of the man broke through in his smile, but his teeth showed gaps.

In a boat Kiah could move as smoothly and effortlessly as the tide, but waiting at the water's edge he shifted from one awkward position to another, reminding Mercy of an uneasy crane. He might have been twenty or fifty, his face told no tales, but Damie, who carried the Cove's statistics in her little black poll, had stated he'd gone twenty-six.

When the dory's bow grated, Kiah seized the side with a surge that almost threw Mercy backwards and increased his painful embarrassment, though she laughed at him reassuringly.

Dan stepped out then to carry her—so tenderly, possessively—and set her gently down upon the greensward of their island home.

A Cove man would have turned to lend his weight on one side of the dory, but Dan gave Mercy his arm with a careless, "Bring the supplies to the house once you've pulled the dory up, Atwood." Mercy was appalled. Did Dan think *that* was the way to treat a man who came to help them out of friendship for her father? Did he consider Kiah a lackey? He would be without a hired man in no time—and worse, he'd become known as stuck-up and high-handed.

She turned her head to see Kiah's face suffused with resentment. Her love for her young husband, her distress at any hurt, her knowledge of how a man's gorge must rise at such treatment, were all there in her wide gray eyes and on her sensitive face. Kiah's anger faded as his eyes met hers and for a brief instant they two of Prince's Cove were close and Dan, with his bewildering foreign ways, was outside the bond of their mutual understanding.

Kiah bent to lift the trunk from the stern. "I'll make out, Mi's Redmond. Certainly," he said.

Reassured, Mercy turned with Dan along the overgrown path from beach to house, while the vibrant perfume of an island spring overpowered the shore's cold tang and silence lay like the sunshine over all.

Set in the face of a crumbling terrace, three steps from a vessel's companionway led up to the front door, which stuck a bit with dampness and disuse as Dan threw it open. They were home.

In spite of recent neglect Zenos Ryder's house was comfortable, even spacious by Prince's Cove standards, with its bedroom off the big kitchen, its spare room and parlor downstairs and the roomy open chamber above.

The front rooms were now heaped with furniture and household goods; Dan's elegant Halifax purchases rubbing elbows with the sturdy tables and benches fashioned in the Nickerson boat-shop, the bolts of wine-colored damask which he had chosen for curtains were piled on the chest of homespun blankets and patch-work quilts, roped rolls of pillows and ticks from the sea ducks' down leaned in a corner.

Untying her bonnet strings, "Dan, my dear, I can scarcely wait to get at all this clutter and set things to rights," the housewife in Mercy declared.

But Dan could wait. He led her through the dim hallway to the kitchen, where everything was tidy and the floor newly scrubbed. A fire crackled in a stove, big and black and more than a little intimidating to Mercy, for though stoves were becoming more fashionable, Damie clung stubbornly to her fireplace. Not so old Zenos; faced with a scarcity of fuel, he had eagerly purchased this black monster from a wracker and in turn sold it to Dan.

The iron teakettle simmered, well back on the stove; Kiah, being a Cove man, knew that a kettle left over the heat would boil your love away. The table against the wall was set for two. Damie had sent on a supply of bread and butter and cakes so that Mercy shouldn't start off with an empty pantry—but the bowl of red and white lobster meat!

"Dan," Mercy pointed out, "now isn't Kiah Atwood thoughtful! He's scrubbed the floor and set the table and boiled off lobsters. Pa no doubt cast a hint as to how fond you are of them." She looked up into his face and laughed, "And do you know, I'm famished! It must be getting on for noon. Do tell me you're ravenous, too."

"It's fainting with hunger I am," Dan replied, taking her in arms anything but faint.

And so, with long pauses for gazing into each other's eyes, with all the delicious delays of lovers, Mercy and Dan had their first meal on New Erin.

Chapter 8

BY MORNING SPRING HAD RETREATED INLAND, ABANDONING THE COAST to leaden seas and driving fog. Even noon welcomed the big stove's heat and at night the chill blankets provided an excuse (little, needed though it was) for Mercy to seek the warmth of her husband's arms.

For a week the wind held southerly while fog dripped from every eave and wharf plank, bent each grass blade and dandelion, veined the faces of rocks with rivulets and put a treacherous grease on the boardwalks between house and outbuildings. It quenched the spring sunshine to a bleary luminescence which lightened reluctantly until noon and then faded swiftly. But only Kiah noticed or minded.

The others were dimly aware of a third on the fringe of their bright world; poor Kiah, hurrying through his mundane days of cows to be milked, pigs to be fed, fields to be dressed, boats to be shifted against wind and tide.

"As for us," Mercy declared, proudly viewing the rich folds of a newly hung curtain, "I'm sure we can't pretend this putting our home to rights is really *work*. And cooking for three! Why, it reminds me of when I was a little thing, playing house among the pasture spruces with my bits of broken earthenware and colored shells."

There came the morning when Dan turned again and again to the window, though the fog hid boats and wharf.

Like every other man, anxious to be out and away, Mercy saw and then admitted honestly. *Just as you're like every other woman, Mercy Redmond. For you've been half wishing something would take Dan out of the house so you could settle down to real work.*

When breakfast was over, "Dan," she said, making a virtue of necessity, "could you and Kiah row off as far as Grannie's Head today? Ma's doubtless in a state, sure some mishap's befell us."

Mercy noted the eagerness with which Dan turned to Kiah before he qualified his first reaction, "But that would mean leaving you here alone on the island."

"Dan," she told him firmly, "no harm will come to me in my island home that mightn't come to me on the main. You will have to leave me often. And what tell of you being gone to

71

Grannie's Head when other women have their men on the Banks?"

She turned to include Kiah in her self-deprecatory smile, "Besides, I prefer my floor cleared of men when it comes time to scrub."

But when Dan bent to kiss her good-by, she burrowed against his stiff sea coat and whispered, "Oh, don't be long," and only pushed him on his way when Kiah, his long face ludicrous with exaggerated patience, reassured her from the doorway.

"We'll be sending back word of our voyage, Mi's Redmond. First ship we speak this side o' Good Hope. Certainly."

A great to-do they'd made over half a mile of sheltered water! No wonder Kiah had poked fun. Of course, he couldn't be expected to understand.

That day both interrupted their immersion in each other and broke the fog's spell. Before Mercy dropped asleep stars were twinkling through her window and she awoke to sunlight dancing on the wall. Dan, opening one eye, murmured drowsily against her neck, "Today we'll explore New Erin."

It was but the first of many afternoons spent tramping beaches or woodpaths until they knew every foot of the island's three-mile shoreline, and each cleared spot of its six hundred acres, but its hours proved such as even lovers seldom know—magic and unmarred.

Mercy tied her sunbonnet, that sure sign of summery weather, as she left the house, and Dan beside her threw his coat open to the soft breeze off the blossoming land.

Then, hand in hand, they pushed through the sworded blue flags at the pond's edge and on to the bold southern shore. Here the land rose sharply from the sea; high deep-fissured ledges thrust out into the turmoil of waves and currents, and the coves between them lay black and deep. Through the years the storms had built a high sea wall of rounded stones and driven it inch by inch back over the sod-land, baring the rocky feet of hills that sloped from the foam's edge.

72

The hillside fields, brightest emerald between the gray rocks, showed scattered patches of catkin-alders and tangles of tender-leaved wild rose and raspberry bushes or an occasional thicket of crippled spruces that hugged the ground and crept away from the sea winds.

While waves foamed at their feet and gulls wheeled above them, Dan's dreams spilled over in words, picturing for Mercy the green slopes dotted with his white sheep and lambs, the ragged fields cropped by herds or waving with grain. Mercy found her eyes going offshore to the blue fields of the sea, to the boats garnering the harvest her people had always known. She kept silence. Who was she to doubt Dan's plans? But did he grasp the work they entailed? Dan, who had never in his life so much as turned a sod or dropped a potato seed. Kiah was perpetually busy with the cattle and sheep and pigs which Dan had bought as a start. But this was no time for such nagging thoughts—she tossed them to the playful breeze ruffling the cove-let ahead.

None of the early settlers had built homes on the wild seaward shore, but when the happy explorers had reached the southern-most point and must turn easterly, the first of the abandoned Ryder cottages came in view. It sat well back in a stone-walled field and they passed it by, for the tide line still held them.

The eastern shore was the island's flattest. Through the light-green inshore water purple bands bespoke protecting reefs, and just beyond them the tiny Thrum Islands lay like a row of plump green pincushions between New Erin and the hazy curve of the mainland beyond.

The southern shore's rugged sea walls and jutting ledges were here replaced by white sands arcing against narrow, pebbled spits. In the flat fields, powdered with strawberry blossoms, waist-high stone piles evidenced past efforts to clear the rocky land. Parallel-ing the beach, well-trodden cowpaths led to a watering place, a shallow brown pool fed by seepage from the island's swampy center.

73

The sun was strong on their shoulders and the wind was held behind the hills. When they reached the white semicircle of Sand Cove, they took off their boots and splashed through its icy shallows with shouts and laughter, then ran across the warm sand like two children. Like children—until Dan suddenly put out a hand and pulled Mercy to him; pushed her sunbonnet back to kiss laughter and breath away.

An unacknowledged urgency upon them, they replaced their footgear with blundering hands and left the glittering beach without a backward look; walking silently, apart. Mercy watched the glade of alder and spruce approaching, while the scent of tassels and resin grew more pungent, more disturbing, at each step. She walked into its flecked shadows without volition, without asking why her heart pounded, why her body trembled with sweet weakness as it waited for Dan's hand upon her shoulder, turning her so he might crush her against him, for his hot face buried against her throat and his hoarse whisper, pleading, demanding, offering, "Wife, my little wife."

The yellow pollen falling like sunflakes, the green earth beneath her, the blue sky above, the far, wild cry of a gull, the nearer lap of the shore, all blended with the tide that whelmed her. Only Dan's face above hers had meaning.

Later, all urgency spent, they wandered leisurely homeward, hand in clinging hand again, up the slope of Further Hill. Looking back from its height they marked the ebb-bared chains of islets and ledge-caps binding New Erin's northeastern corner to the nearest point of the mainland, and heard the short, sharp bark of seals basking on the weeded rocks, then turned down the hollow that dipped to the harbor shore between the two hills.

On the breast of Nigh Hill they came upon the Ryder's unfenced burying ground. Dan, with life and love coursing strongly within him, was disturbed by this reminder of mortality and shocked that bodies should lie so bleakly interred, so far from consecrated soil; but Mercy, who had played among similar mounds and upended granite slabs on Grannie's Head, thought

74

only that this would be a pleasant place to lie in the last sleep.

Their home lay only a few hundred yards away, for they had circled the island, but the abandoned cottage on the slope of Nigh Hill drew Dan through its warped doorway.

Mercy was loathe to tarry in the empty rooms, sadder to her than the grassy graves, for Life clung despairingly to the damp walls and cried from a worn washbench askew in a cobwebbed corner, from a cracked butter bowl on a sagging shelf. But Dan rapped on partitions and stamped on floor boards, busy again with his plans.

They stepped out to see a schooner entering New Erin's harbor. "She's a Yankee; Marblehead-rigged, I think," Mercy told Dan as they watched her drop anchor. "And look! Coming up the bay—another vessel! A Frenchman from St. Joseph's. You remember Pa telling you about the French settlement to the west'rd."

Then shyly, for Mercy was seldom one to put her feelings into words, "I'm proud to think—aren't you, Dan?—that to men at sea New Erin means shelter. And that the vessels putting in for a night's anchorage or to wait out a storm will be part of our life here."

The pressure of his hand agreed as fully as his words. "I'm happy indeed that New Erin provides a haven."

"We must be getting home." Mercy started down the slope purposefully. "The crews will be ashore to fill their casks at the well and like enough the skippers will come to meet the island's new owner."

Hurry was needless, however. The Marblehead master did not call and Kiah helped the crew fill their casks. It was dusk and Kiah gone to bed before the French captain's polite knock sounded at the Redmond door.

Dan welcomed in a slight man, near his own age, who bowed to Mercy gracefully despite his heavy sea clothes, and introduced himself, "Arthur d'Entremont, captain of the *Madeleine Amirault*," nodding towards the harbor where his schooner rode. His pleasant voice held scarcely a hint of accent.

75

"Old Zenos Ryder, he is my friend always when I come to this harbor. In San' Joseph I hear the island has a new owner. I am sorry Zenos is here no more. But I think 'New friends are good, also.' So I come ashore tonight to tell you, the San' Joseph vessels, they all wish you much good in your new home." His smile had retained a boyish sweetness, despite his years at sea, and his soft brown eyes were warm.

Dan thanked him heartily for his good wishes and assured him of New Erin's welcome for each member of the St. Joseph fleet.

The two men plainly liked each other at sight. Over their glasses of wine they found much to discuss. Such a difference, Mercy thought, listening intently, between their studied exchanges and the terse, matter-of-fact visiting among Prince's Cove neighbors.

The candles were growing short before Captain d'Entremont said *bonsoir* and left for the *Madeleine*. A stranger had come to the Redmond home; a friend departed from it.

Chapter 9

THE STORM DARKENED THE EARLY AFTERNOON, SO THAT SHADOWS filled the corners and the fire shone red through the cracks of the stove door. Snow whirled against the panes; not the melting flakes expected of November, but hard pellets that piled along the sashes. A northerly gust swerved to rattle the window in a prankish test of its rising strength, then shrieked past and out to sea.

The storm filled Mercy with a restlessness and foreboding disproportionate to its severity. She crossed the room, peered futilely through a whitened pane, needlessly straightened a curtain and returned to her rocker, deriding herself as she picked up her sewing, *I'm getting as bad as Ma with her gloomy presentiments that never come to anything. Like enough my being on edge is simply a weather sign, like some people's aching corns or a rheumatic knee.*

But the sense of impending trouble persisted and she found herself praying wordlessly for men at sea and giving thanks that her father was safe ashore. Charles and the twins—who knew where they might be? Who but God.

Then to defy the storm she drew the security of her home about her. The wind was powerless against the sturdy walls and full stove, though it might shake the windows and howl in the chimney; might even stir the new red carpet with fingers thrust through cracks in the worn floor, for the "drawing room," as Dan called it, was after all only the old kitchen, changed about and refurnished.

The year and a half on New Erin had shown that Dan was a great one for changes. From the first he had talked of a more imposing dwelling than had served Zenos Ryder, though Mercy had counted herself fortunate to start housekeeping on so grand a scale; many a Prince's Cove bride began married life in the home of her own or her husband's parents and scrimped long years to be mistress of a two-room cottage.

Goodness knows she hadn't intended to complain when she'd mentioned that Zenos' cellar allowed little room for skimming-bowls and butter-butts, even before the winter vegetables were in. She'd known that her mother's cellar (built for Loyalist Abigail) had few to match it in the neighborhood. Pa had explained once that, despite the crazy profusion of rocks on this coast, the early settlers had walled up the same shallow vaults under kitchen trap doors as they had known on Cape Cod's elbow where stones must be boated from a distance.

She'd been taken aback when Dan had declared, without a second thought, "Well, my darling, we need a larger house now we're starting a family. I'll have a big new cellar first of all."

The house at Sand Cove, largest of the abandoned cottages, had been taken down, boated up the harbor and re-erected over the spacious new cellar adjoining Zenos Ryder's. The two houses were joined, or separated, by a long hall. Mercy and Dan retained their bedroom, but most of the original house was now given over to "company rooms" while the new end held a kitchen, Kiah's room, a seldom-used dining room and Dan's combined office and library. This latter room, in Damie's estimation, topped all and proved the heights to which Mercy had soared by her marriage; none of Damie's acquaintances had books to fill even a corner shelf and nobody nigher than Barrington had an office.

Thinking of the tracked-in snow this storm would bring, Mercy felt there was a deal to keep clean. *But it's as Dan said,* she admitted to herself, *now we're a family we do need more rooms.*

She bent to the green cradle at her feet and peered fondly under the hood where three-month-old Patrick slept with his hands softly crumpled and a smile twitching the corners of his mouth.

Damie had boasted on that August afternoon when she had first put the downy head upon Mercy's weary arm, "They claim the first son allus favors its pa, but this is a Nickerson, if ever I see one!" And Mercy had laughed tremulously at the absurd miniatures of her father's wide mouth and broad brow.

Patrick Samuel they'd named him, after the two grandfathers. She often wished Dan could rejoice wholeheartedly, as she did, in the miraculous present that held their love and their first-born and not postpone complete happiness for fulfilment of ever enlarging plans. However, the man must be the provider; perhaps it was right Dan should look ahead and plan for the future.

Mercy's face had rounded and gained comeliness with marriage and motherhood; her gray eyes were soft as summer clouds and her mouth a tender curve as she gazed upon her son. *And Dan does love him truly! So does Molly, as if he were her very own.*

For Molly was now part of the New Erin family. The first island winter safely past, Dan had kept his promise to send for his sister. There had been delays, but one dancing September day they'd seen the *Didamia* rounding the point from Halifax and known she carried a passenger for New Erin. On their way to the wharf, Mercy had fairly run in order to keep up with the happy, excited Dan.

From the *Didamia's* deck Pa had passed a tiny figure to Dan's waiting arms, and stated in mock seriousness that he was afeared he wouldn't be able to sign Miss Molly on as mate, like they'd planned, for she'd never poked her nose above deck since they left Halifax.

Molly, still green from the rough water off Cape Sable and wilted to her very bonnet strings, had been beyond Pa's well-meant jokes. She'd clung to Dan and wept that never, never, as long as she lived, would she lift her feet again from dry land. Dan had hugged her close, masculinely embarrassed at this vehemence, while his eyes besought Mercy's support.

Though she had hidden it guiltily, Mercy had been dreading the arrival of this sister, who would be sure to see that Dan had married beneath him and, being better learned, prettier and more stylish, would by contrast lessen his wife's appeal. But when Mercy had seen the bedraggled little figure in Dan's arms her heart had listened even as it upbraided her, *Shame on me! Why, she's that tiny and frail a good breath would lift her right off the wharf.* Then as Molly had turned her pointed face with its woebegone mouth and brimming violet eyes, Mercy, with her motherhood so newly and wondrously upon her, had taken the other girl into her arms as if she were a child.

And indeed, that's just what she is, Mercy thought tenderly now, as she stirred the cradle with her foot and gazed across the room at her sister-in-law, *a lovable, timid child.*

Molly could not be coaxed into a boat or even for a walk along the outer shore where the waves rioted, so great her dread of the water. She scurried for the house at sight of a cow and feared even the sheep which fled from her with a rattle of beach rocks under their small hooves.

She was terrified by the antics of Skipper, the Newfoundland

79

pup with the huge paws and friendly heart, whose most winning efforts merely sent Molly into hysterics and himself into puzzled and crestfallen banishment.

Mercy felt some impatience when Molly shrank so obviously from the men ashore off the vessels waiting out a spell of weather. Molly could not rightly interpret their rough ways nor their shy, slurred words. But Mercy understood them; knew what a few hours in a home, what the sight of women and a child meant to men so far from their own.

The word soon spread that Mr. Redmond, besides being a fiddler himself, had a piano and a pretty little sister who could play tunes on it. The captains visited politely, if ill at ease, in the drawing room while crew members sat in stiff rows along the kitchen walls and listened with Kiah to the faint music through the open doors.

As for that wonder, the pianoforte; last spring when Long Tom Doty had eagerly accepted Dan's five pounds for "the pie-annie off the wrack," Mercy had wondered if it would ever serve any purpose but to impress visitors. She had ached for the skill to loose its music, but it had sat dumb awaiting Molly's soft hands. She and Dan played entrancing airs together, for Dan had bought in Halifax a violin to replace that lost on the *Morning Star;* but this afternoon the violin lay in its case and, oblivious to wind and snow, the two were singing the Irish melodies they loved.

Molly's voice was high and sweet, but Mercy knew her own to be fuller and truer, a better complement to Dan's rich baritone, and she wished they had chosen songs in which she might join and so release some of the inner disturbance aroused by the storm. Chide herself as she might, she felt excluded when Dan and his sister shared songs and memories in which she could have no part.

"Eileen Aroon" came to an end, and Dan turned with the look which his dark eyes held for Mercy alone and a smile that dispersed her fancies like fog before an offshore wind. He was her husband (still so sweet a word upon her lips, still so marvelous a fact) and surely she'd be a jealous hussy to resent his affection for his sister.

The cessation of the music might have been a signal for Little Obie's round face to appear in the doorway, just as it used to be thrust around the entry door on Grannie's Head.

"Ary person t' hum?" asked Obie, with the familiar jarring snicker. But now his pale eyes sought Molly's approbation; the query had been for her ears. He'd long since finished with the role of Mercy's heartbroken discard; when ashore he frequently visited New Erin, and in the Cove boasted of his friendship with the Redmonds.

His first glimpse of Molly had keeled him over—much to her bewilderment and distress. Nor could she understand the local custom of visiting, by which Obie "rowed on" when the spirit moved him and stayed for days, taking his place as one of the establishment, and then left as unceremoniously as he had arrived.

This afternoon he had been helping Kiah fasten the boats against the rising storm and as he stood in the doorway, he rubbed his red hands and searched out his cud from a cold-stiffened cheek.

"The wind's hauled to the no'theast, and is a'ready freshenin'," he announced. "One good thing, it'll soon cut down the seas."

All ears now consciously caught, under the wind's piping discords, the thunderous and incessant bass of the surf still beating out the measures of yesterday's southerly. To each in the cozy room the weather was no idle topic; even Molly had come to sense that along this shore, life itself hinged on wind and tide, though she could not yet know how dreaded for their bitter cold and blinding snow-squalls were the winter northeasterlies.

Obie, true to his Prince's Cove upbringing, had left his heavy boots in the hall and now padded, stocking-footed, to a seat on the sofa. Skipper, who'd followed him, all thumping paws and wagging tail, caught Molly's look and stopped short at the doorway. He set deligently about routing his fleas.

81

"Fleas!" said little Obie. "Don't talk t' me about fleas. In all yer born days ye never see so many as the' was in that house on Cape White. Thy-ah! Thy-ah!" Obie slapped his knee with his thick, red hand.

Mercy often felt that, in spite of himself, Dan found Obie's yarns amusing, but poor little Molly consistently remained as puzzled at their completion as at their start. However, there was no stopping Obie, and now, confident of their attention, he was well under weigh.

"Me'n Nathan Sears, we'd been a-fishin' on the Ragged Rip when it breezed up sudden with a sou'west fog. We couldn't do nawthin' but run before it and when we made land we was off Cape White. We could see the loom of a house and as it was a-growin' dark b' then, we decided we'd ask if they could put us up over night, even if they only let us bunk in the fish store.

"But lands! Nawthin' would do the man and women o' the house but we come in and have a bite and set by the fire 'n' talk. When bedtime come, they showed us to a room. 'Twas their spare room, I know it must 'a' been. The' was a nice clean bed and the woman had fixed up curtains at the winda, some kind o' lacy stuff with little mashes—like a herrin' net, only smaller o' course. Well, we crawled in and blowed out the candle, and I cal'ate we both dropped right off.

"But purty soon I begun t' feel Nathan a-twistin' and a-twitchin', and by that time, I don't mind tellin' ye, I was doin' some flouncin' myself.

"'Obie,' says Nathan, 'do ye feel somethin' a-bitin'?'

"'Nathan,' I says, 't' tell the story and tell it true, I'm et up alive.'

"''Taint s'bad fer you, Obie,' he says. 'You'm fat: but *my* shinbones is gnawed away like two wormy wharf spiles.'

"'Fat's no help, Nathan,' I told him. 'Jest that much more t'be crawnched on. What kind o' critters do ye cal'ate they be? Can't be fleas,' I says. 'Not so fierce an' greedy as all this.'

"'Wal, the's no tellin',' Nathan allowed, sorry-like. 'What's more, nobuddy'll ever know. By sun-up,' he says, 'the' won't be nawthin' left of us. Our famblies'll think sure we was drownded when that squall struck.' He heaved a sigh right from bottom.

"You mind, Mercy," Obie turned for corroboration, "Nathan was always one t' get down in the mouth, first little thing."

Mercy nodded, not that she was familiar with Nathan Sears' propensities towards gloom, but to avoid starting Little Obie off on another tack. Actually she had been listening less closely to Obie's story than to the sound of the rising wind.

He went on, "Fer all that, I didn't know at the time but what Nathan had the rights of it. I says to him, 'Wal, I can't stand this another minit. I'm a-goin' t' get up and give myself a shake, then jump back in, quick-like, and tuck the bedclothes under me tight. It oughta take 'em a while t' work their way back in.'

"'You'm a-buildin' yer house on a broken reed, Obie,' Nathan argyed in the same dismal-like way.

"I didn't have t' shake. The minit I stepped out, 'twas snick-up! as fleas hit the bare floor. Snick-up! all around; and then hop! hop! and snick-up! The room must 'a' been as full o' bouncin' fleas as a hopper full o' popcorn. But when I turned the kivers back and jumped in, every last one o' them jumped in, too. Must of.

"I was never so glad in all my days as I was t' see the daylight grayin' the winda. I rolled Nathan over a mite t' find out if all the fleas was on my side o' the bed. Thy-ah! Thy-ah! I rolled him right back.

"'Twas snick-up! and hop! all the time we was gettin' into our pants." Obie stopped and blushed to realize he'd been so coarse and carried away as to mention that detail of his toilet before Miss Molly Redmond, and he resumed his saga in a chastened tone.

"When we stepped to the winda t' look out, the' was fleas mashed in them fancy curtains thicker'n ever herrin' mashed in a net. Thy-ah! Thy-ah! The like was never knowed. If . . ."

Little Obie's high drone stopped though his mouth remained open. The sound of heavy boots hurrying down the hall followed the slam of the outer door.

Kiah's lanky figure appeared in the doorway. His thin face

83

glistened, brick-red from the sting of wind-driven snow. Hard white kernels lay along the folds of his woolen cap and in the creases of his coat, and Kiah, the meticulous, stood with melted snow darkening the floor about his boots. He brought indoors with him the storm's chill—and something more that drew every eye to his face.

His short breath showed he had run with his news. "Mr. Redmond—the's a brig piled up on that reef to the south'rd o' the p'int. I catched sight o' her between squalls. She looks to be breakin' up. And the's still men aboard."

He stepped aside as Obie waddled swiftly for his boots. Dan stood stricken for a moment. Then he reached his coat and cap from the hall pegs and turned instinctively to Kiah as to a leader.

"What can we do?" He glanced towards the whitened windows. "This wind . . ."

"Why," Little Obie interrupted loudly, stamping into his boots, "I've put off in many a worse blow than this."

Kiah spoke consideringly, "The's some fair-sized seas a-runnin', Obie."

"Go on!" Obie scorned him. "I've see bigger lumps in my straw tick."

Kiah ignored this wild exaggeration and turned to Dan. "I cal'ate their boats must 'a' been smashed or carried away, else the crew would 'a' left the vessel when she struck. Mr. Redmond, your sloop's too rickety; my skiff's too small. But we might reach 'em in Obie's boat. Once we get 'em aboard we can land in the lee somewhere and leave the boat till the wind moderates. But it's a long row 'round the p'int, and a dirty one, with the wind and tide ag'in them seas; and the's only the three men of us. On the main now, I could have a bigger boat and the pick o' twenty or more t' man her. Certainly."

It was the longest speech Kiah had ever made in the Redmonds' hearing and his voice held a strange lack of confidence.

Something nudged Mercy's memory. Part of some story heard long ago? It escaped her again. Her father's words. They strove

84

against the block that consternation had set up and at last broke through.

"Kiah," apologetically she brought his attention back to the room, for Dan and Obie had struggled into their coats and all three had turned towards the outer door. "Which is safer? Which would take longer? To fight your way around the point in Obie's boat, or to haul the boat across to the leeward shore on the ox-sleds? You'd cut off some of the roughest water that way. I seem to remember Pa telling of some such case as this . . ."

Kiah's face lightened, his eyes commended her. "Mi's Redmond, it's a good thing somebuddy 'round here's got a better head than the turmit on *my* shoulders."

Then, almost like a squall shipping past, the three men were gone.

This, Mercy told herself, *this was the storm's threat; to reach through the strong walls, to pull Dan and the others out into its grasp.*

Her conscience smote her. *And us singing and listening to Obie's foolishness while almost at our back door a vessel was breaking up and men were fighting for life.*

She replenished the fires automatically, and, seeing that Patrick whimpered and mouthed his fist, she put him to breast, holding him close as if the greedy sea and wind menaced even him, and as if her cherishing arms might keep them back. Molly huddled on the sofa, white-faced and staring at the door through which the men had disappeared. Then she bent her head over the rosary in her hands and Mercy saw her lips moving. She thought, *Ah, yes, men can fight the storm, but women—women can only wait and pray.*

As she closed her own eyes she marveled at Molly's faith in the mild Virgin who could know so little of man's fight against the seas. Her own prayers would rise to the God of Storms, to a wrathful Jehovah, omnipotent and inscrutable, who now and then tossed before the bended knees of a supplicating woman a son or husband miraculously spared from the core of the tempest, but whose ears were shut to the cries of so many. Her heart pounded rebelliously. But familiar words came to her, "Like as a father pitieth his children," and the picture of her own father's loving face. Faith and acceptance returned. She prayed though the rising gusts and the surf's diffused roar mocked her.

Chapter 10

THE BUFFETING WIND MADE IT DIFFICULT FOR DAN TO KEEP HIS stiff sea boots on the frosty boardwalk as, with head down, he followed Kiah's racing feet to the barn and Little Obie puffed behind them.

Resurgent memories of the *Morning Star* and the discovery of the stricken brig combined to accuse Dan. He chided himself, *While Kiah was busy with the chores, I should have been keeping a watch along the outer shore; God knows how long the vessel's been pounding herself to pieces out there.* But, wrapped in contentment as he sang the old songs with Molly, he would never have believed that New Erin, the refuge, could betray ships or men.

Even the few yards to the barn took an unconscionable time to cover. At this rate nightfall would be upon them, the brig demolished, before they could reach her, he fumed.

As the three men swung back the double doors the storm rushed into the barn's gray interior. The cattle stumbled hopefully to their feet as the wind, acrid with shore smell and snow, sliced through the mows' fragrance and the ammoniac stable fumes, presaging mangers pitchforked full, the blissful chewing and grinding of stalks, the stowing of a delicious cud for the long black night. Startled and disappointed eyes rolled backward whitely as Kiah ran to the far stall and the ponderous hindquarters of Bright, the ox.

"Over there," he said to the others as he went, and swung his long arm towards a dark corner where, under cobwebs and sifted hayseeds, the wood-sleds awaited the first hauling-snow. The dry runners clung to the rough floor, the chains squeaked and rattled in protest at this too early rousing, as Dan and Obie, one at each shaft, ran the sleds to the open space before the barn.

Bright knew the weather outside was fit for neither man nor beast, and he sensed the portent of the stable's invasion. As Kiah backed him out of his stall he caught with a defiant noose of tongue one last bristling mouthful from his manger. He tossed his head and stamped, tail aswish, as the head-yoke dropped over his wide-spaced horns. At his ill-tempered commotion the other cattle danced about nervously, straining at their stanchions until his heavy hooves had thudded through the swinging half door from the stable into the main barn.

Tranquillity and the gray twilight settled again over the steaming stable; the cows found consolatory cuds as the thick outer doors swung to behind ox and men, shutting out the storm.

In response to wind-snatched words from Kiah, Obie hurried shoreward, while for an intolerable moment—a moment might balance the life of a man—Bright balked and pranced and blew white plumes across the cold wind. Dan felt his hand itch for the whip. Yet Kiah's firm patience would serve them better, he knew, remembering his own early attempt at driving, when the ox's cross-grained stupidity had so exasperated him that he had handed the plaited whip, and all future dealing with oxen, to Kiah in one angry, frustrated gesture.

Today Bright's rebellion was short. He soon submitted to Kiah's exhortations and the cracking whip, stepped docilely between the waiting shafts, holding his yoke steady until they could be pinned in place, while the snow powdered his shaggy brown coat and weighed his long stiff lashes. Then at Kiah's, "Come up! Gee, Bright," he lowered his head and moved sulkily into the wind.

And now all our success hinges on the strength and willingness

87

of this dumb beast, Dan admitted with unaccustomed humility. The first step against the full force of the wind had proved there was no hope of rounding the point by boat.

Under Kiah's unnatural use of the whip Bright indignantly broke into a lumbering trot while the men ran to keep beside the empty sleds as they jolted and bounced over the rocks and frozen hummocks.

On the bank, where he and Kiah had propped her less than an hour before, lay Obie's eighteen-foot boat: tubby and water-heavy, scarred and surface-splintered, but with stout strakes and thick bottom planks and a deep keel that, with the help of an oar in the square stern's notch, would hold her steady in wild water.

"Will she carry us and the brig's crew?" Dan asked dubiously as Kiah maneuvered Bright into position. "And how many should we find—if we reach them in time?"

Kiah's eyes went calculatingly over the broad beam, the curved sides. "Obie claims she'll carry a ton o' fish—or men—and keep lots o' freeboard." Then less positively, "Nigh as I could judge her size, the brig'd carry no more'n six or seven men. We sh'd manage."

Obie approached from the fish shed with an extra pair of oars which he placed in the boat's bottom alongside his own and a handful of tholepins to be tossed into the bow. Together the three men swung the boat onto the sleds, and Bright lurched forward, more willingly now with the wind on his rump, in spite of the load. Neither Dan nor Obie questioned Kiah and he offered no prospectus of his plans. One move at a time—and the next was to gain a launching place on the island's leeward side.

Soon ox and men were past the closed doors and frosted windows of the house and out on the wind-raked point, where the cold drove remorsely through their heavy coats.

Though the end of the point was nearest the brig, trapped some two hundred and fifty yards offshore, the steep bank and tumbled boulders between it and the water precluded launching the boat there. Behind the higher land of the point itself was a low neck three hundred yards across, with Clam Cove on the seaward side matching the landing cove on the harbor. Kiah hawed the ox towards the flat head of Clam Cove.

Dark sweat melted the snow on the beast's heaving sides, but for once Kiah's whip knew no mercy. Dan had never guessed an ox could move so fast; the runners slid with surprising ease, for the wind left over the grass only a thin coating of snow. The three men hurried with heads slanted against the driving flakes. Now and then Kiah turned to face the wind as if to gauge its strength, or lifted the cap from his ear and listened to the veering sounds of the surf.

The outline of the house was lost behind them, land's edge and water's beginning lay unrevealed before them. At the height of a squall the world consisted of wind and snow and frozen ground.

Once Kiah turned and threw this bit of comfort across a gust, "The water ain't winter cold yet. 'Twon't ice up on our boat nor on the brig." And again, "The ebb sh'd last another hour; it's holdin' the seas back some, same as the wind's doin'." But when the outlines of the cove became visible he warned, "It'll be dirty where them combers meet the chop and the run o' the tide."

Little Obie saved his breath for keeping up with the others.

Bright balked when he reached sod's end. An ox, he snorted in protest, was a *land* animal. But a sharp lash across his quivering flank sent him plowing through the piled seaweed at the high-tide line, out upon the firm stretches of gravel and the low ridges of embedded rocks. The cove's ebb-bared bottom made not impossible footing, but the sleds dragged heavily in the softer spots. Bright leaned forward and flattened to his load. Kiah showed him the way, walking just ahead with gesturing arm and swinging whip and a voice that held a frightening urgency.

"Gee up a step, Bright," he shouted when Bright shied in dismay.

And, "Haw over there! Back haw!"

And occasionally, "Whoa!" which meant a delay while the men lifted clear an endangered runner.

89

To Dan their progress was unbearably creeping.

For seventy-five yards Bright followed his driver, placing his feet mistrustfully, taking with his huge neck muscles and the strong head-yoke the strain of sleds lurching over rocks where snow added treachery to always slippery seaweeds.

He reached the swirling line of spent seas and stood, hooves awash, eyes rolling at the turmoil before him, sides filling and collapsing like bellows, the steam of his mighty breathing lost in the whirling snow and spindrift. Bright's part in this venture was complete. Kiah laid the whip across the wide horns and paid tribute, "Most oxen would 'a' balked and we could never have tugged the boat to the water's edge."

The reef should be in view from here and, as the snow lifted momentarily, all three men peered seaward. Before the squall shut down again Dan glimpsed a black hump not remembered as part of the reef. Kiah nodded at his exclamation. The brig was not yet completely destroyed. There might still be time to save her crew.

In spite of the need for haste Kiah paused briefly, gazing out to where coarse threads of slanting snow and tossing spray wove an impenetrable curtain. Little Obie moved impatiently. However these were not wasted seconds, for there would be no time for gauging, once they were in the midst of sluicing seas and yawing gusts.

Utter desolation surrounded the small group at tide-line. The wind off the land howled over the men and out to sea, while along the waves' crests, the surf's thunder rolled in from the outer ledges, adding an awesome note to the dull slop of shallow waves and the hiss of snow melting in brine.

The smell at water's edge rasped the nostrils with an easterly's evil chill, the sting of snow, the fierce salt spume, the rankness of repulsive sediment now bared by the full-course tide and churned by the breakers.

This was Dan's first close acquaintance with any of those dreary acres below high-water mark—half New Erin's, half the sea's. *No,* he almost voiced his repudiation, *let the sea have them. New Erin and I claim no part of them.*

The approaching flood would exact them, rolling its broken combers in until the cove's mouth (where he might now wade from shore to shore) would be fathoms deep, indistinguishable from the vast expanse outside. He had never before completely realized the power of the moon's spell nor the inexorableness of the bewitched tides.

The ceiling of swirling snow and laden clouds pressed down upon the raw sea bottom on which they stood—three puny men and a panting ox of no more significance than the empty clam-shells underfoot or the torn rockweed awash in the shallow pools; and as easily tossed aside.

As Dan looked about him he knew stark fear and he kept his eyes down lest either companion read them.

In his brief terror he hoped that Kiah would turn from his gazing with an acknowledgment of their impotence. Dan had a vision of three men plodding back across the field, bound for home and safety, but defeated and somehow shamed.

However, when Kiah moved it was purposefully. The others bent with him to swing the boat from the sleds to a flat rock. Then he turned the ox and started him towards dry land; Bright could be trusted to pick his way to the lee of some building.

Little Obie spoke then and there was no hint of boasting in his voice, nothing ridiculous in his round figure and red face. "Kiah, I talked big back thyah in front o' the wimmin, so as not to scare 'em. But the chances don't look noan too good. Mr. Redmond here, he's got a wife and fambly. I been thinkin' I could manage the oars, with you at the sweep and the wind on our starn."

At this Dan's fear was pushed aside and forgotten. "Do you think my wife would want me safe ashore while you men . . .?" He gestured out into the storm, "I may be no rower, but I can take the for'rd oars and match your stroke, Obie."

He turned to his hired man, as a novice to a master. "Unless you think, Kiah, that I would be a hindrance, a useless weight that might cut down the chances of bringing those poor devils ashore."

Kiah's flat brown eyes met his with a new respect. "We'll do better with two rowing. Certainly." No hint that they all might stay safe ashore. "You'm a strong man, Mr. Redmond, if you ain't got Obie's heft t' come back on the oars. You take the for'rd thwart, like ye say. I'll be at the tiller oar and con ye what I can."

Dan took his seat and thrust the oars into place, waiting with tensed muscles and pounding heart for the moment to use them. He knew much depended upon a good start. He'd heard tales of boats swamped, and swamped again, as men strove to force them through the first line of breakers.

Braced against the wash, Kiah and Obie at either gunwale watched the seas beyond the bow and, after holding firm against three breakers that threatened to whelm all, they ran the boat out into the backwash. Obie tumbled to his seat, grabbing his oars. Then with Dan carefully pulling stroke for mighty stroke with him—a fouled oar would mean disaster—they drove the bow through the swirling water and gained way enough to swing her true and meet the next sea. Kiah, who had pulled himself over the stern from water to his middle, thrust his sweep into place and threw his weight against it. They were launched.

The first spray hit with a patter and ran down Dan's salt-stiffened coat like rain on a window. What followed was like flung bucketfuls. When they were clear of the low shore the wind slammed them. They rode quartering into the shallow seas, keeping all possible lee from the point, but turning to meet the larger waves bow on. Though the chop peaked into white plumes that leaped sidewise into their open boat they worked upshore, across wind and sea, towards where the brig should lie.

Occasionally Kiah shouted an order, "Back, back and hold," or, "Steady as ye go, now," but mostly he swung his own big oar to ease them through the confused seas that all about them toppled and collapsed. Crouched in the stern, he was perpetually drenched by flying spray as the wind flung the crest of one breaker back upon the next.

The two pairs of oars moved as one; Dan found the short unbroken rhythm less difficult to maintain than he had feared, though he dared not lift his eyes from Obie's broad, steady back. If it were no worse than this!

But he knew the real struggle would come farther offshore when they met the billows that, encountering wind and tide, climbed into crazy pyramids or sprawled in a smother of rage as a hidden shoal tripped their speeding feet.

They soon reached the more contentious water. While Kiah struggled to prevent the boat from swinging broadside to, the northeaster put its hands against the wide stern and pushed them relentlessly out into the turmoil. The chop, although flattened by the wind, nonetheless pounded them savagely. Below the broken surface, the ebb grabbed the keel and steadily pulled them away from their goal. For minutes at a time Dan and Obie dug their blades in and pulled, while the boat was lifted and dropped and bludgeoned, but seemingly denied gain.

They were taking in water, too; over the bow as they met a cresting comber, over the gunwales as the boat fell off and a peaked chop toppled. Their efforts at the oars must not lessen for even a stroke, and Kiah could shout no orders, for spume and snow hid everything but the white crests at the bow and the churning water at their oar-tips. Again and again Kiah brought the boat's head into a sea in the very nick of time.

Driving snow and blown spray lashed their faces as with whip-ends. Eyes smarted and filled and overran; there was no looking into the wind.

They rode on crests above roiled water, they dipped into hollows where rolling waves blotted out the gloomy sky and made briefly a windless valley. In each valley between crests, Kiah edged them westerly towards the reef, gaining a few feet before he was forced to swing the staggering bow to meet the next billow.

After what seemed an interminable struggle, Kiah cast a white-faced look ahead and half rose from the stern-sheets. He shouted, "*Now,* b'ys! Now!" and braced himself against the tiller.

Obie lifted to his oars as the bow climbed and Dan rose with him, putting every ounce of weight and muscle against the heavy blades, pulling until a white-hot pain replaced the nagging discomfort that had been gnawing his shoulders, until his chest screamed for a breath. He worked now, not for the unknown crew of a lost brig, but for Mercy and Patrick—for life. He felt a moment's pity that the sea might so soon take from Mercy the husband it had brought her.

They seemed at the center of a maelstrom; demoniac waves climbed above them; slewed them crosswise; tossed them to gray-green crests; sucked them down into black-green pits; pitched them headlong to bury the boat's nose in the oncoming sea. Yet the billow that would have ended its fellows' sport broke always a bit to this side or that, never directly upon them. Kiah still fought the lashing oar, Obie's blades rose and fell and, to his astonishment, Dan saw his own oars were rising and falling in unison though he was no longer conscious that his hands gripped them.

They would never live to reach the brig. They would break their hearts fighting and fall across their oars in defeat before the sea scattered them. (How sweet that moment's respite would be!) In all probability the brig that had called them out into this cruel welter no longer existed; such murderous surges had no doubt demolished her and with every send were tossing broken timbers and broken bodies across the reef.

Still he did not regret he had chosen to take his place with Obie and Kiah, who, knowing what they faced—as he hadn't known—had pitted their few planks, their arms and backs, their men's hearts against this fury. He was proudly one of them.

Water was washing about his legs. What had Obie said about a ton of fish and plenty of freeboard?

The little boat seems tired and slow. She lifts her head uncertainly. She drags her tail piteously. Kiah's long face is white and his lips drawn in snarling effort. Obie's oars lift slowly . . . more slowly. They find the water less surely. The starboard oar fum-

94

bles . . . catches the stroke again. The white snow is throwing a black blanket over the water. The white snow . . . The black water . . . The running waves are blacker. Blacker and smaller.

Kiah straightened. "We've made it, b'ys," he gasped. He paused to take a great breath. "We're inside the reef."

The breaking seas were now kept back by the rocky barricade, while wind and chop pushed the boat along, low and sluggish, but still afloat.

Obie's oars took up their old sure rhythm, but Dan could only pull his in and lie across them gasping. Though it seemed they had fought the sea for hours, he saw the afternoon's snow-blotted light was not perceptibly dimmer.

When he looked over his shoulder through the snow and flying foam, there dead ahead the shattered brig lay at a hopeless angle. Vicious seas leapt up the ledge to tear at her with white fangs, to dribble foam from her gnashed sides and broken back; but the low tide had saved her from complete destruction.

Four figures crouched in the bows, pitiful, helpless, seemingly beyond hope or despair, as Obie worked the small boat towards them and Kiah dropped his oar for a bailing scoop.

Chapter 11

OUTSIDE THE FROSTED KITCHEN WINDOW THE NIGHT WAS FAST RIDING down on the storm. Candles sputtered on the table but the shadows were deep. Molly, seated in the warm corner beside the stove, shivered as the wind rattled the latch and somewhere on an exposed corner found a board to bang.

Mercy opened the oven door and, as she tested the molasses cake with an experimental finger, its spicy fragrance filled the room; but for the two women anxiety soured all the kitchen's good smells of good food cooking. When she straightened, Mercy's eyes went yet again to the mantel clock and Molly's followed them.

"Mercy, you believe in your heart Dan's lost—they're all lost—and you won't tell me," she accused her sister-in-law in tones which held tears and terror.

"No such thing," Mercy valiantly denied, clasping to herself some of the courage she mustered for Molly. "Though it seems so terrible long, they've been gone little more than an hour. I made up my mind at the first I'd give them two hours before I started to worry."

What can I do but wait? she asked herself.

To Molly she added, "Just so they make the shore before pitch dark. For from the rote it's plain the tide has turned and will bring heavier seas."

Molly could detect no change in the surf's voice that always told so much to Kiah and to Mercy—but not to her, nor as yet to Dan.

Mercy busied herself with the simmering fish, and sizzling pork scraps at the back of the stove. She mused aloud, "I mind we had duck stew the night Pa brought Dan home."

Molly wanted her fear dressed out in words, wanted it expressed in order to have it denied. She went on with unwonted spirit, "Dan wouldn't listen to *me;* but *you* knew he might not come back. I saw it in your face. How could you let him go?"

"Let him go? Did you hear him ask my leave?" Mercy admonished her. "And if he had, could I keep him safe behind my petticoats and let other women's men perish? Would you want a man who'd *stay?*"

"But for strangers? Perhaps for wicked seamen who might murder us all in our beds?" Molly persisted solemn and big-eyed.

In spite of her heavy heart Mercy laughed, "You've heard stories of a different breed of seamen from the ones I know, Molly. Can you imagine Pa running around murdering people that had been good to him?"

96

"Oh, no! Indeed, I can not," Molly repudiated the thought. "Captain Sam is goodness itself.

"You, too, Mercy. You are truly good," she continued with timid earnestness. "I must tell you that when Dan wrote he had taken a wife in this strange land, one outside his church as well, I was troubled. I was afraid he had let gratitude and loneliness lead him. That he would be unhappy, and make his wife unhappy, too."

Molly's triangular little face twisted as she forced herself to go on. "How can I tell you, Mercy, how good and kind and brave I've found you? So patient with my notions, too. You consider everybody, Obie and Kiah, even a boy off a fishing vessel, before yourself." She put out a hand pleadingly. "Let me be truly your sister. Teach me to forget my silly fears. Then," she added shyly, "perhaps people will love me, as they do you."

Mercy could only stir the pork chops intently while Molly dabbed at her eyes, then ventured a trembling smile. Damie's daughter did not open her heart easily but this outpouring forced it through surprise.

"Why, Molly," she finally managed. "Why, dear little Molly, whatever gave you such ideas? As for loving you, we *all* do. Everyone on New Erin, all the folks on Grannie's Head. You're so little and sweet, Molly, we don't want you to change. Except maybe Skipper, so he wouldn't have to spend so much time tied up in the barn."

She tried for a light tone, feeling humble and unworthy of Molly's admiration. *Me! Kind and brave and good! My gracious, I don't know what to say to her.*

What Molly needs, she reflected, *is a mother, or a husband. Someone to lean on.*

Suddenly the silence, with its mingled embarrassment and intimacy, was broken by the sound of voices above the wind.

Mercy turned to face the door and the drops from the forgotten spoon in her hand spat on the hot stove unheeded. "Oh, Molly!" The tears were in her own voice now. "They're *back!*

97

Listen! I hear Dan! And that's a strange voice. At least some of the crew are saved."

Molly had used up her courage for one afternoon. "Mercy, I couldn't meet strange men now; I'd be sure to burst into tears. You do better with me out of the way. Now that I know Dan's safe, let me keep the fire and the baby in the drawing room."

"You goose!" Mercy chided her affectionately. "Run along, then." She heard the hall door close softly as she gave her kitchen a final scrutiny.

The stove gave out a mighty heat, the full teakettles steamed, the pot of fish and potatoes bubbled, the table was set with high-piled plates of bread and cake. *Ma was never one to be caught with an empty pantry. And tonight I'm glad that's one lesson she taught me,* Mercy rejoiced.

Blankets and mens garments were draped over chairs to warm. She had brought them forth with misgivings, for Mercy had her share of the prevalent superstitions. Was it tempting Providence to prepare so openly for her men's return? Then she decided bravely, *Better to put all away in grief and bitterness later, if need be, than for wet and hungry men to find a tardy welcome.*

Her glance showed nothing amiss; she smoothed her apron and tucked in a strayed lock as with a heart like to burst with relief and joy she threw open the door.

Dan came first and close upon his heels were four strangers. They crossed the doorstep with effort, lifting one foot in its squelching sea boot, putting it down and waiting (it seemed) till their numbed brains could command the numbed muscles to lift the other. The single low step into the kitchen was an obstacle to be stumbled over. As she stood at the open door and urged them in, Mercy thought she had never seen men so exhausted, so near collapse. Kiah and Obie completed the procession and then she quickly closed the door against the wind and snow, while rescued and rescuers alike dripped and shivered as the warmth hit them.

The strangers' faces were gaunt with fatigue and, under the

98

stubble of beards, blue with cold. Truth to tell the New Erin men looked little better.

"Mrs. Redmond, this is Captain Larkin of the wrecked *Osprey*," Dan was saying. "Captain, my wife."

Mercy saw a big man in his early thirties, with red hair that curled as he removed his cap. "We have put you to a great deal of trouble, ma'am," he said, glancing around the room, and even in this extremity Mercy felt his charm; clean and rested he would be uncommonly attractive.

She had heard of handsome Richard Larkin, out of Hines' Harbor, who, if stories could be credited, had a way with women, and used it to his own ends. At another time Mercy would have felt ill at ease with a man of his reputation, but the blue eyes he turned to her now were lost and boyish. Mercy took his wet hand warmly in hers.

From that moment she was mistress of herself and of the kitchenful of distressed men. Customarily she left the words and gestures of hospitality to Dan; but tonight she was fulfilling the coastal woman's duty and glory—succoring those whom her men had rescued from the sea.

"You are each welcome, and more." Her smile added assurance to her words. Then piling bedding and garments upon the woodbox she found seats for them all: the couch near the stove for the older man who appeared dazed and a little hard of hearing, a chair for this one, a stool for that, the washbench from behind the door for Kiah. She pulled all as close to the stove as possible.

"I've supper ready," she told them and heard Obie sniff appreciatively. "There's gruel, too, for any who might be sick or hurt. But before I set you to the table you must get out of your wet clothes.

"Now, first of all, a hot drink." She had put the mugs out in readiness; now she filled them with the bitter, hot brew from the teapot and a generous lacing of rum. She pressed one into each pair of chilled hands. "Drink now," she adjured them, "before you catch your deaths of cold and wet."

They drank with noisy slurps, their hands about the hot mugs shaking.

"Wet!" Little Obie could not resist such an audience. "I sh'd say 'wet.' The finishin' touch was when we got pitched out amongst them plagued big rocks on the p'int. I ain't been so out-and-out soaked sence the day I was baptized." He chortled at his joke despite chattering jaws.

Mercy asked quickly, "Your boat, Obie, is she smashed?"

"One garboard stove and a broken thwart, nigh as I could tell," he rejoined cheerfully. "We snaked her up above tide-line till the weather moderates."

Throughout the evening as she bustled about, Mercy heard, from one voice or another, the story of the *Osprey* and the rescue of her crew in just such disjointed snatches:

"The brig was jumpin' along like a singed cat."

"I sent all hands below except the man lashed to the wheel with me," this from Captain Larkin.

"Without a stitch of canvas and the seas stampin' over us."

". . . foremast went and took the main-topmast and yards."

Unreal yet familiar words evoking pictures of terror and destruction, heard and heard again throughout her life in many such stories. It was days before the pieces fitted together to tell how the *Osprey* had been crippled offshore, driven into the bay and finally cast upon the reef, how the rescuers had gained the ledge and how Obie's laden boat had run before the seas for the nearest shore and made it, though she had dumped them out at the last.

All that evening, however, while the wind howled and the snow hissed upon the windows, it was enough that Dan and Obie and Kiah were home again and that they had cheated the sea of four victims.

When the hot drink had revived them somewhat, Kiah's first thought was for Bright, left out in the storm after he had served them so well.

"Bright's in his stanchion, Kiah," Mercy was happy to tell him.

"I heard him rubbing his yoke against the kitchen wall and went out to see what I could do. He followed me to the stable door and stood so patient whilst I took the yoke off! But," she apologized, "I had to leave the sleds where the shafts fell.

"Then while I was about it I filled the mangers and milked the brindle cow for tonight's supper. The others can surely wait till morning. I filled the water buckets and put Skipper in the barn; so there's no need of your going out again in this storm, Kiah," she ended triumphantly.

"Mi's Redmond!" The words started in amazed remonstrance and ended in weary gratitude.

"I thought it better to keep busy than to wear the window through with useless watching," she belittled what she had done. "And Molly rocked the baby and tended the fires for me."

The men had finished their mugs of tea, and Mercy pointed out the heavy garments on the woodbox. "I've set out every stitch I thought might serve—Kiah's and my husband's. There should be enough to go around."

She hesitated and looked at Captain Larkin, "I thought the brig might have a larger crew."

He answered her, "I'm awaiting command of a new East Indies ship out of Salem. The *Osprey* was small and old and I took her only to fill in time. We were Halifax-bound with sugar and molasses from Mantanzas when the storm struck us two days ago." He paused at memories of the storm and continued heavily, "I had a crew of five, but I lost a man to the comber that carried our boat away last night. And one man, a boy really, was hurt bad when the mainmast crashed. He died just before your husband's boat reached us."

He and his men stared into their empty mugs and Mercy's eyes filled for the lost shipmates. Not only the evil perished while the righteous were spared, as she had once believed, for plain to see they had all loved the dead boy.

But the living were still to do for. She gave Dan garments for himself and the captain and sent them to the stove in the drawing room while she began to sort out clothes for the others. Almost immediately, however, Dan beckoned her from the hall and Mercy excused herself. "Kiah will see to your wants," she told the strangers.

On entering the drawing room she noticed Molly's absence and the empty cradle. *She's slipped away with Patrick into our bedroom when she heard Dan and Captain Larkin approach,* she thought with loving amusement.

Dan's discarded clothes were spreading a wet stain across the new carpet, but that seemed unimportant, for lifting her eyes to where Captain Larkin sat, she saw his startlingly white face and his right arm held stiffly across his chest.

"Mercy," Dan explained his summons, "Captain Larkin is hurt. We need your help in getting these soaked clothes off and in binding up his arm."

"It's really nothing," the captain assured her. "The flesh got torn when the topmast fell. Now the arm has stiffened and it bleeds too freely when I try to get it out of the sleeve."

Mercy's inspection revealed a jagged tear and adhering ends of cloth matted with blood. "I see," she said calmly, as if she'd often coped with such wounds, though her heart was quaking. (Folks told her she was like her Grammie Abigail, but she had still to earn experience, to gain skilled fingers.) "We must cut these sleeves away. My scissors are here, but, Dan, the men will be changing their clothes about the stove so you'll have to get me a basin of warm water to soak these ragged cloth ends free."

She remembered her father's account of cutting a fishhook from a man's cheek, at sea where a vessel's master must be its doctor. "And Dan, a good stiff drink for Captain Larkin before we tackle this."

At last it was over: the blood-soaked sleeves in the stove, the sweating captain in dry clothes and his torn arm bound in soft linen rags saved for just such emergencies. Mercy, proud but trembling and nauseated, could send Dan to join the others at the kitchen table.

102

As he opened the door, the clatter of dishes and the mutter of men's voices came across the hall. Kiah and Obie, bless them, were caring for the strangers. This was as it should be, people helping one another and acknowledging their interdependence.

"Captain Larkin," she said gently, "if you will lie down here on the sofa I'll bring you some gruel." She picked up the basin and bloody rags, anxious to get them out of sight. It would be the final straw to have Molly faint, she thought.

As the captain rose to his feet and moved unsteadily towards the sofa, Molly, who had dropped asleep beside Patrick and wakened from a troubled nap, chose this moment to open the bedroom door and slip silently into the drawing room. Although the light from the candelabra blinded her, it was apparently insufficient to reveal another presence to the exhausted captain. Swaying, he brushed against her.

Molly, not fully awake and worn by the day's emotions, went completely to pieces. She screamed and pushed against the big stranger wildly, as if he were one of those murderous seamen she had mentioned to Mercy.

He turned and staggered, weaving from weariness, from the close heat, the searing pain in his arm and the fumes of Dan's generous sedative. He put out his good arm as if to encircle the feminine figure before him.

"Don't touch me, you savage, drunken brute," Molly cried and aimed a hysterical blow. It landed on the freshly dressed arm and the captain came stiffly upright. He shook his red head, trying to focus his eyes upon Molly's white face and trembling mouth.

In spite of her dismay Mercy realized, *My bold Captain Lady-killer finds this strange treatment!* Then she noticed a red stain mottling the new bandage. *Is all that to be gone through with again?* She could have wept with distaste and weariness. Then swiftly, *The poor man, how his wound must hurt.*

"Molly Redmond, I'm ashamed of you!" Alarm at the damage to the injured arm lent an unusual edge to her exclamation. "Is

103

this the way you mean to grow brave and kind? Striking an injured man! Look at his arm . . ."

Captain Larkin interrupted, "Mrs. Redmond, your little girl is not as kindly, nor as well-bred, as yourself. I hope it's not been a case of sparing the rod and spoiling the child." He deliberately closed one eye.

Mercy was almost as confused as Molly. *The wretch,* she thought. *A few minutes ago I was afraid he'd keel over before the last bandage was on. And now, here he is, thorning Molly.*

"Captain Larkin," she said severely, "this is my husband's sister, Miss Redmond."

He expressed his pleasure at the meeting; then protested his clumsiness, his lack of manners, with a charm that belied both.

Molly lifted her brimming violet eyes from the reddening bandages and looked into his dazed blue ones, while her pointed face lost the last of its fright. "I'm terribly sorry," she told him contritely and put her soft little hand on his good arm. "I shall never forgive myself if I've done you harm."

"Indeed, Miss Redmond, the sight of you does me good, but," weaving again, "if you'll excuse me, I think I'll lie down."

Strange, Mercy mused afterward, *what makes a man and woman fall in love. And how opposites attract.*

A few days later Little Obie informed Mercy secretly and sorrowfully that he saw what way the wind was settin'. He bade Molly a significant and reproachful farewell, bent a blackly accusing glare upon the puzzled Richard, and left in his patched boat.

"His heart is broke. Certainly," Kiah told Mercy. "He swears that as long as his head is above the sod he'll never come anigh the island again."

In the meantime, with the variableness of early winter, the morning after the storm broke fine and warm, and the *Osprey's* crew were taken to the mainland. However, for two weeks Captain Richard's arm, although it appeared to be healing cleanly and well, gave him a great deal of trouble, especially after Molly

104

kindly relieved Mercy of its care.- When he left New Erin he was a firm friend of the Redmonds and, avowedly, a changed man. It was understood he would be back in the spring and that Molly would be waiting for him.

Chapter 12

ALTHOUGH NEARLY A YEAR SEPARATED THEM, MERCY ALWAYS REmembered the northeaster that wrecked the *Osprey* as linked with the first real storm of her marriage. That storm, which sadly tossed her about and left her adrift, struck out of an apparently clear sky; but there had been weather signs, could she have read them.

As Mercy crossed the hall, a September sunset was gilding the bay and no whisper of the sea reached her, only Molly's letter in her hand recalled that wild evening of the previous November.

How good Kiah had been, when near midnight, with everyone else finally abed, she had wearily faced the kitchenful of wet clothes and dirty dishes. "Let me glaum onto that dishrag, Mi's Redmond," he'd insisted, though he must have been bone-weary. "'Twon't be the first time ever I waded through dishwater. Certainly."

Deftly putting things to rights, he'd told her shyly how as oldest child he had helped his frail mother with her housework until a sister had grown enough to free him for the sea. Mercy's heart had yearned over the homely, awkward boy (Kiah could have been no other!) tied to broom and dishpan. She had laughed with him at his wryly sketched predicaments, and had forgotten fatigue. Later, hanging her kitchen apron behind the door, she'd thanked him, "Why, it's been almost like washing up with Bethiah."

He had answered in a quiet voice, "Bethiah?" Then, "Aye-ah; like Bethiah. Certainly."

Since then he had found ways to lighten many small tasks for her. Dan was never one to see how work piled up at times and as for Molly helping, as Kiah had often hinted she should—all last winter and spring Molly had been in love, sewing and dreaming of Richard's return.

They'd all shared Molly's plans and helped them along so that the winter of waiting and preparation had been cozy and happy, and the May wedding, after Richard had returned impatient to claim his bride and join his Salem ship, had been a merry one.

Molly had worn one of the Dublin gowns from her scarcely opened trunks. How sweet a little bride she had been—like a flower in the rose taffeta with the full, full skirt beneath her tiny waist. Prettier than Mercy could have believed possible, remembering the pathetic figure she had greeted at the wharf; but over winter Molly's face had rounded, color had come to her fine skin and a glow to her violet eyes. That day no one had wondered at Richard Larkin's choice of such a shy little body, though many a girl, watching the resplendent groom, had sighed and wished herself in Molly's slippers.

Dan had spared no trouble nor expense for his sister's wedding and as host had charmed the guests that crowded every room: merry Larkins by the sloopfuls; Barrington business acquaintances with their wives and children; all the Prince's Cove friends and neighbors. Bethiah, sparkling and pretty in a new lilac silk, and—all of a sudden—grown-up, had been a magnet drawing the oldest Doane boy (of the Barrington Doanes) from his companions. Pa's fair head had moved above all and a happy laugh had followed him, while Ma (who'd come a week ahead—bless her—to aid in the preparations) had bustled about, lending a hand to every task and a clinching word to every conversation.

Contrasting with the stiff local manners had been the easier French courtesy of Captain d'Entremont who with his brother-in-law had brought the priest to New Erin in their shallop.

Strange, it had been, to see a priest at a Prince's Cove wedding!

Father Burke, a youngish man with a hearty laugh and a keen blue eye, had joined in toasts of wine and in those from the rum-puncheon in the kitchen where Little Obie (his head still above the sod and his vows forgotten) held sway.

Yes, the priest, despite long-rooted local prejudices, had made himself popular, "spinning yarns" in a rich Irish brogue and exchanging pleasantries with Dan, who answered him in the same accents, "put on" for the occasion. Perhaps it had been only to amuse the guests, perhaps it had lessened some homesickness in the hearts of each, to assume the speech once so familiar.

Together they had grieved over the tender, mournful isle of their birth, her wrongs, the ebbing of her lifeblood across the Atlantic. Mercy had been surprised at Dan's vehement protestations of love for the Old Country, the nostalgia in references to familiar spots as well known and loved by the Irish priest. Listening, she had known an unreasoning jealousy for New Erin.

At other times she had been painfully aware of the priest's sharp eyes upon her and had recalled the belief that some men could tell at a glance when a woman was in the family way. Nonsense, she had scolded herself, even *I* am not sure. Nevertheless she had hurried self-consciously past the laughing groups that formed about Father Burke.

There'd been little time to consider anything but her guests' welfare, yet all day the sight and smell of the huge roasts of island beef and mutton, the mounds of cakes and crusty bread, the rows of pies, had turned her queasy.

That evening the wedded pair had left in a Larkin sloop to the fluttering of kerchiefs, and shouted good wishes from the guests gathered on the wharfside, and to the echoes of Skipper's hoarse, delirious barks. Only the St. Joseph shallop need await the morning tide, so that before dark the Barrington and Prince's Cove sails had all disappeared behind Nigh Hill or Narrah.

Then Mercy had been overtaken by weariness and complete nausea and had known surely she was again with child.

She smiled a bit ruefully now, remembering her mingled joy and dismay, for Patrick had not yet been weaned. Dan had been no comfort. After sitting late with Father Burke, he had stumbled into their room and had reeked of spirits, so that instead of sharing her knowledge in the tender circle of her husband's arms, Mercy had lain awake against the wall and listened with a vexed heart to his heavy breathing. She had never seen him affected by drink; never, until then when she had needed him clearheaded and responsive to her mood.

But when the last guest had gone and life had resumed a slower rhythm, Dan had rejoiced at her news and encompassed her days with solicitude. . . . Only this suppertime he had stood at the cradle's head, laughing with her because their son had already outgrown its narrow sides, agreeing it would be sweet indeed to have another baby under the green hood.

Mercy knew she was favored beyond other women with such a young, handsome, well-to-do husband, who loved her with a passion and tenderness that kept her wondering and humble.

Her heart was light as she opened the parlor door. The room had scarcely been entered since the wedding and she made a mental note to air out its stagnant dampness the first sunny day, lest mildew form on the fine furniture or the new carpet.

When she pulled the lace curtain back from the western window, she stood for a moment drinking in the beauty of the sunset anchorage.

Then she turned to the leathern-bound family Bible, lying sacred and aloof on the center table. Pa had bought it for her and Dan that never-to-be-forgotten time in Halifax, as a symbol and consecration for the new family of which they were the heads. In it were pages set aside for Marriages, Births and Deaths; the events of Life. Under Aunt Grizzie's beaming eye Dan, in his scholarly hand, had recorded their marriage—the first entry. There'd been additions, Patrick's birth and Molly's marriage.

Molly's letter would be kept in the Bible, for letters were rare

108

and treasured. Although Mercy knew this one almost by heart she opened its folds and read it again, forming each word with her lips and relishing it. *I can almost hear Molly speaking as I read,* she thought affectionately, aware of how greatly she missed the piquant face, the high clear voice of the sister-in-law she had learned to love.

"Dear Brother and Sister," Molly had begun in her lady's hand. "We have sighted the Boston ship *Success* and Richard says he will send a letter across as we pass, so that you may have News of us that this leaves us both in the best of Health as I trust it finds you dear Ones."

She went on to describe their setting out from Salem and the first weeks at sea. "I sometimes think this cannot be me, my Home a Ship's Cabin that Love makes as safe as a rock Castle. I do not fear even the Storms so much on a Ship under Richard's Command. Richard is teaching me Navigation and many things about the rigging of the Ship."

Mercy glanced along and laughed a bit impatiently, *"Richard, Richard." I'm sure I don't boast so of Dan, who's far superior.*

The letter closed with many protestations of gratitude for kindnesses received and, "My Husband sends his obedient Regards to all on New Erin and Grannie's Head. I trust Little Obie has gotten over his Romantick Despair and will find one more suitable than

Your loving sister, Molly.

"P.S. Tell Patrick his Aunt Molly would dearly love to see those blue eyes and golden curls and tell him not to grow too big before she comes sailing into New Erin anchorage some 'sloppy sou'wester.' "

So this was timid Molly, who could never be persuaded to cross the harbor even when Kiah pointed it out lying "all starched and ironed." Molly, writing somewhat condescendingly to the stay-at-homes from the after-cabin of the *Margaret Scott,* somewhere "in the Mozambique Channel."

She refolded the letter and placed it in the Bible, against the page that held Molly's name and Richard's.

Then she must add to her happiness by turning to "Births" where another name would soon join Patrick's. A girl's name? A boy's?

The leaf folded back. There was the name "Patrick Samuel Redmond" and the date, "August 14, 1842." Just as Dan had entered it. But above it in the same clear hand—unexpected, unbelievable, senseless words. "Born out of Wedlock."

The smile left her lips slowly as the color drained from her face.

Her eyes traced the words again. They had made no mistake. She stood motionless, too surprised for anger as yet.

When had Dan penned such a lie? And *why?* "Oh, I must find him," she whispered, and found herself trembling.

Unconscious of what she did she picked up the thick book, and because her arms shook so uncontrollably she clasped it to her breast as she moved toward the door. She had the queer lightheaded feeling that once before she had walked thus with dragging feet through the familiar rooms, that every sick thud of her heart was an echo of a former experience, now recalled faintly as one recalls a sad elusive dream. Most troubling of all was the sense that she went forward to greater unhappiness and went without choice.

Between one breath and the next her contentment had been turned to a pain that she refused to acknowledge lest it overwhelm her. She would keep it down until she had seen Dan. He had written those false words in the sacred pages of the Bible, their wedding Bible. *But, he'll explain it all. I'll understand in a few minutes,* she told herself without faith in her own words.

Chapter 13

SHE REACHED THE OFFICE WHERE DAN WAS WORKING AT THE AC-
counts which absorbed so much of his time and kept him so
distrait. She seldom intruded here, for lately Dan resented any
hint of interference or advice.

As she opened the door, warm air came to her in a soft rush
and in the grate of the Franklin stove she saw the gray ashes
of burnt papers. Black sunset shadows lay outside the eastern
windows, which dimly outlined Dan at his desk. In the poor
light Mercy thought he lifted his head from his hand with a
startled movement, as if he had not heard her at the latch but
had been dreaming, and not happily, in the dusk.

He rose slowly to his feet, but as his eyes went to her face and
the clasped Bible, he braced himself against the desk at his side
—almost as if he faced an expected trouble. Dan, whose arms
came out for her so eagerly always when they two were alone
as now! *He knows why I'm here,* Mercy realized, and her hope
of repudiation or simple explanation died.

She went forward and, looking full into his face, opened the
Book upon his desk, covering the clutter of papers. "Dan," she
said, "I found this entry in the Bible. What is the meaning of it?"

In her new pregnancy Mercy had lost the color and flesh she
had worn so entrancingly after Patrick's birth; but never had Dan
thought to see her like this, with each bone outlined under the
strained white skin, with her gray eyes deep-sunken. A ghost of
herself, an accusing ghost.

He dropped his eyes to where her finger pointed but he had
no need to peer through the fading light to read the words.

"Mercy," he said in a tight voice, "Mercy, listen to me. You
know, you've always known, that I belong to the Holy Roman
Church."

What has his Church to do with this? Mercy wondered as Dan continued.

"I was thrown on this shore, in a land of strange ways and a different religion, but of great kindliness. I came to love you so that your love meant more than Heaven itself." His eyes were seeking hers. "So I married you in the manner you and your parents wished, forgetting (or pretending to forget) that for a Catholic no ceremony is a true marriage unless a priest performs it."

Mercy cried out at that, "But you agreed beforehand! Pa would never have heard of our marriage else. You stood beside me and spoke your vows as I spoke mine, before God and man. No marriage, Dan! Think! What do you call *me* then? What would you make of Patrick?"

He moved towards her but she turned away, her thickened figure under the snowy apron held unyieldingly. Dan dropped his arms.

"You know I love you, Mercy," he said, trying to break through to her with words that had reached her heart so often. "With a true love, the noblest thing my life has known—not a sinful love, as Father Burke . . ."

"Father Burke!" Mercy exclaimed in astonishment that brought her about to face her husband. "What has Father Burke to do with our love?"

"He is a Catholic priest. At the time of Molly's wedding he urged me to have you adopt my faith so that we might receive the sacrament of marriage. He reminded me that I was living in sin."

Was that why the priest's sharp eyes had been upon her? She recalled the night she had left the Irish priest and her husband alone before the fire. She cried, "Father Burke!"

Dan's brow furrowed angrily. His words were cold rocks thrown to bruise her. "As a spiritual director of my Church he was bound to speak. He was performing his duty—pointing out mine."

112

No thought of me, Mercy cried inwardly.

Dan's voice softened again as she remained silent. "The morning after he talked to me, I saw the Bible as it lay open at the record of Molly's marriage. I wrote . . . what I did. Not to hurt you but to remind myself of the wrong I had done both you and our son. I meant to right it as soon as possible. Then you came to me with the news of our second child, and afterward . . . well, other things came up. So I planned to wait until you were yourself again before broaching the matter."

He regretted that she had come across the written words and been wounded by them, but the priest had wakened in him a sense of guilt; and generations of persecuted Catholic forebears had added their silent upbraiding.

Mercy, uncomprehending, looked at him in despair. He could break her heart, shame her and her child for a creed which, she could have sworn, he had given no more than a passing thought since coming to Grannie's Head.

She had continued in her quiet faith. The meetinghouse in Prince's Cove had a pastor only when Mr. Allbright arrived on circuit each spring and from the island it was impossible to attend the evening prayer meetings, but like her Pilgrim forebears, Mercy felt every man to be his own priest, needing only the Word as guide. So she read her Bible long and carefully, that the Lord's way for her might be plain. She had not demanded that Dan tread the same path with her, neither had she dreamed they had been walking so far apart.

"I didn't ask you to give up your faith," she reminded him, "since I couldn't give up mine. Pa warned me that different religions in our home might be like rooms closed against each other. 'Half the joy of marriage,' he said, 'is turning to the mind and heart of the one you love, without let or hindrance. But if there must be closed rooms, let each one respect the other's. It's not so good as open doors, but you can make a happy home and marriage that way, if you've both a mind to.'

"I'd forgotten his words till this minute. But, Dan, you know

113

I have never so much as touched your door latch, yet you tell me you planned to come storming into my room and drag me, willing or no, into yours."

Dan seemed touched. "Not that, Mercy. I would have led you gently. Even Father Burke cautioned patience."

She brushed that aside.

"Dan, neither you nor Father Burke had a right to blemish my good name or Patrick's. Tell me you will erase those ugly words from the Bible and from your mind."

His eyes were shadowed and she could read nothing from his closed lips. She had always delighted in the strength of his chin —could it be merely stubborn? Certainly it was now set against her pleading. She knew, and did not care, that her own face was frozen under his gaze; let Dan prove his intent before ever she opened her heart to him again.

His answer came at last, "As my wife you should be guided by me. Father Burke was right. The Church believes . . ."

"The Church believes . . ." her voice changed from faint mockery to impatience, "Dan Redmond, what do *you* believe?"

Dan answered flatly, "I believe what my Church teaches."

They were strangers staring at each other across widening waters. Mercy closed the Bible, clasped it again to her bosom and left the room.

Dan stood and watched her go.

The twilight had deepened suddenly or had this nightmare been of long duration? Mercy crossed the darkening rooms like a sleepwalker, placed the Bible on the marble-topped table and foolishly dusted an edge with a finger. She fitted Molly's happy letter between the pages as she had planned to do. "Ah, Molly," she cried brokenly, "if you could know what your letter has done!"

She stepped to draw the curtains. A gray fog swirled past the window, blotting out the sunset. She mused forlornly, *The warmth, the colors, the beauty are gone. From the sky and water; from my life.* She believed they would never return and couldn't dream that she would find in softer tints on deeper waters a beauty more satisfying.

She turned from the blank window, went through the seldom-used front hall—no chance of meeting Dan here—and out into the fog. Its chill struck through her gingham dress but, shivering, she rounded the corner of the house. Then she hastened her steps as if to outdistance the pain she carried with her, until she was almost running towards the southern shore where the surf was moaning and mourning softly under the fog.

"Out of wedlock. Oh, Dan, how could you? Living in sin!" She was crying the impossible words aloud as she came to the head of Clam Cove. Here was the low dike which last spring had been built between the cove and the shallow pond. One mother-of-pearl evening she had walked along the top with Dan and watched the seas creaming. . . .

Oh, no! No memories left now but of the black words before her eyes and of the blow that Dan had dealt her after all his protestations of love. Dan, her husband, sworn to honor her, to cleave to her above all others.

She was gasping as she ran along the dike top, dragging her wet skirts through the rank, hip-high burdocks, lamb's quarters and coarse grasses. From the shore rose the stench from rotting banks of seaweeds, the ugly slobber of the tide licking amongst them.

An hour ago, recalling the night when she had cared for the *Osprey's* crew, she had pictured herself a serene matron whose husband and children might any day rise up and call her blessed, even as the Scripture promised. She laughed in ragged scorn at her pride and its downfall.

She knew herself to be only a child, lost and helpless when her bolstering love for Dan was removed. She tried to pray, but bitterness got between her and God. She wanted desperately to run to her father's arms, so blessedly familiar and unchanging. For Dan was a stranger. Her heart might never have answered his pounding heart so close above it; her body might never have

115

cried out to his, or stirred in response. They were aliens, of different blood and beliefs, incapable and undesirous of understanding.

Each step was a struggle with saturated skirts and entangling weeds. The child within her leapt—a basin of cold water in a hysterical face. She stopped short. *What am I doing? This child, and Patrick, left alone in the cradle. What have I been thinking of?*

She was drenched to the waist and her breath was coming sharp and shallow. Beneath the wet apron she put her hands under her distended abdomen, easing the downward pull. No one would see, here in the fog and the gathering darkness. She forced her breath to come deep and regular. The feeling of being lost and wandering in a broken world ebbed and in its place came a flood of realization. She must get herself and her unborn child out of this poisonous night air, away from the chill off the sea, out of the dripping grasses.

Life allowed no escape, no running away. She must go back, take up her duties as wife and mother. With her decision came the relief of tears, but unheeding them she began to retrace her steps slowly and carefully. She must not remember Dan and her slain love; she would school herself to be one of those women who live for their children, whose husbands are merely a cross to be borne. The tears flooded afresh at the dismal picture of such poverty after riches. She felt a creeping lassitude and numbness, grateful after the sharp agony.

She reached the curving cove-side with its steep banks. She must watch her steps now, in the half-dark, over the black, wet rocks under foot. Almost at the cautionary thought she felt her foot suddenly twist and catch—whether on her dragging skirt or on a bit of fog-greased kelp, she never knew. She flung up her arms and had barely time to push a cry into the muffling fog as she fell. The boulders beneath the bank rose swiftly. There was a red-hot jolt, pain and blackness.

Skipper was barking to be let out. She couldn't come wide awake or push the quilts back from her legs to get out of bed.

Ah, there was Kiah's voice, soothing Skipper. Kiah would see to things.

She didn't drop back to sleep, though the barking stopped. She was too cold. That Dan! He must have all the covers again! Then troubling words were close against her hair and face. Troubling because they came on Kiah's voice and not on Dan's; and because anguish was in them. Kiah, too, must be caught somehow in the pain that flooded her.

"Poor Kiah," she murmured.

She felt herself lifted and carried through breaking seas of agony. Finally she knew the softness of her own bed beneath her racked body. Then Kiah's voice came faintly once more, "You'd best care for yer wife, Mr. Redmond, whilst I go fer M'is Damie."

Chapter 14

" 'TIS AN ILL WIND THAT BLOWS NOBODY GOOD," DAMIE ALWAYS maintained, and Mercy's weary sickness brought the boon of Serena Swim to New Erin.

Kiah suggested her while Mercy lay uncaring and Damie fretted. "Her mother and mine was cousins," he told Damie. "I've heard tell she's a good cook. And *clean!* Certainly." He swallowed hard and went on in an embarrassed rush as if his conscience drove him, "She's a good woman, too. No fault of hers she's had man trouble. Oh, he married her. Made out he did, anyways. But it 'peared he a'ready had a wife down Liverpool way. Serena's well quit of him, certainly. But she made heavy weather of it fer a spell, so they tell."

Even had the need been less, Damie could not have resisted a woman with such an unfortunate history; so on the first moderate

117

day Kiah had taken his skiff and fetched his second cousin from Cape White to help out "for a time."

Folks said Serena had a tongue bitter as a no'theast squall; certainly her face held some of a northeaster's bleakness. Her thin colorless hair was drawn back so tightly that Kiah was once moved to inquire innocently whether she slept with her eyes open, or loosened her halyards a mite to lower her lids. Serena's thin lips never smiled at such good-natured jibes, her wintry eyes never twinkled. Kiah 'lowed her trouble had soured her some. Certainly.

Though she was scarcely older than Mercy it was impossible to imagine her ever young and madly in love with a rapscallion; but through the years she seemed not to change, remaining to the end gray and angular and quick as a steel trap.

It took Damie but a few days to judge Serena's cooking and housekeeping, then she had handed over the affairs of the New Erin household and, since the doctor had declared Mercy out of danger, gone back to her own home. "Not but what Bethiah, fifteen years old 'n' all, couldn't keep house," she explained, "but Philip's started to shoot up lately and tongues might wag."

Serena boasted she spoke her mind no matter who she 'fronted, and she greeted Mercy, lying still and white in bed, "Well, I must say I can't see noan o' the prettiness Kiah was braggin' up. I d'know as ever I see a woman more like a blowed-out candle than what you be, M'is Redmond." Her pale eyes showed no sign of sympathy.

For many mornings, as regularly as she appeared with a bowl of gruel, Serena announced, "Don't ye go a-countin' on me fer long, mind. I allus vowed and declared I wouldn't stay on an island if every beach rock was a gold piece."

Nonetheless, Mercy soon knew, somehow, that Serena was to stay with her through the years—another right hand and a stanch friend.

In all those years Serena referred to her own troubles but twice and then briefly; but understandably she judged men a cross the Inscrutable had fashioned for women's backs. They cluttered and dirtied the house and devoured grub at a disgusting rate when home, then were off to sea leaving the women to worry their hearts out—and like enough a new baby on the way to top off everything!

Captain Sam had noticed from the first that Serena and Damie didn't pull strings, but each grudgingly gave the other her due and Damie had seemed content to leave Mercy and her family in Serena's hands.

It can't be Serena's not feedin' 'em, he decided, passing through the Nickerson kitchen where Damie was working her butter after a morning visit to New Erin. Yet the furious little spurts of yellow fat, the resounding thumps of the wooden bowl, declared plainly that Damie was upset. He moved more slowly so that she might unburden her worries, if so inclined.

"Sam, Mercy's no better," she blurted, "and I can't fathom out why. She's had a hard time but other wimmin has lost a baby and lived to bear a dozen more. 'Tain't all that."

Sam waited.

"She fell on the rocks after sundown! Kiah says he heared her cry above the cove's wash. What was she adoin' there at that hour, I sh'd like to know? Mr. Redmond says nawthin'. But it 'pears t' me he blames hisself. You heard him swear that night he'd foller Mercy if she died. Talkin' wild, like he'd make 'way with hisself."

Damie paused and rested her hands upon the golden butter island in the buttermilk sea. "Could be, Sam, that's what he's atryin' to do." Then more darkly, "By way o' drink."

Sam was startled. "Nonsense, Damie! You and your Temp-'rance! Always jumping in a puncheon when a barrel would do ye. Dan has his glass at meals, and like o' that. But he doesn't *drink.*"

"Well, he's a-drinkin' now and not at his meals," she retorted, and fell to kneading butter until the bowl rocked perilously.

"Sam, you've got t' have a talk with them two. Nobuddy pays

me any heed, but Mercy's allus thought the world o' *you*. Mr. Redmond, too—as well he might!" Sam recognized this as what Damie had been leading up to.

"It's five weeks gone sence Kiah routed us out that night. I thanked God when it was over and Mercy's life spared. But if she's agoin' t' lay there and pine away . . . Well, I d'know . . ." Damie was deeply moved when words failed her, as now.

Sam recalled that black night. How the skiff had seemingly refused to respond though he put every ounce of muscle against the oars and Damie had urged him on; how once on New Erin the long hours had crawled until the early morning when he had looked down into his daughter's ravaged face. He remembered his bitter reflection, *What men do to the women who love them!* Though it was ordained women should travail, surely 'twas not God's will that Mercy's eyes should look so stricken, so like those of a dumb animal in pain. And before she turned her head as if to rest, why had she reached for his hand and not for Dan's? The lost baby had been Dan's—hers and Dan's.

Serena's latest report to Damie had been that Mercy still lay white-faced and big-eyed. Each morning she kissed Patrick when he was brought to her and a few tears crept down her cheeks, but she was content to see him go, though once she couldn't bear him out of her sight, for loving his every glance and movement so.

Serena's most tempting dishes each brought a wan smile and "That's tasty. But you shouldn't have gone to so much trouble." Then the spoon would fall from the listless hand and the broth or pudding grow cold.

"Sam," Damie spoke in a whisper, "I'm tempted t' ask Nabby Nolan, or Old Gypsy Bess, for yarbs, or sech. Only, I've tongue-scoured them so, they might take their spite out on Mercy."

"No!" Sam's anger was sharp. "Don't let me hear another word about witches' yarbs for one of ours.

"Pass me a clean shirt from the peg, wife. Midafternoon or not, I'll run on to see Mercy before this fine weather breaks."

Under a small sail his skiff was soon on the course that, since Mercy went to New Erin, had become familiar as a well-used footpath, so often Captain Sam's keel had cut the water.

He went to the Redmond kitchen door, for, as in Prince's Cove, the front door was reserved for strangers. After due and polite exchanges as to weather and health, Serena informed him baldly, "M'is Redmond and the baby's sleepin'. Mr. Redmond's in his office. A purty mess you'll find it in, too. But he won't let me come anigh."

As Captain Sam went along the hall he ruminated that for all Serena did well, a house changed terribly when its own woman was laid aside. Even so he could scarcely hide his consternation at the office's dusty neglect and the usually immaculate Dan slumped at his desk coatless, his white shirt rumpled and stained. The young man sat staring at nothing over the top of a brandy bottle and a clouded glass, trouble and despair written large upon him.

At the other's entrance he turned a gaunt, unshaven face, but he said no word and made no gesture of greeting.

"Dan! What's wrong with ye, man? Shut up indoors this fine afternoon! And what's that doing here? I thought better of you." Captain Sam pointed sternly at the bottle. If he was going to have things out with his son-in-law, he might as well have them out, no backing and filling.

"That? Oh, I'm not drunk, if that's what you mean, I opened the bottle with some such idea . . . but as you see, I've barely touched it." Dan shrugged.

"I'm glad," Captain Sam said simply. "For I've come to have a talk."

It was none too easy to begin.

"You must know, Dan, that even before you married into the family, from the very first, I've set great store by you."

"I know, Captain Nickerson, you've been kinder to me than a father."

121

But he might be telling me the price of codfish, Captain Sam thought in frustration.

He tried again. "I'm sticking my oar in where it wasn't asked, and likely isn't wanted. You know I don't hold with interference most times. But Damie thinks Mercy should be out of bed before this, and she is worried."

The young husband's face encouraged him to go on.

"I spoke true when I said I thought a heap of you, but Mercy —*Mercy's* my girl! If aught befalls—well, Dan, I don't like to think of it, much less talk."

"Captain," Dan replied simply, "I'd kill another man who harmed Mercy. But I've hurt her myself. Not really meaning to."

He flinched from the mental picture of Mercy lying quiet and white as she had lain these five endless weeks. A dream was the loving Mercy walking beside him, listening to his grandiose plans, his foolish enthusiasms, or like a warm fragrant breeze through his home and his life dissipating all the small vexatious fogs of daily living. Only as a dream she had turned into his arms with her warm lips waiting. In reality she had always lain beyond his reach, uncaring while the island shrank to insignificance and the sea lost its sparkle. Last night from Further Hill even the moonlight across the water had been a barren path, promising only disillusionment and loneliness. With Mercy's hand in his, how different . . .

It would be a relief to tell Captain Sam what had happened and to meet his censure.

He explained Father Burke's rebuke to a Catholic who had fallen away, and his own contrition. "I don't know, now, just why I chose to write what I did, except that the Bible was lying before me. And when a man's had too much wine the night before he's apt to feel full of penitence and high resolve in the morning . . ."

He had meant to appeal to Mercy gently, he told her father, to her love and her desire to please him. Then she had stumbled on the written entry and had read more into it than had been meant, had accused him angrily. "But the wrong is this, I let her go from me, alone and hurt. Some devil held me from her. That's when the blow was dealt, Captain, not when she fell."

The older man's face was black; he kept silence with an effort.

Dan went on, obviously sincere. "The world was never a happy place for me until I found Mercy. It's nothing to me now without her."

"Have you told Mercy this? Have you tried to explain to her as you have to me? Talked to her from your heart?"

"I *can't* talk to her. She says no more than 'yes' and 'no' to me, or gives me a listless nod. Her eyes—Mercy's eyes!—look at me as if she didn't know me, or wish to." He turned his open hands hopelessly towards Captain Sam. His mouth was twisted and hurt.

The captain replied, "I never knew Mercy to look at a man before you came. It must have cut her deep for you to brand her as a wicked woman."

At Dan's gesture of dissent he added quickly, "That's what it sounded like to Mercy. That's what it sounds like to me. And you recall, Dan Redmond, we thrashed all this out before I consented to Mercy's marrying you."

He paused and ran a long hand over his face as if to smooth out the marks of agitation. He stood up and said slowly, "One thing's certain, we can't let Mercy pine away. It seems to me you're not doing a great lot to prevent it. Go to her and tell her you didn't believe what you wrote and Mercy will be cooking your dinner inside a fortnight."

"But I can't deny, Captain, what is true in the eyes of my Church."

"You and your Church!" Captain Sam's great fist thundered down on the desk, shattering the room's quiet and setting inkwell and books jumping. "Breaking the heart of my girl! By the Lord Harry, Dan Redmond, if Mercy dies I'll see ye back in the water I fetched ye from."

His voice broke in anger and he glared at the young man.

Many a man had flinched from that ice-blue gaze; Dan returned it, morosely, but with no sign of fear.

Captain Sam sat down again limply. With his great yellow head between his hands he said wearily, "I'm sorry. Forget my words. All are tools in God's hands, your Church and mine. But, man, what are ye going to do?"

Dan made no reply; but after a pause he burst out, "Captain, you know only half of the miserable story. I've lost Mercy's love and I'm about to lose New Erin."

Captain Sam decided worry had proved too much for his son-in-law's mind. "Lose New Erin? Do you expect it to sink beneath ye? Or go adrift?" His tone showed he was prepared for any notion.

"It might as well do either, as far as it concerns me," Dan replied despairingly. "My books are a mess, but I know all too well where I stand. My money's gone. I borrowed for Molly's wedding and since then I've gone deeper in debt; to Mr. Robertson—and others. My fine cattle and sheep give me small returns; my crops have failed. Mercy will soon know what an ignorant, incompetent fool she married.

"As for me, I planned that if you and Mrs. Nickerson would give Mercy and little Patrick a home—for a time only—I would seek work in Halifax. I considered appealing to John Chetwynd since I have had some experience in the mercantile trade . . ."

His voice trailed off, wretched, beaten and astonishingly boyish. Captain Sam felt his liking for the young man surge back.

"Well, I must say this takes the wind out of my sails." The captain's face bore out his words. "Money did seem all-fired plentiful around here, but I cal'ated you knew your own business."

Strangely enough the captain did not seem particularly downcast at this revelation of disaster. After a moment's silence he rose and laid a hand lightly upon Dan's shoulder. "Don't take all this too hard, Son. I think I see a way to the light.

"But I must visit Mercy. For her sake, no more o' that," with a nod towards the brandy. "My womenfolks have never held

124

with drink. Nor do I, far as that goes. And since I'm talking to you like a Dutch uncle, 'twouldn't hurt your looks if you shaved and spruced up a bit. Mercy would grieve to see you like this."

He turned towards the door. "Where's Kiah?"

"Oh, Kiah's getting in the last of the turnips. He won't admit ruin though he must see it staring us in the face. He scarcely speaks to me now, but if his looks speak truly, he could hardly blame me more if I'd pushed Mercy off the bank with my own hands."

Captain Sam nodded absently. "I'll see you and Kiah both before I go, Dan," he said and left the office.

Mercy lay deep in the feather bed, and, although she looked as if the weight of her thick braids was too much for her thin shoulders, her father pretended to see an improvement in her.

He stooped to kiss her forehead and pat the white hand lying strangely idle on the quilt. "I'm glad to see you're looking up a mite." *That's a lie, the Lord forgive me, for she's looking more peaked than the last time I saw her.*

"And noan too soon," he went on. "The house don't seem the same at all, and if ever a man needed his wife up and around to keep him on a straight course, it's that husband of yours."

He pulled his chair to the bedside and looked into the white face. Heavens knew he didn't want to shock Mercy beyond her strength, but he must shatter her apathy; he was sure, knowing Mercy, that an appeal for a weaker one would do it.

"But Serena said she was managing fine." Mercy's frail hand stirred in distress.

"She keeps him fed and clothed. But you know Dan thinks of her as a servant. Can you see him going to Serena with money troubles?"

"Money troubles? Dan! Pa, what are you saying?" She was weakly incredulous.

"Oh, it isn't as bad as he thinks, but he's taking it hard and he's terribly downhearted. I was taken aback when I found him drinking this hour of the day. All alone in his office. You know,

125

Mercy, that's a right cheery room with the morning sun shining in, but it's amazingly doleful in the afternoon."

Ah, yes, Mercy knew how doleful a room it was in the dim afternoon light.

Captain Sam hastened on. "A man misses his wife when he's been used to her pulling shoulder to shoulder with him. The husband's only half the team, after all."

Mercy's blue-veined lids hid her eyes and what she thought of this.

Her father went on, "Dan looks thinner, and older, seems to me. Only natural, worrying over you; thinking you won't love him when you find his money's all gone. Afraid he's going to lose New Erin, to cap it all."

"Pa, you wouldn't tease me *now,* surely. Oh, I know you wouldn't. You'd best tell me all."

So Captain Sam told her how her husband's money, never so much as they had believed, had melted away. "He's always had his pa to pass it out to him, so he never learnt it goes quick and don't come back. But he knows now. He won't be so free another time.

"Now, Mercy, I have a plan. You listen and see if you don't think it will work, once you're up and around again."

He laid the plan before her briefly; he and Dan would form a partnership, Dan contributing New Erin's wharf and shores and its ideal position, himself offering the *Didamia* and his knowledge of the sea and fisheries. "Dan's been keeping his eyes on the ground, we'll look to the water."

They would catch and cure fish, buying from the Cove fishermen to make a full lading for Boston or the West Indies, and in return bring to New Erin a general cargo and ships' stores for the local trade and New England vessels seeking the harbor. "You might remember, Mercy, I suggested this to Dan when he first hinted about the island.

"It'll be sailing dead to windward at first, perhaps, but it won't be long before we make headway. I think John Chetwynd will back us for a start, especially when he sees there'll be a penny in it."

These were plans Mercy could grasp, and she nodded gravely as her father concluded. He thought her face had taken on a faint flush of interest.

Captain Sam took a desperate big breath. What had gone before was easy. He reached for his daughter's thin hand. "Mercy, I mistrusted 'twas more than a fall and your lost baby that kept you so near Death's door. Dan has told me his side of the story. Would it help you to talk to your pa?"

Her hurt and shame showed in her brimming eyes and choked voice, but she recounted the cruel words she had inadvertently read, and Dan's stunning support of them; she told him of her running out of sight to hide her pain and of her fall.

"When I came to enough to remember it all, I wanted to die. I kept seeing Dan's face so cold and hard when we quarreled. I grieved for my baby (a little girl, Pa) gone from me before she could know my love."

The captain felt his own eyes fill.

"Perhaps I'd been too joyful. Perhaps Ma's right, we aren't meant for happiness in this world, and the Lord was punishing me for setting such store on Dan, human like myself. But it was bitter, bitter punishment, when I'd meant no wrong and I never once said my prayers but what I thanked God for Dan and Patrick and all His goodness to me. I can't understand, Pa, it's like I'm lost."

Her head moved piteously on the pillow, and the uncontrollable tears of physical weakness coursed her white cheeks.

Captain Sam cleared his throat tremendously. "We all get lost by times, Daughter. I don't know about the Lord punishing you, though. Seems to me we mortals cause one another enough troubles and sorrows, blundering about and running foul of each other, without the Lord adding to them because we relish the happiness He sends.

"But that's all over. Now that you'll soon be up and about

127

you must find a way to go on in peace and happiness with your husband."

He was no stranger to religious strife, to brother set against brother, family against neighboring family. From their beginnings the churches along the shore had been rocked and split by recurrent controveries and disputes. Free Will Baptists and Free Christian Baptists were even now attacking each other's doctrines hammer and tongs; searching their Bibles, not for their soul's enlightenment but for clinching arguments to discomfit a neighbor. Captain Sam often grieved that, to the disputants, dogma and the letter of their beliefs had almost obliterated the Master's creed of brotherly love.

He recognized, however, that the difference between Mercy's beliefs and Dan's went even deeper; it scraped the very bedrock of her family's long-rooted Protestantism.

"I've prayed over it," she told him simply. "I can see now that Dan had no wish to hurt me nor little Patrick. But I blame Father Burke. He had no right to interfere. What could *he* know of the love a woman bears her husband?

"Captain d'Entremont told me Father Burke was not even the St. Joseph priest, but one who had come until Father Sevigné was better of his illness. Why did Dan listen to *him* and turn against me?" Then in a cry torn from a sore heart, "Dan killed my love for him. It's dead."

"Now, Mercy," her father chided her, "love is stronger than that! You'll feel different once you get your health back. Dan has the makings of a good man and he loves you. Bear this in mind: The strong must help the weak and Dan has not your strength."

Mercy looked at him in astonishment.

"'Tis the Lord's truth I'm telling you. Dan is easy lifted up, easy cast down, perhaps easy led astray. You're not. You have inner strength—part of it is your woman's heart and understanding. Right now you're sick; that's a different weakness. You think, no doubt, your pa's a strong man, because you've seen me lift what mostly takes two men, and I've swung you up so light

128

when you were a big girl. Many's the time I've leaned heavily on your ma."

This was indeed a new picture to Mercy.

"If Dan needs you, you need him every bit as much. A woman like you must have someone to spend herself for, children and her man. Nine times out of ten the wife makes the marriage, good or bad. Dan won't change—much. There's often a terrible stubborn streak in a man like Dan, for all he's so agreeable."

He tried to lighten their conversation, "But if there *is* anything stubborner than an Irishman it must be a Nickerson!"

Mercy responded with a feeble smile.

He continued, "Remember, a man's God is his own. You wouldn't expect a farmer who never sees any water but what's in the well, or a puddle come spring, to know the same God I've found in the smashing seas and in the whisper of the rigging with the stars all clear overhead. Some people turn to one faith, some to another."

Mercy began to look exhausted.

"Now I must go, my dear. I didn't mean to tire you, just because I found you better. It'll be a proud day when I see you at the helm again."

Outside the door the captain paused and wiped his face. *Damie won't send me visiting again in a hurry when she learns about this new stroke o' business. But I do believe I'm on the right tack.*

In the kitchen, he asked, "What are you giving Mercy for supper, Serena? *That* swill! You take her a taste of the haddock I brought, in a little cream sauce. Suppose she hasn't been touching a thing! She's got to start some time, hasn't she? You give her what I say; she'll eat it."

And to Serena's astonished gratification, she did.

Chapter 15

THE CANDLE WORE A MISTY HALO, FOR THE AUTUMNAL FOG HAD penetrated even into Mercy's bedroom. At the back of the bed Patrick slept, his hands (baby hands still) softly open, his curls damp upon his forehead. Her son; Mercy leaned and brushed his cheek lightly with her lips.

She must go to the kitchen and set sponge for tomorrow's bread. How good to have strength for such daily tasks, to be once more the woman of the house; after long weeks of illness, to be herself again. Herself, but oh! never again the old Mercy.

The house was quiet; Serena and Kiah were in their beds, but she knew Dan still sat in his office, or she would have heard him go to his room. She must tell him the flour barrel was down to the scrapings and that another should be brought from the storeroom.

She opened the office door and stood until her eyes found Dan's figure in his chair before the dying fire. Suddenly he was on his feet and coming towards her with a cry that held so much loneliness, so much hope, that pity rose within her; pity for Dan and for herself.

"My little wife, Mercy mavourneen."

How I used to love his Irish endearments, Mercy thought numbly.

He had her in his arms, fast against his leaping heart. "I've waited so long. So long. Praying you'd come to me like this. Of your own free will. In my dreams you've come. Turning in my arms; lifting your face in the old sweet way. Your warm lips waiting."

He kissed her hair, her eyes, her mouth; buried his face in the hollow of her neck. His hand against her cheek trembled

130

revealingly. For a moment the wild, swift tide that once had lifted and swept them along to rapture rose again. Then it ebbed. He was straining her to him, hungry and aflame; but she let herself sag wearily in his arms. He released her gently, then. Only from his eyes the passion and tenderness blazed as he begged her brokenly with the one word, her name, "Mercy."

She did a cruel thing that was long to accuse her. Out of her own pain (Dan had dealt it to her!); out of the love she believed he had slain, she said, making her voice cold and flat, "I have no wish to bear more children, 'out of wedlock.'"

As she turned from him the burnt sticks in the stove's open grate fell in a small heap of gray despair. But in the center a red coal glowed. It reminded Mercy of something, although she was too sick at heart, too shaken to think of what. From the doorway she saw Dan kneel and pile chips carefully about the ember, blowing attentively until it should burst into flame again.

Chapter 16

THE WINTER WAS EXCEPTIONALLY SEVERE. IN PRINCE'S COVE EVEN Captain Ephie Doane could scarcely recall one of longer duration or more intense frosts; but the drifts, no more than over the windows, *they* were nothing to some he had shoveled through as a boy. The inhabitants of New Erin, being two generations younger than the captain, had never seen a winter to compare with this.

The early onset of cold denied the shore to Indian summer; instead of dreamy haze against the mainland hills Mercy saw white frost rising when she stepped out of a November morning.

Then came winds and rain. On the island slopes the ragged copses of stunted spruces turned gray; under matted tops like streaming hair they strained their twisted limbs to flee the wind. Shingles, silver-sheened by summer sun and fog, were cut and darkened by driving sleet, so that the New Erin buildings, like the huddling cattle, wore their rough winter coats.

The tempo of living slowed as the hours of daylight diminished and the cozy fall evenings were come. Wind and sea might mourn the lost summer, but indoors the full stove purred and, each in its tiny orbit, the candles defeated the night. Kiah got out his net-twine, his mesh-board and needle, and sat steadily knitting while the net piled in folds across his feet and the slumbering Skipper. Dan read, or with Kiah discussed plans for the spring. He was avid now for information on local fishing, on the curing and shipping of the various catches. While the men talked Serena and Mercy spun carded rolls of wool, or knit the balled yarn into stockings.

All sat about the kitchen except on Saturday evening, the beginning of the Prince's Cove Sabbath, which stretched from "even unto even" as laid down in Leviticus. In the drawing room the closed pianoforte stood under the old spell of silence, while Dan and Mercy spoke often of how greatly Molly was missed. Mercy took pride that before the others she and Dan might have been last winter's loving couple, and she showed Dan true care and consideration in all the small things of daily life. His courtesy was as unfailing as her own and as much a surface covering for the lack of inner communion.

By the first of December the surrounding sea had become heavy, sullen, and the air above it was laden with salty cold. Thin slush slopped along the shore and clung viscidly to wharf spiles and seaweeds as the tide receded. At the head of the bay where the salt water was thinned by the Dreen's trickle, solid ice formed, melted and formed again, was lifted by the tide and, as a thin line of broken shards, was carried out past the island—harmless forerunners of the marching cakes that would soon trample the gray waters under.

Wild ducks crossed the point in their flights between the bay and the inner flats where at low water the succulent eelgrass roots lay exposed and its long ribbons were black with periwinkles. From offshore the old squaws screamed their weird forecasts of storms; or lifted in snarls to settle again, each bird dropping heavily with untidy splashes that brought an exaggeration from Kiah, "I've seen killicks heaved over and less water flying. Certainly."

Black powder's residue and greasy rags made a stench in the close kitchen as Kiah and Dan cleaned their muzzle-loaders after a gunning expedition, but the tantalizing aroma of prime black ducks roasting, the savory steam of a whistler stew, were more than recompense.

A low overcast continually hid the sun and intermittently spat a few hard flakes or licked across the island with a snowy tongue that curled away and out to taste the brine of the bay. The December days were short beyond belief; candles and sea oil for the lamps disappeared at an alarming rate.

New Year's had a clear, brilliant sunset and Mercy joyfully pointed out the few minutes gained from the solstice's sundown hour. Serena countered bleakly, "As the days grow longer, the storms grow stronger, I've allus heared."

As if to prove the old saw there followed a fortnight when snowstorm followed blizzard; and while the storm-wrack scurried for fresh snow, the wailing wind drove and tossed the frosty drifts already down. The seas along the shore were no more than a faint hissing under the slob-ice and the air held only the almost-rustle of snow which, noiseless itself, deadened the few small sounds of island life. Nothing stirred on the water. Outside the windows there was only the drifting snow and its dim light.

Most of the point was swept as clean as if Serena had taken her broom to it, though in small hollows and in the rocks' lee snow rested momentarily from the whip of the wind; among the clustered buildings the banks were head-high.

Ice now jammed the shore. Only here and there in some freakish eddy the cakes sagged off and left a narrow band of open

133

water. This filled as if by magic with diving ducks, whistlers, old squaws, sea ducks, bluebills; all the familiar varieties and others whose plumage marked them as ice-driven strangers. But all had grown so poor and strong-tasting that it was a waste of powder to shoot them. The black ducks died in increasing numbers and their frames, picked clean by the crows, were found near the trickles of fresh water.

For a month New Erin was cut off from the mainland by the drifting cakes and miniature icebergs, too loosely packed to walk across, too thick to thrust a boat through. It was when Mercy considered this barrier's implications that she knew fear. Fear for the men who might fall on the wharf's icy planks, or have a frosty ax slip in their hands, be victims of one of a hundred frightening possibilities that would demand a doctor. Most of all she feared for Patrick, since death so loved babies. At bedtime and when she wakened during the night she listened with a pounding heart to his breathing, in dread of the croup that so often choked out a little life in the black hours. If only her mother were within summoning she would rest easier, for Mercy had lost her self-confidence, her faith in her own courage and ability to meet an emergency. Grammie Abigail would have disowned her.

However, of them all Patrick minded the cold least. He prattled happily as he played about the kitchen, a roly-poly bundle of clothing topped by a round, fair head that was mostly two blue eyes and four white teeth gleaming in an already boyish grin.

The January thaw came. The drift ice was pushed out by a smashing easterly, was caught in the Fundy tides and did not return. For three days the sea lay open, leaden under somber skies; eaves dripped, water lay above the ice on ponds and puddles. Everyone breathed a bit easier.

Captain Sam sailed on to see that all was well, to exchange family news and to discuss business with his new partner. He had been to Barrington and could relieve Dan's worry as to the fate of New Erin, since Mr. Robertson had decided to carry Dan's debts until the new partnership should have time to prove itself.

"He understands how you might miscalculate here in a strange land. He thinks the island has great possibilities for a business such as we have in mind," the captain assured his son-in-law. "I offered my shares in the *Didamia* for surety, but he laughed. Said my word was enough, for all Robert Robertson has the name of being so shrewd and nigh a man." Sam Nickerson was obviously surprised and flattered that a lifetime of integrity should have this effect upon a neighbor.

He brought to the island dwellers a quarter of beef from a recently slaughtered critter. Hung and frozen this would provide welcome variety from the salt fish and salt meat that had been the staple diet since the ducks had failed them. "You can pay me back next winter," he salved Dan's pride.

When these matters had been concluded he turned to his daughter. If he noticed her cheeks were still too thin, her limpid eyes too shadowed, he made no mention.

All on Grannie's Head were keeping well, though Damie complained of rheumatism in her arms. Philip was helping his foster father and Long Tom Doty in the boatshop where they prepared barrels for the spring herring and mackerel. The boy was developing quite a knack. Mercy could see her father was setting more and more store on Philip now that his own sons were grown and gone.

"Looks like I'm to have plenty of help this winter, one way and another, Mercy," he said with his old twinkle. "That young Doane from Barrington, Gilbert. Well, he walks to Grannie's Head every so often to see how I'm getting along with the coopering. Don't look at me so, now! That's what he always *says* he comes for. And I haven't a doubt but that's what he and Bethiah talk about till all hours of the night."

Captain Sam's face was blandly innocent.

"Bethiah! Do you mean Bethiah's 'setting up' with a boy? What's come over Ma? Why, Bethiah's only . . ." Her voice trailed.

"She's sixteen, Mercy." Her father sighed. "And Gilbert's over eighteen. A nice boy and comes of good people."

"Well, of course, I marked how he followed her about at Molly's wedding. But *Bethiah* . . ." Mercy spread her hands. It seemed disloyal of Grannie's Head to have all this going on and she not there to share in it. She knew a knotting homesickness for the kitchen and the hearth where she and Dan had "set up" and made their happy plans. Pray God Bethiah would be luckier—marrying one of her own kind.

Mercy's face had always betrayed her feelings. Her father said gently, "Your ma cal'ated my telling you would give you something nice to think about during the long winter."

Then he slapped his knee and leaned forward. "Damie charged me to be sure and tell you *this*. Never let on that I most forgot. Obie's got himself a woman at last." He sat back in satisfaction.

"No!"

"So they say."

"Tell me, Pa."

"Well, 'tis this Cynthie Goodwin, from Pilot Point. She came to care for his ma, who's bedridden now, poor soul. This winter Obie took to staying at home and folks naturally suspicioned something was up. Then it grew plain Cynthia was running the house with a high hand. She's given out they intend to be married when Mr. Allbright comes around in the spring."

"Well, I never," Mercy declared, interested in spite of herself. "What's she like?"

"She's a good cook and housekeeper, your ma says. She's sweet spoken, but *I* don't like her hard eyes and tight lips. However, it's Little Obie's got to live with her. Some think that now she's got what she wants, Cynthie's noan too kind to the old mother. I notice Damie's taken to going across fields or sending Bethiah with bowls of stuff. You know your ma's covered bowls!"

Mercy knew, she'd carried many a one to homes where there was sickness or trouble.

On leaving, Captain Sam said, "When the cold sets in again

136

it'll stay. 'Tisn't likely I'll be seeing you till the middle o' March, or later." He strove to minimize the import of his next words. "I'll keep an eye this way. If you should need help, fly a red cloth on the point. If you need a doctor, make a fire. Keep it blazing till you see an answering one on Grannie's Head. Some of us from the Cove could doubtless work our way with boats and sleds across to Narrah, and from there to New Erin."

He then turned to his son-in-law. "Dan, to save me a lot of worrying, please promise me you or Kiah won't attempt to get off through the ice. I doubt one man would make it; two would leave the womenfolks alone."

Dan assured him they would not challenge the ice.

Captain Sam retrieved his enormous white mittens, warming under the stove; gave his little grandson a slap on his well-padded stern; sent a smile to Mercy and was gone.

Throwing her shawl about her shoulders, Mercy went to the parlor window to watch him. In his boat her father stood long in serious talk with Kiah on the wharf above him before he cast off.

Pa puts great trust in Kiah's judgment, Mercy reflected with an instinctive and unreasonable jealousy for Dan, whose judgment had proved so fallible. Standing at the window she watched the dory disappear behind Narrah. She had never felt so alone, so deserted; until she remembered Patrick and his need of her.

Through the night winter struck again with the beginning of a three days' blizzard. Greater cold followed, until Kiah reported that even from the high southern shore he could see only white fields of ice where once blue water had stretched to the horizon. Through the blanketing ice, vapor from the sea rose and condensed in the colder air. Thick as a low fog, this vapor burnt mouth and lungs and pinched nostrils into uselessness.

Outdoors, Kiah's long nose perpetually wore a freezing drop, his breath built up miniature ice-walls upon his muffler; only his patience, his willingness to lend a hand at any task, showed no sign of frost.

Serena hovered the stove every spare minute, her chapped hands clutching the heat from the red lids, the cords of her scrawny neck standing out in her efforts to absorb warmth.

All winter Mercy was conscious of being too easily chilled, too tired and weak. Doubtless her blood had been thinned by her illness; she faithfully tried to eat heartily of the fat pork scraps, the rich suit puddings, by which the others seemed to hold their own against the weather's rigors. She added first one and then another extra petticoat, spun and knitted from New Erin's warm wool. She pulled on over-stockings of the same, but the cold crept up from the floors and her feet and legs were like blocks of ice from morning till night.

At bedtime Serena put her faith in a length of heated hardwood, but Mercy, reverting to a childhood habit, warmed two smooth beach rocks in the oven and placed them, well-wrapped, in the frigid foot of her bed.

Patrick and Dan slipped easily away in sleep, but Mercy, lying between them, could seldom follow them at once; through the closed bedroom door she often heard Kiah creep into the drawing room at midnight to refill the stove.

Often it was agony to lie still; for when the warm rocks had restored their feeling, her feet were tortured by chillblains, unbearably itching and tender.

Last winter she had put her cold feet on Dan's and giggled like a girl at his startled yipes, had turned laughing and eager into his arms; but now she could not seek the warmth of his body while her heart stayed cold to his. She yielded him her duty as a wife and told herself he did not miss the inner flame.

Some mornings she wakened to find her errant body had shaped itself to the remembered curve of his back, or she felt his warmth along her own spine. She would lie for a moment empty. Empty of the old thrilling sweetness or of complete belonging; then hurt pride would rush in to fill the emptiness; she would lift his hand from her breast and move away.

It was indeed a cold, bleak winter on New Erin.

Yet Mercy often gave thanks for her full storeroom and cellar, for she knew that some in Prince's Cove were empty; as she fed the New Erin stoves she thought of windy fireplaces that seldom knew full fare. Before late winter, neighbors would have banded together to share their little with the less fortunate. *Many a trip Pa's made down the hill to Nabby Nolan's with fish and potatoes and the wood to cook them, I'll warrant.*

Nabby could not depend on driftwood this winter; the mouth of her cove must be frozen across, for Mercy had seen men walking on Narrah, evidence of solid ice between it and the mainland. Only the racing tides prevented a similar bridge to New Erin.

The bright sunshine on Candlemas Day killed all hopes of an early break. Just so far as the sun's rays filtered into the house on that day of omen, so far would the snow lie. Serena marked this truth many a time during the next weeks as she swept up the white lines sifted in through cracks or doorjambs—wherever a sunbeam might have slipped.

But imperceptibly changes came about during those weeks. When the ice showed a lane, no matter how narrow, the water blazed back at the sun and returned the sky's blue, deepened and enriched a hundredfold. From a gray flatness pressing upon them the sky had sprung back to its mighty arch with New Erin under its zenith.

For days at a time the wind left the drifts in peace; the sun found them like waves caught and held at the moment of cresting, and sent its blue shadows across their voluted faces, down their pristine flanks.

At night across the frosted windows stars and moon shimmered, cold but not inimical.

There came an afternoon in late February when Mercy could not resist the pure and sparkling world that lay beyond the crisscrossed paths between house and outbuildings. Dressing warmly she walked to the end of the point. Here she stood and looked across to her old home without sighting any movement; gazed at the glittering, heaving sea of white; gauged the amazing speed

139

of the inner cakes winging past on the tide; felt the sun strong on one cheek, though the light breeze nipped the other. She turned home tingling and refreshed.

Looking back, she saw how her footprints had sullied perfection and knew a moment's regret. Then thought, *Who wants an untouched world? It's time life began to stir again. Suppose it does leave marks!*

All winter it had been a struggle to dry a scant sufficiency of apparel in the empty upper chamber, or about the stoves. The morning after her walk Mercy's outdoor clothesline bore a brave array of well-washed garments. True they froze stiff on meeting the air, but they would dry and bleach and sweeten in the sun. As if she had run up signal flags, from the line on Grannie's Head similar bunting answered her—a message of faith in the ordained seasons.

With the blood mantling her cheeks, the crisp air awakening her lungs, she was laughing as she lifted her emptied basket and ran towards the kitchen. She turned the corner, stamping the snow from her feet, and bumped into Dan.

His arms came out, swift and hard and familiar, to steady her; for a moment his blue eyes—like the patches of dark-blue water —blazed into hers; almost his mouth came down on her smiling lips. He straightened and released her. "What's so funny this morning?" he asked.

She was a bit breathless and not from hurry alone. "Oh, Dan, March can bluster and freeze all it likes—I know it will do both —but on New Erin the backbone of the winter is broken."

"I wish I could think so, Mercy," he said soberly and went along the snowy boardwalk towards the barn, his boots squeaking through scattered diamonds.

April was almost come before the wind left its northerly stronghold. Then an easterly gale swung huge seas into the bay to smash the floes; it drove the cakes past holding headlands and presented them to the powerful spring tides to carry off. A southeaster brought torrential rains and a following fog to rot the

140

crystal blocks into drab honeycombs. When the sun broke through again, only the sagging sheets in coves and harbors awaited its final stroke.

Chapter 17

SHY SPRING HID LONG BEHIND THE CHILL SKIRTS OF THE FOG, BUT slowly the surface water of the bay and harbor lightened in density and danced in a livelier chop. The waves among the rocks replaced their sullen winter blows with jocular slaps and nudges, while the last brittle shore ice lifted and bobbed out to dissolution. The little pond behind the dike throw off its ragged winter blanket and quivered under the wind; but for too many weeks the trees stayed gray and weary, the fields lifeless.

Then green flowed down the fold between Nigh Hill and Further. Among the hummocks on the barn's sunny side Dan found the first violets and brought them to Mercy. She took them with thanks, but she stubbornly refused to recognize the ardent spring in her husband's voice, in the touch of his hands.

The winds still smelt of arctic seas and icebergs, but they brought exhilaration and they rushed to fill sails as boats ventured forth from all the coves and harbors.

Kiah and Dan plowed the gardens, hauled sea-dressing for the fields, repaired fences and buildings. Mercy felt her old zest for life returning as she and Serena turned out room after room in a frenzy of housecleaning.

One dawn when the anchorage was a silver mirror Dan, in vast excitement, called the women to the front door. From behind the low spur of Nigh Hill, Indian canoes appeared until fifty or more spread across the harbor. The paddles flashed in rhythm, above their broken reflections the well-laden craft slid forward with astounding speed. Soon the foremost canoe swung out of sight around the end of New Erin.

Dan was thrilled with his first sight of the red men and their graceful craft. "What brings so many through the harbor?" he asked.

Serena explained, "Them Injuns gather every spring and go in a flock to St. Joseph's."

"But we were on New Erin last spring; I saw none then."

"Could be 'twas foggy this time last year," Serena replied flatly. "Could be the tide was low so they paddled outside and you didn't catch sight of 'em."

"Where did they come from this morning?"

"From Cape White. They always camp overnight on a small island offshore from my father's house. A sight t' behold is all them canoes hauled up, side by side. When I was a girl we used to stand on the shore of a night and watch the squaws moving around in the firelight."

"Why do they camp *there* overnight?"

"Well." Serena shrugged. "It's just a good day's paddle from St. Joseph's."

"St. Joseph's?" Dan was still puzzled.

"Why, t' be sure! They'm bound for St. Joseph's and what they call Easter Mass. The priest holds one fer 'em, special. Mass!" Serena unrolled her arms from her apron. "La! They'm nawthin' but heathen yet, if ye ask me." She stalked back to her kitchen.

Mercy explained what she could of the ancient friendship between Acadians and Micmacs. Each spring the Indians gathered, from Liverpool westward, and followed the shore to St. Joseph's, where exiled Acadians had returned to rebuild their community.

Dan soberly watched the last two canoes disappear beyond the point. He turned to Mercy. "These red men shame me. I shall take the sloop and sail to St. Joseph's for Easter Mass. I'll visit Captain d'Entremont, since I can't go and return in the same day."

142

He explained briefly that he had neglected his attendance at Easter Mass, since the nearest Roman Catholic Church had seemed so far away. "But if Indians can come faithfully from so much farther, surely I can make a lesser effort." He spoke defiantly, as if he expected opposition.

Mercy felt no hurt at his plan. She put a friendly hand upon his arm. "Do go, Dan. You *should* attend your Church. But I beg you, don't attempt the boat trip alone this time of year." Then her face brightened. "Why not take Patrick and me off to Grannie's Head for a visit? You can hire a rig in the Cove and drive to St. Joseph's; stay with your friends a day or two, then bring us back to New Erin."

It was so arranged. But Mercy found that, much as she loved the old home and all in it, welcome as the family made her, she was only a visitor on Grannie's Head. She couldn't help but feel that Patrick, at the into-everything age, was often a nuisance in his grammie's long-childless house.

Gilbert provided the chief topic of conversation: Gilbert was this, Gilbert said that; Gilbert had sailed away on his father's barkentine; Gilbert was coming home in the fall to marry Bethiah.

At times Mercy, seeing the wonder and adoration so plain in her sister's eyes, could have cried out, "Don't love him so greatly, "Thiah. Don't lay your heart so bare. The more you love, the more you'll be hurt. A heart is tender and easily bruised. Keep a wall about it from the first, for once the harm is done, no wall helps then."

Instead, she joined her mother in weaving and spinning, seaming and hemming, so that Bethiah should not go among the Barrington Doanes ashamed of her blankets and linen.

It was when Mercy again stepped ashore at New Erin with Dan and Patrick that she felt what she had expected at Grannie's Head, the sense of being home. Plainly Dan felt the same, and they walked from shore to house in something of their old companionship.

Mercy saw much of her family that summer. Captain Sam spent most of it on New Erin, putting the new partnership upon its feet. Often Mercy saw the Nickerson dory pull into the dock with Philip at the oars, Bethiah perched in the bow, and Damie prim on the stern thwart, her "second-best bonnet h'isted" as Captain Sam said. No matter how busy he might be, he found time to meet the dory and lift her small figure ashore.

"Ye know very well this is my visitin' bunnit," Damie would retort. "Some wimmin might be satisfied to throw on a shawl and set off, but I hope I know what's fitten 'n' proper; even if Mercy *is* my own dorter."

Mercy cherished the new understanding and equality between herself and her mother; she was touched by the love that must have lain all these years under the sharp tongue, to be revealed when Damie felt the danger of "spoiling" her child was past.

Dan had never before worked with his hands, but he learned their use that summer as he shared the labor of preparing mackerel and herring, pollack and cod. After the busy day, when the last boats had landed their catch and slipped away for the Cove, he spent the long twilights with Kiah and Captain Nickerson at the splitting table. There, in leathern apron and heavy boots, he worked until the last fish was in the butts, and Captain Sam raised bloody, brine-shriveled hands to pronounce the traditional benediction and prayer, "Ever more and never less."

Wharf planks that wind and rain had scoured and sweetened were once more encrusted with scales and gurry and smelt to high heaven. To Dan the offal and odors were offensive and at night his face was drawn by more than fatigue, but he never complained and what he lacked in skill he made up in persistence and effort. Barrels of pickled fish began to fill the cold black shadows of the fish store, butts of brined fish lined the wharf and drying flakes extended from the wharfhead towards the barn.

Mercy and Serena walked the long rows between flakes, expertly turning the hardening triangles of fish. They also milked the five cows, freeing Kiah for other work. Mercy found it good to feel again a cow's soft flank under her forehead and to hear twin streams hum into the pail, good to see Serena's sunbonnet bent to a neighboring flank. All the world was their barn those summer mornings and evenings, and the sea sang along with the streaming milk. As Captain Sam had hoped, Mercy was responding valiantly to an appeal for help.

In the house there was no knowing how many to expect for a meal. On "leew'rd days" (which had to be explained to Dan as days so windy as to necessitate a lee, hence a day to stay ashore) fishermen were hired to work on the island: building new flakes, transferring fish from wharf to store, from butts to flakes. Two extra or a dozen, all sat down to a plentiful well-cooked meal.

When Kiah's whetstone rang against the scythe and on the crisp breeze the sweet perfume of cut grass rose above the ever-present tang of the sea, Mercy and Serena lent a hand haymaking, while Patrick stumbled about the swathes in excited rapture.

With Mercy's lassitude from her illness gone, she and Dan might have drifted into an easier relationship based on the need of healthy young bodies, each for the other, a mutual dependence that would have covered without excising the old sores; but before Kiah had fitted scythe to sheath and taken the first experimental swing, she had known she was again with child. She felt no desire to run to Dan with this news. Rather it was something to be kept from him, as if her body had betrayed her. She suffered none of the discomforts of her previous pregnancies, yet she knew no mounting happiness at the thought of this child, no impatience to see its face, to hold it in her arms. At times she forgot about it entirely.

So that she was caught unaware one September morning as she slipped from bed to dress before Dan wakened. Glancing up, she caught his eyes moving from the outlines of her body to her face.

"We are to have another child, Mercy?" His voice betrayed no feeling and his face was stilled.

She nodded, ashamed of the rankling hurt that had kept her from telling him. Dan had planned so proudly for the boys and girls they were to have—little princes and princesses of New Erin.

"Yes," she answered him, hurrying to don the full apron that hid her figure, "in March."

"Ah.

"Do you hate me for this, Mercy? Do you hate to bear my child?" His voice held expectation of an affirmative answer and this shocked her.

"Oh, no, Dan. Believe me. I bear no hatred. Have I seemed so to you?" Not waiting for an answer, *"My* child, too, Dan."

"My dearest," he said in broken tenderness and put out a hand as if to draw her down on the bed beside him.

"I must go. Patrick will be crying for his breakfast."

The hand dropped. "Yes, Patrick. He, at least, is well-beloved," Dan said bitterly.

Mercy admitted to herself that she had indeed turned upon her son much of the adoration, she had once given his father, but she justified this stubbornly, *I must have someone to love, and Patrick will never fail me as Dan has done.*

But although they remained friendly strangers, they two who had been such fond lovers, it was not an unhappy summer. It was a busy one and in the fall the *Didamia* carried a load of fish to Halifax to trade for the goods with which Nickerson and Redmond hoped to start their business. Several years of hard work lay before them all, but the start had been made.

Chapter 18

IN HER ROCKER BY THE WINDOW MERCY HELD THE NEW BABY TO breast; but sweet as was the tugging child, she lifted her eyes now and again from its silken head to the sun-scattered diamonds across the blue harbor mouth.

March had been a dreary month, with high winds driving off the frigid land or across the ice floes lining the coast. Today the sun, having wiped the frost-ferns from the western window, was pouring gloriously into the drawing room and, after pregnancy's long sluggishness, Mercy's avid body rejoiced in its tonic rays.

Spring was surely on its way. Already lambs were arriving in the sheltered hollows, and the calf-pen had been readied. Spring and birth, how wonderfully things were ordained! She herself had this three-week-old daughter. How exquisite a baby—and how greedy! Her arms tightened in laughing adoration as she laid her cheek gently upon the fuzzy head.

It was then Dan entered the room. He was seldom about the house these busy days and she looked up in quick surprise, her lips still curved in tenderness, her eyes still dark and deep with love. He strode towards her and without a pause was on his knees beside her, his black head buried in her lap, his arms about her. His voice came raggedly.

"Mercy, my beloved, don't think me ungrateful. You have given me so much; so much more than I deserve. Yourself—the great gift, believe me—my son, and now this precious daughter with my mother's red-gold curls."

He lifted his face to hers. "I've given you little enough in return; but, Mercy, the best of me is my love and you have that. Selfish, arrogant and blundering as I've been, I do love you. Sweetheart, give me your full love in return. You are kind to me—but I remember kisses that stopped my breath and set my heart aquake. Kindness isn't enough after more. Take me back to the haven of your heart and come home to mine."

Through the window she had watched the ice caps on the shore rocks crumble under the strong sun and slide into the rising tide. Perhaps the shell of ice about her heart had long been softening and shrinking and had needed only this last touch of sun to melt and disappear.

Only those who have endured a frozen winter feel the full glory of spring. She leaned to meet her husband's lips in the first

147

sweet passion for over a long year. Then she was weeping, sweet tears of release from the thrall of remembered hurt. Dan's arms were again a refuge, his face against hers an aching tenderness, his touch an ecstasy.

She laid the baby gently in its cradle and with trembling hands turned Dan's face towards her own, that she could read his eyes once more. It was for the moment so open, so boyish, that she urged him, "Dan, you say the baby has your mother's curls. Tell me of your mother, of your home, so different from mine. Now, while we are close in love and understanding, let me learn about the little Dublin boy I can never know except from you."

"There's little to tell." He began gropingly but soon found words for his flooding memories.

The earliest were of his mother, of her laughing blue eyes and the hair that he afterwards pictured as firelit, because so often she used to sit with him before the nursery fire. Sometimes his father was part of the memory, a thin, dark man with his face buried in the red-gold curls as if he absorbed their warmth and gave it out again in tenderness for his wife and son. Or he recalled his mother with her rosary, and such love and goodness shining from her face that it was natural a little boy should think those qualities were connected with the beads.

"Mercy, don't let me hurt you again, but in the pictures I painted of you before our marriage, you were before the fire in our home—and there was a rosary in your hands."

Mercy drew his head close; this was no time for words from her.

"That first night when I saw you standing in the doorway, the fire behind you made your hair golden-red. And (this sounds silly now) next morning I felt cheated when I found it was silver!" His lips upon it told her that, silver or gold, he now found it precious, and Mercy smiled tremulously.

The pictures of his mother ceased when those of Baby Molly began. His father turned into a taciturn stranger who spent his time in the dark office and warehouses near the Corn Exchange.

Dan was a quiet little boy who kept out of the way because he felt unwanted; but from a dark turning on the stairs he often watched his father leave and enter the house, hoping that his presence would be felt and rewarded with a smile or a word.

"As I grew bigger I thought blows would have been kinder than my father's cold ignoring of me. Now I see that in grief for my mother and the old days, I distorted and magnified the change in my father; I think he must always have been reserved.

"Do you know I could scarcely bear at first to watch your father's companionship with the twins or to see his love for you and Bethiah so plain on his face while I remembered my own father's cold features. You all had so much. I—I felt beggarly beside you."

"And we," Mercy remembered wonderingly, "envied you your education, your travels, your money, your opportunities."

Dan had been a sober seven and Molly a delicate baby of two when their father brought the stepmother home. The memories of that day were undimmed; the waiting in the drawing room, where Maggie, the nurse, tried to hide her misgivings; the red-faced confusion of the maid who stumbled in and out and wept noisily into her apron. A chill had settled over the room that for Dan still held a faint fragrance from his mother's hair and the half-heard rustle of her skirts.

There came the sounds of arrival, and the boy's gleam of bitter pleasure because his father's voice speaking to the new wife re-called no echo of what it had once held.

This woman brought no flame in which a man, or a boy, might warm his heart; not in her bright black eyes, her thin smile, her bony height, nor in the stiff row of curls across her narrow brow. She brought, however, money to bolster her husband's sinking business and a driving determination for more.

The renovated home soon became *her* house, Dan's father *her* husband. Maggie, the loved and loving, left to join her brother in Galway and Molly was given a new and capable nurse. Dan

149

was packed off to a school near the Sussex home of his English mother.

The teachers were kind, for he was an obedient child; the boys were neither more nor less cruel than boys have always been. In time he lost the loneliness of the first weeks, but nothing came to fill the place in his heart where love had lain. At home he found some comfort in Molly's clinging affection, but he was not welcomed in the nursery.

The stepmother was not cruel, merely indifferent, Dan admitted. She had no little ones of her own ("For which the Lord be praised! The heartless thing!" Mercy interjected), and no love for her husband's two.

Dan was twelve the summer when the children for the first time visited Maggie in the Galway cottage where she dwelt alone since her brother's death. Dan had never understood why his father, who ordinarily showed so little interest in his children, had gone to the trouble of conveying them across Ireland, a tiresome journey. Perhaps his wife had wished them out of the way, perhaps some incident had aroused compassion towards the forlorn reminders of his lost happiness.

In either case, one misty evening when the Atlantic was smothering the Galway rocks in foam, Dan and Molly were deposited at the door of a low stone cottage. Their father's farewells were lost in Maggie's welcome. Dan saw that Maggie's sober town gown had been replaced by a warm red skirt and blue shawl that made her eyes bluer than ever, but did not alter the love in them.

In her care the contented children watched the boats put out and return, joined the haymakers garnering the rocky hills, and spent hours gathering shells and mosses along the shore. The sea that began at the foot of Maggie's field might be gray as stone or blue as the Virgin's cloak, but always it thundered or whispered of a land beyond its curving horizon.

"Can you see now, Mercy, why I lost my heart at sight of New Erin? On a smaller scale its hills and shore are like Galway's."

Those were enchanted days he and Molly spent with Maggie,

but all at once the bleak morning for good-bys was upon them. They left with backward looks and yearnings; the smell of mingled peat smoke and sea followed them far inland, like the perfume of a loving one deserted. At the turn of the road Molly crumpled and wept damply, but Dan sat stiff and silent, holding her hand and presenting a manly (he believed) composure to the jolly driver of the cart.

The magic Galway summers stopped when at sixteen Dan entered his father's office. In spite of the difficult times in Ireland, the business prospered moderately. For eight years Dan tended the books and traveled on business.

Then one October day, he had been summoned from Cork by a servant; his father had been fatally stricken. He had made all possible speed, hoping to be in time to catch one last gleam from those days when his father's smile and his mother's arms had sealed a little boy's happy world. Haste, however, had proved fruitless, and his father's face in death was no softer and no harder than it had been in life. Dan had turned from it to comfort Molly.

His father had left each child a moderate sum while the business she had nurtured went to the stepmother. She had wished Dan to continue with her, but he already . . . . join his uncle in Boston, that city of which such fal. . . . . . me back to Ireland.

"The rest you know, Mercy." When he. . . . . he gray skies were weeping and Molly had wept wi. . . . . . . .y could picture them there on the quay, Dan so tall . . . . .e in his beaver hat and traveler's cape, his black hair gleaming in the rain, his eyes dark with the pain of farewell, his smile plainly assumed to cheer his sister; and Molly, her violet eyes flooding and her mouth most doleful, caring never a bit that her eyes were reddened and her nose rubbed raw by the wet kerchief she used so assiduously.

At the last minute she had clung to Dan and begged him to change his mind, but it had been too late for that. So she had slipped a little crucifix into his hand and managed a twisted smile as he released her and stepped down into the boat that would row him to the *Morning Star* and start him on his perilous way to Mercy.

As the story ended Mercy sighed and slipped from her husband's arm. "Oh, my dear one, why didn't you tell me all this before? I might have understood many things better. We on Grannie's Head pictured you one of Fortune's favorites, though you did say you had lost your mother young. You told us so little about your former life and Ma warned Bethiah she was not to pry! I felt that what had gone before I met you didn't really matter. But I see now a life can't be cut off in lengths, so much here, so much there; what went before always matters."

She paused and then asked, "Dan, what was the name of the lovely mother you lost?"

"Catherine," he said, "Catherine Agnes."

She gestured towards the cradle, "Shall we call our first daughter Catherine Agnes? Would you like that?"

His face showed that he would. "But," he said, "I heard you and your mother planning to name her after your aunt Tamsin."

"We'll call our next girl Tamsin," she assured him simply. "This is Catherine Agnes.

"And Dan," her voice was shy but eager to proffer this proof of her new understanding, "if you like, you shall teach her the ways of your Church. Perhaps you'll see again your mother's rosary, as well as her red-gold hair."

Dan smiled and kissed her tenderly.

Why had she wasted so much time over their religious difference? How quickly love and understanding could have conquered it. She mused, *It's not so much what difference comes up, I guess, but the selfishness and contrariness in each one of us that differences bring out.*

She had gone on with her marriage because she had promised for better or for worse, and because the alternative of discarded wife forced to return to her father's home was unthinkable; but she had treated Dan selfishly. Giving him the husks alone of love. Torturing herself, she now admitted. Many a night she had cried herself to sleep remembering the first glory of their love. "Pride is a cold bedfellow," she had often heard; but pride was a strong one.

She had not been willing to accept in place of the Dan she had created for herself the imperfect human upon which her girlish heart and imagination had built. From now on she would love, not only a man, who might again grievously wound her, but also the little boy who had had only the memory of a mother and her rosary to cling to.

Mercy had grown from a girl in love to a woman who loved.

Chapter 19

THE DAY AND THE DAY'S TASKS WERE DONE. THE STORM THAT WAS brewing outside the cozy room would tomorrow force an interlude in spring work, both outdoors and in; it made the evening one for planning the future, for dreaming over the past. In her rocker beside the center table Mercy's thoughts were not upon the mending in her lap, though her needle flashed steadily in the lamp's orange glow.

Seventeen New Erin years seemed to have touched her gently; but they had been womanhood's full years; love's ecstasies and tendernesses, dragging pregnancies and racking childbirths, blissful suckling of babies, anguished night vigils above a cradle, could not have left her unmarked.

Bright sunlight would have picked out their fine transfiguration, but the lamplight and fire's glow were less revealing.

Near the hearth Serena's knitting needles clicked off the rounds in her never-ending race to produce stocking heels faster than the boys' boots chewed them through. Some women might hold that knitting was restful work; fiercely erect, with mouth clamped and eyes intent on the darting needles, Serena illustrated the mistakenness of such a notion. If the years had mellowed Serena, no surface changes bore witness to their amendments.

Across the table from Mercy, Philip was helping Catherine and Tamsin with their lessons. Beyond them Dan sat reading, his slippered feet covered by Skipper's shaggy head. Between

Mercy and the fire were the three youngest children: Will, past nine; Charlie, who had followed him so closely; and Adria, just turned five.

Seated on the low hearth-stool, Adria thrust her bare toes fireward from under winding folds of nightgown. She had her mother's gray eyes and tawny hair aglint in the firelight. Sprawled on either side of her, Will and Charlie hugged the fire, hoping to absorb enough of its heat to temper the chill of their imminent beds, never damper nor surer to set jaws a-chattering than when the east winds of early spring went searching through the house as they did tonight.

Will's handsome black head and regular features were outlined against the fire. His thoughts were noble and far-removed, should Mercy judge from his expression, but she caught the sly movement of his arm behind Adria's back and saw Charlie's involuntary jump at the swift pinch. The younger boy, estimating chances for reprisal, slid his blue glance up to his mother, but at her admonitory nod he admitted his purpose and its abandonment in the same wide-gapped grin. He was a sweet-tempered boy. "Just like his Uncle Charles," his grandma Damie often boasted, sorrow for her lost son and pride in his namesake mingling in her voice.

The large room in which the family sat had been recently built to join the kitchen ell and the front wing. Its walls were plastered and papered in garlands of dark roses instead of being ceiled as in the older rooms; but, although stoves had proved marvelously heat-producing and fuel-saving, it had an old-fashioned fireplace which had become the heart of the home. This middle room was the sole portion of the Redmond house not formed from a Ryder cottage, for through the years all the island's scattered buildings had been incorporated into the dwelling.

Mercy found this helter-skelter marrying of houses had produced a brood of inconveniences: different floor levels, doors opening the wrong way, odd jogs into the rooms, and the interminable roundabout walk from the kitchen to the front door.

The irregularities that preserved the island's early cottages somehow endeared his home to Dan and although he recurrently planned improvements, Mercy had resigned herself to its present rambling state.

However, she thought now, bending to bite off a thread, *the front wing does provide ample space for the family and guests, and we certainly need the kitchen ell for the hired help. It seems each season brings its special tasks and extra men to cope with them.*

Dan's chief pride still lay in the island's rocky acres and in his livestock; visitors were proudly escorted over "the farm." Sheep and cattle now dotted the hillsides as he had pictured to his bride; pigs wallowed behind the barn; hens, ducks and geese filled the dooryards with their foolish alarms and squawking retreats, and kept Serena forever chasing with apron aflap. Increase from all these supplied the kitchen pots or was eagerly purchased by vesselmen hungry for fresh meat; but behind New Erin's apparent bounty lay much labor.

Men were hired for spring plowing and planting, for although crops were limited to those which had proved themselves against fog and sea winds, the gardens and potato patches must supply the family table for the year.

The skimming-bowls were always yellow-clotted, the butter-butts full; but haymakers toiled all summer filling the big mows, other men spent the fall spreading the sea-dressing to assure the abundant grass.

In May the dike-sluice was raised and, sown to oats, the drained pond's mucky bottom yielded bounteously. In autumn the sluice was lowered and by January the pond was producing the second crop—smooth crystal blocks to fill the icehouse and the holds of the halibut fleet. Dan might glory in the green swords of springing grain but money came from the white harvest reaped in winter winds and hauled home by oxen whose breath froze in clouds about their heads.

Ten years ago Captain Sam had returned from a Gloucester

voyage with the news that the George's* halibuters had begun carrying ice to preserve their fares. "There, Dan," he had said, pointing to the pond, "there's what will bring more and more vessels to New Erin."

Then had begun a great bustle: digging a deep cellar, drilling and splitting granite blocks for a foundation, boating lumber and sawdust packing, drying rolls of eelgrass for insulation. Soon a high blank-walled icehouse, fifty feet long and more than half as wide, had risen between shore and house.

Each following winter, after frost had set in strong but before the salt water caught, twenty men and two teams of oxen were ferried on from the main to garner the ice. The chamber above the kitchen was lined with tiered bunks, while Serena, though she made the two hired girls step lively, was hard put to it to keep the workers fed.

Where the fishing schooners sheltered, there they traded; increasing numbers put in at Nickerson's and Redmond's after word spread of available ice.

Their coming meant that the tipsy old store at the wharfhead had been replaced by a new one; the wharf had been repaired and extended (though it was called Short Wharf); Long Wharf, bearing a big warehouse at its waist, thrust new spiles and strong cribbing fifty feet beyond its companion and broke the westerlies from the snug dock between them. The partners now held shares in local fishing vessels and in West Indies traders and owned outright the *Didamia II* and the *Pride of Erin,* 60-ton schooners plying to Halifax and Boston.

New Erin was bound to feel the brisk and ever-increasing world traffic, since much of the trade to and from American ports passed the island as ships made the old landfall of Cape Sable.

Nova Scotia itself was rapidly launching a sizable fleet of smaller craft and the tales of local mariners held new place names. Listening, Mercy felt these names carry her along ocean currents, catch her up in boisterous winds. Almost she knew, for an in-

*George's Bank, between New England and Nova Scotia.

stant, the run from Rangoon to Baltimore and what it was to lie wind-bound off Otago, on the underside of the world.

The Redmonds saw the bulky timberladen New Brunswickers, their new sails like fine-weather clouds, standing out by Cape Sable, bound for Liverpool or London and the Australian emigrant trade. Now and then they watched a steamer drag its smoke through the clean sky like a black and evil wake.

The more ships the more wrecks. Seldom a storm but was followed by news of some brave craft clutched by the almost unmarked coast between Cape Sable and Cape Forchu.

Dan had never forgotten the stricken *Morning Star* and the seas that had reached for her clinging passengers, nor the *Osprey's* bowsprit raised as in prayer to the merciless sky. He had early sworn to erect a lighthouse on New Erin and thus diminish the danger at one spot on the cruel shore.

His vow had been fulfilled last fall. On the point's tip a square one-story tower stood and, in the lantern atop it, five lamps sat in a zinc trough, one before each seaward window. After sunset the ruby chimneys and the polished brass reflectors behind them sent a red glow into the night. A ship's bell swung from a bar before the tower and was rung in answer to the blown conch shell of a fisherman, or the weedy horn of a vessel.

Dan had named his beacon St. Catherine's Light and hoped that his oldest daughter, who bore the saint's name, would learn to tend its lamps while her name became a benediction on seamen's lips.

Catherine, however, showed interest in nothing that involved work. Serena declared bitterly it was *her* belief the whole halibut fleet would be dashed to kindling wood on the rocks beneath the unlit windows and every man jack drowned, before milady would dampen her pretty gowns on the lighthouse path or soil her dainty fingers with the oily lamps and sooty chimneys.

The quantity of truth in this harsh appraisal disturbed Mercy. Yet the spoiled Catherine should not be blamed too severely. At thirteen, usually an awkward age of change and uncertainty,

Catherine had a figurine exquisiteness that drew admiration from all. She could wheedle her father as smoothly as she wound an errant curl about a slender finger. Even her brothers found her drenched-violet eyes hard to resist, while the vulnerable boys off the vessels brought her their cherished curios, their scrimshaw treasures, as they would bring tribute to a queen.

It puzzled Mercy that Catherine, child of a heart bitterly bolted against Dan, should have an ethereal beauty not approached by the children of rapturous and mutual giving.

Catherine's selfishness and comeliness aside, the fact remained that tending the light, like so much else, usually fell to the willing and overworked Kiah. Still, most of the seamen who used and blessed the beacon had never heard of St. Catherine—or her name-sake—and cared little who lit its lamps. They called it "Red-mond's Light" after the man who had erected it for their safety, and whom they liked for his warm hospitality and trusted for his fair dealing.

Dan, it seemed to Mercy, was near the fulfilment of his early dreams. He had his farm, his wharves and boats, his comfortable home, his family of strong sons and pretty daughters.

Now that the hard, dirty work lay behind him, Dan dressed as a gentleman always. His white linen shirts were tucked and seamed by Mercy's own hand; his boots fashioned of the finest leather; his outer garments made by Halifax's best tailors. By a single glance from the house window Mercy could distinguish her husband's finely garbed figure among a dozen men gathered on the wharfside.

She looked across at Dan now as he stared into the fire, his open book forgotten. He did not look up to meet her eyes and nothing told her where his thoughts were. The demands of business on him, of the growing family on her, had pushed away the companionship of the early island years. Yet Dan remained her lover, faithful and true. Though he was prone to override her cherished prejudices, he could still stir her with a dark-blue glance or a touch of his slender hand. As tenderness rose within her, she

160

searched his face again in the flickering light and was vaguely troubled by something she saw there, some unhappiness or unrest. Not, she decided, the same sorrow that stirred in her own breast as the storm gathered.

Yet, she thought, glancing about her, *there's nothing in the room to disturb him.*

In his rich voice Philip was explaining a sum to the girls.

Tamsin's soft brown eyes were fixed on him. Her dear little tilted nose—so like Bethiah's!—bore an ink smudge as if she'd attempted to erase her errors with that absurd feature, and her curls, at which she tugged when perplexed, appeared to shrink before coming struggles with what Philip was calling Medial and Alternate Alligation.

Catherine, her eyes veiled by their long bronze lashes, was obviously not listening.

What does she dream of, Mercy wondered, *this beautiful daughter who is such a stranger to me?*

Philip might have been pondering the same. "A penny for your thoughts, Catherine," he chided her smilingly.

Philip had been one of the New Erin family for six years. Before that he had been like a brother to Mercy and a good son to her parents. He had tried to hide, lest it grieve them, how his heart turned from boats to books, though he had absorbed all the Prince's Cove schoolhouse held for him. But Captain Sam had known that a fifteen-year-old boy who loves the water doesn't prop a book beside him on the thwart and memorize long lists as his oars rise and fall on the way to herring nets, or to the rip where the pollack leap. So when the new term opened, Philip had left the Cove to be enrolled at the Yarmouth Academy.

Patrick had been eight and Catherine five when the eighteen-year-old Philip, his schooling completed with honors, had been engaged as teacher, bookkeeper and general help on New Erin.

Philip was a handsome young man, brown-skinned, black-eyed, fine-featured, but slender and barely of medium height. His slight build added to a certain bookishness in his speech and his "dry-handed" means of earning a livelihood drew condescension from some bigger men who followed the sea; but the Nickersons and the Redmonds knew his worth.

Mercy's children had always loved gentle Uncle Philip; they learned to love him more when they took their places in the schoolroom, as the new chamber above the middle room became.

On winter evenings Philip, reading aloud, brought to the gathered family such friends as Mr. Pickwick and Rob Roy. On the arrival of the *Yarmouth Herald,* however, exciting stories were forgotten for even more exciting news. News of shipping, of the provincial railway's inching progress, the marvels of the telegraph, the records broken by transatlantic steamers, the latest political furors. Mercy noted that Dan listened closely to Philip's opinion and put a high value on the younger man's judgment.

Ah, yes, it does us all good to have Philip with us, she thought, looking at his dark head bent attentively above Tamsin's difficulties. *Strange that with such a teacher, Patrick never came to love his books. If only he had turned to Philip, perhaps . . .*

An easterly makes healed wounds throb and rouses sleeping pain. As the wind whined and rain spattered, Mercy cried silently, *Two years is a long time, too long for one of a family to be away; it brings too many changes to growing boys and girls. Patrick will be like a stranger to us and we to him.* Her longing to behold her son again, before the years had stolen his boyhood, rose choking and bitter.

On nights like this, she told herself, *when the rain lashes the deck and the wind moans through the rigging as it is moaning in the chimney, Patrick on watch must dream of New Erin's safe anchorage, of his brothers and sisters about the fire, of his own snug bed.*

Memories of scoldings and punishments for boyish misdemeanors rose to upbraid her. *Oh, Patrick,* her sore heart wept, *I meant them all for your own good—because I loved you so.*

Surely out of all her care for him he must—oh, he must—find a tender memory or two of his mother.

Chapter 20

ON THAT STORMY DAY TWO SPRINGS AGO PHILIP HAD BEEN IN SHEL-
burne on business, the schoolroom deserted and the restless children underfoot until the rain had ceased. When the afternoon
sun had burst through the last clouds, Mercy, grateful for a breath
of outdoors, stepped around the corner and spread her milk-cloths
on the May grass to sweeten.

A movement of Short Wharf drew her eyes. Kiah in his glistening leather apron stepped from the barrel shop and flung a bucket-
ful of offal into the dock. Patrick, his yellow head gleaming as
the sun found it, followed him out the door and in again. Her
son's voice came to Mercy clearly through the rain-cleansed air
and, though the words were lost, the tone was agitated. *He and
Kiah with their men's arguments,* she thought fondly and then
sighed because it was to Kiah and not to Dan that the boy turned.

As she re-entered the kitchen Serena met her. "Oh, thyah ye
be! Ye can mind this little Tartar whilst I gather the eggs." She
whisked through the door, glad, as Mercy had been, for a few
minutes in the spring air.

Adria ran to bury her head in her mother's skirts. "Little Tartar," she said complacently.

Even while Mercy stooped and smoothed back her baby's
clustering hair her thoughts were with her first-born; as she
straightened she saw that the open door framed Patrick hurrying
across the yard.

*How he's shot up over winter! Not quite fourteen and as tall
as his father! Steady and dependable as a man, but sensitive and
loving under his manliness,* she mused as he paused in the doorway, feeling him especially near and dear this afternoon.

Her smile wavered and fled. Patrick's eyes were at once deso-

163

lated and wrathful, every freckle stood out on his white face. Her heart contracted. *Dan had hurt him again—and cruelly.* In spite of her love for her husband she thought impatiently, *Why does he show his preference for all the others? Not only for Catherine, the favorite; Patrick could overlook that.*

It had long been so. She recalled the small Patrick, his yellow curls bobbing against his collar, his skirts swinging as he ran to lay a dimpled hand on his father's knee, and plead for approval. "Pat-wick's a *good* boy, Papa?" She could hear again the yearning in the childish voice, see again the soft mouth's quiver at Dan's indifferent or impatient assent, little better than a denial.

Once she had besought her husband, "Dan, can't you see you're hurting a loving son, just as your father hurt you?" But he had replied coldly that the boy was too big to be babied.

From earliest boyhood Patrick had come to his mother with proffered help or with precious gifts of pretty stones and wild flowers, never for her approval or for consolation. Now she watched his face anxiously as he strove for words.

"Kiah won't talk about it," he blurted out. "He says—he says I must ask *you*." Each short breath was audible.

Mercy could only wait.

"Mamma," he demanded when he had his voice under control, "whose child am I?"

She could see the boyish heart thumping under the rough jersey and the thin young arch of breast; but she knew she must not move to take him in her arms. "Child?" she echoed, completely at a loss. "Why whose child would you be but mine and your papa's?"

He laughed. Such a sound on a boy's lips! "Yours. But not Papa's. And that's why he never loved me." His voice rose and cracked, "All the others. Not me. Let me tell you I don't blame him." His eyes in the shadowed doorway were black with pain. Mercy had seen such eyes—in a young steer gored by the ox—holding the look from a death wound.

She groped for a chair and lowered herself into it.

164

Her voice was deceptively calm. "Patrick, come in and shut the door. Now, tell me what you are talking about."

As the boy's words poured out she reproached herself starkly. Her own wound had healed in the reconciliation following Catherine's birth, the scar had faded during succeeding years. But to think that she—even if Dan had neglected to do so—that *she* had not torn that page from the Bible, had not burnt and scattered the words before they again dealt pain.

Patrick told her how, seeking to fill the rainy hours, he had wandered into the parlor and had examined first the curios on the whatnot, the daguerreotypes in their wire rack, then turned to the Bible on the marble-topped table. He'd been idly riffling its pages when his own name had caught his eye. From above it, in what he recognized as his father's writing, cruel words had leapt at him, "Born out of wedlock." Soon he had closed the Bible and crept from the room, down to the wharf and Kiah. Kiah, who admitted that for him the sun rose and set in Patrick, certainly.

Kiah had failed him. "*I* don't know the rights of it," he'd repeatedly declared. "Ye'll have t' go t' yer maw."

Mercy explained that those words had been a mistake, long ago. "Didn't you notice they'd been crossed out? If you'd turned the page you'd have seen your name above Catherine's and the others' in a new list."

Patrick would not listen. "I know you were already married to . . ." He was struck by the thought that he had no right to the word "papa" and the shock tightened his tender mouth. "I know you were married," he resumed a bit shamefaced as if he might be accused of prying. "I looked up the dates."

Poor hurt and bewildered boy; how little the scant records could tell him.

"Patrick, you must harken to me. You are your father's dear son—no different from his other children. Except that you were our first and perhaps a bit more precious for that. Papa was so proud of you! But he, he . . ."

165

She must not criticize Dan to his son, "You will come to see, as I did, that your father's religion . . ."

He broke in bitterly, "Religion!" Tears were not far from his voice and he hurried lest they overtake and shame him. "Religion isn't what those words mean! Do you think I haven't heard the men talking? I know what they call a boy like me. I'm a . . ."

"Patrick," she besought him, "don't! Don't say it! You'll break your mother's heart. Oh, how can I make you understand?" She wrung her hands upon her aproned lap. Then with forlorn acknowledgment, "You *can't* understand. No more could I." The wound she had thought so well healed was a running sore.

Patrick was stricken to see his mother weeping, her face twisted away from him, her head bent to the chair's back. No matter if the world had slipped from under his feet this afternoon and she was to blame for the void, he loved her. He put his hand clumsily upon her hair, then bent and laid his smooth boy's face against hers. He kissed her cheek shyly with lips atremble, a sweet and heartbreaking kiss Mercy never forgot.

The soft closing of the door, in place of Patrick's usual bang, started her tears afresh. But tears wouldn't mend matters. She must find Dan, have him straighten out the wretched misunderstanding and reassure his son.

Adria, who had stood big-eyed while Mamma and Patrick talked, now began to whimper and, for her own reassurance, brought her doll to be kissed. Mamma crying was a thing not to be borne.

So Mercy dried her eyes upon her apron corner and when Serena returned was busy about the evening meal.

Not until they were at last in bed could Mercy find opportunity to tell Dan of Patrick's discovery.

"Poor lad," he said with pity and self-accusation roughing his tones. "At that age, when everything stabs so keenly!"

Mercy, hearing the love in his voice, felt that good might come

166

from the day's trouble; that Dan would now show his son the affection he had so stubbornly withheld. She clasped to her this gain from the years—now, instead of flying apart to nurse their pain as they once had done, she and Dan found solace in sharing it, a lash not inflicted upon one by the other, but laid across them both by impartial life.

Before sleep claimed her, Mercy thought, *Tomorrow will bring us the greater intimacy that must follow Dan's righting of a wrong.*

The foggy morn brought, instead, the disclosure that Patrick was gone from New Erin. Slipped off, apparently, in the *Effie* of Marblehead, which had dropped down the bay on the early ebb.

Mercy, forcing herself to go about her work, could see nothing but Patrick's accusing face. What a struggle between love and bitterness must have twisted the young heart as Patrick pushed boyhood behind him into the fog over his island home.

The good hand of his God would be upon him, afloat as on New Erin; but Mercy remembered, with a stab of pain, the dangling shirt button awaiting her needle, a symbol of motherhood's small duties and great joys.

Often during the next months Mercy compared herself with Rachel, who mourned her first-born and would not be comforted. Her mind went perpetually seeking Patrick's somewhere in the space dividing them, and she brought it back reluctantly to meet the demands of his brothers and sisters. Sometimes she returned to these safe and near ones with sharp words; then their stricken faces would reproach her and she must assure them of her love, and of Patrick's return—for they missed their big brother woefully.

Dan was both the man who had given her Patrick and the man who had driven him away. She made her arms gentle when at night he turned to them as to a haven from unvoiced remorse. When an uninformed seaman asked the whereabouts of Patrick, or the children's prattle probed unbearably, she pitied him for the bleakness that washed over his face. Whatever else she felt, she hid, knowing it would pass.

His grandson's departure shook Captain Sam, when the *Didamia* next made New Erin. He told Mercy soberly, "It would have been better for the boy if he'd had less Nickerson and salt water in his make-up, perhaps. I'd hoped, what with the business for your boys to step into, you'd be spared the heartache and worry your ma's known."

"There's more to it than the call of the sea, Pa." Mercy told him of her son's white-faced accusations and Dan's inadequacies as Patrick's father.

He listened gravely, only the tightening of his wide mouth giving any sign of his disturbance. When she had done he reached out and stroked her drooping head with his big hand that could be surprisingly gentle. "There, there, Mercy girl, don't take it so hard. I've knowed more than one man not his kindest to his first son. Almost as if they were jealous. A pity, it seems."

Jealous? Mercy recalled Dan's voice the morning he had discovered her pregnant with Catherine. "Ah, yes, Patrick!" he had said, and his voice had troubled her even then, so that it came back to her clearly now, "Patrick, at least, is well-beloved." Did even their son's running away have some of its roots in her stubborn coldness after her quarrel with Dan?

Her father was continuing, "Patrick will understand the how of it, if not the why, before he's been long away and rubbing elbows with all kinds and creeds.

"Perhaps some night when the trucks seem to be moving in the stars, there'll come to Patrick the feeling I first got when I was no older than him, and have never lost for long; the feeling that everything, stars, currents and winds, every splinter of the ship, every drop of blood in each man of the crew, are all sweeping along swift and sure, on a voyage where the storms and the fair weather, the making port or the shipwreck, are all planned —and all necessary for the working out of a greater Plan."

168

He went on more matter-of-factly, "Boys have always been running away and mothers' hearts have always been torn at their going. Patrick will be home before many months; growed and changed, no doubt, but still your own." He patted his daughter's hand and turned away.

Patrick did not come home in a few months. Mercy heard of him only from the seamen who, remembering her hungry eyes, made inquiries among their kind so as to have a scrap of news for her when they should put into Redmond's again.

Once after Mercy's starved questions had brought no news, Serena volunteered flatly, "The' was a time when *I* used t' pester anybuddy an' everybuddy fer news. Not of a b'y. Of a man, 'twas. But I give it up. His people found out he was married an'—so's the men wouldn't take t' laffin' at me behind my back—they told me so, plumb and plain. They was good people," she ceded, gently for Serena. "An' what he done wasn't no fault o' theirn."

"Just who *was* your husband, Serena?" Mercy's sympathy for another distracted her thoughts, as perhaps Serena had intended. "I haven't asked, because you've never mentioned him till now."

"Well," Serena said shortly, " 'taint no secret. Manasseh Swim brung him up, though he wasn't no blood relation." Then bleakly, "Truth t' tell, he was one the devil blowed a-flyin'."

Mercy winced. Patrick had heard that obloquy—and worse. Suddenly weeping, she turned from the amazed Serena.

Chapter 21

No good could come from grieving; Mercy brought her mind back to remaining riches, while the family group gained in security as the weather outside worsened.

Despite signs of storm no vessel had sought the harbor before dark and none would be apt to put in while fog and rain-squalls hid the light's red beam; yet no one in the middle room showed any surprise when a heavy knock sounded—with that sixth sense engendered by island life they had been half expecting it.

The dog growled and came to his feet. He was the third Skipper, of the same black Newfoundland breed as the first and as faithful a watchdog.

"Quiet, sir!" Dan commanded, and the big dog sank down obediently.

His master crossed the room and opened the door upon a man's blurred outlines. A high thin voice announced, "Dellie Watt Hines, master o' the *Bluebell*."

"Come in, Captain Hines, come in," Dan urged cordially. "A nasty night out. A raw wind. Come over to this chair by the fire." He turned to Mercy. "Mrs. Redmond, this is Captain Hines."

Mercy's smile lit up her face and softened her eyes as, pausing briefly with lifted needle, she gave the stranger good evening and bade him make himself at home. Serena knit on as if every foot in the house were bare and she alone to cover them, but Philip and the girls politely pushed their books aside. To make room, the smaller children crowded close to their mother, for the New Erin hearth was shared with all comers as a matter of course.

Captain Hines refused a seat and the request to shed his sea coat and round-rimmed hat, glistering with rain; but he stood for a few moments thrusting thick hands towards the flames and shivering in their delicious heat, while his heavy pants gave off small plumes of steam. A catechu-kettle of a man, black and round on short, wide-spread legs.

Rivulets of tobacco juice crosshatched his flat chin and he spat towards the fire through a gap in discolored teeth. His blue jowls drooped above his short bull-neck and his weather-mottled face looked haggard.

Surely if his vessel were in trouble he'd say so at once, Dan thought, puzzled. He excused himself and returned with a glass

170

of brandy. "Try this. It will warm you, Captain," he said.

The other snatched at the glass and drank its contents at a gulp, smacking his lips hugely when it was down. When Dan made no move to refill the glass the *Bluebell's* skipper stepped forward glumly to set it on the table.

With affected heartiness in his reedy voice the stranger then turned to Will and Charlie, and they answered him politely but briefly, sensing that he had no real interest in them. When he laid his gnarled hand on Adria's soft hair it was with surprising gentleness, and Mercy afterwards held that tender gesture in his favor.

That the captain was ill at ease and his mind not upon visiting was plain before he blurted out, "I come t' see ye on business like, Mr. Redmond. Ain't the' ary place me 'n' you can have a talk?"

Dan led him into the office and closed the door.

"Now here it is, without any backin' and fillin'," Captain Hines said vehemently in his thin voice, as soon as candles had been lit and the men were settled in chairs. "I'm in a tight pinch and I've come t' ye for help." He brought his hands down heavily upon his spread legs as if he were laying his cards upon the table.

Dan was frankly bewildered. "I'm always happy, Captain Hines . . ."

"Call me Dellie Watt," the other interrupted. "Everybuddy does. Too many Hineses in Hines's Harbor, too many of 'em captains." He made an expansive gesture of comradeship, a strange combination of arrogance and fawning.

He went on, "Ye mought 'a' heared o' Hazelitt Morris, who owns the *Bluebell*. Married to my dorter, he was. She died 'most a year ago, poor girl. But no matter! Haze 'n' me, we'm partners, in a manner o' speaking."

Dan had heard of the prosperous but slippery Hazelitt Morris, whose name was a scandal and a reproach on the tongues of upright Prince's Cove folks.

Under the black rim of his hat the skipper's small eyes were sharp upon his host. "I dassay ye've heared that Haze 'n' me, we don't declare all we bring in."

Dan agreed noncommittally that he'd heard rumors to that effect.

"Well, believe 'em," the other advised shortly.

He went on, shuffling his heavy boots restlessly. "Anyways, here I be, with a cargo from St. Pierre. As we rounded the Cape at dusk we nigh run across the bows of the Cutter! Her skipper, Sparrow Smith, he sighted me sure as hell-fire and he's been awatchin' and awaitin' this long time fer a chance at me.

"Off Newfoundland and the French islands now, I can mostly bow-peep the cutters, and then it's hurray-mi-b'ys! try an' catch me. I got a trick or two besides, like carryin' an extry set o' sails and name boards. When Excise men have been a-chasin' a suit o' white sails it confuses 'em to sight a tan mains'l and jib. And t' other way around. Confuses 'em when they come up t' what they figgered was the *Bluebell* and read she's the *Robert Manning* of Marblehead or the *Mary Ellen* o' Yarmouth."

He snickered gleefully, then sobered. "But that's up Newfoundland way. I can't pull the wool over Sparrow Smith's eyes. I'd like t' . . ."

By a sharp gesture Dan cut off the trenchant recital of Dellie Watt's desires.

"You'm pretty finnicky about yer langwige, Mr. Redmond, I can see that," the other resumed, none too pleased, "but I tell ye true, we never had noan o' this trouble till a year or so back, when they put Sparrow in charge of the *Beagle*. And him born and brung up right around here!" This local background apparently added to what Dellie Watt considered treachery.

"Sparrow," Dan said. "Isn't that an unusual name for a man?"

Dellie Watt brought his flat face and his small eyes about suspiciously. "What's so onusual about it? His grandmother was a Sparrow. Same as mine."

"I see." Dan backed warily away from the trap of local nomenclature and possible relationships.

The other continued, "Sparrow's cracked—cracked, I tell ye—

172

on Temp'rance. In Meetin', so they tell, he's allus a-gittin' up in the high seats an' spoutin' off about it Haze has tried t' talk reason t' him. He won't listen." Dellie Watt spat disgustedly into the open grate of the Franklin stove and raised a flurry of ashes.

Dan understood from all this that Sparrow Smith, master of the Revenue and Fisheries Cruiser, had refused Morris' bribe to close one eye against the *Bluebell's* unloadings.

Dellie Watt continued "Now Hines' Harbor ain't like this open one o' yourn, or I'd scratch my way in tonight, low water 'n' all. I know the anchorage and, let me tell ye, I'd be a hard rooster t' beat on my own dunghill."

Dan could credit that.

"Ordinary, I'd ride out this blow at sea. But didn't the *Bluebell* spring a leak for'rd in that rough off Halifax, so I don't dast risk it."

He paused, and though the fireless office was too cold for comfort, his face was beaded with sweat from the effort of so many words and the maintenance of an ingratiating manner despite anxiety and frustration. He looked sharply sidewise at Dan to mark possible headway.

"I can understand your reluctance to put out tonight," Dan replied, beginning to see the form of Dellie Watt's coming appeal, but undecided as to how he would receive it.

The high voice went on, "I was a-ponderin' on things when we come abreast o' them outer islands in the bay. But them's too small, too bare; ye couldn't hide a flea on 'em! An' then, before the fog shut in, I catched sight o' *your* island. 'What a spot,' I says t' myself. 'If only I had a friend there.' I remembered the good 'counts I'd heard o' ye. I thought, 'Now if me an' Haze c'd go mates with Dan Redmond and use New Erin, we c'd all be rollin' rich in no time. No time a-tall.'" His big hands patted his knees confidingly.

Dan made a gesture of repudiation, but a desire for excitement was stirring. He had been depressed all evening, feeling the easterly counting out every one of his forty-three years and whittling the towering trunks of his early ambitions down to the splinter size of his moderate success. This seaman, matching his wits and his *Bluebell* against the government boats, began to take on color as a bold sea dog with a dash of pirate in him.

Dellie Watt Hines was not discouraged by what he saw in his host's face. "I don't ask ye t' lift a hand, Mr. Redmond. Ye don't even need t' know where anything is hid. Sparrow don't suspicion I slipped in here; he's high-tailin' it fer Hines's this very minute." Dellie Watt appeared to derive a morsel of grim pleasure from this diddling of Sparrow.

He went on, " 'Count o' that blasted leak I'll go to Barrington t'morra, all innocent-like, an' clear what's still aboard. Then some foggy night one o' Haze sloops will slip in here—the crew will know where t' look—and in the mornin' the stuff'll be gone." His eyes glinted in the candlelight and he moved his cud as if the matter were settled; then as Dan kept silence he said begrudgingly, "I can promise ye a good lay in the trip's profits if ye'll help me out o' this pinch."

Dan answered slowly, "I wasn't thinking of profit. Only that I wouldn't wish to tangle with the law."

The other exploded with an oath. "Law! Whoever heared tell of an Irishman who didn't glory in a bit o' law-breakin'? Fur as that goes, I'd wager the brandy you'm so blasted savin' of came from Miquelon under a Gloucester skipper's bunk."

This was so near the mark that Dan could only laugh.

Dellie Watt's high voice took on new assurance. "Blasted revenue laws! Nobuddy pays them any heed. Ye know that yerself, you."

It was true. The Banks vessels all had their French liquors and their bits of feminine finery tucked in the forepeak; many schooners back from Boston slipped into home port at night and rode noticeably lighter in the morning when they set out for Barrington and the tidewater. Few merchants along the shore paid duty on all their stock and no one expected them to.

Dan found it difficult to deny any appeal and nearly impossible to refuse help to a mariner. This storm-shrouded night had

174

been bred for the *Bluebell's* skipper; Kiah and the hired boys were abed in the far end of the house; who was to know what took place in the fog and rain? *Just for this once,* he thought, *for the anomaly and to help out a fellow man.*

"I'll be going to bed shortly," Dan heard himself stating. "And I'm a sound sleeper. My buildings aren't locked and I seldom inspect them closely."

Grinning, the other slapped his sodden knee.

Dan rose then and crossed to the wine closet in the corner. "Now," he said, "shall we toast the *Bluebell* in tax-free St. Pierre brandy?"

The schooner was gone by dawn. Dan never sought to discover where the liquor had been hidden nor when it was removed.

In the rush of spring and summer trade Dellie Watt had almost been forgotten when one August night the *Bluebell's* master again came ashore. In the office he produced a generous pouch of coins ("wharfage 'n' sech," he called it offhandedly, pushing it towards Dan) and sweeping plans for further and greater co-operation.

By now Dan had learned more of Hazelitt Morris; of his association with Yarmouth merchants, of the finger he had, not only in the affairs of that thriving town, but in many a provincial pie as well. Apparently few of his business friends concerned themselves as to his ethics, while all agreed that Tariff Regulations were relics of a barbarous age and Customs Officers the natural enemies of all lovers of freedom and a good round turnover. Dan had decided that friendly dealings with Morris would open new doors to the island partnership.

Besides the enticement of expanding business there was the thrill of intrigue and the matching of wits with the law's officers to assuage a growing restlessness; the knowledge that smuggled spirits had long flooded the province. He was no Puritan, he thought a bit irascibly, remembering some sour looks when wine had appeared at Molly's wedding.

175

Afterward Dan was never clear just when and how he became so deeply committed in the illicit trade, or just when he began to sense that, like Dellie Watt of the unsavory reputation, Dan Redmond was Hazelitt Morris's man. On that August visit the *Bluebell's* skipper had been well primed by a cunning and unscrupulous employer and had proved a more fluent and persuasive talker than Dan had suspected.

Dan argued to his own conscience that what use he and his new associates made of New Erin need not affect his partnership with Captain Nickerson. He strove to justify the venture under the long, unblinking stare of Kiah, for the hired man had to be told. Something in the steady look called Mercy to mind. Mercy would not approve but, completely occupied with her household and family duties, she need never suspect that Dellie Watt was other than a skipper who periodically made Redmond's Harbor and came ashore for supplies.

At first Dan's part was small: a few kegs and demijohns of New England rum were landed by Gloucestermen on their way to the Banks, a much larger quantity from St. Pierre and Miquelon on the vessels' return—little more than the haphazard movement of spirits that had always gone on. The work and excitement, the risk and the large profits lay in the *Bluebell's* cargoes. She made several trips a year, carrying contraband to Newfoundland and returning liquor laden. She had other hiding places along the shore but more and more often she put into Redmond's.

There each cargo was widely dispersed, hidden in the abandoned Ryder wells, in the haymows, among the eelgrass in the icehouse or the barrels of oil in the lighthouse; then, after a time, in specially constructed hiding places. Some of the smuggled drink was sold locally, despite the strong Temperance movement sweeping the shore, some to the crews who used the harbor, but most of it awaited Hazelitt Morris's small boats which carried it to his tavern and the much larger Yarmouth market.

Chapter 22

BECAUSE, AT THE START, THE *Bluebell's* VISITS WERE WIDELY SPACED, a year elapsed after her first unloading at New Erin before talk reached Captain Sam's ears. He came to Dan's office, one morning and laid his cap on the desk with the air of casting down a gage.

"I'm breaking away from our partnership, Dan," he said bluntly. "I won't inconvenience you to settle up right off. That'll take time and I'm content to leave it to you and Philip."

Though Dan now realized he had known this was bound to come, he was none the less dismayed. He straightened a pile of papers with lowered lids as he asked, "I suppose you have a reason for this, Captain Nickerson?"

"Yes," the other answered wryly. "I have a good reason for any who might inquire. Old age."

That brought Dan's dark gaze swiftly upward. He had continued to think of his father-in-law as the *Didamia's* stalwart master who had rescued young Dan Redmond. He saw with a shock that the once-golden hair was now silver. The crows' feet about the clear blue eyes, formed as much by a humorous crinkle as by squinting across water, had deepened. So had the downward brackets about the wide mouth. There was no ounce of superfluous flesh on the big frame, but its movements were no longer loose and quick.

Why, yes, Dan silently conceded, saddened by the truth, *Captain Nickerson is an elderly man.*

However, the strong voice had lost none of its timbre as the captain resumed, "I have a better reason to tell *you,* Dan. I won't be mixed up—even by name—with the likes of Dellie Watt Hines and Hazelitt Morris!

"I could give you many a chapter and verse as to why I despise the pair of them," he went on. "I'll quote you but one and that's the *Henrietta*. Put on the Cape Ledges for her insurance. Haze Morris gave the orders and Dellie Watt carried them out."

Dan recalled the rumors rife at the time the bark was lost.

Captain Sam continued. "That wrack cost two men's lives and Abel Stoddart of the Cove left four small children. You helped some of us see his family through last winter, remember? But a basket o' food now and then, a few cords o' wood—what tell o' them when the man of the house is gone? I want no part nor parcel of men who would make widows and orphans for money's sake." The captain's fist thumped the desk and his blue eyes blazed.

Dan reminded him that the charges against the skipper and owner could not be proved.

"Proved!" The word was almost an oath on the good captain's lips, but when he spoke again his voice was moderate. "I understand you plan to help those men break the law. You should give the matter some thought."

Dan shifted uneasily and turned his eyes out the window.

"You've come to fill a big place in the district; many a man will watch how you set your course and follow your wake. If they see you breaking one law they'll use your example for their own ends. I mind you spoke bitter enough last winter when Cape Whiters helped themselves to your sheep. No doubt they justified their action by saying they were hungry and you could stand the loss; but what would become of us if every man picked out what laws suited him and cast the rest overboard?"

Dan shrugged impatiently. "Captain, you know as well as I that most people along the shore evade the tariff—a different matter entirely from thieving."

The other could not deny that smuggling went on. Instead, he pointed out earnestly, "There's another side to this new business. You claim any man has a right to drink if he pleases. That's fine for you, since you're not one to be bothered by liquor. No more am I. But I've seen many a man pour the food for his wife and

178

children, the roof over their heads, his own manhood, out the bunghole of a rumpuncheon."

Stubbornly, Dan told himself that Captain Nickerson sounded like the old woman Dellie Watt labeled him.

The captain brought out his final argument. "You've got boys of your own growing up. Don't break Mercy's heart and don't be tempted by money from other women's heartbreak. For that's what this smuggling, this having 'the ardent' cheap and plentiful, always comes to."

He stopped, reached his bandanna from his back pocket and wiped his face.

Dan straightened desk papers and remained silent. The new venture was already showing fine profits, without risk, and he had no intention of giving it up.

Captain Sam's smile, if wistful, was without rancor. "I put my case as strong as I could, Dan, but I hardly hoped to sway you. And I'm not one that holds it must be a fault in another to differ from my opinions." He put out his hand.

Dan took it warmly. "I hope we shall continue friends, Captain Nickerson."

The captain nodded. "I hope so. Life would be empty for Damie and me if we couldn't run on to see you and Mercy and the children." He asked, "Mercy doesn't know what's going on?"

"There's no need for Mercy to know the details of my business," Dan reminded him stiffly.

"I judged not," her father said. "Damie has promised me, no matter what she hears, Temp'rance or no, she won't breathe a word to Mercy."

It was an old man's voice that went on, "Though Philip's like a son, still Mercy is the last hereabouts of our own."

Bethiah and her Gilbert had been drawn around the Horn by '49's gold and had remained in California; their parents were not likely to see them again in this world. Levi had married ashore in London, Isaac was master of a steamer out of New York; Grannie's Head saw them no more.

Dan's voice was gruff with emotion; he himself had an absent son. "I know, Captain, I know. You'll always be welcome on New Erin. What kind of a man would I be . . .?"

His father-in-law nodded. "All the years we've been partners, Dan, I wouldn't have asked for a better man to work with, a fairer man to deal with. Perhaps a mite too openhanded with some who plan to slide through life on a little soft soap, but generosity's a fault not hard to overlook. I'm downright sorry we've come to the parting of our ways and I pray the Lord you won't have cause to regret the road you're taking."

What could Dan do but murmur thanks for the generous praise? It would be useless to suggest this new undertaking need not infringe on the older partnership; Captain Sam knew not the meaning of compromise.

To break the growing constraint, Dan asked, "What about Philip? I suppose he, too, . . . disapproves?"

"Philip's his own man, he decides things for himself." The captain picked up his cap and fumbled the latch of the outer door.

When the books were in order and a fair settlement reached, Philip, too, said good-by to New Erin.

Dan hated to see the old associations broken up, yet there was a headiness in being without a partner's strait-laced and old-fashioned notions to consult or consider. Time he was standing on his own feet!

His new self-confidence was shaken when, after the landing of the *Bluebell's* next cargo, the *Beagle* tied up to the Long Wharf. Captain Smith left his crew lounging about the deck and strolled the wharf's length to smoke a pipe in the lee of the icehouse.

Sparrow Smith, contrary to the picture Dan had drawn from Dellie Watt's invectives, proved a mild, undersized man in his forties. His bowed legs and toothless mouth corroborated stories "spouted off" at Temperance Meetings, stories of a drunken father and the perpetual hunger of children cursed from birth by the ills that followed the rumpuncheons. A fanatic against liquor he might be, and stubborn purpose was marked on his

180

face, but from the first Dan liked the little man who snipped off his words between the blades of his sharp nose and his pointed chin.

He announced at once, "Mr. Redmond, I'm out t' catch Dellie Watt. Randall Duncan, the Excise Officer at Hines's, he's out for Hazelitt Morris. That man Morris, with his licker, he's made more widders and orphans than George's and Brown's put together."

Then mildly, but leaving no least doubt as to his meaning, "Man dear, I hope sech as you wouldn't be mixed up with sech as them." Nose and chin closed sharply.

Dan made no reply to this and the other continued as if he'd expected none. "Years ago I sailed on a v'yage under Sam Nickerson and a better cap'n couldn't be found. I'd be loathe to do him or his business any hurt."

"Captain Nickerson is no longer a partner here," Dan replied rather acidly.

The little man looked up at him swiftly. So the talk was true that this foreign son-in-law had kicked the old man out!

"Oh!" Having snipped the word off, he smoked on it a while. Then, "I've heared tell 'twas Cap'n Sam picked you up, all but drownded, that time off the Ragged Laidges?"

"He did. And I've always been grateful. But that doesn't give him the right . . ."

"Don't give him no rights," the other agreed softly. "Man dear, anybuddy fool enough to risk his life and his vessel around the Ragged Laidges after a storm, he don't deserve no rights. Noan a-tall."

Before Dan could meet the implied accusation in this speech, Captain Smith knocked the rank dottle from his pipe and started down the wharf towards the *Beagle*. Dan, who had no wish to be rude, fell in step beside him, for on New Erin one saw a guest to the wharfside as elsewhere one might see him to the door.

With a foot on the cap-log the visitor paused. "You'm like t' have me under yer bow every so often, if Dellie Watt keeps

181

finding this anchorage so handy. I'll be dropping ashore and looking around, like. I cal'ate you have an idee as t' what I'll be looking fer." A tame enough challenge.

As his men cast off and began to hoist sail he stood gazing shoreward from the *Beagle's* deck. He raised his voice to carry across the widening water, "A right nice spot ye got here. A shame t' dirty it." His bowed legs took him swift and sure along the deck to the wheel aft.

Watching, Dan's anger rose at the meddlesome Sparrow Smith who had practically accused him of ingratitude to a benefactor. *I never heard that Captain Nickerson ran any great risk to rescue me!* He kicked a wharf spile wrathfully, and absent-mindedly, but he was forced to admit he never *would* have heard such a thing from the captain or from one of his family.

At any rate, he decided in his ill temper, *I'm tired of having Captain Sam Nickerson held up to me as a model. And what the devil do I care for the good opinion of a bowlegged little Cape Islander?*

The atmosphere of New Erin changed from the day of the *Beagle's* visit, or Dan began to sense the change.

When seamen came ashore they wanted liquor from the cached supplies. Some skippers were often so far in their cups that Dan hesitated to ask them to join his family. Kiah no longer welcomed all crew members to the kitchen for the long evenings when one of the seamen tuned up his fiddle and the others tapped out the old tunes, or joined in the long, doleful ballads beloved by simple folk asea or ashore—songs of too-lately repentant pirates, of lost ships and drowned crews and of lily-white maids in early graves.

However, money became increasingly plentiful. There was money to replace Captain Sam's share in the business; to spend on the wharves and boats; to repair and re-shingle the big house and to keep it always dazzling in its white paint, so that sailors told of catching its gleam far out at sea and setting their course by it; to purchase fashionable furnishings for the home and expensive clothes for his wife and family, to invest in the varied undertakings of his new business associates.

Yet, while the smuggled liquor brought its share of this money, Dan was well aware that more came from the undertakings which Captain Sam's foresight had founded, and was part of the shore's prosperity.

Provincial fishing flourished, since the rival New England crews and vessels were depleted by the Civil War. The war also brought trade with both factions though sympathies and blood ties were with the Union. True, towards the end of the struggle word seeped out that Irish Fenians had enlisted in the Northern Armies with the understanding that, once the South had been defeated, they would be free to turn upon Canada and the British provinces across the Bay of Fundy. But no one worried too much about the Fenians while there were well-paying cargoes to be carried and bottoms to carry them.

Not only the Atlantic seaboard knew Bluenose craft; more and more of them were turning to the foreign trade; wherever the winds blew across the deeps their blunt-bowed ships pushed, nosing out freight. The flags of Nova Scotian shipping-houses floated from the skysail poles in Far Eastern ports and in the harbors of Europe and South America. In the coastal homes women wore the exquistie shawls of Cashmere, the bright Paisley cottons, the silks of Shanghai, brought them by their seafaring menfolk.

Village streets were empty of able-bodied men most of the year and black-clad women, with eyes burnt-out by vigils on the too-well-named widow's walks, showed the price of prosperity; yet in Yarmouth, Shelburne and Barrington, as in other towns, new firms sprang up and established businesses knew miraculous expansion. The early gray cottages found themselves flanked and overshadowed by imposing replicas of homes seen in foreign ports.

Times were strange and stirring and prosperous.

Increasing numbers of vessels put into New Erin for supplies and the ice to keep their fares from souring. Forty or fifty craft

183

often snuggled together in the round anchorage so near the fishing grounds. From the shore they appeared packed like herring in a barrel, yet two vessels seldom fouled, even in a storm.

Dan was flattered to hear himself referred to as one of the shore's "merchant princes," yet restlessness and self-dissatisfaction frequently walked beside him.

New friends flocked to the hospitable New Erin home, but though Dan had always felt a need to make an impression, to establish himself as superior to the fisherfolk of the shore, their flattery proved less congenial than the reserve of Mr. Robertson and his kind, whom Dan seldom saw now; their boisterous fellowships less satisfying than that with Captain Arthur d'Entremont, who still came ashore when his schooner was in harbor, despite a growing constraint. When Dan felt distaste for his partners' lack of principles, as he did with growing frequency, he asked himself if a similar revulsion colored the feeling his former friends had for him.

Captain Sam visited New Erin only occasionally, while Damie professed growing reluctance "t' go strammin' over boats and wharves." To Mercy and the children Grampy Sam was unchanged, but, in spite of their efforts, the two men grew stiff and increasingly ill at ease with each other.

Chapter 23

For Mercy the time following Dellie Watt's appearance was one of decrements which she intuitively connected with the *Bluebell's* skipper.

Her eyes filled when her father declared himself too old to eat Fundy fog and said that he was retiring to be "Square o' Grannie's Head." The picture of Captain Sam as squire of his rocky headland brought the smile he sought, and Mercy admitted it was truly time he took life easier.

Philip's going was another loss, though she respected his expressed desire to teach a larger school. "But what shall *my* poor children do, Philip?" she cried. "I've come to depend on you for much more than their book learning!"

"I want to talk about that," he answered, his grave young face concerned, and Mercy sensed that his leaving was a severe wrench for him. She felt that neither he nor her father was being quite frank with her—and yet, what could there be to hide?

He continued, "I've made inquiries and find there's a Miss Thankful Newhall in Barrington who wishes to teach. She's young and has had little experience, but I think she might do."

So Thankful Newhall was engaged to replace Philip, and a poor substitute Mercy judged her from the first.

Thinking it could not be easy for the new teacher to come thus among strangers, Mercy went to the shore in welcome, but Miss Newhall showed herself quite self-sufficient. As she stepped ashore from Kiah's dory with an air of infinite gentility, every mousy hair was in place beneath her stiff bonnet, her unwholesome-looking skin still shone from the morning's soap and water. She glanced about her coolly with pale blue eyes, a trifle protuberant and, as it proved, nearsighted. She gave Mercy the tip of a gloved hand, then picked her way among the lined barrels and fish flakes at the dock's head, clutching her many petticoats close, holding her thick nose high. *As if fish scales and shore smell were strange and unbearable, as if she'd not been brought up amongst them like the rest of us,* Mercy thought with amused annoyance.

An orphan, Thankful Newhall had been taken by a childless couple who paid for her schooling and boasted of her quickness at book learning. She soon took to spelling her name "Newhall," as more elegant than the local "Newell," and plagued her simple foster parents with so many notions that they secretly rejoiced when, a scrawny, high-strung sixteen, she left them for New Erin.

Mercy might tolerate Miss Newhall's airs; Serena slammed

185

stove lids and banged dishes whenever she was exposed to her "high-falutin' foolishness." But, though her mouth puckered against the grudging words, she admitted that Thankful was an excellent seamstress and that Mercy had growing need of such.

As teacher the newcomer gloried in authority and ruled the schoolroom overstrictly, but she possessed the ability to pass on her limited knowledge and her employers were perforce satisfied. Still, Mercy felt the substitution of this notional, narrow-minded young woman for Philip, with his warm companionship and gentle leading, was another debit.

Thankful had been warned of the dangers that would beset her in a household headed by a Papist and had arrived bristling with readiness to defend her faith. To her disappointment she met no insidious attempts to weaken her Free Will Baptist dogmas; instead, the Redmonds showed what she considered unnecessary zeal in sending her, with the children, to Sunday school.

Sunday afternoon, when the weather proved stormy, Mrs. Redmond read from the Scriptures to the family gathered in the Sabbath hush of the middle room, while Kiah in his good black coat sat at rest from his week-long labors and Serena's cambric apron proclaimed the kitchen forgotten.

Although born and bred a good Baptist, Mrs. Redmond never mentioned creeds; Thankful judged her a weak-spirited creature and one lacking true Christian zeal to let her husband go his doomed way. The girl's small nature could not gauge Mercy's inner strength and true charity, nor estimate the influence of the Grannie's Head home.

Sam and Damie had made many sacrifices to pay for their children's schooling, for they themselves had grown up without this advantage. In the Cove's early days every pair of hands was needed, the girls' to ease the never-ending household tasks, the boys' to clasp a pair of oars. Yet respect for learning was part of a Pilgrim heritage and the meetinghouse was soon followed by a log schoolhouse.

On the day when Sam and Damie first watched Charles set

186

off with his slate, they had resolved not to shame their children. That evening they had taken down Abigail's big Bible and, as Damie later told it, "larnt each other t' read." Damie, with her quick black eyes and darting mind had first made landfall across the tossing waters of the printed word, but Sam had steadily over-hauled her, until in time she became content to listen as he read.

The Bible and the key of reading unlocked for them treasures of solace and inspiration. As they read and pondered they never doubted their competence to interpret the written truths; the Word was God's, their souls were God's; one was meant for the other. They strove to follow the Lord's instructions to teach His words diligently unto their children and Mercy had her parents' utter faith in the Scriptures as a fixed truth to steer by.

As her father had foretold, she and Dan, in their life together, each had a closed door marked *Religion. Perhaps,* she told her-self, *every marriage has its locked doors.*

True, after that one intense period, Dan took their difference in beliefs most lightheartedly. Mercy found more puzzling than his Catholicism the fact that Dan was not at bottom a religious person, not concerned with spiritual matters. He attended Mass at Easter, but he spent no time at devotions, as Molly had done, and nothing seemed to hold for him what her Bible held for Mercy.

For many years now she had understood that God did not dwell exclusively in the Cove's unadorned meetinghouse nor on St. Joseph's rich altar. He spoke from the birds' song, the sun's warmth, the seas' thunder, in her own heart and in the hearts of all good people.

And Dan was good. Never a charitable enterprise but could count on his support; never a man in need came from vessel or main and left New Erin with empty hands or belly.

Indeed, Pa often scolded that many took advantage of Dan's open hand, and Mercy had noted how easily swayed her husband was by sugared praise or a bit of bootlicking; she grew disturbed at the men now gathered about him.

She had no liking for the coarse-spoken Dellie Watt Hines, yet he gained by comparison when his more polished partner, Hazelitt Morris, came on his first business call. Remembering tales of his many conquests, she had expected a handsome man or one of striking presence; she was repelled by his fat figure, his moist lips, curved and red as a woman's, by his hot, quick eyes. She turned faintly sick when she saw those eyes upon Catherine.

Since Catherine's swift growing-up, Mercy was accustomed to seeing in men's faces the recognition of her daughter's desirability. The girl, however, had shown no interest in the Cove swains and young New England skippers, who treated her with shy adoration and respect. Respect was not in the glance Hazelitt Morris swept over the girl and Mercy felt an absurd desire to use a washcloth on the fine hands, the soft face, as she used to do when fastidious Catherine had come to her bespattered by her rowdier brothers and sisters in their play.

On his next trip, a month later, Hazelitt brought Boston gifts to them all; but every stone in the pearl and opal brooch for Catherine proclaimed its special value and disturbed Mercy, since it obviously impressed and flattered the girl.

Dan grew profoundly troubled as it became plain that this man was paying court to his favorite; he tried for a time to pretend that Hazelitt's interest was merely avuncular. How tell his daughter that her father's associate was not fit for her to wipe her slender feet upon? When Mercy, with every persuasion that concern for her child's happiness could muster, urged him to refuse his home to this newcomer, Dan, unhappily knowing himself too involved and helpless to do as she asked, could only plead the urgencies of business.

"Oh, Dan! What difference would the trade of one schooner make?" Mercy sounded a trifle impatient. "Sometimes it seems the harbor can't hold all the vessels that put in! I know you can't deny the anchorage to any of them—I wouldn't ask it if you could—but show Haze Morris and his skipper the door of your home. Harm will come of those two; there's something evil about them."

How could Catherine bear the man near her? Mercy wondered. Catherine, something a man might dream up under the pure stars of a midnight watch, with her silken curls against her milky neck and brow, eyes like the bluest violets along the dike, and a mouth fashioned for the kisses of some clean youth. Mercy often sat and looked at her oldest daughter as at a picture; Tamsin and Adria were dears and would be pretty, but Catherine! *Oh, my daughter, my darling,* she would moan in her heart, *how can you?*

But Catherine could do many things beyond her mother's comprehension. She could accept the suit of this vulgar man, who was twice her years and lacked an inch of her proud young height, with the same cool possessiveness with which she accepted his gifts. She could listen to Damie's blunt recital of the unsavory stories concerning Hazelitt and calmly reaffirm her intention to marry him. She could set her will against her mother's and, using the charm that had served her since babyhood, inveigle her father into giving her her way. She could start out proudly for Aunt Molly's in Boston and return with trunks full of dresses fit for any lady. She could name her wedding day and make plans for a celebration that would impress the length of the shore.

After that wedding, self-possessed and queenly, a bride of sixteen who made the stumpy figure and balding head of her triumphant groom the more obvious, Catherine could wave farewell from the deck of Hazelitt's new sloop, her hand light upon the arm of her husband.

That night, for the first and only time of their marriage, Dan was soddenly drunk. Kiah took him to the bedroom off the kitchen—the hired man's sole retreat—and refused Mercy entrance. Surprisingly, she felt no more than weary pity at Dan's dereliction and she left him in Kiah's good hands.

Catherine apparently found it possible to overlook any defects revealed by marriage; blinded, if not by love then by the glitter

189

of Hazelitt's possessions and lavish gifts. Months later when she returned for her first visit to her old home, she made no secret that she rejoiced to be free from New Erin's demanding tasks and her mother's determination to bring her daughters up as good housewives. "Now, after all your fussing to train me in tidiness, Mamma, I don't even hang up my own clothes! When I step out of them a servant girl picks them up."

Mercy was shocked. "Why, Catherine," she remonstrated, "you mustn't say such things before Tamsin and Adria! That's a sinful way to live. Such sloth and luxury!" Her gray eyes softened. "Those first few months . . ." she offered, "I know I always found bending . . ."

Catherine's red-gold head tossed, her full lips curved scornfully. "Now don't start *that*, Mamma," she said. "I don't need any such excuse not to be forever toiling like you, when Papa can well afford more servants." Again ignoring her wide-eyed sisters, "I'm not in the family way; and I don't want to be, so there!"

Mercy's lips firmed to hide her hurt and she said no more.

From all accounts Catherine made a perfect mistress for Hazelitt's big home; if she did not lift her own hand she saw that others lifted theirs to good effect; no children came to disrupt the order of the well-kept house. She and her husband entertained lavishly among the newly rich merchants and shipmasters, and the fame of her beauty spread.

After winning his bride, Hazelitt Morris's visits to New Erin became infrequent, though Dellie Watt Hines came and went in the *Bluebell*. Once or twice a year Dan made the trip around islands and headlands to Hines's Harbor and returned looking unhappy. As long as she lived, Mercy never set foot in the home of her eldest daughter and Catherine seldom came back to the island.

Often Mercy's heart knew a great emptiness for the two absent children. She judged the separation from Catherine a sadder one than that from Patrick; her marriage to such a man as Hazelitt

Morris erected a greater barrier than Patrick's misunderstanding and far paths.

Ah, yes, the years brought prosperity but they were draining away the dear ones who had made New Erin for her. There was, however, an addition to the island's population, though Mercy was anything but pleased at the arrival.

Shortly after Captain Sam had retired from the sea, he appeared one morning at the kitchen door with an uncouth boy whose shyness translated itself into awkward contortions. Mercy saw a slack good-natured grin, a ragged mop of dark hair, heavy black brows and brown eyes which betrayed the terrible loneliness of the slow-witted.

"This is the hired boy I was telling Dan about, Mercy," her father said.

"Hired boy?" Mercy echoed. Dan seldom mentioned such things to her any more and hired boys came and went, for none would stay ashore once they had grown enough to go handlining on a vessel. She tried to place the boy's look, for something about him brushed her memory.

"What's his name, Pa?"

"Waits'l Nolan." At Mercy's involuntary exclamation Captain Sam went on half apologetically. "Seems like as long as there's a Nickerson there'll be one of Gypsy Bess's breed clinging to them. This is Nabby's boy. You mind he was born the same summer as Will."

"Nabby Nolan's boy!" Mercy could not cover her dismay; but seeing the grin fade from the boy's face, her heart smote her. "Well, Waitstill, come in," she managed. "I'll call my boys."

As she stepped out her eyes went to the outer shore of Grannie's Head and the gray oblong of house at the water's edge. Premonition chilled her like a March easterly.

Chapter 24

NABBY NOLAN'S WEATHER-BEATEN HOME HAD BEGUN LIFE INNO-cently enough as Prince Nickerson's fish store and outwardly still resembled other Cove shanties, except for its squalid dis-repair.

Bare spots and canvas patches on the roof showed where winds had clawed out shingles as they tore inland. Under the seaward peak a salt-rimmed window, like an eye dulled by distrust, peered at incoming boats; cocked awry in the sagging opposite end, its mate watched over a dreary swamp. The single lower window, with its rag-stuffed sashes, faced the shore; the door beside it opened crookedly against the beach's seaweed ruff.

The house was cut off from the Cove by Grannie's Head and from Pilot Point by the Dreen and swamp, but its utter isolation was due less to its situation than to its inhabitants, alien and darkly suspect.

The villagers had inherited not only an abiding faith in a just and jealous God but also a superstitious respect for the Prince of Darkness. An introspective breed, each had searched his own soul too unsparingly to deny the existence of evil, and had pried too intently into neighbors' lives to doubt the ubiquity and power of Beelzebub and his agents. Gypsy Bess's black looks and out-landish tongue had marked her as Old Nick's from her first ap-pearance in the Cove.

That event remained one of the sea's insoluble riddles, tossed up to be mulled over and elaborated as years passed. And many years had passed, for Sam Nickerson had been an unmarried youth when the shanty received its first tenants.

The spring night (not fit to be out in) had fallen early. Prince and his wife were thinking of bed when a knock sounded at the kitchen door. Abigail, as village nurse, was accustomed to a summons at any hour, but the height of local ceremony was a rattle at the latch and a scraping of boots to warn householders unprepared to receive company; this knock, though imperative, was formal.

While Abigail mentally braced herself for some emergency, Prince strode to the door, which in those days opened directly upon the steps. There in the swirling mist stood a strange woman. Globules of fog glistened on her wilted bonnet and on the dank hair beneath it, while her cloak and skirts showed wet-black to the knees; but Abigail saw that the clothes had quality and that even in her deplorable state the woman retained a bold beauty.

As she moved into the room, or was pushed by the dim shape in her shadow, a man's arm in a fine serge sleeve reached into the light, a voice muttered something about a trunk, coins clicked dully, and Prince found himself holding a heavy purse. The door was pushed quietly shut and when Prince came to himself enough to fling it open and run out into the fog, there was no one to be seen, no sound of footsteps to be followed.

Urgency was in the woman's haggard face and distorted figure. She fixed her black eyes upon Abigail and dragged herself towards the fire, her sodden skirts hissing like a spent sea. She stopped and gasped out a few unintelligible words.

"To be sure," as Abigail afterward said in her quiet way, "it could be seen at a glance why she had gotten herself into a house. And none too soon, poor creature."

By morning the home on Grannie's Head held two strangers and Prince's Cove buzzed with the news of their arrival.

The woman gave her name as Elizabeth and that of her shadowy husband as Edward Nolan of Boston. "Did you ask to see her marriage lines, M'is Abigail?" Ephie Doane's wife later inquired with sly righteousness.

"Indeed I did not," Abigail replied calmly. "I saved my breath to cool my porridge."

In her strange accent (not French and not West Indies Spanish) Elizabeth told a simple story. In Yarmouth she and her husband had taken passage on a snow to visit Edward's Shelburne relatives, but the vessel had run up into the bay as the fog shut down. Before the anchor was over Elizabeth had known her time was upon her. This had sent the snow's master into a fine frenzy but one of the crew had known of M'is Abigail Nickerson's skill and kindness. The couple had been hurried into the down-haul boat and landed on the empty beach, whence they had followed the knowledgeable seaman's directions through the darkness to the Nickerson's door.

There, apparently, Edward had deserted his companion. Next morning Prince found, above tide-line, a trunk and a corded box containing clothes for the woman and child. There was never a further trace of the man.

On being questioned Elizabeth didn't remember the name of the snow or its master and Prince intimated her story failed to hold water. She shrugged her shoulders sullenly and offered no other—then, or later.

The baby, whom its mother named after the kind Abigail, was a puny mite that received scant maternal attention.

When the woman was up and about she made no attempt to help with the augmented household tasks, but instead sat darkly brooding by the fire, while her vital dark handsomeness and her bold manner reasserted themselves. These and her mutterings in a strange tongue won her the name of "Gypsy" among the neighbors; "Elizabeth" became "Bess" and "Gypsy Bess" the woman remained.

When she grew well enough to travel, Prince offered to carry her to Shelburne in his sloop. She laughed in his face—Shelburne relatives did not exist. She had no one, anywhere. She countered with the astonishing suggestion that Prince sell her his empty fish store for a home.

At first he wouldn't hear to such a thing, but Abigail pointed out they couldn't keep the woman and child, neither could they, as Christians, turn them out on the road; as long as Elizabeth's purse lasted they weren't a problem for the poor-overseers; the store, with repairs and a hearth, would make a tolerable dwelling, tighter and cleaner than some on Pilot Point, and it was never used since Prince had built the bigger one on the inside of the Head.

"I don't like t' be the one responsible for keeping her likes in the Cove," Prince objected. "The woman's a born trouble-maker, Abigail."

"There's truth in what you say, Prince," Abigail agreed, "but the Lord may have sent her into our care that her feet be kept from evil ways."

When her husband snorted his scepticism Abigail added gently, "I know what it is to be a woman without friends in a strange land. What might have become of me, Prince, if the Lord hadn't sent you to Shelburne when He did?"

Prince could argue no more. Though he explained, "It's not only that Elizabeth and her child will be a drag on us and, like enough, on Sam after us. I feel—and feel it strong—that trouble and grief will come to ours through them, though you and me, Abigail, we may not live to see it." His blue eyes were troubled and Abigail's heart misgave her momentarily. "But let it be as you say, wife," he went on. "As far as the store goes, she can have it and welcome. I'll make a hearth and chimney."

The kindly Cove people contributed household furnishings but Gypsy Bess proved a slattern who neglected her child and house. (" 'Twas better kept as Prince's fish store," the women declared in disgust) and village donations ceased.

Prince could not see a woman and child go cold and hungry and Abigail could not neglect them in sickness; Gypsy Bess in return lent an indifferent hand in the hayfield and at the fish flakes. Thus, as time went on, a chafing tie was woven between the two families, a tie that was to hold for three generations and be broken only when the last of Gypsy Bess's alien blood was gone from the Cove.

Prince's family grew up and scattered, all but tall and flaxen-haired Sam, who at nineteen wedded black-eyed little Didamia Crowell from over Meetinghouse Hill, and brought her home. Damie, of the quick ways and quicker tongue, had no patience with the likes of Gypsy Bess and her fatherless offspring, but Sam could be stubborn for all his easy-going ways and he had inherited his father's grudging responsibility for the store's tenants.

To Damie's relief the child became known as Nabby; she hoped the Cove would soon disremember it had been called after Sam's dead ma—a 'front to the memory of a good woman.

When Nabby had survived the first years of her mother's neglect and appeared likely to grow up after all, folks got a turn when they first looked into her pinched face, for under her mat of black hair, one eye was a clear green and the other a golden-flecked brown.

Little Nabby soon showed an evil disposition. She stoned all village children who ventured within range of her accurate throwing arm or, meeting them on pasture paths, she flew at them with whatever came to hand. Even the timidest could not forgo staring at Gypsy Bess's daughter, with her wild ways and queer eyes, and their stares enraged her. Bolder spirits braced themselves for running before taunting her with "Two Eyes," for she became a fury, spitting out strange curses and raking with sharp claws any unfortunate she caught up with.

Yet she loved to watch little Mercy Nickerson playing about the dooryard, and Mercy prattled to her happily, though Charles ran and hid each evening when Nabby came to the kitchen door for a jug of milk. Nabby was eight when Damie's sister Griselle —she who had done so well for herself in marrying John Chatwynd of Halifax—came to visit at Grannie's Head. At twilight the ragged child slid into the kitchen, darting sharp glances from under tangled black hair, thrust a milk jug into Damie's hands and, while that housewife bustled to the cellar skimming-bowls, stood like some frightened wild thing under the piercing eyes of the strange lady in the rocker. Her pointed face lit up when Mercy toddled towards her, laughing, but it resumed its dark secretiveness the instant Damie reappeared.

Damie noticed her sister's intent glance as Nabby slipped away with the tightly clutched jug, and rather sheepishly explained, "The poor thing allus looks half-starved; and what tell of a little skim milk each night?"

Grizzie was not thinking of her sister's charity. "Those eyes!" she said, rolling her own heavenward and lifting her soft white hands in the same direction.

"Yes, they *do* give a buddy the creeps," Damie agreed as she flew about. "She's a pinnickin', plain little thing in the first place, and why the Lord saw fit . . ."

" 'Twasn't the Lord's doings, Damie. At least not in a manner of speaking." There was a weighty pause. "I don't suppose you have any notion of who the child's father might be." Grizzie was smug with superior knowledge.

"I d'know as I ever give it much thought," Damie apologized a bit resentfully, for the solution of such puzzle was one of her chief delights and apparently she had missed something. She briefly sketched the story of Gypsy Bess's arrival. "Nabby's father must 'a' been a stranger t' me; I couldn't be expected to recognize ary look."

"You would have," her sister assured her triumphantly, "if ever you'd seen Commodore Stanwood! 'Old Two Eyes' he's called. Behind his back, that is, him being so high up in the dockyards and all. But that child's his spit 'n' image. Mark my words, she'll make a tall woman. Besides, those eyes! One green eye he has, and one brown one and both glaring to match his brimstone temper. It comes back to me now, all the talk there was about him and that Portuguese woman years ago."

Damie interrupted, "Sam's pa allus claimed the snow that brung Gypsy Bess hadn't come from Yarmouth. Halifax, more like!" She tsch-ed in vast disapproval. "What lies that woman told!"

Her sister rocked gleefully. "And the airs Mrs. Stanwood gives herself because her husband's own cousin to a lord! La, 'tis a queer world, I must say!"

Grizzie appeared to find it a highly entertaining world as well as a queer one, and Damie knew tongues would wag in Halifax drawing rooms when her sister returned, just as they would wag in Prince's Cove kitchens as soon as she herself found an excuse to visit the nearest.

Later she informed Sam of Grizzie's deductions. "So ye see, Sam, Nabby's got good blood in her."

She jumped as Sam's clenched fist thumped the table. "Good blood, woman! You call that 'good blood'? Bad blood. On both sides—for the Lord knows how far back. If poor Nabby heirs some brightness from her father it will only make her life the harder. She's swamped before she's launched, ye might say." There was no understanding Sam sometimes.

Though Damie relayed her news with less gusto after this talk, she remained unyielding in her views of what should be done with the likes of Gypsy Bess, with her spells and her dirt and general disrepute. Not that Damie was free from the superstitions that kept her neighbors from offending the foreign woman, merely that it was not in her to curb her tongue.

Nabby's visits to the Nickerson home ceased when Mercy reached the age of parroting all she heard. With the addition of some of the most scandalous words to the child's vocabulary, Damie, as she said, "riz in rebellion." Where could such language have come from but Nabby? And Sam, troubled by evil on his darling's innocent lips, agreed that Damie should do what she thought best.

Damie could not soften a blow. Next evening when Nabby slipped unsuspecting into the kitchen and thrust forward the empty jug, her erstwhile benefactress caught her startled attention with a threatening gesture.

"Mark now, ye little besom, what I'm about to tell ye, an' mark it well. You'm t' keep away from Mercy, out o' my yard—

198

'ceptin' when ye come fer yer milk. Foul-mouthed little hag that ye be, you'm not fit t' come anigh a good girl."

The child said no word, but her lips and nostrils grew more pinched and the two eyes, for once in their black pain almost alike, looked piteously into Damie's flushed face. An instant later the eyes blazed, green and golden-brown, the tangled thatch of black hair was flung back, the ragged figure whirled through the door and flew down the sloping field, over the stone wall like a wild thing and past her desolate home, to disappear behind the stunted spruces at the swamp's edge.

Damie stared after her, the forgotten jug in her hand, secretly aghast at the effect of her words.

The child Nabby never darkened the Nickerson door again. The milk set aside for her turned to bonnyclabber and was thrown to the hens, while for many evenings Damie felt her heart smitten by a remembered look and the knowledge that a jug of skim milk might have been standing between Nabby and gnawing hunger.

Sam, troubled, said perhaps he should have spoken to her himself, since she liked to follow him about the wharf and boatshop and seemed fond of him in her wild way.

A few days later, Sam, searching for the brindle cow, came upon a pathetic figure, face-down across Abigail's grave and a posy of wild flowers lying stiff and out-of-place near the mound's head. He cleared his throat to warn her of his presence, then bent to pat her shoulder. She sat up and he saw that tears had grooved the grime of her face. She said simply, "I make believe M'is Abigail's my Grammie." Then to his amazement she demanded forlornly, "Why didn't ye marry my ma? Then ye'd be my pa and Mercy'd be my little sister. I wouldn't larn her bad words then, would I?"

"Well . . ." Sam was taken aback by this.

"Ma ain't much," the child continued, judiciously, "but she ain't no worse'n that sour-faced Mrs. Damie, always a-jawin' and a-goin' on."

"Hold on, now, saucebox!" Sam answered her sharper than he meant, but Damie' scolding was a sore point. "No more o' that. I never had a mind to marrying your ma. I don't know where you got such a notion!"

Nabby's swift temper was rising and she sprang to her feet. "Well, let me tell ye, I don't give a hoot. My father's a fine gentleman. An admiral, he is. High above the skipper of a stinkin' clamshell, like ye be." The bare hard feet stamped the sod, the strange eyes snapped. "I hate ye, Cap'n Sam! I hate that saip of a Damie. An' I hate that nasty little Charles. Yes, an' I hate Mercy, too. So thyah!" She whirled and was gone through the spruce and alders before Sam could put out a hand.

Damie never heard a word of this encounter.

Cold weather brought further proof of Nabby's stubbornness. Gypsy Bess was a great one for dozing before the evening's last coals and waking to find the fire out. It had been her custom to send her blue-lipped daughter to beg a brand from the well-tended Nickerson hearth. The young 'un would race down the slope, leaping rocks and hollows with sparks flying and smoke streaming from the blackening brand. Damie could not guess how they managed this cold winter, unless Nabby, child though she was, had taken over the banking of the hearth rather than ask a favor of her neighbors. Damie felt more shamed anger and less relief than she had expected at being so completely quit of Nabby Nolan.

Bess had become a bent and withered harridan muttering between toothless gums. When she clutched at folks with dirt-caked claws and peered so balefully into faces, nobody suspected it was to bring features into focus out of an inchoate blur, for her failing eyes looked as black and sharp as ever. Such a crone was certain to be suspect and it was known she held long conversations in a strange tongue with some invisible One—and who but the Lord Harry? (It was thought wisest not to tempt the wrath of his black Lordship by naming him too openly.)

Her mother took Nabby through the woods in search of roots

and herbs, or to the Indian grounds at Squaw Lake for ingredients of the charms Gypsy Bess dispensed on occasion. The child never saw the inside of a schoolhouse.

Older, she patched a discarded skiff, calked its gaping seams, begged lines and a piece of net, and caught fish for herself and her mother; she planted potatoes in seaweed "lazybeds" and, though she would never work for Captain Sam, she earned a few shillings at Cove fish flakes. Admittedly, she showed more gumption than might be expected.

She inherited her mother's swarthiness without any of Bess's early beauty. Sharp features under the tangle of black hair made a setting for the strange eyes. She dressed in unsavory castoffs which she altered to fit simply by tearing off what got too much in her way; in summer she went barefoot, in winter she thrust her feet into a pair of men's warped and shrunken sea boots.

She kept her wild ways and temper, her thin face and bitter tongue, but she developed a tall, slender figure, beautifully strong and lissome under her ugly garments, and she carried her wild black head with an air that made folks remember her supposed paternity. She gave no cause for "talk," for she was as waspish with men as with her own sex, and so Nabby Nolan grew to an unloved and unlovely womanhood.

She had reached her middle twenties when she set Prince's Cove by the ears and sent good housewives, their morning's work not half done, hastening across back pastures towards neighboring kitchens.

A few weeks before, an autumn gale had sent a British frigate into Redmond's Harbor, and before it left, the storm ridden out, a pinnace came ashore to inquire about a missing seaman. Nobody had seen him. Nobody would have. More than one citizen along the shore had arrived out of the woods after a naval vessel had heaved up anchor, and had been asked no embarrassing questions. The independent fishermen could understand how easy it would be to get more than a bellyful of Her Majesty's Navy, and there were those who remembered too well the press gangs that once scoured the woods and seized men working on their own lots.

A fortnight went by and no half-starved man appeared from hiding; the poor devil must really have fallen overboard, or he had perished in his attempt to swim ashore.

Then one morning Damie Nickerson received the shock of her life, as she later vowed and declared. She'd gone to answer a knock and there at the door stood Nabby, who'd never been anigh all those years! As if that wasn't surprising enough, a strange man towered behind her. He was huge, with shoulders that would scarce squeeze through a doorway, but his black-bearded face was gaunt and his eyes had a washed-out look as if he'd been long sick. As for Nabby, she was that clean and combed that Damie thought at first she faced two strangers.

Damie was struck speechless. "We've come t' borry Cap'n Sam's boat," Nabby said. "We aim t' go t' the magistrate in Barrington an' git married."

"Well, I cal'ate likely," was all Damie could put her tongue to. She added as the two turned away, "The oars is kept in the right hand corner as ye go in the fishhouse; the sail's in the loft."

She found strength to hurry to the front window where, behind the curtains, she watched the man run the boat down the slip and take the oars. Noting his short, apparently effortless, strokes, "You'm a dory-man, milud," Damie muttered. "Navy or no." For, of course, she had enough wits left to suspicion at once who the stranger was.

The Cove soon learned that Nabby had found the deserter on the outer beach, unconscious and bleeding about the head; she had got him home with her mother's help; hidden him in the loft and nursed him back to health.

Many were glad to see the love-changed Nabby and spoke her kindly; but her loutish husband made no friends. To succeeding inquirers he gave a different surname but always "Joe" preceded it and always he twiddled his huge thumbs 'round and 'round in black embarrassment, until Little Obie aptly called him "Joe

Twiddle" and the name stuck. No one asked Nabby what was written on her marriage lines, as far as the Cove was concerned she remained Nabby Nolan.

Before the winter was out Joe took to stumbling home from Pilot Point, roaring drunk. Dorymen, edging across the small cove, often heard his thunderous oaths and Gypsy Bess's shrill vituperation seeping through the shanty's broken windows.

In the spring Joe Twiddle signed on for a trip with Captain Eldredge Gardner. He proved a smart fisherman but quarrelsome and truculent, using his enormous strength to harass his shipmates oftener than to ease the common labor.

Though the crew were accustomed to rough language, the profanity that poured from Joe's bearded mouth disturbed them. This was no railing against the contrariness of wet canvas and slatting rope, against repeated soakings and long spells of cold grub—the Lord must know these things would try the patience of a saint. Few men defy their Creator from the empty face of the sea; Joe Twiddle flung bitter blasphemy against God Himself. The crew feared that when His wrath descended, as descend it must, they too would bear its weight. Some of the older men remonstrated with Joe on this score, but he guffawed scornfully. The others grew quiet and took to watching sea and sky anxiously, to judge whence the blow would fall.

In a rising storm they'd run clear of Brown's shallow water and the vessel was jogging off and on, waiting for daylight. She was pitching and tossing nervously and taking a little water aboard, though nothing to worry about, as Joe Twiddle braced himself under the swinging forecastle lamp and lashed his jacket tight for a turn on watch.

Hearing his running oaths, a shipmate demanded, "Ben't ye ascairt t' go on deck with sech words on yer lips? I sh'd fear the Lord would brush me from His sight an' hearin'."

Joe lurched forward and up the ladder. He paused at the top, turned and laughed down at the dim, shocked faces, then doubling his great fists he thrust them upward, under the very nose of heaven, turned his face to the black sky and bawled, "I defy yer God t' send a comber big enough to wash *me* off a vessel."

All seamen know those giant billows that make up in the midst of moderate seas. It was as if one of these had been towering there in the night, awaiting the challenge. It struck quartering and shook the vessel like a blow from a colossal maul. In the spouting yeast, smashed gear and the white blur of Joe Twiddle's face vanished into the blackness alee. But although an ugly flood poured down the open hatchway into the forecastle, not another man aboard was more than bruised; the forward watch had jumped into the stays and the man at the wheel had by some miracle clung to its spokes. Clearly God's hand had plucked the blasphemer from the midst of his fellows.

Captain Eldredge was forced to put in for repairs. Once ashore he begged that his friend, Captain Sam, accompany him to break the news to Joe's widow.

"Yes, I'll go with you, Eldredge," Sam said. "It's not a job a man should face alone."

Nabby must have seen their approach and guessed their errand, yet when Gypsy Bess opened the door of the miserable dwelling, the younger woman sat at a rough table eating her breakfast porridge with an air of great unconcern. Her face wore its old sullenness, her hair and dress showed their old neglect.

Hat in clenched and sweating hands, Captain Gardner told Nabby that her husband had been lost off Brown's. In his heart he considered the death a judgment and although he tried to think of comforting words, the best he could dredge up was that in all his years of going to sea he'd never shipped her husband's match for strength.

Nabby listened in silence, with a look neither man could fathom. Then she returned her gaze to the greasy plate before her and resumed her spooning of porridge. "If ye want t' wait till I git my breakfast down," she suggested, "I'll show ye some o' the fanciest takin-on ever ye see." Then broke into ferocious laughter as ill-matched to the occasion as her eyes one to the other.

The men hastened out of the sordid room and up the slope of Grannie's Head, but the laugh stayed with them long after they were out of its hearing.

Nabby's baby was born in blueberry time, a big boy with his father's black hair and heavy features. She named him Waitstill.

After her brief blooming Nabby Nolan withered swiftly. Her snarl showed irregular gaps among her yellow teeth, usually clenched about a stubby pipe; her hair fell in lank strings about her face; her tongue spat increasing venom, while her eyes glared (one greener, one browner) more spitefully than ever.

She and her hobbling mother became an infamous pair. Stories of their spells were heard more frequently and gained greater credence. Cows lost their calves or died for no reason after their owners had offended Gypsy Bess or Nabby Nolan. When rheumatism stabbed, its victim was apt to picture Nabby busy with red-hot pins about a waxen image of the sufferer. Young Jamie Kenney, passing the shanty on his way to cut swamp spruce, shouted a ribald greeting; within a few minutes he had gashed his leg and come nigh bleeding to death, there alone in the swamp; worse, his cut festered and sprangled; not until his father took an offering of fresh meat and bespoke Nabby civilly, did it begin to heal.

The shanty was visited by the trash of Pilot Point and the rougher crews anchored in Redmond's Harbor; the noisy singing and drunken brawling therein was fit to lift the roof of sturdier and more law-abiding buildings. Authentic reasons for shunning the shanty added their weight to suspicion and superstition.

Though Nabby neglected her son as she had been neglected, he thrived and was soon clambering about the boats, and fishing for sculpins and cunners off the wharves—like other Cove boys. At twelve he had attained a man's height and was continually outgrowing his rags so that he always looked like last year's scarecrow. His alien blood and his mother's stigma set him apart and he became the butt for the cruel jokes and tyrannies of small-natured men and boys. He developed skill at getting his arm about his head to ward off a blow, but his heavy features remained perpetually lightened by a good-tempered, if puzzled, grin.

Captain Sam pitied the lad's plight without seeing any way to lessen it. Then, one summer afternoon with the tide far out, the captain strolled leisurely down to the end of his wharf where four half-grown boys, flat on their bellies, were shouting and prodding at something beneath them—and raising an intolerable stench of disturbed flat mud and fish offal. When he reached them, only the youngsters' lack of size saved them from his anger.

Waitstill Nolan, his ragged clothes heavy and stinking with mud and gurry, his face and hair well begobbed with the stuff, was clinging desperately to a slippery spile. Every muscle strained to hold the few inches he had gained above the roiled mud and water, for no crosspieces here offered a grip or a footrest, and the tight lines about the boy's mouth—for once without his grin —showed he must soon relax his hold and slide down to flounder again in the muck beneath him.

"What's the meaning o' this?" Captain Sam demanded angrily. "Throw that boy a line, smart now, and haul him up out of there."

The large boy addressed merely laughed. "Why, what tell o' Waits'l Twiddle, Cap'n Sam! He was asettin' here with his legs adanglin' and Ezra run down quiet-like an' give him a push. Ye sh'd 'a' see the mud fly! We most died alaughin'." The boy bent double in remembered enjoyment before continuing, "Waits'l clumb up the spile, mud 'n' all. Grinnin' he was. Too addlepated t' git mad! Then we took a couple o' gafts an' pushed him back afore he could catch holt o' the stringer here. He got nigh t' the top three-four times and we druv him down. Now he's jest a-clingin' on by his toenails and ascairt t' come up."

Leaning over, he called derisively to the gray-faced boy below, "Waits'l Twiddle dasn't come up, dasn't come up." Another boy joined the taunting singsong, but Captain Sam's foot pushed them roughly aside as he bent forward with a noosed rope in his hand.

"Here, Waits'l," he called encouragingly as the rope snaked downward. "I'm dropping you a line. I cal'ate, though, you'll have to slide down into the muck, just this once more, so you can slip it under your arms. Can you make it, son? Would you like me to come down? That's fine. Get your breath now, before I haul away."

He turned fiercely upon the crestfallen boys, "Get off my wharf—every mother's son of ye—and smart! Or I'll warm your backsides so as your britches'll smoke."

This from kindly Captain Sam! They fled, their bare feet whispering along the soft planks and through the red dust at the wharfhead. They stopped there until they saw Waitstill's black poll rise above the planking, then they turned homeward, disconcerted and unwilling to meet one another's eyes after the unexpected ending to their sport.

"Aw, 'twas only Waits'l Twiddle," said one. "What fer would Cap'n Sam want t' make sech a ti-yi over him?"

"Well," said the bold Ezra dubiously, "I fergot his maw's a witch. If Waits'l sh'd tell on us, I guess we'd be in a bad fix." They looked back over their shoulders fearfully, and though no sign of the witch's house showed above the ridge, they hastened their steps.

At the wharf end Waitstill stood panting, a sick grin on his filthy, exhausted face. He spat and tried to make a joke, "Even Maw's cookin' is better'n flat mud, Cap'n Sam." Then the man saw run across the boy's slack face the dread of his mother's reception.

207

"Son, I wouldn't have dast go home to my ma in the state you're in right now," Sam said, establishing a bond between this miserable lad and the cherished boy he had been. "You run down to that ledge." He pointed. "There's a deep pool on the far side. Take off your clothes—every stitch—and let 'em go. Souse in, head and all, mind, and scour yourself well. I know where I can lay hands on some clean clothes."

Later Captain Sam watched Waitstill disappear behind the gray shanty and thought of his own boys, grown and away from home; thought, too, of all boys who lacked a father's care. Instinctively, as he worried the problem of Waitstill, his eyes went across the mouth of Redmond's Harbor.

New Erin! He slapped his thigh briskly. *That* would be the place for Waitstill, away from the tormenting boys and men, and out of the wickedness in his ma's house. *There's always work for another pair of hands on the island. If only Dan and I hadn't come to the parting of our ways, I could see to it easy.* He paused and admitted, *Dan would see to it for me, if I'd a mind to go asking favors.*

When Dan had agreed to make a place for Waitstill, Sam braved Nabby's tongue. She lived alone now, for Old Gypsy Bess had been laid in the Nickerson burying ground.

At first it looked as if Nabby would refuse to let Waitstill go and would back her refusal with one of her obscene tirades, for her eyes glittered and her fingers shaped themselves into claws. Then suddenly her face dulled and darkened; she looked tired and old, old. She reached for her blackened pipe and Sam saw that her hand was shaking.

"Take him. Nobody nor nawthin's ever stood by me. But take him, I say! Let someone else fill his big belly and wash his filthy clothes." The door slammed and rattled in Captain Sam's face.

Chapter 25

By 1865 each Nova Scotian headland sheltered a slip where men scarfed and bolted a keel upon its blocks, walked the length of a planked hull to the time of their calking mallets, or spiderwise spun webs of rigging. Above the sea's wash floated the grating whine of saws, the measured stroke of broadax, the chattering of hammers and, cutting through the duller wooden tones, the anvil's clear clangor. Black smoke from forge and bubbling tar caldron drifted downwind, acrid against the shipyard's resinous fragrance and the tide's salty tang.

Scarce a seaward cluster of gray houses but held at least one man who could whittle a half model out of a pine block and his dreams of a sweet-running hull, a yard foreman to translate the model's lines, a blacksmith to forge the ironwork, a carpenter who doubled as ship's joiner and men who, between voyages, could shape their hands to any tool required in a vessel's construction.

Only the humming town yards launched big ships, but every brown stream had its sawmill and nearby ways from which sturdy barks and barkentines, speedy schooners, neat brigs and snows, slid into the sea. Where no running water lent itself, men, nothing daunted, squared timbers with broadax and produced piles of plank with the arduous whipsaw; then fashioned the shallops, the pinks and sloops, the little blunt-nosed schooners, that dotted the coastwise waters and the offshore fishing grounds.

New Erin's horizon was seldom empty. Sails shone white in the sun; were dark, wet patches under clearing storm-wrack or lifting fog. Hugging the headlands or skimming the skyline, they winged past.

With the bustle of building and sailing on every side, Prince's Cove had not been surprised when Captain Sam, restless ashore,

209

voiced plans to give the sea yet another vessel from the Grannie's Head slip whence his father had launched the settlement's first.

Since early spring the happy hammering of wood on wood had been slipping past the end of Narrah to ring faintly and out of tune among the New Erin buildings. Then, above the ridge of Grannie's Head, Mercy had seen two masts in place against the sky, slender signposts of progress. Now on this perfect June morning she and the children were bound for the launching of the *Didamia III*.

Cloaked and bonneted for the boat, she stepped from the front door and into the sweet clarity of the new day. New Erin was lush with late spring; Mercy could almost feel the upward push of grass blades beneath her feet; the climbing sun's ardent touch upon her cheek went like a lover's caress all the way to her heart.

By nine o'clock the full moon's swollen tide would be brimming Prince's Cove and lying clear and deep at the foot of the ways, awaiting the new *Didamia*. It was barely half tide now, she saw, and the morning shadows lay long upon the wet grass. No need for hurry.

Across the mirroring harbor Grannie's Head wore a white frill at tide-line and June's verdancy upon its sloping shoulders. So it had looked and so the air had smelt that morning when she had first crossed to New Erin. Twenty-four years ago! Oh, surely not so long since Dan had rowed her home and lifted her ashore. She knew a flash of envy, and of compassion, for the young Mercy, untouched by all that the years were to bring; she turned to gaze at the shore as if she might glimpse a girlish figure in a new bonnet and shawl.

Rounded pebbles lay where New Erin greensward had first kissed her feet, yet to balance the sea's gain there, behind Long Wharf a mat of weeds and grass now claimed the old tide-line. So many changes! Only Dan's love had not varied; in spite of his faults and blunders, *that* had remained steadfast; more constant in quality than her own, which had altered like the island shores, portions washed away, others built up and reinforced through the years.

Standing quiescent in the morning's radiance, she was stabbed, as she had often been recently, by a recognition of beauty's inherent transcience and by a poignant sense of imminent change. So, she had heard, impending death (one's own or that of a dear one) laid its warning finger on the sensitive spirit. But, she told herself, perhaps all woman who bore children late in life and after long barrenness, felt a similar foreboding, no matter how welcome the expected child.

Twelve years before when Adria had almost cost her mother's life, Dr. Whitehouse had told Dan there would be no more family. Later Mercy had pushed the green cradle under the attic eaves and wiped away a tear for each little face that had smiled up at her from under its hood. Now, at forty-two, she was to prove the doctor mistaken; the long-empty cradle would be wiped clean of attic cobwebs before the snow flew, if all went well. If all went well.

She forced her mind away from doubt and moved leisurely down the terrace steps. Along the dock-path the grass was high; soon the mowers would be busy and summer begun in earnest. Again the inexorableness of the rolling seasons, the mutability of time!

From the icehouse a wagonload of glittering blocks creaked towards the Gloucester schooner lying across Long Wharf's end. Among a murmur of voices at the wharfhead Mercy caught her husband's. *What will Dan do if I am taken?* she asked herself. *Even the children would fare better than he. They have tough Cove fiber in their make-up, their heritage from me and them behind me; for good or for evil, they will all be stronger than their father.*

She knew that Dan, despite his pleasure in the hopes of another child and his freedom from feminine premonitions, was not happy. What gave him that harassed look when he believed himself unobserved?

He saw her approaching, gave a few brief orders to the work-men beside him and hurried to meet her. Side by side they slowly walked the grassy path, Mercy deeply conscious of the dear familiarity of the arm beneath her hand, the thrust of Dan's stride along the fullness of her skirts.

"I wish you were coming with us, dear," she said, looking up to meet his dark gaze. "I feel lonely, going without you; as if something might happen and I'd want you there to turn to." A girlish dependence in her voice matched his youthful erectness, his air of proud possession.

"I wish I *could* go." He put his hand over hers. "But the boys handle the boat as well as I. Of course, if the wind springs up, Kiah will come for you in the sloop. I can't leave, as you know, while the bay's alive with herring and I have these extra men working from dawn till dark."

Both glanced to the busy wharves, where leathern-aproned figures moved among the splitting tables and barrels, and herring flashed in the sun like bits of looking glass. The men worked silently but every sound came across the dock, clear and ringing: the splash of a tossed herring, the plop and drip of a bucket lowered for clean harbor-water, the swish of its flung contents, the uneven stream and dwindling patter as water escaped through the wharf's cracks and rejoined the creeping tide.

Dan turned again to his wife. "Are you sure you feel well enough for the trip?"

It was heart-warming, Mercy thought, to be so precious and considered. This belated child had drawn Dan and her closer than ever in the deep happiness of maturity, in appreciation of the miracle of new life begotten by love—a miracle they had accepted unawed, when younger. But she had been most miserable in her pregnancy.

"I feel better than for many a day," she reassured him. "The fresh air will do me good."

She looked back over her shoulder. "I suppose Charlie will be all morning, once I sent him back to comb his hair! And Tam-

212

sin is all in a flutter to think she's going to christen the new schooner. Aren't you happy, Dan, to have her home again?"

Dan had decided that the younger girls should in turn finish their education in Boston at Miss Symington's Day School for Young Ladies, highly considered by the quality of Barrington and Yarmouth, and Molly had been delighted to have her niece, now that she and Richard were settled ashore in their Boston home.

Dan answered Mercy, "Indeed I am! She informs me she still prefers New Erin above all other spots. Just as her father does."

They had reached the dock where the big red skiff waited afloat with its nose grating upon the pebbles and its reflection brightening those from brown barrels and silver spiles.

Dan had spread his boat-cloak over the dew-wet after-thwart so that no dampness should reach her. "Indeed, you spoil me." Mercy smiled as he half lifted, half handed her to the seat and helped her settle herself.

Mercy was thrifty by breed, nature and past necessity, and preferred simple clothes, but Dan loved to buy her pretty shawls and gowns; her wardrobe was full of lovely things scarcely used.

Today under her cloak she wore a new rose-sprigged challis, though there'd be only Cove neighbors to see it; enough to know that Dan thought her beautiful and worthy of adornment.

Dan *was* thinking her beautiful, though his heart contracted at the thinness and transparency of her face and the deep shadows under her gray eyes.

Both turned and smiled as shrieks and laughter from the path announced the children were on their way.

Then Waitstill, in gurry-stiffened boots, lumbered across the shore to help launch the boat. He was now an accepted part of New Erin and, at sixteen, the island's biggest man. Will alternately patronized and bullied him, and even Charlie could not resist teasing him occasionally, but Adria had taken the uncouth boy under her motherly wing.

213

She spoke to him now. "I wish Kiah could spare you to come, Waits'l. You'd love the launching."

"Oh, I've see aplenty o' *them*," Waitstill assured her airily with his slack grin.

It proved as well that Nabby Nolan's son had stayed to help Kiah.

Dan splashed through the shallow water, tucked the cloak about Mercy and, hat in hand, bent to kiss her tenderly.

Then he said, "Now, Adria," tugging one of her long yellow locks to gain her attention, "you sit aft here on the keg in front of Mamma."

"Tamsin, on the forward thwart." He reached into his coat pocket. "Here's the christening wine," and he handed her a bottle gay with dangling ribbons.

"Papa!" Regardless of rocking the skiff, Tamsin threw an arm about his neck and kissed him. "You've fixed it so pretty!" Her happy smile and brown curls made an entrancing picture under the rosy brim of her bonnet, while the reflected sunlight danced across her face.

Dan turned to his sons. "Mind, boys, no rocking the skiff to tease your sisters, no quarreling. We must all take special care of Mamma this summer."

"We'll be careful," Charlie assured him, his face instantly sober. But Will's silence showed he resented being given orders.

The brothers placed their tholepins, eased the boat into deeper water and climbed in.

"Off ye go!" Dan said, stepping back while Waitstill sent the skiff skimming with one thrust of his broad shoulders.

Tamsin tucked her skirts happily about her and clasped the precious christening wine closely. The boys slipped their oars between the tholepins, found their stroke and swung the skiff close under the end of Long Wharf, past the smooth black sides of the Gloucesterman. The crew were busy packing the ice into holds, but the cook leaned upon the rail to watch them by. From the skiff he was a pair of hairy arms crossed beneath high-pushed red flannel sleeves and topped by a head bald as a capstan. The boys put on a special burst of speed for his benefit, but he spat morosely into their wake, unimpressed.

Mercy watched the skiff's red reflection swim alongside, topped with a patch of blue (Adria's jacket) a streak of rose (Tamsin's) and the white of the boys' shirts. The gurgling blade-pools swirled gently past in endless procession to flatten and lose themselves. Now and then Tamsin leaned to trail her hand in the silken water, but Adria sat motionless, lost in daydreams, her back pressed against her mother's knees.

Wonderful, Mercy thought, *to be on a holiday with the children.* The creak of tholepins, the plash of blades were rhythmic and soothing; she relaxed as the boys sent the boat straight and true across the harbor.

Soon it turned into the channel between Grannie's Head and Narrah, where the tide raced green and crystal under its keel. Its passengers began to sniff appreciatively, for here spicy gusts off the land overwhelmed the sea tang that had been in their nostrils. Almost they could distinguish the various perfumes that made up the intoxicating whole; alder tassels, spruce cones, berry blossoms, sweet white clover.

Ahead of the skiff Prince's Cove opened and the village on the far side wavered out to them across the brimming water.

The plain old meetinghouse had been pulled down and atop the hill the new church spire pierced the blue sky, a landmark for passing ships, a heavenward-pointing symbol for all. A frame schoolhouse had for many years replaced the log structure where Mercy had conned her lessons. Mercy could see seven new houses on the nearer side of Meetinghouse Hill, for Prince's Cove was prospering and growing like other shore settlements.

Now the skiff was opposite the end of Nickerson's wharf, the boys were spinning her swiftly. There, on the slip before their eyes, lay the *Didamia III,* poised stern-to, awaiting the full tide and destiny.

Chapter 26

A JUNE LAUNCHING, AFTER THE SPRING BANKING HAD DRAINED THE able-bodied men from the neighborhood, could not be expected to draw a large crowd. However, this schooner belonged to Captain Sam, in whom the sturdy best of his New England forebears had united with his Scottish mother's gentleness to produce a man who was widely loved and esteemed; so a dozen or more oldsters, as many shoresmen and other dry-handed citizens, were clustered under the bow. Here the strong scents of salt water, fresh timber, pitch and rope, gave them back youth and voyagings as they leisurely discussed the schooner's lines and recalled other launchings.

Though the *Didamia* was but 65 tons, her bow, seen thus out of water, towered amazingly, her two masts reached farther skyward than masts afloat, her bowsprit angled more sharply.

Her temporary rigging was heavy with dangling boys; her decks were cluttered with boys racing from bow to stern, from larboard to starboard; from the beach, boy's heads appeared like so many turnips laid along the bulwarks. Where all the boys came from was a puzzle, for those of twelve and fourteen were on the Banks, hardy fishermen with a roll in the sea boots that had waded through fish guts and green water. Yet the schooner swarmed with boys and, on the wharf, mothers continually snatched the skirts of smaller boys "teetering on the feather-edge of nothing."

The women, some in primly starched sunbonnets and calico gowns, some in sober cashmere second best, had gathered at the wharfside where they could watch while keeping the young 'uns from under the men's feet and out of danger. Although most vessels slid into the water smoothly, now and then some un-guarded or unforeseen weakness brought tragedy.

Captain Sam and his builders looked for no trouble with the *Didamia,* a neat little lady if ever one was shaped from hack-matack and oak; she should take to the water like a duck and ride as lightly there.

They had given her a clipper bow but otherwise had kept to the older, fuller lines of the cargo-carrier; painted her green up to the bends, put black on her upper works and picked out her name on the headboards with chrome yellow. The Redmonds, viewing her from the skiff, thought her beautiful as she sparkled in the sunlight and yearned for the water.

Mercy had heard Little Obie's voice, all importance, before she glimpsed his figure. He waddled down the beach to assist the Redmond ladies ashore. Mercy was grateful that she always car-ried her babies well; no one could detect her condition under her long, full cloak. She thanked Obie for his voluble offer to find her a vantage point, "—but Ma and I plan to watch from the house. We'll have an excellent view and keep an eye on dinner at the same time."

The girls started towards the wharf, the boys went to clamber aboard the *Didamia*—for more exciting than watching was being part of the schooner as she took the water. Mercy followed the familiar house-path winding upward between the rocks.

She saw the bent figure of Nabby Nolan ascending the slope from her home and instinctively hastened to avoid an encounter, then shamed herself into resuming her leisurely pace. When the woman drew near, Mercy gave her a pleasant "Good morning."

She might as well have greeted the gulls above the beach. Nabby fixed her eyes on the new schooner—eyes as piercing and ill-matched as ever. Mercy's passing glance told her that Nabby was dirtier and untidier and much older-looking than when last seen.

This was brushed from her mind by the sight of the open front door and her mother's figure—still rounded like a cunning

217

little bird, Mercy thought. She smiled, *This is indeed an occasion, if Ma is using the front door!* Out of habit she continued a step along the path to the stoop.

"Come in, come in this door." Her mother beckoned impatiently. "No need t' walk around Cape Horn."

Mercy bent to kiss her mother, rejoicing to feel the flesh still firm under the softly withered skin, noting the snapping black eyes, the pink scalp through the sparse hair, for Damie was never one to wear a cap in the daytime. Thank goodness, in a changing world, Ma remained the same.

As Mercy moved aside Damie caught sight of Nabby Nolan hunched in her tattered black shawl. "What's that crow of a woman doin' on my path, I sh'd like t' know!" she burst out suspiciously.

"Now, Ma," Mercy soothed her, "most like she's only come to watch the launching like the rest of us."

"Oh, *you* can talk! When ye've lived next door to her as long as I have ye'll know better," Damie retorted darkly. "But come in, do, and lay off yer things."

So Mercy followed her mother politely and "laid off her things" in the long dim hall, whose corners mustily protested the prying sunlight. She felt like a guest in a strange house until Damie opened the door at the end of the hall and kitchen smells rushed out, then Mercy hurried into the dearly remembered room with the hearth fire and the sunlight across the dresser's face. There was her mother's rocker, worn through to the gleaming wood where the small quick hands had rested briefly, there was the mending basket, even the waiting needle woven into a patch on her father's red flannels.

"Oh, this is restful, Ma." She sighed, sinking into a rocker. "Everything neat and shining. In spite of all I can do (Serena and the girls, too) my kitchen and the middle room are always in a clutter. They *never* look like this!"

Her mother's eyes came sadly to her face. "Mercy, the day yer kitchen looks like mine, ye'll sit ye down and weep. For the last of yer children will be gone from ye."

"Why, Ma!" Mercy's voice was quieted. Here again was the cruelty of time and change. Had her mother ever wept for the old days when her children "kept the kitchen in an uproar," as she used to scold? Had she loved them so much in spite of her sharp tongue? Now even Philip was gone from Grannie's Head, teaching school in the Valley.

"What do you hear from Philip?" she asked as lightly as possible.

"Hear from Philip? Why, nawthin' but books an' teachin' an' studyin'." Pride vied wtih impatience in Damie's voice. "Bound an' determined to ruin his health! He's gone far and is well liked as a teacher, but it's three years sence he's been home fer so much as overnight."

Then moving gently in their rockers, mother and daughter talked of the distresses of pregnancy, of Tamsin's return, of Damie's settin'-hen, of what's-for-dinner and of how hard it was to plan when there was no knowing how many extra Sam might drag home for dinner after the launching.

A meaningful shout from the shore brought them hurriedly to the window. Men were moving towards the ways with smoking oil pots; others with mauls in hand were approaching the props shoring up the schooner. Mercy and her mother went back through the hall and out upon the front steps.

The women on the wharf, the boys in the rigging, the men on the bank, were motionless as those along the *Didamia's* under-sides swung their mauls and the sound of props being knocked away came up the slope.

This was the moment. Now the schooner should feel her freedom, should quiver with delight, should start to slide, gathering speed as she rushed to the water's kiss. Mercy found herself holding her breath until it was a pain in her chest. Then, even as she let it out, slowly, reluctantly, lest she need it before she could gasp another, she saw the *Didamia* was stock still on the ways. Bewilderment and disappointment settled on the surrounding figures and a murmur of consternation rose from the shore.

"Oh, what's gone awry?" Damie moaned. "It's the worst o' signs t' have a vessel stick on the ways!" Then catching sight of Nabby, solitary on the brow of the hill, she pointed a trembling finger. "Thyah's the trouble. Right thyah! I knowed it. I *knowed* it. Nabby Nolan's put a spell on yer pa's schooner, Mercy."

A babble of voices, a few shouted orders came from where the *Didamia* lay as if some evil spell did indeed hold her. Then men with ropes and mallets began to move purposefully.

Mercy thought, *They'll start her any minute now and, though the launching won't be quite the same, still, no harm done.* But minutes passed. The men regathered at the ways, their voices too low for Mercy to distinguish words. She recognized Tamsin on the platform near the bow and Adria on the beach below; they would be dreadfully disappointed girls at this setback to the christening.

Earlier Tamsin had overcome the withdrawn shyness of the feminine group on the wharf with her merry delight in all that went on, her appeals for instruction in the proper way to christen a vessel, her ridiculous accounts of the things she got backwards —nobody could resist Tamsin long. The girls' tongues were loosening when Captain Sam shouted an order and chatter ceased as all eyes turned towards the schooner.

Little Obie and two companions reappeared from around the boatshop corner, wiping their mouths with the backs of their hands. The old days were gone when enough rum was drunk in the building to float the completed craft and, in deference to Damie and the Temperance Division, Captain Sam had not even broached the time-honored launching cask; but it would be too much to expect a vessel to take the water without her health having been drunk in "the ardent," even if surreptitiously behind the steam box, safe from the eyes of crusaders.

220

Tamsin's full skirts billowed and rustled reassuringly as she hurried forward. Captain Sam proudly helped her up the small platform near the bow, where she stood holding the beribboned bottle and blushing under her bonnet. *Like Damie, years ago; like Bethiah; and sweet as this morning's cream,* her grandfather marveled. She leaned forward, ready, when the schooner should stir, to smash the bottle on its bow and call aloud its name.

She hoped the girls on the wharf would hear her. She thought again of the name she could call out, *Didamia.* Gramma Damie was old and homely; she seldom smiled, while her scolding tongue could flick the tenderest fault. Tamsin wondered briefly how such a one had inspired devotion in kindly Grampy Sam. She was too young to understand that truest love depends upon the lover and that rich natures find and inspire lovableness where others turn aside. *Anyway,* Tamsin decided, *it's his schooner and she's his wife and if he wants . . .*

"All ready?" Captain Sam was demanding, the pride and anxiety of last moments plain in his voice. Even the schooner seemed to gather and tense herself; wharf and shore and water waited with the quiet spectators for the morning's climax.

Finally, "Knock out the for'rd pin," Captain Sam ordered.

Tamsin raised the bottle and held her breath.

The vessel did not come to life.

A long sigh from wharf and beach broke the hush.

Tamsin stood bewildered, clutching the bottle with its dangling ribbons.

Men stepped out of the groups and walked along the hull, searching for some impediment. They scratched their heads and rejoined their companions, thrown off balance by the unexpected hitch.

Captain Sam helped Tamsin down and she made her way to Adria. She gripped her smaller sister's arm hard—no tears, for Grampy Sam's sake.

Suddenly from the ridge of Grannie's Head a laugh rang out, shrill and mocking. Every figure turned as if pulled by the same

221

string towards where Nabby Nolan stood, ragged and unkempt, her features a pale blur but her black pipe plainly smoking under the lank locks streeling about her face.

She pointed to the helpless vessel, then bent over with laughter, if such a sound could be called laughter.

The women on the wharf shrank together and drew the children nearer their spreading skirts. Captain Sam turned his back angrily upon the figure on the ridge. He glanced at the faces of his two builders; both were staring at Nabby.

Bradford Sears' thin face was blank.

Little Obie's round countenance, recently moist and flushed from his visits to the steam box, was pasty. His bulging eyes seemed hypnotized. As Captain Sam swung around to follow their gaze, Nabby Nolan took the black pipe from her mouth and blew a contemptuous wisp of smoke in Obie's direction.

"Obie and Bradford," Sam said sternly, "you mind I warned ye not to let Nabby about the vessel or shop, nor let her get her hands on anything belonging to one of us."

"She's never been anigh," Bradford swore solemnly, "to my knowledge." But his face was troubled, for there was no mistaking that this was witch work.

Little Obie swallowed convulsively but said nothing.

"Spew it out, Obie," Captain Sam ordered grimly. "Let's hear it. Has Nabby been about the vessel?"

"I d'know about that, Cap'n," Obie stammered reluctantly. "But t' tell the story an' tell it true . . ." He paused as if the truth would not bear telling, but the men pressed closer and every eye glittered with determination to hear it.

"Yes, yes," Captain Sam encouraged him, striving for patience, while his big hands moved as if feeling a need to wring the truth from the perspiring Obie.

"Well." Obie gulped. "Jest afore ye come down this mornin', I was a-settin' on the doorsill o' the boatshop thyah." He pointed dramatically, getting into his story, "a-waitin' and a-whittlin'

222

like, an' when I looked up, who should I see but . . ." It took another gulp to bring this out, ". . . Nabby Nolan."

"Obie, don't tell me you let her into my boatshop after all that's been said!"

"Now, Cap'n, what do ye take me fer?"

His captain didn't say.

"She was right perlite an' talked friendly." Several shook their heads at Obie's failure to recognize this bad sign.

"She said as how 'twas a fine mornin' and I 'lowed it was an' she said . . ."

Little Obie jumped at the goaded sound from Captain Sam and hurried on, "Well, the truth is, she wanted suthin' t' put in that pipe o' hern. Bein' a chawin' man, I hadn't nawthin' fer her, but I remembered where you'd tucked a twist over the doorway, Cap'n Sam, and I knowed ye wasn't one t' begrudge . . ."

"Oh, no! Never!" Captain Sam groaned in disbelief. "You *never* gave her my tobacco, you . . . Obie, you chowder-head!"

Obie shrank back. An angry murmur rose from the men about the two. Any fool should know that a witch bent on casting a spell would first obtain some personal belonging. One or two men turned aside and, evincing their opinion of Obie, spat scornful brown streams into the trampled shavings, but most of them were too disturbed to take their eyes from Captain Sam's face.

The captain looked at Obie and back at the watching Nabby. He pretended to be less shaken than he was. "Best try again to get the schooner movin, b'ys," he said patiently.

They could not budge the *Didamia,* though her every line yearned for the water and she seemed struggling against invisible bonds. Then men muttered of bewitchment and spells while the women turned hostile but frightened eyes upon Nabby, clear-cut against the sky as she puffed her pipe and pointed its stem at the struggling men. She sent laughter like a loon's unearthly mirth down across their useless strivings; it wilted them like a blight.

They gathered anew in a knot near the bow. Old Ephie Doane

223

spoke then. His thin voice shook with the palsy that had all but taken him off during the winter, but his words carried the weight of ninety-odd years. In one pendulous ear a thin gold thread remained from the earrings marking a man who had been—if not on pirate ships, as many suspected—much in pirate waters. His bleared eyes had beheld many a sight.

"Plain as the nose on yer face, what's wrong," he squeaked, thumping the ground with his cane. " 'Course the vessel won't take t' the water. She's 'witched. That's why." He nodded towards the schooner's naked side. "An' don't noan o' ye get under her, neither. I've seen men crushed t' chum by a spelled ship afore this."

The men involuntarily jumped away, then stopped, ashamed; they had been beyond danger.

Captain Sam was agonizingly conscious of time being lost. "It's slack water now, the tide'll race out when it turns. What's to be done?"

"Done! Only one thing t' be done." Old Ephic spoke querulously. "Do like I've see done aboard ship. Shoot the witchery out o' her." His head shook perilously but he continued, for it was strengthening to be again a leader of men, to have them await his instructions. "Ye need a plank and a silver slug."

"A silver slug! Where'd we git a silver slug?" Obie must put in his word though his voice piped with fear, both of Nabby's spell and his fellows' wrath.

"*Git* it, ye fool!" Ephie's paper-thin hand clutched the cane as if to splinter it about Obie's fat head. "Why, make it. Somebuddy's surely got a silver luck piece on him."

Somebody found a lucky shilling, spat on it and passed it to Reuben, the blacksmith, who disappeared behind the boatshop, whence the sounds of short blows on his small anvil reached the waiting men.

Captain Sam turned to Obie, who wavered between fright and pride in his important role in an exciting event. "Can you draw?" the older man demanded.

"Draw?" Little Obie said with some of his old glibness. "I might draw water out of a well!" He cackled discordantly, but glimpsing the captain's face he hurriedly changed his tone to one of apology. "Draw pictures, ye mean? No, I couldn't draw nawthin'. That is," he explained, "not so as it would look like nawthin'."

"Well, then, you git to the house and tell Damie you want my duck gun and the powder horn from over the mantel."

As Little Obie's fat legs made the shavings fly in his haste to be gone, Captain Sam turned to his other helper. "Bradford, you're handy with a piece of chalk. Draw us a picture of . . . of a woman. On this plank. Nothing fancy."

Ephie quavered, "We all know who 'tis. We all know."

Under a ring of straining eyes Bradford bit his tongue and solemnly outlined a woman's figure upon the plank. Though he meant no likeness (no need to call down trouble), so powerful was the conviction in every mind that men exclaimed at the reproduction of Nabby's tall figure.

From the front steps Mercy and Damie had looked down upon the inexplicable delays and movements at the ways, becoming increasingly disturbed at the men's attitudes and gestures. They saw Little Obie puffing up the slope, haste and consequence in every swing of legs and arms. "Now what?" Damie queried the empty air.

They met him at the kitchen door, but before Damie could ask the first of many questions crowding her tongue, Little Obie panted, "Cap'n Sam says gi' me his duck gun, quick."

"Lord, save us!" gasped Damie, even as she hurried towards the mantel. "What does Sam want with his duck gun this time o' year?"

"T' shoot *me*, I cal'ate," Obie told her lugubriously. "An' I *don't* know but what it'll be a good riddance." Then more practically, "He'll need the powder, too, Mi's Damie."

Seizing the gun and horn from her hand, he made haste towards the shore, keeping well away from the ridge and Nabby. His account of Damie's amazement was shut off by Old Ephie, still reveling in authority. "Quiet, ye fool. This ain't no time fer yer blabbering." Even Obie fell silent before the malignancy centering upon the crude limning on the plank.

In the kitchen Damie faltered, "Mercy, ye heared what Obie said. Ye don't suppose yer pa's really agoin' t' shoot him? What do ye cal'ate Little Obie's done now? I've often heared Sam declare he'd like t' wring Obie's neck. But shootin'! He'd never, surely, even in a rage. Why, it'd be murder! And all them witnesses! Mercy, you run now, an' tell yer pa I said he's to do no sech a thing."

Mercy had never seen her mother so distraught. "Now, Ma, wouldn't I be a fine figger running down the hill? The men might well shoot *me*." She laughed. "I don't know what happened but this I do know, if Little Obie doesn't die till Pa makes away with him, he'll outlive Methuselah! So don't worry." She turned. "Ma, let's go back to the front door where we can see what's going on."

Fascinated, they watched Bradford Sears set a plank upright beside the boatshop door. The group of silent men stepped back and Reuben passed Captain Sam his gun. On the wharf a child's shrill cries were being smothered against its mother's skirts.

Damie's hands fluttered as if undecided whether to shut out the sight of Sam with his musket or to stop her ears against the coming shot.

Out of the corner of her eye Mercy caught a movement. "Look, Ma!" she called her mother's attention to Nabby moving down the slope towards her shanty.

"Ay, she'd better go," was Damie's grim reply, but she scarcely took her eyes off her husband's figure.

Reluctance and compulsion were in Sam's every movement as he put the gun to his shoulder. Several of the men dropped their heads as if in prayer.

Rolling black smoke hid everything near the boatshop, but the sound of the shot was less than Mercy had been tensed for. She heard a shriek and turned.

Halfway down the slope Nabby Nolan cried, "My God, they've shot me!" clasped her hands to her forehead and fell upon her face. At the boatshop Reuben walked to the plank and laid a blunt finger upon the splintered bullethole in the outlined head.

Mercy and her mother stared white faced into each other's eyes. Mercy found her voice first. "Pa *can't* have shot her, Ma. You saw—the gun was pointed the other way.

Nabby did not long lie still but staggered to her feet and up to the ridge's crest. She stood once more facing the tranced vessel and the men, but her attitude had lost its insolence.

"You want that schooner to reach water t' day?" she shouted.

There were angry mutterings and an ugly cry or two, for the gunshot, the familiar heavy fumes of black powder, the silver bullet's work (they had not heard Nabby's cry nor seen her fall), together had momentarily broken the spell of superstition. Nabby sensed that the mood to be revenged for their fear was growing.

She pointed to a yearling steer grazing in the pasture that bordered the boatyard, innocently unaware of the (later-detected) hellish red glare in his eye, the mark of the cloven hoof blackly outlined upon his white flank. "Fasten him to that block and tackle rigged under the bow."

This brought an angry jeer. A dozen men had laid their weight and muscles to the block controlling the cunningly rigged ropes without budging the schooner. But no chance must be passed up, for a widening wet line along the shore showed that the ebb had begun. Reluctantly, sheepishly, men brought the steer and led him in a crudely knotted rope harness to the space before the ways.

Mercy could see only the swift passing and knotting of ropes. Then a man lashed the calf—he was little more—across the rump with a rope end. Startled, he sprang ahead and was almost upended as the makeshift harness brought up. Someone laughed, someone swore, an incredulous murmur rose and swelled. The *Didamia* was stirring.

A few feet away on the beach Tamsin, caught unaware, gathered her skirts and ran, still grasping the bottle of wine. She reached high and swung towards the bow, crying in a loud clear voice, "I name this schooner the *Gramma Damie!*"

She wiped the spattered wine from her face, dropped her hands to her sides and burst into tears. She had muddled the proudly awaited christening. She wished the tide would cover her, or the shore open and swallow her. She saw Adria loyally hurrying to share her shame, while her ears tingled for expected laughter.

But people had thought only for the schooner. Men had leaped to clear blocks and ropes as the vessel quivered. Now the *Didamia* slid slowly, creaking and protesting; then gathering speed, sang down the greased way; sent the spray from her stern leaping to wet the deck; pushed one wave to splash up the wharf spiles, another to wash the rocks of the landing-side; gave herself to the water; yielded to the ropes which checked her movement; was at last upon the sea's bosom.

A halfhearted cheer broke forth. Men and women began to move about and speak in natural tones again. Boys shouted and scampered about the deck of the schooner, no longer a bound hulk upon the slip, but a live thing beneath their feet. Yet on the front steps Damie threw her apron over her head. "Yes, there she rides. But I wish she'd stuck till she rotted!"

The morning's events were not yet over. A wild cry came from the ridge and there again stood Nabby, the proven witch. Her face showed white as she moaned and pressed her hand to her head, but rage and spite quickened every shake of her clenched fist and her shrill voice betrayed no weakness.

"So ye'd put a silver bullet through Nabby Nolan. Daughter of an admiral. Above the lot o' ye, she is. Ye'll rue it! Listen t' me, every man jack o' ye. The *Didamia* won't so much as wet her jib but she'll drownd every man aboard. Drownd 'em! Her voice trailed off into a howl.

She turned and pointed a finger. "As fer you, Sam Nickerson, the curse o' fire and water on ye. And on yer schooner. Ye'd steal a widder's only son! Try t' find a crew, my fine skipper."

She again included the others. "Ship in the *Didamia* if ye dast —after Nabby Nolan's put her curse upon her."

She flounced about and stumbled down the slope towards her squatting shanty.

The watchers looked into one another's eyes and looked away from what they glimpsed in those few open seconds before the shutters were closed and the curtains drawn against fear.

Damie cried, "What'll become of us! Yer pa's put every penny into that schooner."

Though she herself was shaken, Mercy set about reassuring her mother. Captain Sam Nickerson, loved and respected, had never known what it was to seek a crew; what tell of Nabby Nolan's wicked talk; the *Didamia* could be manned twice over with the pick of the Cove.

Little Obie went far towards redeeming himself when he stepped up to prove his loyalty to Captain Sam was greater than his fear of Nabby's worst. Despite a treacherous voice, he forced the words past his lips. "Don't fergit, Cap'n, ye've promised me the cook's berth; I'm a-countin' on it."

But even Little Obie refused an invitation to dinner and the crowd melted rapidly.

Captain Sam and his grandchildren were a silent group as they climbed the slope. He paused often and stood looking back at the schooner for long minutes at a time. He wouldn't want anybody to guess he stopped to catch his breath, which this last while had taken to acting peculiar by spells.

Chapter 27

Tamsin poked her brown head through the middle room's western door. "Mamma, I'm off to the lighthouse with Kiah. I haven't lit the lamps since I've been home!" she said and was gone.

From the hearth, where she was laying the evening fire, Adria lifted her wide gray eyes in shy confidence. "Home's much nicer, Mamma, when Miss Newhall's away."

"I know, dear." Mercy must admit this though she never criticized the teacher. "No doubt Miss Newhall needed a change and a rest from us, too, and her people will be glad to have her visit them."

Adria couldn't quite imagine joy at Miss Newhall's presence. "I suppose her *own* people . . ." The eastern latch rattled. "Grampy Sam!" she cried, Miss Newhall forgotten.

Mercy anxiously searched her father's face for ill effects from last week's unpropitious launching and found to her relief that his mouth was quirked for a coming joke and his blue eyes twinkling.

These signs sent Adria's gaze to the shadows behind him. She flung the chips from her apron with an incredulous "Uncle Philip!" and ran open-armed to greet the visitors. Then eager to share happiness, she hurried out to find Tamsin.

Mercy kissed Philip affectionately and told him, "It's so good to see you, Philip!" Then after a second look, "But you're thin, and pale. You've been ill?" Had he contracted the dread lung trouble? So many young men returned from promising careers looking like this; "sent home," as the common saying was, "to die."

"Don't be alarmed, Mercy." He understood her fears and sought to quiet them. Mercy's own face was drawn and white, she should not have concern for him added to other cares. "The doctor tells me I must put my books aside and get outdoors for a few weeks. That's all, truly."

The office door opened and Dan came to greet Philip warmly. Between the two larger men Philip appeared too delicately built, with features too finely drawn, eyes too bright and large under his white brow. Mercy's heart misgave her.

Then Tamsin blew through the western door and into her grandfather's arms like a warm wind.

"And now, here's Philip," he said, releasing her.

Tamsin's confused hands went up to smooth her tumbled curls and down to straighten her rumpled dress. "Adria didn't tell me," she accused her sister with a sidewise glance. "You said 'Grampy Sam'!"

"I saved Uncle Philip for a surprise; but I *told* you not to jump the haystacks," Adria exonerated herself.

Adria had run to Philip's arms but Tamsin put out her hand as to a stranger, so changed she found him or so changed she knew herself to be since those days when she had adored her teacher openly and striven hard to please him.

Where Captain Sam had beheld a laughing child, Philip saw a young woman who, with curly brown head aslant and face colored by mingled embarrassment and pleasure, was altogether so appealing that he wished he had taken her into his arms as he had her sister. Not altogether as he had held Adria, perhaps; but he was one of the family, why should he hesitate to show his affection?

"The middle room seems right again with you here, Uncle Philip; it has missed you," Tamsin said, dimpling.

He had just assured himself he was one of the family, why did he instantly request, "Don't call me 'Uncle Philip' now that you're so grown-up, Tamsin. Won't 'Philip' do?" He wanted to ask if *she* had missed him, but Will and Charlie came rushing in; he must visit Serena in the kitchen; the evening became one of "do you remembers" and nostalgic laughter.

During the next weeks, as Philip divided his time between

231

Grannie's Head and New Erin, his face lost its hollows and tanned in the sun and wind, to Mercy's rejoicing.

The merry, busy days belonged to the young folks, but evening brought mature discussions that often dragged far beyond normal bedtime and left Mercy wearily nodding by the time her father and Philip took their leave to row home.

Up and down the shore the disputed issue of Confederation was first on every tongue. Those who favored the union of British provinces were locally in a minority, but they battled no less vigorously for that, and feuds arose that were to split Prince's Cove for generations.

On New Erin, arguments, while they engendered no personal rancors, waxed long and hot. Captain Sam was a strong Confederationalist and Philip his staunch ally, but Dan, like many others, propounded that New England was Nova Scotia's natural market, that the ties of blood and memory, of affinity, as well as the trade routes, led across the Bay. Sam's Loyalist blood would boil and bring to the surface Abigail's long and bitter, bitter memory of Revolutionary America, memories passed on, little dimmed or sweetened, to her children.

Philip sometimes brought up the threat of Fenians, now that the War Between the States was ended; but the people of western Nova Scotia, despite raids by American privateers during two conflicts, were unable to imagine harm from their neighbors—especially since many Bluenose lads had fought and died in the Northern armies. True, the militia was drilling, but many derided that fact as a "scare" device of the Confederation party.

Mercy wished merely that the arguing among her menfolk would cease; the upheavals and perturbations of the outside world did not touch her this summer, wrapped as she was in her persistent forebodings and her private worries.

However, the summer brought joys as well as apprehensions. She would not speak, even to Dan, of the growing intimacy between Philip and Tamsin, but she hugged its implications to her inner heart. She watched Tamsin grow in womanliness and heard

Philip's rich voice gain happy overtones. Philip and Tamsin! That would go far towards balancing Catherine's choice.

Serena's bleak eye was keen, but Mercy made light of its observations. "Philip is fond of us all," she said. "And Tamsin has always loved Philip as an uncle."

Serena sniffed. "Mebbe Tamsin thinks he's an uncle. Could be. But have ye marked how Philip looks at *her?* Not like ary uncle ever I see!"

Full summer lay upon New Erin. The fish-butts on the wharves splashed over, the flakes between shore and barn were bared and covered again and again while the piles of dried fish mounted in the store. Strawberries and raspberries, drowned in cream, had in turn filled the supper bowls and decked Serena's melting short-cakes; now August was passing and on Israel's Burnt beyond Further Hill, the blueberries were ripe for pies. The garden yielded sweet new vegetables; fresh fish were to be had each evening from the homing boats. A bountiful time.

A busy time as well. When they could be spared from household duties Tamsin and Adria went berrying with their brothers and Philip, or to the hayfield to lend a welcome hand. The days slipped by until there came the last of its perfect kind and the beginning of changes.

From the point's far side the laden hayrack creaked barnward, topped by two sprawling boys and an upright Adria, escorted by Kiah and Waitstill strolling at Bright's head. Philip turned to speak to Tamsin and realized himself miraculously alone with her in the sun-washed field. Her eyes had been upon him and he rejoiced as she looked away, for this tacitly acknowledged her awareness of him as other than a family friend.

No use to remind his heart that he was almost double her eighteen years, that she had kept much of her childish gaiety while he had always been a dull and bookish fellow; that crazy organ persisted in paining exquisitely when she was near and in aching dully when she was not.

Now he took her rake and, bending, looked into the shy face

233

beneath the sunbonnet's frill. He caught a little sun-browned hand and, stifling his desire to kiss away the blisters raised by the rake, laid it upon his arm. Through the motionless late-afternoon air, across the long rock-shadows on the velvet sod, they walked homeward, close, close, and in Philip's breast were music and glory.

When they reached the lighthouse path they turned as one to scan the glassy bay. Tamsin broke their silence, "See how Pilot Point looms! And that schooner—she seems to be floating across the sky." She sighed. "But a loom is a sign of change. Things are perfect now."

So she found things perfect now. Philip was enchanted. He managed to say teasingly, "With your bad signs you sound for all the world like your Gramma Damie!"

"I *do,* don't I?" She laughed in a swift change of mood and, taking off her sunbonnet, she swung it lightheartedly by its strings while Philip watched the sunlight among her curls. "Perhaps," she went on, "it's the schooner that's a bad sign. Perhaps she's a Phantom Ship—a forerunner." She was poking fun at herself now.

"She's real enough," Philip assured her, "but she has no import for us, good or bad. You'll see, because there's a fog-breeze making up outside that will soon bring her to Redmond's Harbor."

"Now, who's prophesying?"

They laughed into each other's eyes and moved along.

Inside the door of the empty middle room they paused. Philip's arms went about the sweetly curving figure, drawing it to his bursting heart. He felt Tamsin trembling and forced his arms to gentleness but, still holding her, he put one hand under her downcast chin and raised her face to his. Between the widely parted lashes her eyes were black and deep, with no flame to match what must show in his. She made no pretense of coyness but begged him soberly, "Please, Philip, not yet."

He watched her slip through the door into the long hall while his arms and heart alike ached with their emptiness.

A few weeks later he was to tell himself, *Fool, you should have held her when you could.* He was to remember also that arms cannot encompass unwilling love and to justify his gentleness. *No, you were right to give her the time she asked for.*

That evening Mercy found herself pausing as she came to the end of each knitting needle and halting her rocker's swing to listen at every sound that might be Will and Charlie returning. She chided herself for worrying. *Great boys that they are! And only to row home from Grannie's Head.* But following Philip's prediction to Tamsin, the wind had sprung up and brought the fog.

Chill had driven all but the boys indoors. On one side of Mercy, Philip pretended to read in the light from the softly sizzling oil lamp; on the other side Tamsin pretended to embroider, refusing to lift her eyes to Philip's glances; between them Mercy pretended not to notice their pretences.

Ah, voices and the thud of sea boots along the boardwalk! The boys were safe ashore. They hated her to fret over them; the turning of a heel took all her attention as the door opened.

Philip looked up from his *Yarmouth Herald.* "So it proves our schooner had business with the Redmonds, after all, Tamsin," he said softly, under cover of voices and scraping boots. He was pleading for a sign that she remembered their shared afternoon; one sign before greetings to the stranger in the doorway precluded it.

But Tamsin was already staring at the young man between her brothers. Not often New Erin welcomed such a dashing stranger. Medium tall, he stood straight as a picket. Above the breast of his well-fitting frock coat, white linen and a carefully knotted cravat showed. The lamplight gave a copperish glint to his flowing moustaches and to his thick hair, worn long enough to curl up from his coat collar in the back.

Dan came quickly to his feet. The stranger bowed slightly. "Your sons rescued me from the fog at the landing and assured me I wouldn't be intruding even at this late hour." He reached in a pocket. "I have the honor of presenting a letter from James

Redmond, your cousin, I believe, sir." He stood rather stiffly erect while Dan opened and glanced over the sheet.

When in Boston, Dan occasionally called upon his cousins, but blood ties had not overcome a lack of mutual tastes and interests, and they remained little more than acquaintances. However, he said warmly enough, "Yes, indeed, I'm James Redmond's cousin, and happy to welcome any friend of his, Mr. . . ." (another glance at the letter) "Mr. Clark."

"O'Shaughnessy Clark." Under the moustaches, magnificent teeth flashed in a smile that swept the room. "My friends call me Shaun." His voice implied his hope that the Redmonds would be his friends and call him Shaun. Mercy could not be sure she caught a hint of condescension in the proffered friendship.

When Dan said, "My wife, Mr. Clark," the young man took her hand with a deep bow. Other introductions followed: to a demure Tamsin (the stranger bowed deeply again and lifted his eyes to hers with what Philip considered a studied effect), to a stiff Serena, a shy Adria, a cool Philip.

New Erin hospitality was not forgotten. "Can't we find you some supper, Mr. Clark?" Mercy asked, and Serena started to her feet.

"No, indeed, thank you, ma'am. I dined not·more than an hour ago with Captain O'Dwyer on the *Resolution*."

He accepted a glass of wine and, settling back in his chair and crossing his legs so that his varnished boots gleamed, he addressed himself to his host, though every ear was tuned to his words.

"I'm in this country as a representative of the Liberty Fish Company." He paused and looked closely at Dan, but the name was unfamiliar.

"A new company, I presume?"

"New, yes. Yet its formation has been under consideration for some years. I thought you might have heard of it."

Dan shook his head.

"It has much solid backing, I assure you."

"I wish it and you every good fortune," Dan replied, "but I've dealt with the New England Halibut Company for many years, and our arrangements are highly satisfactory to me."

"Perhaps you'll let me talk further about the matter after I have seen other merchants." Something lay behind his words, but there was no rude persistence. "I'm to visit various towns along the shore, Yarmouth, St. Joseph's, Barrington . . ." He tapped a pocket. "I have a list. I'm to get information on available quantities of fish and warehouses. Your cousin thought you'd be kind enough to advise me about this district. Captain O'Dwyer must go on to Halifax; he will pick me up at the end of a fortnight."

Tamsin thought, *A fortnight never before sounded so short a time.*

"Indeed," Dan assured him, "you must consider yourself New Erin's guest and make this your headquarters. It's as central a spot as you'll find. My small sloop *Katie* will be at your service and the boys will like nothing better than to ferry you about."

The boys chimed an eager assent. Who wouldn't be glad to sail the coastline in such August weather?

"Why not send for your luggage now and spend the night with us?" Dan suggested.

The other explained there were plans to be finalized with Captain O'Dwyer, who also had shares in the new venture. "Like me, he's a young man, interested in the future. The end of the war has made a difference in many things, Mr. Redmond." Again there was a faint but perceptible emphasis behind the words.

"You were in the war?" Mercy asked. But she had already noted the military bearing and had decided, *He has the moustaches and the bold eyes of a soldier,* though she had seen no soldier, save in pictures, since her long-ago visit to Halifax.

"Yes, I was one of the boys in blue," he answered with a vocal swagger. Behind Tamsin's eyes a picture formed of this handsome soldier astride a black steed and charging, sword awhirl, to the rescue of Uncle Tom and Eliza.

237

"From your speech I would guess you from Boston—or that vicinity." Mercy smiled, encouraging him to give them information about himself.

"I'm Boston Irish," he replied proudly. "My parents came out from the Ould Sod, like yourself, Mr. Redmond," turning again to Dan and assuming an accent that reminded Mercy of Father Burke and set her heart against the young man. "Many's the sad story they'd be telling me, about Erin's cruel treatment by the English. And niver a doubt but what you could be tellin' more of the same." He looked to Dan for corroboration; his tone was laughing but his eyes were not.

Dan did not answer him lightly. "As a boy and young man I heard many such tales, to be sure. However, I often fear I'm no true Irishman, much as I love my birthplace. You see, my mother was English, and I was at school in England for several years. I've found the English no better, and no worse, than the Irish. Different certainly. Others speak of the cold English, the warmhearted Irish, but it was my mother who was warm and laughing, my father cold and severe."

For a moment Mr. Clark appeared inordinately rebuffed at this quiet speech. His eyes chilled and his jaw set in an ugly line. Then his smile flashed out again, "Ah, well! Everyone to his taste, as the old lady said when she kissed the cow. I'd heard you called a true lover of Ireland."

Dan replied quickly, "So I am! But what have you and I to do with the old wrongs and hatreds? We are citizens of this New World and should not be bringing old quarrels to it.

"Your country, both North and South, has bitterness and sorrow enough in the present, and scars that will be livid for many a year. Its sons should not be seeking more.

"As for me, here on this tiny New Erin I've made my home and my life. I didn't leave all the Old World's evil behind; man carries greed and intolerance with him, wherever he goes. But at least I have made every man welcome here and have never asked his nationality nor his creed, nor what wrongs his fathers suffered or inflicted."

The family sat in silent surprise, for Dan never spoke any but surface pleasantries to visitors. Mercy was stirred and proud.

"You take my nonsense too seriously, sir," O'Shaughnessy Clark said nonchalantly. "We Irish talk too much perhaps." He turned to the ladies then with a rallying smile and conversation became general.

Mercy felt that the stranger's glances deprecated the much-used middle room, and her pride in Dan and his home rose unreasonably against the handsome, well-dressed young man. Tamsin, sensing her mother's coolness, perversely warmed to the newcomer and ignored the silent Philip.

Mr. Clark's departure at the end of an hour left Mercy depressed by his obvious interest in and for Tamsin. Not that Tamsin would be long impressed by the shallow charm of such a man when she remembered Philip's deep devotion.

It was as well for this belief that she could not overhear her daughters in bed.

"Tamsin, what's wrong with you?" Adria complained. "I'd as lief sleep with an eel."

"Isn't he the handsomest thing, Adria? And did you see how he looked at me?" Tamsin twisted restlessly again.

"Uncle Philip looks at you nicer, Tamsin; only he does it when you don't know." Adria was forthright. "I thought you liked Uncle Philip."

"Oh, I do! But he's like a relative; we've always had him. And, he's old." Tamsin twitched her nightcap with troubled fingers.

Adria could not gainsay this. Uncle Philip was over thirty, really old—still, when he was with Tamsin he didn't seem old.

Tamsin continued excited and talkative while loving Adria fought sleep to provide the required audience.

"You know, Adria, opposites are supposed to attract; I think

I always preferred blue eyes, really," Tamsin concluded, forgetting the recent nights when Philip's gentle brown gaze had followed her into the first sweet dreams.

Adria was loyal, and as sleep closed softly about her, she remained convinced of Uncle Philip's superiority over the stranger. She reached drowsily to pat the soft hand lying on her arm. Tamsin was so sweet and loving; she should know nothing but tenderness. Adria could not picture O'Shaughnessy Clark as tender. She was glad his stay on New Erin would be short, a few days—then the happy summer would blot out his coming and going.

But the stranger did not leave in a few days; he accepted Dan's invitation to make New Erin his headquarters and made long stops between excursions along the shore.

He returned from St. Joseph's in a black and disgruntled mood. He called desultorily at Prince's Cove, where Captain Sam greeted him and, after a brief conversation and a long, blue regard, watched him with a puzzled air. Kiah later agreed, "Yes, Cap'n Sam, fer a man in the fish business Mr. Clark knows precious little about fish. Certainly."

On his returns to New Erin, Tamsin came to life with a new gaiety, a sweeter glow. She walked with him, over the dike to watch the Caldron boil and froth with the flood tide, along the lighthouse path to tend the lamps at sunset and to saunter home in the twilight.

Evenings there was music about the piano; but now the young Irishman, not Philip, turned the pages of the music book; though all joined in the refrains, his tenor and not Philip's baritone blended with Tamsin's light soprano when the other voices dropped out. They chose songs to which the Northern Armies had marched or old Irish tunes.

Too, Tamsin and Shaun had mutual memories of Boston to share while Philip sat silent, his dark eyes seeking Tamsin's only to find them absorbed in laughing blue ones. Philip's visits became less frequent and Mercy did not urge his coming. Shaun appeared to find the gay Tamsin irresistible; Mercy could have shaken her well.

"Dan," she asked her husband one morning, "how much longer does Mr. Clark expect to be with us?"

Dan's reply was unusually sober. "That I can't say, Mercy. Surely not much longer, he's had time to find out all he needs to know. I can tell you this, I shall have nothing to do with his new firm."

"I think you're wise, Dan," she said. "And I *do* wish he'd go before he turns Tamsin's head completely."

Dan gazed at her in surprise. "Are all fathers so blind? I hadn't guessed that Tamsin might account for his lingering." He considered the new idea gravely, but he expressed no opinion and Mercy thought with a sinking heart, *Perhaps he'd prefer O'Shaughnessy Clark to Philip for a son-in-law. Clark is Irish and of Dan's Church.*

"He's a stranger, Dan," she suggested hesitantly. "We know nothing of him . . ."

"A true Prince's Cover!" he twitted her affectionately, coming to brush his lips across her hair and draw her into his arms. "How did you ever marry *me*, when you consider everyone outside the Cove a foreigner—and suspect?"

"Oh, Dan," she repudiated his taunt. "From my first sight of you, you were no foreigner to my heart." She didn't voice her fear that Tamsin's heart might have recognized its own in the same precipitate way.

The *Resolution* was an answer to prayer when at sunset she dropped anchor just beyond Captain d'Entremont's *Arthenese*. Mr. Clark prepared to rejoin his friend O'Dwyer.

In his office that evening Dan and Captain d'Entremont nursed their glasses before a glowing end of beach log while fog ran down the glittering window. Once the affairs of the *Arthenese* had been completed, the men ordinarily would have joined the family in the middle room, but by mutual, if unacknowledged, consent they made no move to do so.

241

Arthur d'Entremont broke a lengthening silence. "I see your friend, Mr. Clark, he is here."

"No friend; an acquaintance of my cousin's merely."

"So." The Frenchman groped for words that would not say too much. "This Mr. Clark, he is interested, I think, in strange fish."

"Yes, strange fish. Not fish he and his friends will catch in New Erin waters."

The captain was pleased the other had got his meaning. "Also, in San' Joseph's Harbor he catches no fish."

They sipped again, each still thinking more than had been said. "Mr. Clark is, like you, an Irishman?"

"I'm proud of my Irish blood, Captain. Perhaps here, away from my homeland, I've boasted of it unduly. My mother was English; she died when I was small, but I loved her dearly."

"Ah, but yes. The mothers . . ." Captain d'Entremont nodded, his warm eyes sympathetic.

"Yet I was never English, I'm no longer Irish. I believe I'm Nova Scotian." Dan smiled rather sheepishly.

"*Et moi*," the other agreed quickly. "Acadian. As you say, Nova Scotian." He considered French and English had both been wrong to spew old poisonings over the new land. Their quarrels had brought long sorrow and trouble, especially to the Acadian French. "But the blood and the tears, they are ended now. And we French, we want no Fenians." He brought the name into the open.

Dan explained, "Until today, when the *Resolution's* arrival forced Clark to lay his cards before me, I wasn't sure just what 'fishing' he had in mind. I had held him off, not *wanting* to know, I suppose, and content that he was meeting only disappointments." He set his glass down and turned to face his friend. "The whole scheme was harebrained and bound to come to naught. Apart from spying out the shore—and why, in Heaven's name, not buy themselves an Admiralty chart?—Clark and O'Dwyer had some

242

woolly idea of organizing the French, whom they pictured as waiting to rise against the English."

There was no need for Captain d'Entremont to comment on this. He listened carefully as Dan continued, "Most of all they counted on using New Erin as a base and arsenal—and me as a leader!" He laughed scornfully. "When I called the whole thing treacherous and evil, apart from its errant foolishness, Clark was enraged and talked wildly of revenge for my betrayal of the cause, as he called it."

Dan's voice changed, "My wife has worried because of Clark's attentions to Tamsin—he *is* good-looking and he can be charming. But no matter what business had brought him here, he's not the man for Tamsin."

"The little, laughing Tamsin!" The captain smiled at memories of an affectionate child who had climbed his knee and begged for a French song. He sobered. "No, Mr. Redmond, he is not the man for your Tamsin. In San' Joseph he boasted of the Irish girl he is to marry. Her father is rich; he hired Captain O'Dwyer and backed the *Resolution's* trip."

Dan swore bitterly at Clark's deceit.

"I hope the little Tamsin, she will not be brokenhearted when this Clark is gone," his friend said.

"She'll get over him," Dan spoke with conviction. "Philip Cadell is home; her mother and I, we hope . . ."

Arthur d'Entremont smiled and nodded. "Philip's a fine chap."

Dan resumed, "Another thing bothers me. Clark says he got my name and the names of a few dissident French from Father Burke, who's one of the Boston Sinn Fein." He blushed to remember his ultra-Irish flights of patriotism, voiced as he and the priest had talked long ago at Molly's wedding. He had forgotten his wine-inspired agreement with the other's bitter views; but Father Burke had remembered them, if Clark could be believed.

"Father Burke was never at home in San' Joseph." Captain d'Entremont dismissed the Irish priest with a wave of his hand.

"Father Boudreau, now, he comes to watch the young men when they drill."

"St. Joseph men are drilling?"

"What do you think? Like in Barrington, in Yarmouth, all along the shore. Over two hundred men—English and French, it makes no difference—they come from both sides of the harbor. Four companies we have. Benoni, my brother, he's captain of one company. When Mr. Clark has talked to me (roundabout, like you say, but I know which way the wind blows), I said to him most polite, 'Come with me, my friend, and see how we play soldier now at San' Joseph'."

Small wonder Clark returned from the French settlement angry and chagrined, Dan thought, amused. "Perhaps it's as well," he told the captain, "that these men have visited our shores and got a clear picture of the welcome awaiting invaders."

While the men talked it had grown late. The captain expressed his regrets that he would not see Mrs. Redmond and her charming family this trip, but he must have his cargo of fish in Boston before the week's end and already the fog had cost him a day. "I will be dropping down the bay tomorrow morning about three o'clock—before you wake, my land-loving friend." The old cordiality was back in Arthur d'Entremont's tones.

At the door he pulled his jacket up and his cap down against the cold fog. "No, don't come with me," he entreated his host. "My down-haul boat, she lies at the wharf end. I will get my men from Kiah in the kitchen. We'll find our vessel. A good vessel-man, he can smell out his own on the darkest night."

Two hours later fog and darkness had thickened. Tamsin dropped her skirts and clutched the high sides to prevent herself from falling as the dory tipped and lurched. Though Shaun was not even a darker blot in the fog, she could hear the splash of his boots at the bow, his alternate panting and whispered oaths. Charlie's new dory was stuck at tide-line.

Well, I was a goose to wear my good rose silk in the first place.

244

Even though, Tamsin mused with a catch in her throat, *it's to be my wedding gown as well. But the damage is done now. Even my petticoats are wet to the knees from the grass and dory-slop. I may as well forget them and lend Shaun a hand instead of sitting here like the Queen on her throne!*

Letting the bedraggled skirts fall as they might, she pulled an oar towards her and, standing up, thrust it over the side. When it had found secure bottom she whispered, "Now, Shaun! Push!" and put her weight against it. She heard Shaun's sharp expulsion of breath, felt the boat give, and dropped suddenly back upon the stern thwart, her heart pounding. The first big step was taken, they had left the shore of New Erin.

Shaun stumbled to his thwart and slipped the oars into place. Slowly he backed the dory from the shore. The music of water lapping among spiles came from either side of the dock, the shed on the wharves loomed huge and close, leaning to watch Tamsin as she stole away between them. She had the feeling that one of them might reach out and pull her back.

"Hurry, Shaun," she whispered. "Row quietly but *hard* until we're clear of the wharves." Though who could be around to see them? The fog was dark as sin, with no faintest hint of dawn's lightening behind Further Hill where the sun slept.

She remembered her satchel and lifted it from the dory's bottom to her lap. No sense in letting its contents get as soaking as the clothes she wore.

Away from the shadows of the wharves, Shaun was a dim figure moving to the oars' time. Dim and frightening. Without his strong hands imprisoning hers, without his arms turning her to his kisses, his blue eyes that melted everything but her love for him, O'Shaughnessy Clark was a stranger. She knew a moment's panic, caught with this man between black fog and black water.

"Shaun, dear," and she had to push her voice through her dry lips as well as through the woolly folds between them, "Captain O'Dwyer will think me a bold creature to run away and be married at sea." Though Shaun couldn't see her hands twisting upon the satchel, he might hear the agitation in her voice. "Perhaps," she went on timidly, "it would have been better for me to coax Papa around, like I said. Then, when you came back, we could be married in the parlor, like Catherine . . ."

"When I come back there'll be no time for weddings," he told her grimly, putting a savage thrust into his stroke.

Oh, dear, I've only made him cross, Tamsin thought in dismay, but she went on. "Papa isn't really unreasonable, and I don't think . . ."

Shaun stopped rowing and leaned towards her on his oars as the boat tipped slightly in the uneven swell. "Shall I land you and let you sneak back to your precious home and family? You've only to say the word. Then I'll go to the *Resolution* alone and set Charlie's dory adrift as we planned. You'll never see me again— but perhaps, like the rest of the Redmonds, you'll be pleased to be quit of me." His voice was hard, angry.

For a moment Tamsin's heart hammered. *Yes! Yes! Tell him to turn around; leap ashore, run through the wet grass, through the dark halls; toss off these sodden clothes and be warm and safe again in bed beside Adria. Wake to find you've only dreamed the long long hours of lying tense, nightgown over underclothes while Adria slept and the soft night sounds of the house filled your straining ears like thunderclaps; only dreamed the rattle of gravel against your window, the hurried dressing with hands that fumbled and shook, the groping for the packed satchel under the bed and the dark-lantern hidden beyond the bend of the stair rail, the stealthy passage down the stairs and out the creaking door into Shaun's arms.*

Only dreamed this change from the impassioned lover who had pleaded with her earlier, for there on the stone wall in the birch grove on the hill behind the pond Shaun had been tender and eager, his plan had sounded romantically right for them. All else might have been a dream, but not to see Shaun again, not to have his kisses, the thrill of his touch, not to watch that white smile

246

flash out—*that* would be a nightmare from which she would never awaken.

"Oh, no, Shaun. You are my world now." She tried for one of her merry laughs, for Shaun liked her laughing. "Steady as ye go," she commanded.

"Aye, aye, sir." But his voice sounded as taut and unreal as her laugh.

They seemed to have been rowing endlessly and Tamsin knew Shaun had allowed himself no great margin of time, thinking that once they were aboard the *Resolution,* the sooner that schooner was beyond the reach of possible search, the better. She stirred and her voice was scarcely a whisper, "Stop rowing a minute, Shaun." She listened, head on one side, island ears alert.

"Over there." She pointed beyond the larboard oar where water rippled along a ship's side. Shaun caught the sound and swung the dory towards it.

All at once a bow loomed above them; a schooner lay dipping her hawser and lifting it with a running tinkle of drops. Plop-plop-plop, fog dropped upon her deck from boom and mist-soaked rigging. If a watch was on deck he was asleep in the bow shadows. They drifted silently aft along the vessel's side.

Shaun carefully drew his oars in and steadied the dory. "Hssst," he whistled upward and listened. There was no answer, and no amount of staring could fashion the darker loom of a figure out of the fog-sheets.

"Here," Shaun spoke softly to Tamsin. "We'll get aboard, then I'll go aft and wake O'Dwyer. Let me help you up."

In spite of her dragging petticoats Tamsin stepped to the middle-thwart, to the dory's high side, then she grasped the bulwark above her and, with Shaun's help, was up and over and standing on the deck, among a double row of mackerel barrels. She leaned over and lifted the satchel, then Shaun's heavier valise, as he passed them from the dory. Then with a light leap he was beside her, obviously relieved at having finally made the schooner.

Charlie's dory rocked violently and sent wavelets slapping along the schooner's side, wavelets which rebounded to push her away. Still nodding to the impulse from Shaun's leap, she melted into the fog and the night.

Oh, I hope no harm befalls it! Charlie sets so much store by his new dory. The ebb will ground it safe on the point, Tamsin told herself, *and he won't begrudge me the use of it for a start to . . . to happiness.* She peered after the last and disappearing link with home until her eyes stung. She blinked and when she opened her lids she saw that the east was lightening faintly. Under her feet the schooner was winding to the tugs of the beginning ebb.

Suddenly, from what must have been the forecastle hatchway, came a sleepy voice, twisted by the fog. Tamsin did not catch its words, but at them Shaun started and laid his hand swiftly across her mouth. She pressed close to him, spine tingling, absorbing her lover's incomprehensible but mounting alarm. When she moved and raised a hand to brush the fog from her face, Shaun hissed impatiently, "Now, don't start sniveling!" Sniveling, when she was being so brave!

Then he held her close and sent the blood pounding warmly under a strange, swift kiss. He swung her quickly about and, bent double, urged her along to the small boat's fuzzy gray outlines. He raised one corner of the wet tarpaulin and lifted her up into the boat.

"Quiet now," he whispered. "I'll stay out of sight among the barrels until we're clear of the bay and I can approach the captain. Here." He dropped her satchel and then his valise beside her, pressed her down with a hasty hand and drew the tarpaulin back over the boat.

Tamsin flattened as if under a weight. She pulled her cloak about her sodden skirts, wriggled herself into a less painful position, put her head upon her satchel. What a sorry mess she had gotten herself into! Was this fear and furtiveness what a runaway marriage meant? She was sure she would never stop shivering, never feel like Tamsin Redmond again—no, never. Her tears were scalding as they joined the cold fog upon her cheek.

She heard running about the deck, cries as the anchor came

up, creakings and rattlings as the mainsail was hoisted. Once she lifted her head, thinking she had caught a familiar tone, but it had not been Shaun's and she could know no other voice on the *Resolution*.

The ebb was grabbing the keel, the mainsail whispered as it began to draw, water talked lightly along the side, the schooner was dipping as she met the ground swell in the open bay. Tamsin nodded, caught herself, moved an arm, pulled the satchel closer. The long, sleepless hours of waiting for the sound of gravel on a window overtook Tamsin, there on the bottom planks of a none too clean small boat.

Chapter 28

GOLDEN SUNLIGHT FLOODING THROUGH THE WESTERN WINDOW AND a chip supper-fire filled the Nickerson kitchen with the close heat beloved by old bodies. At the hearth Damie tended a fry-pan of crisping mackerel roes; the September mackerel run had started and Philip always relished a mess of roes.

On the couch Sam was finishing his afternoon nap; the red bandanna across his face fluttered, filled and collapsed. His heavy breathing, the small fire's soft crackle, the roes' sizzle, were the only sounds in the kitchen, so that the protesting creak of a board overhead hit strongly on Damie's ear.

What's Philip a-doin' up thyah, this hour o' the day? He's been a-movin' back an' forth, back an' forth, acrost the floor of his room this past hour. Why'd he come back so quick from New Erin an' go upstairs without ary word? She bent to turn a browned roe, still listening. *I'd been a-thinkin' that slow, heavy tread of a sick man had slipped from him durin' the summer, but here 'tis back. Eatin' his heart out fer Tamsin, that's what ails him! I'd like t' box her ears. Little vixen, a-keepin' a good man on pins an' needles.*

She heard Philip coming slowly down the steep back stairs. As he opened the little door and stepped down into the kitchen, she saw he was dressed in his sober schoolmaster clothes, which he hadn't worn since the day he arrived home on the coach. His tall hat was under one arm, his carpetbag in his other hand. He had never looked more mature and never reminded her more strongly of the child Philip.

He stood looking around the kitchen. "Almost," as Damie later told, "as if he knowed he was seein' it fer the last time."

"Philip," she said in dismay, her long fork upright in her raised hand like an exclamation mark of surprise. "You'm never leavin'?"

Without waiting for an answer, she moved to the couch and shook it with her foot. "Sam! Wake up! Sam'll!"

Her husband obediently swung his feet to the floor and sat up, shaking sleep from his eyes. He looked at Philip's face. "Mercy," he whispered and seemed to shrink. "Something's gone wrong with Mercy." He pressed his hands tight upon his knees to stop their shaking.

Philip saw again how the captain had failed recently, how the shock of hair had thinned and stood soft and light upon his head like dandelion seeds, how the color had left his cheeks and new lines formed there. He dreaded adding more lines, yet the old people must be told and he had promised to tell them.

"Not Mercy," he reassured them. "Mercy remains a tower of strength as always. Dan seems more likely to break; he blames himself, for some reason." He added miserably, in explanation, "Tamsin has run away. With that Irishman—that O'Shaughnessy Clark."

"Tamsin run away! What kind of foolishness do you talk?" Damie might have launched into scolding, but she caught sight of Philip's lips, so tightly pressed they drew lines of pain down the sensitive face. "Oh, Philip," she said compassionately. Then with a touch of temper, "Tamsin has no right t' do the likes o' this to you."

Philip answered quickly, "You mustn't blame Tamsin for my

250

folly. I forgot I was only her uncle and teacher." He paused and voiced a trouble unguessed by his foster parents. "I forgot my wife could never know what my family may have been. Now I remember Cynthie Obie drawing her skirts aside from me as a child and her veiled hints about a 'Tar-brush.' "

"Cynthie Obie!" Damie sputtered. "That know-nawthin'! The trash o' Pilot P'int." Anger at Obie's wife gave her back her positiveness. " 'Tar-brush.' Why, you'm only the least mite darker'n my people. Everybuddy who knows ye vows ye must come o' good stock."

Philip's missing background had always nagged Damie's imagination and she had never given up hope of some day unraveling his story, though she held but the single thread. Could she but follow the twists and undo the knots, the strand would lead to a noble Old World family. Of this she had convinced herself —and many others in Prince's Cove.

Captain Sam was not concerned with Philip's ancestry. "I cal'ate you'd best tell us about it, son."

There was little enough to tell. Adria had wakened to find her sister gone and a note under Tamsin's pillow. The note told her parents that she loved Shaun and was running away with him; Captain O'Dwyer would marry them at sea. She begged their forgiveness if she caused them pain; once she was settled in Boston they were all to come and visit her and Shaun.

The written words had seemed impossible to believe, but no Tamsin was to be found. The anchorage had been empty, the *Resolution* and the *Arthenese* both gone long before Tamsin had been missed.

Philip told the old couple of the Irishman's real purpose and of his threats against Dan. Damie was aghast, filled with swift visions of invading armies and a return of the American raiders ("pirates" the shore called them, ignoring the euphemistic "privateers") that had threatened the coast during her childhood. But neither man had thought for Fenians; their fears were with Tamsin.

"And so," Philip concluded, "I'm driving along with the after-

251

noon mail to Hines' Harbor and I'll finish the walk to Yarmouth during the night."

"Yarmouth?" Damie's face was blank.

"I'll catch the packet that sails tomorrow and be in Boston almost as soon as the *Resolution*."

Her face remained empty, her eyes waited for explanation.

He gave it starkly. "Dan fears Clark will not marry Tamsin, since he boasted of his coming wedding to the daughter of a wealthy Irishman. Dan can't leave Mercy now; I'm going to find Tamsin."

He turned his eyes away as realization rushed across Damie's face. She crumpled into her rocker and covered her head with her apron.

Philip said fiercely, "I swear that if I'd guessed the black heart of Clark I'd have choked the life from him—a righteous God would have given me the strength—and thrown him to lie with the fishbones off Long Wharf."

Such words from Philip startled Damie into smoothing her apron back into place and saying, "Ye mustn't talk so, child. 'Vengeance is mine, saith the Lord.' We must leave all in His hands."

To show her his violence did not include her, he lovingly gave her the Cove title. "Mrs. Damie Sam," he said, "if harm comes to Tamsin I'll kill O'Shaughnessy Clark, or he'll kill me trying. Let the Lord take His vengeance then."

In her heart Damie admired him for this, but she remained silent and a bit frightened before the black look on his face.

"I'll be on my way, now that you know," Philip told them in an evener tone.

"Let me git ye a mug o' milk an' a piece o' johnnycake—an' yer roes I was a-cookin' special fer ye," Damie pleaded with resurgent faith in the power of "a bite t' eat."

Philip smiled a refusal.

Captain Sam came wearily to his feet. "You'll be needing money, for traveling and expenses, Philip."

252

"I have some. When it's gone I'll get work. I can care for Tamsin once I find her," he answered proudly.

But Sam went to the bedroom and returned with a purse. When Philip waved it aside he begged it be accepted as a loan.

"Sir, you and Mrs. Nickerson—you are getting along in years, you might need this money and I not here to repay you."

"I'll have security, Philip. The Yarmouth Bank holds money of yours that is still in my name."

It was Philip's turn to look bewildered.

"Have you forgotten your share of the reward for Yappy, that winter v'yage you saved the old *Didamia?*"

"I had forgotten. But you've spent that many times over, all the years you cared for me!"

"I never intended to touch it. I haven't. It's yours and has grown to more than is in that purse. I thought to save you time and trouble in Yarmouth. As for the other—if I've put out a mite of money on you, if ever you owed me aught, and I never thought you did, you're repaying it now with usury. Tamsin is worth . . ." The captain cleared his throat but could not go on.

Philip took the purse without more ado. He went to Damie, sitting stricken in her rocker. He lifted the worn and thin-skinned hand, where the veins showed knotted and purple, and carried it tenderly to his lips. All three in the silent kitchen were filled with memories of the big-eyed boy who, his first night on Grannie's Head, had made that astonishing gesture. When Philip bent and laid his cheek against Damie's withered face, her small black eyes filled with tears and overran.

"You'm a good boy, Philip," she quavered, patting his sleeve, "t' be a-settin' out t' find Tamsin 'spite of everything. Ye allus *was* a good boy. Ye've never give me cause t' do aught but bless the night Sam brung ye home."

Her voice steadied. "An' Tamsin's a good girl. Why, only yestiddy morn when Kiah come off t' the main, she come along t' see her Grammie. I wasn't out o' bed yit, an' she come in an' rubbed her soft little cheek ag'in mine—fresh as the dew on the

253

fleece 'twas—an' kissed me. Teased me a mite about bein' a lazy layabed, told me my cap was squee-gee an' sot it proper."

Her eyes filled again and both men regarded the floor steadily as Damie continued, "The' was no wrong in that curly head, nor in that lovin' heart. Oh, I know what Cynthie Obie and her like will be a-layin' their tongues to." The old face crumbled piteously. "But even if she *has* brung shame on the fambly, Tamsin's a good girl."

"God bless you," Philip said. "Pray for Tamsin—and for me."

He clasped Sam's hand and turned to go.

To Damie's annoyance, she couldn't see him clear as he strode to the entry door, paused for one final look and was gone. *The last time I'll behold him, like enough,* she scolded herself, *and my eyes blinded with tears, old fool that I be.*

Chapter 29

THREE WEEKS AFTER PHILIP'S DEPARTURE, A SMALL ANXIOUS GROUP stood on the point of New Erin, sniffing the fog as it swirled past and watching for the main's outlines to break through. Overnight the wind had pulled in and now, at dawn, the low fog was rolling out to sea across the surface of harbor and bay. The rising sun was still hidden but, overhead, patches of blue sky and high, white clouds reflected its rays.

Serena twisted her apron corner into a tormented ball, smoothed it carefully and rerolled it, unknowing. Dan had thrust a steadying arm through Mercy's and she leaned gratefully against him. A few steps away Adria clung to Kiah's hand.

Mercy broke a long silence as she turned her face to the freshening breeze, "Why, Kiah, you said the wind was northerly."

"It might be a p'int west o' no'th," Kiah admitted shamefacedly. His voice was determinedly controlled, but his big fingers plucked nervously at the outer seams of his pants.

"Don't try to spare me, Kiah," Mercy replied. "It's drawing directly from Grannie's Head and that smoke is from no forest fire; there's hay and timbers in it and the smell of a burning house."

Kiah abandoned well-meant deceit. "Ay-ah, seems so.

"I called Waist'l and the boys and sent 'em off t' help first-along when I smelled it, Mi's Redmond. Certainly." His homely face twisted in earnest denial of neglect. "But from the smoke I cal'ated the damage was done and I'd be no help when I got there."

He couldn't tell her he hadn't wanted to be gone with all the menfolks of the place, lest bad news should prove too much for her and someone had to row for a doctor. Brave, she was, but white as a sheet and her eyes a day's march in her head as she strained them to pierce the fog between her and her old home. He'd give a good deal, himself, to know Captain Sam and Mrs. Damie had come to no harm in the fire.

"Yes, from the smell I think the fire has burnt itself out," Mercy continued. "I know, Kiah, you'd never be one to hang back and there'd be neighbors to do all possible before you and the boys could have reached Grannie's Head.

"But Kiah," her gray eyes were huge in her drawn face as she turned to him pleadingly. "Won't you go now and find out . . . what's happened? The boys won't think of me at home, worrying; they'll stay till the last minute."

There was nothing for him to do but turn towards his skiff, but before he'd taken a dozen steps a cry from Adria brought him about. She was wiping the uncombed hair and the tears from her face with one hand and with the other she was pointing towards the harbor.

Under the growing light the fog coils revealed an alien yellow-ish-brown stain. As the wind hurried them seaward they broke here and there and left between their ragged ends a piece of blue water reflecting the sunlight. Out of one fog whorl into a sunny patch came the nose of a dory.

No one moved or spoke as two oars appeared, fell heavily,

255

grasped the water and pulled the remainder of the dory slowly into the band of clear water that edged New Erin's shore.

Captain Sam was at those leaden oars. Captain Sam, who rowed with such effortless rhythm; Mercy felt tears start, as much from pity as from relief. On the stern thwart, a shawl neatly about her shoulders, her hands primly folded in her lap, sat Damie, so motionless that Mercy was reminded of tales about boats found with bodies frozen where they sat. Mercy was crying, not caring who saw, as she hurried, clinging to Dan's arm, through the dewy grass towards the dock. Kiah scrambled across the beach, ready to seize the dory the instant its keel grated.

They waited in silence as the boat rounded the end of Long Wharf and came neatly in to the landing place. Captain Sam shipped his oars unhurriedly, stepped out into the shallow water and laid hold of the gunwale. But Dan and Kiah left no weight for him to pull. At their tugs, Damie came to life enough to clutch the side and steady herself. She spoke no word and made no movement until Sam splashed out to her and held out his arms. She went to them like a tired child, and he lifted her with the accumulated tenderness of well-nigh fifty wedded years. He set her safe and dry upon the flat-topped landing-rock, only a step or two from the greensward. She stood stock-still until Mercy stepped forward and took her into her arms. "There, there, Ma," she said tenderly. "There, there."

Under the shawl, Damie stood clothed in only her nightgown, warm flannelette and modest as any dress—but for Damie! Beneath its sopping hem, discolored by smoke and ashes and soaked in dory-bilge, showed a pair of Sam's sea boots. Most pathetic of all, perched on her head and tied neatly under her chin, was the second-best bonnet, sacred to visiting.

Dan saw that Mercy had her mother close; he spoke to Captain Sam. "We didn't smell the fire till after the wind changed, Captain Nickerson. The boys set off at once but I felt I shouldn't leave Mercy. God be praised you're both safe and sound."

Captain Sam's voice was dazed and unbelieving. "Burned out. What money I had. Everything but a few broken sticks of furni-

ture tossed out on the grass and what we stand in." His garments, Dan saw, though less incongruous than his wife's, were
scanty.

"The neighbors were good, Dan; they flocked to our aid, but
the fire had great headway before we wakened. Seems to have
started in the barn—always too close to the house—and ran
through the kitchen ell in less time than it takes to tell it. The
well was low and it's a long way to the shore. We could do
nothing."

Dan groaned. Mercy's old home, his first sanctuary on this
shore. New Erin itself would be poorer now that the house on
Grannie's Head was no longer part of its view.

"Every home in Prince's Cove," Sam added with sorrowful
pride, "was thrown open to us. But Damie had made up her
mind and none of the women could budge it. 'We'll be agoin''
to our dorter Mercy's, she's got lots o' room,' she told everybody
who coaxed her. 'Sam will row me on,' she said, 'like he allus
has.'

"As for me, I never expected to have to turn to ary man for
a roof over our heads. But when the time came I found, like
Damie, that I could turn to my own easier than to outsiders."
He paused and straightened his sagging body. "I can still do a
good day's work, Dan, and you say you can always use another
man. I won't be too choosey now, as to who I work with—or
for."

This was too much for Dan. "Captain Nickerson," he cried in
a choked voice, "don't tell me I've made it galling for you to
turn to me in your trouble. Man! Do you think I forget all I
owe you? I'd be proud if I could pay even a fraction of it. It's
been a shame to me, many a time, that I pushed you from New
Erin, the best friend I ever had!" His sincerity and his affection
could not be misread. "Mercy and I will be *proud* to have you
and Mrs. Nickerson in our home." Dan was never nearer being
the man he wanted to be than when he offered refuge to Mercy's
parents.

He promised himself, *I'll break now with Hazelitt Morris and*

257

Dellie Watt Hines. Have New Erin again to myself. He felt freer after making the bare resolution. *Yes, once Mercy is herself again and I can leave the island I'll go to Morris and ask for a settlement.* His mind raced on. *There's been too much business done by word of mouth.* He hastened to answer a doubt that had nagged him lately, *Not that I distrust my own son-in-law, but I'll tell him I'm through and break away.*

He came back from these thoughts to find that Captain Sam had more to say. "I don't come quite empty-handed, Dan." With a ghost of his twisted grin he waved a hand. Above the trees of Narrah the spars of the *Didamia III* showed. "The schooner is yours in return for a home. Neighbors will tow her into Redmond's Harbor on tonight's ebb."

Dan was wise enough not to question this local custom whereby the older generation, when their working days were over, passed on to one of their children what goods they might have accumulated in return for care and security in their old age. "I need her," he said. "I was looking for a good vessel for the Boston trade. But we shouldn't be talking here! Come to the house."

They moved towards the landing rock, where Mercy stood with her arms still about her mother. Damie's frozen calm was broken at last; she was trying to crowd all her fright and loss into words. "I smelled it fust and heared a roar—like a high wind 'twas. I woke Sam but it come anigh bein' too late. I grabbed my bunnit from the drawer—seems all I could git into my head was my bunnit—an' I d'know but what I'd 'a' been roasted to death, only Sam half carried me out."

Mercy asked, "What could have caused the fire? Pa's always so careful about not putting in hay that might heat and he wouldn't be needing a lantern in the stable this time o' year. I can't understand."

"It's easy understood, Mercy. Surely ye ain't fergot Nabby's curse. 'Fire 'n' water,' she said, 'the curse o' fire 'n' water.' *She's* the one that's brung all this upon us. She's in league with the Evil One; 'tis well-knowed he has no lack o' fire."

258

Mercy murmured soothingly but Damie was not to be diverted.

"I ain't the only one as thinks so, either, Mercy. The Cove people this morning was a-talkin' o' puttin' an end t' Nabby's spells once an' fer all. Rightdown ugly, some of 'em was. But ye know yer pa! Nawthin' t' do but he must talk 'em out o' blamin' Nabby. Then a young feller—Theodore Ryder's nephew from Halifax, 'twas—he spoke up an' said about bein' fer a walk last night an' meetin' a tramp jest where the Grannie's Head path turns off the main road. The tramp was a-smokin', so he said. 'Course, tramps *has* sot fire t' many a barn. But," she added stubbornly, "ye can't tell *me* anybuddy but Nabby Nolan was at the back of it."

Damie's tossed her bonnet and moved briskly forward out of Mercy's arms, much like the old Damie despite the bedraggled nightgown.

She'll feel better now she's found somebuddy t' put her tongue to. Certainly, Kiah thought, and nodded his head in relief.

Perhaps tears blinded her, perhaps Sam's sea boots with their unexpected spaces were too much for her tiny feet; in either case, as Damie stepped down from the landing rock to the beach, her left foot slipped and she pitched forward with a sharp cry.

Dan reached her first but she pushed him away and sat up. She moaned and turned a gray face to her husband, now kneeling beside her. "Oh, Sam! On top o' everything, I do declare I've gone an' broke my ankle. I heared the bones scraunch."

Chapter 30

OUT OF THE ATLANTIC NIGHT THE SOUTHWEST FOG-BREEZE DROVE IN over the point, almost obliterating the half dozen scattered torches lashed to Long Wharf spiles-heads. Fog condensed upon the rigging and spars of the schooner made fast at the wharf's end and fell like huge raindrops upon her deck.

Now and then the *Bluebell* speared a gleam of torchlight with her bowsprit and tossed it back into the slack jib, but mostly she nodded contentedly, at rest from the buffeting of the open sea, indifferent to the crew moving about her slippery deck.

In the lee of the warehouse her master stood, his head drawn down between his thickset shoulders, so that his sou'wester's trickle was lost on the misted width of his sea jacket. The light from a smoking torch glinted along his fat jowl and left the rest of his face in shadow.

He spoke without turning his head. "So ye don't like me runnin' in here t' night, eh, Mr. Redmond?"

Such a thin whine should speak for less bulk, Dan Redmond thought, not for the first time. Under his cloak he, too, was hunched against the searching rivulets of coalescent fog, but he showed head and shoulders above his companion. His voice made no attempt to veil his dislike for the present situation—or the man confronting him. "I can't say I do, Captain Hines."

Dellie Watt swore. Though why should Dan Redmond's use of his proper name roil him? From Cape Race to Cape Ann, men called Dellie Watt Hines a slippery bla'guard to his face and worse behind his back. He paid them no heed when some threw up to him incidents like that wrack of twenty years agone, when he had chosen to fill his boat with the rich cargo before taking off the exhausted crew—and had enforced his choice with a show of pistols.

It's still held ag'in me. But how was I t' know the bark would break up afore other boats reached it or I could get back myself? That wrack's what give me my start. Me an' Hazelitt Morris. Young Haze he was then. What's more, us bein' shipmates in that fracas was what got Haze for poor little Nancy.

He never liked to think long of his daughter and her marriage to the man her pa had "got" her. Nor of her death. Now Haze was married to Dan Redmond's beautiful daughter. It tickled Dellie Watt that Haze, from his own tell, had found slob-ice when he had expected leaping flames.

Haze's domestic problems did not concern Dellie Watt. For

260

many years the bodies he loved had been of pine and oak, their finery had been canvas trimmed with rope. Even men who scandalized him worst had to give him credit when it came to handling a vessel, though he had reached the age when most of his kind became shoresmen, if they lived that long.

He had a good bit salted down, too, if it came to that. Why should this furriner, this Irishman the sea had spewed up, be so all-fired high and mighty with him? "Captain Hines" in a tone that said, "I wouldn't wipe my feet on you and I wouldn't be that familiar as to call you 'Dellie Watt.' "

Well, my fine laddie-dah, you'm in fer a jolt afore tonight's over, Dellie Watt presaged silently and grimly.

He turned his back on his companion and rolled heavily towards the wharf end and his vessel.

In and out of the torches' smudged orange his crew moved up the sloping planks that formed an improvised gangway, humpbacked under a keg or deftly footing a cask to its place at the wharf's waist. Under sodden woolen caps their mist-enameled faces momentarily reflected nebulous torch or lantern light, then vanished.

The men slipped on the fog-greased planks, cursed, and regained their footing with a jig-step that gave a false touch of levity. They were chilled and dog-tired but warmed themselves with thoughts of their shares in tonight's profits. Too, they'd known when they signed on that a berth with Dellie Watt meant more than shutting one eye to the Customs and keeping a tight mouth.

Dellie Watt cocked his head towards the harbor. He couldn't see his hand before his face, but fog was tricky for sound. Another craft might have followed the *Bluebell* into Redmond's and be waiting off there. If so, some small noise like water's slap-slap under her stern, or a rope's flogging, should betray her.

He heard only the lazy squeal of the *Bluebell's* sheaves, the groan of her tautening hawsers, the protesting creak of timbers as the vessel rubbed the wharf, the tide's chuckle among the spiles, the plop of fog-drops.

261

To the listening captain these spelled silence.

Though the fog muted nearer sounds, it magnified the roar of the sullen surf on the outer shore; picked it up and pressed it down upon the working men until it became a rushing through their heads, a pounding on their eardrums. They were putting their backs into the job, though; Dellie Watt was convinced of that as he looked about. One huge bustling figure caught his eye. *That hired boy of Redmond's—what's his name—Waits'l—he'll make as able a man as ever I see,* he calculated admiringly.

Satisfied with the men's progress, he blew his nose between blunt fingers and returned to the lee of the warehouse and his interrupted conversation.

"An' suppose ye don't like it!" he resumed as if there had been no break. "What about me? You 'n' Haze, you'm the fine gentlemen with yer white shirts an' dry hands. Yer stuff's landed fer ye, either by me or the Yankee skippers—and nobuddy's agoin' to bother *them* much! Who's out a-playin' hide-an'-go-seek with Sparrow Smith all over the face o' the waters?"

He spat a high thin arc in the general direction of the dock. "Who's a-comin' in past Cape Sable on sech smotherin' nights as this, when a vessel'd fetch up on the keeper's backhouse or run the bloody lighthouse down, fer all ye can see of their fine new beacon? Fur as that goes, how'd ye like t' be making Redmond's about now?"

Dan looked towards the lighthouse, more than ever his pride since the installation of kerosene lamps. A diffused ruby glimmer showed and disappeared in the fog-flaws, though the tower stood within two hundred yards of him. He admitted he'd rather not be running for harbor, wearing the fog's blindfold.

"Now," Dellie Watt went on triumphantly, "ye're bellyachin' about me onloadin' here so often—fer all the's not much goin' ashore t'night. I grant ye the onderstandin' was that ye'd take only every third cargo, besides handlin' what the Gloucester boats dropped. 'But circumstances alter cases,' as the lawyer feller said. Truth o' the matter is, the's no place else *to* land it. The

262

Temp'rance crews is awatchin' Haze's wharf in Hines's Harbor like cats at a mousehole."

Dellie Watt spat out his opinion of Temperance Bands along with a huge cud, reached automatically for his tobacco plug and went on. "Lamb Died Island is out o' the question from now on. They found the well there—most full, too, blast 'em! 'Course, they can't prove who owned the ardent.

"As fer movin' the stuff from here quick like ye want, Haze has got more'n he can handle right now. He's run into a mite o' trouble lately and most of his big Yarmouth customers is playin' it cagey for a time. Ye can lay to it that Haze ain't agoin' t' git caught, no matter what comes or goes.

"It's *me* Sparrow's after right now. An' I can tell ye, he's harder t' shake than the seven-years' itch."

Dan Redmond sounded tired. "So they've found the well on Lamb Died. It won't be long before my hiding places are known, too. There are people in this district who would like to see me caught and disgraced. I think some of my workmen must pass word on to Captain Smith; he's been close on your heels these last few trips."

"Could be so," Dellie Watt admitted.

Dan shifted restlessly. "Already I daren't spot stuff in the mows or icehouse. Lately I've had to use an old cellar under part of my house; but only for wines and fine liquors. I don't like having even that . . ."

He couldn't tell this man he feared it would kill Mercy, frail as she was this summer, if the illicit liquor should be discovered in her home.

Dellie Watt thought resentfully, *You'm above discussin' yer fine home with present company, eh?* He shrugged his heavy shoulders and sneered to himself, *Especially sence yer woman don't know all that goes on and you'm afeared to tell her. More fool you; the's nawthin' like a woman t' diddle men out o' lookin' too hard fer what don't consarn 'em.*

Aloud he retorted impatiently, "Well, hidin' the stuff's supposed t' be your lookout. Surely ye can afford t' pay a fine out

263

o' yer profits, if so be if ye do get caught. As fer the disgrace, as ye call it, what tell o' bringing in a little liquor an' fergettin' t' pay the taxes? You'm not the only one!"

Dan made a weary gesture, his hand white against the black night. "No. And I don't care much for the company in which I find myself."

That's p'inted enough, Dellie Watt told himself bitterly.

Dan continued, "Nobody seemed to mind what the Gloucestermen brought in, but people have changed their attitude towards the traffic. My friends are . . . some of them . . . no longer my friends." His words were acrid on his tongue like the stinging torch-smoke in his nostrils.

Dellie Watt spat again. " 'Tis the same up our way. The's great demand, what with the good times, the militia drillin' ag'in them Fenians and all the political get-togethers to chaw over this here Confederation. But Haze can't do much until the old hens stop cacklin'."

Indignation stretched his thin voice still thinner. "Ye mind Old Peg-leg Lumsden? Well, anyways, his wife's got bit by the Temp'rance bug and when she thinks Peg-leg's apt to go off on one of his tears, what does she do? (This just shows ye that wimmin is takin' to actin' out of all reason!) She hides his leg! Now ain't that horrid?"

Dan stifled a laugh at Lumsden's plight.

Dellie Watt continued, "Every time a pair o' young fools gets t' fightin', or some old rum-pot stivers t' the poorhouse, them Temp'rance Sassieties holds a meetin'. Now they tell me the priest at St. Joseph's is after the young men there, layin' into the evils of drink. Not that we ever sold much to the French. But it shows which way the wind is blowin'."

Any inclination to laugh had left Dan before the end of Dellie Watt's recital. He'd long realized the wind was strengthening against the liquor traffic.

A man approached out of the darkness. "S'all out, Cap'n."

Dellie Watt moved away and, once out of the building's lee,

he stopped and sniffed. "The wind's backin' in a'ready, you," he flung over his shoulder to Dan. "We'll hafta hustle."

He raised his voice, "To the head of the wharf with it, b'ys; an' step lively."

Dan picked up a lantern as Dellie Watt seized a flare and together they turned towards the wharfhead. Here barrels, some empty, some heavy with salted fish, lined both sides of the wharf, leaving only a narrow passageway.

"Now, men," Dan said quietly, "some of these barrels must be moved. Pile the empties here, the full ones there."

The men spun the barrels away to reveal a trap door, some five feet square, set in the wharf planks. They swung it up and the fog eddied and settled into the wide black pit beneath it. When a lantern was suspended from a projecting spike, the "well," already containing some kegs and demijohns, was seen to be a board-lined cavity set above tide-line and running back under the greensward at the wharfhead. None of the men who commented on its perfect disguise gave a thought to how Dan Redmond had weakened the structure of his wharf to provide this hiding place.

A wiry man immediately leaped into the well and called, "Lower away." In no time the casks and kegs were stored, the trap closed and hidden under the rows of barrels with a narrow walk between.

Dellie Watt beckoned Dan with a heavy air of secrecy; the two walked to the schooner's side and paused, with the short skipper peering up into his partner's face. "Afore we cast off the's suthin' else. An' *you* ain't a-goin' t' like it." His truculence hid misgiving and a hint of reluctance.

Dan was weary of the night's work and of his companion. "Well, let's have it," he replied shortly.

"The long an' short of it is—I want ye t' hide a man."

"Hide a man! Why should I hide a man? And what has he done that he needs hiding?"

Dellie Watt gained confidence; Dan Redmond had not refused

point-blank. "Why, he ain't done nawthin', so t' speak. The Excise men found him 'dispensin' illegal licker.' Ha! Ha! you." Dellie Watt's high voice reached a new pitch but he thought better of a contemplated poke in the ribs to point the joke for Dan. He continued his explanation. "They plan t' have him up before the magistrate next week. He swears if we don't git him to the States first, he'll blab all he knows."

He held his breath. *The Lord knows that yarn's thin enough to see through! But the way he's feelin' Dan Redmond 'd never help if he suspicioned the truth. Now, if I can get away quick an' not give him time fer questions . . .*

"Where is this man? One of these?" Dan gestured towards the grouped crew, awaiting orders.

"No. He's on the *Bluebell*. I'm t' give him the word."

"What's his name?"

"Josiah Barry."

"I never heard of him."

That's jest as well fer me, Dellie Watt congratulated himself. Aloud he said casually, "Likely not. He belongs on Cape White. Yesterday as we came along by he rowed off t' the *Bluebell* with his story. He sailed with me a v'yage or two; he's helped land cargoes at Hines's Harbor and at Lamb Died. He knows too much. We *got* t' hide him."

"But why should *I* hide him? He can swear to nothing about New Erin. You're asking me to put myself in his power just as you and Haze have apparently. Let one of you look after him."

"You ain't fool enough t' think that if we git caught that yo'm a-gittin' off! Haze himself—son-in-law or not—would swear to your share in the business. And more. Fur as that goes, what's t' prevent me takin' my oath 'twas you, and only you, who'd hired me? Haze'd make it worth my while . . ."

His threatening voice trailed off and before Dan could speak for the sick anger that rose in him, Dellie Watt went on in a changed tone, "No, in fer a penny, in fer a pound. After all! It ain't sech a great thing we'm askin'. The' must be hidin' places galore on New Erin. You can slip him onto the first Gloucesterman that makes harbor, nobuddy the wiser. Then Sparrow and his crew can look till they're cross-eyed."

He whistled twice and then again. A dim figure stepped from the schooner to the wharf, an undersized, furtive figure with the reek of stale rum revoltingly strong about it.

Dellie Watt turned to his men in a great bustle to be away. "Cast off lively, there. H'ist the mains'l, we'll work her into the bay an' be outside before the fog's gone.

"Good night t' ye, Mr. Dan Redmond. See that Josiah don't talk t' nobuddy. An' git him off yer hands first chance."

While he was speaking the lines had been deftly slipped off the spile-heads and coiled down aboard, the last of the crew had stepped from the wharf. The schooner now began to sag away in answer to the tide. The captain jumped to the deck as lightly as a man half his age and size. The *Bluebell* swung slowly into the foggy night. Muffled voices, the slap of wet sails and the creak of their hoisting came back to the shadows on Long Wharf.

Though the fog was still heavy, the wind plainly had shifted and was blowing off the land; already a few pale stars pierced the mist overhead. Soon the last of the obscuring fog would be blown out to sea and there remained work to be done under its cover.

Brusquely Dan told the disgusting Josiah, "Come along. I'll find you a hiding place."

He turned to Waitstill. "Now, my boy," he said, trying to put into his voice a heartiness he could not feel. The lad must be almost dead on his feet; his loyalty, which Dan had hitherto taken as a compliment and a bolster to his pride, seemed suddenly an accusation. "We've only these few cases of wine to stow away. But we must be quiet, you know. Fetch the wheelbarrow."

Dan followed as Waitstill trundled the load along the grassy path from the wharf to the front door of the house. Josiah slipped like a noisome shadow behind him. Thank goodness Captain Nickerson and his wife had been given Serena's bedroom in the kitchen ell. The thought of the old people and how they would judge the night's work reminded Dan of his resolution to break with his partners—a resolution he had had no opportunity to carry out tonight. Instead he had bound himself to them more closely than ever.

Once inside the house, the three moved silently, their feet muffled by the rich carpet of the wide front hall. Dan led the way, lantern in hand, to the jog under the stairs, raised one end of the carpet and rolled it back from a trap door which in turn revealed stone steps leading into black depths. The safest place on the island for illicit goods, for after more than twenty years who would remember that the front of the big Redmond house had once been a cottage and its present hall a kitchen with the usual cellar under a trap door?

When Waitstill finally closed the trap and straightened up, Dan told him, "Get some rest now. You've worked hard. Don't be in a hurry to get up in the morning. Kiah and the boys can manage. Good night, Waitstill."

Then he beckoned to the shifty-eyed Josiah, who had remained in the shadows. "Follow me," he said shortly, and turned up the broad stair, holding the lantern low and moving cautiously. His wet boots left dark stains on the fine stair-runner and the stench of foul breath and bilge-saturated clothes mounted behind him.

The railed stairs ended in a square upper hall, an open room with furniture grouped along three sides of it. Dan stopped short at the top step and his heart leapt to his throat. But that highwayman's figure with a light partially hidden in the skirts of a long cloak, with its air of stealth and evil secrecy, was himself. *That then, is Dan Redmond, proud owner of New Erin,* he thought with weary distaste. He went on, motioning again for silence, for behind the door to the right little Adria lay asleep.

The doorway leading to the other portion of the chamber was closed by a pair of heavy, red curtains. He pushed the deep folds aside and listened. Nothing stirred. He stepped then into a narrow passage with closed doors on either side, his unwelcome guest on his heels; he opened the second door on his right and set the lantern on a chair. Both men stood and looked about them in the close air of a long-shut room.

A boy's room; pants hung on the wooden pegs behind the door;

the model of a top-rigged schooner sat on a highboy, the tiny sails time-darkened. The bed was empty, the patchwork quilts long undisturbed.

This was a hateful thing Dan was about to do, but even as Dellie Watt's ugly threats had been urging this wretch upon New Erin, Dan's mind had gone to Patrick's empty room and his Secret Place.

How pleased eight-year-old Patrick had been to have for his own the bedroom with the boy-sized door, cut low in the boarded wall and leading into one of the lost spaces resulting from the joining of houses that differed in height and construction. Under the roof's steep slant, it was barely three feet wide though it ran the width of the bedroom: a stuffy little hole that only childhood's magic could have made intriguing. With the low door hidden behind the bed, the space had become a repository for Patrick's treasures and a retreat for boyish dreaming. His Secret Place, though known to all the household.

The lantern showed the cramped recess to be empty of all but dust and cobwebs. Josiah Barry, wiping his nose on his hand, declared it was roomy enough for him; he didn't plan to be standing much; he was going to catch up on his sleep.

Dan left the room and came back with a quilt for Josiah. "Stay hid till you hear me speak. Leave the little door ajar for air, but be sure to shut it—quietly—if you hear anyone approaching," he adjured in parting. "I'll bring you food and drink tomorrow as the chance occurs, but we may have to wait until night for you to stretch your legs. By then there should be a vessel in the harbor."

The other nodded without meeting Dan's eyes.

Dan pushed the bed back into place; straightened the mat, and left his son's room. By the fuzzy gray of predawn he made his way to the cot in his office, where he hoped to catch a nap before the family stirred.

He felt spent after the day's work and harassed by a sense of dissatisfaction that of late seldom left him. How had he let himself become involved with such a man as Dellie Watt? Dan Redmond, who had hoped to found a respected family on New Erin;

who loved his wife and hated to hurt her pride in him? By hiding from Mercy all knowledge of his true business with Hazelitt Morris and Dellie Watt Hines, he had barred himself from his accustomed refuge in Mercy's tenderness, her brave serenity. To be able to turn to her now with his mounting difficulties would be like making harbor before a rising gale.

Chapter 31

ADRIA WOKE TO THE DARK NIGHT SUDDENLY AND COMPLETELY, HER heart pounding fit to shake the bed to pieces. She pushed the smothering quilt off her chest and turned upon her side to escape the engulfing feather bed. The knotted ropes beneath it squeaked alarmingly. She huddled down into the feathers again and listened achingly to catch a repetition of the sound that had broken her sleep.

What was that? A human scream out of the night? Or a shriek from the stormy petrels that came out of their fetid nests in the bank to ride the fog-breezes, chattering and cackling their crazy laughter till daybreak?

Was that her heart pounding or a muffled thump from the wharf? Was that a faint flicker thrown by a torch at the wharf-head or one of those ghostly lights of which Gramma Damie and Serena told so many tales? Both sound and light were soft distortions with fuzzy edges, her ear and eye could not catch and classify them.

Adria had wakened on other nights to strange noises, which she had come to accept with the resignation of a twelve-year-old in an adult world. Bit by overheard bit of talk she had pieced out their explanation. Not a comprehensive or reassuring explanation, however; always when she heard the stealthy sounds from the front hall she cowered under her covers until they had ceased. Not that the noises ever threatened *her,* for Papa's was one of the muted voices, his steps sounded along the hall with the others.

Adria loved open things: the unclouded sky, the wide sea, the hearts of daisies lifting to the sun, people who looked at her straight and said what they meant. She loved New Erin, of course, but there was no denying it held an ugly secret, tied up with drunken men and making money. If hiding smuggled liquor held no wrong (as Will claimed), why did it need the double screen of fog and night? Why must it never be mentioned to Mamma?

Adria suddenly realized that a contraband cargo could not be the explanation of her present wakefulness. It was only last night she had lain listening to the half-heard, half-imagined sounds from the hall, the longed-for opening of the front door, the in-rush of the sea's voice, the deeper silence after the door closed, signifying that the night's work was over. She had fallen asleep instantly. Long weeks usually separated the landings of illicit cargoes, but here she was, wakened the very next night, by a fur-tive sound.

There it was again! It didn't come from the downstairs hall, either. Creak. It sounded near. Terrifyingly near. Will and Charlie slept at the far end of the hall; it would be useless to call out to them, even if she could force a scream through her tightened throat. She wished Tamsin were beside her, but Tamsin was gone from their shared bedroom—gone from New Erin.

Suddenly Adria wanted her mother desperately. A long way lay between her and her parents' bedroom; could she find courage to creep downstairs and through the front hall that held fright-ening shadows even on a sunny day? Would she dare pass the trap door under the stairs, pass the Secret Cellar? Yet, once through the hall she'd be in the music room next her mother's bedroom; safe from whatever-it-was that creaked and soughed through the upper chamber.

She lifted herself on an elbow. Suppose something was behind the red curtains, just beyond her door. It always took courage to pass through the shifting folds of the draperies separating the open front hall from the narrow, windowless passage beyond. The

271

red curtains might be making that slithery rustle, might be writhing away from the opening they guarded, might soon be across her door!

That settled it. Holding her breath, she stepped out of bed. The painted floor was cold under her bare feet, but it was solid and familiar. She lifted the door latch, striving to make no sound; though it grated harshly against the silence, nothing stirred. She drew a long breath, straining her eyes towards the curtains' place. She couldn't see them, but she could almost feel them—feel them waiting to smother her in their woolly, boneless embrace.

She whirled about to face the stair well's upward pressing blackness and felt her stomach go queasy.

Rubbing the sweat from her palms upon the front of her nightgown, she forced her feet to take the first step down. Safely. She pressed close against the inner wall, away from the open bannisters and went down from broad tread to broad tread, her feet making no whisper through the runner's pile. She paused on each step to listen, hearing only her heart. The night pressed upon her, malignant and soft—soft as feathers that floated away when she put out her hand, but that clung to her tight throat and to her weighted legs.

Not until she had turned the newel post and gained the opposite wall did she think that whatever-it-was might not be behind her; might be in the front hall, between her and her mother. She stopped and held her breath again. Perhaps she should turn back. The remembered warmth of her bed drew her. But suppose It was waiting at the stair top. Suppose It had crept into her room, was lurking under her bed—*in* her bed! No, she couldn't go back.

She put one hand over her mouth to stifle the cries she could taste there, hot and ready to pour out. The other hand she kept along the wall, feeling her way with it and with her feet along the carpet. She'd never get anywhere this way; and suddenly she felt a need for haste. She'd gather up her nightgown and *run!* Run for the door at the hall's end, past the blackest shadows under the stairs' slope. She wouldn't even turn her head towards the trap door of the Secret Cellar.

She took the hand from the wall, the hand from her mouth, to snatch both sides of her nightgown; she lifted them high and took a long, free step forward.

Before her eyes the trap door was rising! A thread of light along its edge widened into a pale wedge as the door came slowly, soundlessly, up and back. Above the faint must of carpet, the dankness of a mud cellar and moldy straw packing that rose, liquor-laden breath was all at once strong.

Adria could not lift a hand to cover her mouth again or to brush the tumbled hair from her eyes. Starkly rooted, she awaited the dreadful apparition that must rise before her.

In the angle of the rising door a hand appeared, holding a candle stump. Then a face, loosened and emptied by drink. The feeble light flickered along the hand's black hairs, across a stubbled, hollowed face, was reflected from two beady eyes. A man, with bits of straw and cobweb clinging to his foul clothes, rose gradually, emerged completely.

He wiped a dripping nose upon a stringy cuff and, without glancing around, lowered the door with a dull thud. The candle wavered in the puff from the closing door; Adria thought she *must* cry out, but a second hand curved fumblingly about the flame until it steadied, then dropped to pat a pocket where a bottle bulged.

The man swung about then and caught sight of Adria, pale and wraithlike as any ghost with her fear-blanched face above her full white nightgown. His features, which had knotted into a scowling tightness, all at once went slack with superstitious horror. Before they could reassemble themselves in a different cast, the candle fell, sputtered and went out. There was a smell of scorching carpet, and utter darkness.

The screams came pouring out, breaking the horrible stillness. Adria found her legs and darted forward in blind necessity to reach the door. She heard a startled oath, felt a fetid breath, smelt a dirty hand as it grabbed. It grasped her nightcap, but, like her sunbonnets, Adria's nightcaps usually dangled untied; this one slid from her head.

She was through the door, had slammed it shut, was stumbling through the music room while screams came, not from her aching throat, it seemed, but (part of the harrowing night) were thrown against her from the enclosing walls, down upon her from the low ceiling, up from the floor.

She heard the door of her parents' room open and her father's alarmed tones, "Adria, Adria. What is it? What has happened?"

She was clinging to him and sobbing herself empty of fright, shivering in delicious safety against his nightshirt, which smelt thickly of sleep and bed. She had never known that such gentleness and strength lay in her father's arms, never heard his voice reveal such love for any but Mamma. He drew her through the door, to the bedside, took her upon his knee and folded her close.

Mercy had wakened to the first scream of terror and the slammed door, but for several seconds her mind refused to name what had roused her. The bed jumped as Dan left it; she heard his feet hit the floor and his hand at the latch.

Now she raised herself awkwardly and lit the candle on the bedside chair. Adria, the least timid of her daughters, was obviously sick with fright. Dan was comforting her. "What startled you, darling? Tell Papa. A nightmare? A noise? The wind and the creaking house make strange sounds at night sometimes, I know, but they won't harm you." Mercy lay back, glad to let her heart pound itself into order, glad to let Dan, for once, comfort one of the children.

Dan's voice was calm but his soul was sick as he remembered the proximity of Josiah's hiding place to Adria's bedroom; dreading to learn what had sent his daughter shrieking through the house; realizing suddenly that the last of his little girls was no longer a child. If harm had come to her! If the man had been in her bedroom! Blast Dellie Watt Hines. Blast Haze Morris. Most profoundly of all, blast Dan Redmond, who would never listen but must go his own way if it broke his wife's heart and sent his child out of her senses.

When Adria's sobs had lessened Dan questioned her gently,

anxious not to disturb her, but equally anxious to find out the cause of her fright.

It was a relief to hear of the noises, of the terror-stricken walk down the stairs, of the man in the hall. "I never thought you hid *men* in the Secret Cellar, Papa." Even at this juncture Adria remembered to whisper this for her father's ear alone.

The Secret Cellar! Adria knew of his hidden cache. Little Adria. Then every one of the children knew. What a fool he had been to think otherwise! What a fool not to know that Josiah Barry must have seen the wines and brandies stored in the old cellar, not to realize what they would mean to such a man after a long day in the cramped recess. Apparently Josiah, passing through the upper hall on his way for a drink, had awakened Adria.

She was repeating, "And, Papa, there was this horrible . . . smelly man, a black stranger, with a stump of a candle in his hand . . ."

Mercy interrupted with troubled patience. "But, Adria child, there wouldn't be a *stranger* in the front hall. One of the boys sleep walking perhaps, though I never knew either of them . . . Black, you say? Waits'l's black enough when he misses shaving. Dan, could it have been Waits'l roaming the house for some queer reason?" She answered herself, "No, Waits'l's would never frighten Adria."

Dan's reply was heavy. "It wasn't Waitstill, Mercy."

"Now, Adria, you must crawl in bed beside Mamma." He lifted her gently though she still clung to him. Then he drew the quilts over her with continuing tenderness. "You must lie still, acushla, and not cry any more. That would bother Mamma and she must get her rest. See, the morning is almost here."

True enough, the window showed a faint gray and, opposite it, the looking glass glimmered. Mercy blew out the candle.

Dan hastened into his trousers and coat, stooped to pat Adria's cheek and left the room.

Mercy reached over and took her daughter's hand. "Cold as a

clam," she scolded tenderly and tucked it under the covers. The child within her would not let her take Adria in her arms, but she said, "Put your feet on mine, we'll soon have you warm. Don't fret any more now, dear; things that seem black at night always brighten in the morning."

After a short silence Adria demanded in a voice still taut from recent terror, "Mamma, do you know about the Secret Cellar under the front stairs."

Not until later years could Adria appreciate the love that kept her mother's voice flowing evenly that night, that hid the restlessness and discomfort of her tired mind and swollen body.

"Well, I never thought it a 'secret' cellar, but many's the time I went up and down its stone steps."

"You *did?* That horrid place! Why?"

"Why? To put butter in the crock, to bring up potatoes and turnips. Why does anyone go down cellar?" Mercy was puzzled at the cellar's part in her daughter's fright. She told Adria then of the cramped cellar under the early kitchen, of how the big house had robbed cottage after cottage from New Erin's fields and left their cellars open to the sun.

Adria knew those cuplike hollows with their moss-faced walls where fern and raspberry bushes sprouted from the crevices. She tried to imagine the Secret Cellar with the front hall lifted from it (like the lid off a kettle) and lined by the infinitely tender and tiny plants that first appear from drifted soil and seed. Almost before she could pull the quilt over her shoulder she was asleep.

But Mercy lay awake. Dan had been nearly as frightened as Adria at tonight's happening, yet he had hidden the cause of his fear from her, his wife. *If I can find strength to go on until this child is born—and if I am spared,* she promised herself, wearily, *when I'm up and around again, I'll look into this—and other things.*

Her burdened body refused to make itself comfortable, the child within her beat upon its confining walls. She lay, breathing sharply and shallowly, and watched the dawn run gray fingers over the room's furnishings.

Chapter 32

On Long Wharf a few hours later Dan shrugged his coat into place across his shoulders, glanced down to see that his trouser leg was neatly strapped under the instep of his polished boot; well-groomed and punctilious, he was waiting to greet an arrival at New Erin.

Yet under his calm Dan was relieved that his father-in-law was already aboard the *Didamia,* a hundred yards offshore; that the boys had gone skimming down the harbor on some errand of their own. Glad, too, that this was the season when local boats caught pollack for their own winter use; the New Erin wharf would be empty of splitters and salters when the *Beagle* docked.

The sighting of the *Beagle* had been a relief. Better to have things over with and, no matter what the night's fears, his spirits could not fail to rise on such a morning.

The fog was gone; not a breath of it diluted the wine-sweet air, not a wisp blurred the horizon. At the mouth of the dancing blue harbor the lighthouse tower gleamed white, its landward window giving back the morning sun in a beam that shamed the small lamps' nightly efforts.

In the lighthouse, at least, Dan could take pride. He could swear to his conscience that although he had believed its erection would aid his business, yet he would have built it had he known that every craft to set its course by the white tower and the red lamps would pass Redmond's to take their trade elsewhere.

He turned to look across the dock. On Short Wharf Kiah's lank figure was disappearing through the barrel shop's open door. *Thank Heaven for Kiah!* Dan thought with warm affection.

Kiah, who had steadfastly refused to soil his hands with "Hazelitt Morris's gurry," as he called the smuggled liquor, but whose loyalty to the Redmonds would drive him to protect Dan from the consequences of his folly, now that he knew the latest difficulties.

Dan was too tense to relax in the quasi relief that often accompanies the postponement of a disagreeable issue; again he turned impatiently towards the harbor mouth. There at last was the *Beagle* coming about close under the point. *She's a pretty thing,* Dan admitted, *no matter what trouble she's bringing me. And devil take it, I like her master!*

Dan considered Sparrow Smith a man of queer and strait-laced notions, but one who wore honesty and his purpose as simply as his sea clothes. Any dealer in liquor was ripe for the punishing hand of the Lord (Sparrow had no foggy ideas as to *that!*), yet Dan often felt that the *Beagle's* skipper returned his liking. Not that Sparrow would hold his fire because of liking; drink was his mortal enemy and he pursued it relentlessly, let all else stand from under.

The tide was low so that, when the *Beagle* came neatly across the wharf end, her deck was several feet below the planking level. Dan caught the tossed-up lines, fore and aft, and dropped them about the spiles. The ropes groaned, drawing the vessel close, while Dan nodded down at the crew with the careless smile and the air of welcome which he knew always disarmed and angered Sparrow Smith.

"Like we was b'ys playin' a game," the puzzled and forthright skipper had muttered more than once. Today he swung himself up over a crosspiece and, removing a stubby pipe from his mouth, said soberly, "G'day, Mr. Redmond."

Dan forced the customary heartiness into his voice. "Good day, Captain Smith, a splendid morning for a sail. I take it you're hot on the trail of the demon rum?"

"Well, yes an' no," Sparrow snipped his words off neatly between nose and chin. "Man dear, ye can be sure I'll not overlook a single illicit bottle I might come across. An' the more the merrier. But this mornin' I'm-a-seekin' too fer a crim-in-al."

Dan hoped his face looked as stiff as it felt and so would not betray him. The taint of Josiah Barry was almost palpable in the morning air. "Indeed, may I ask what criminal? and why you're seeking him on New Erin?"

278

"Yes, ye can ask. An' I can answer. I'm a-lookin' fer Josiah Barry. That's who. Why? That's a dog with a longer tail."

As the captain's words fell in neatly cut lengths of the planks between them, Dan was conscious of his wet palms and the tight band of his cap.

"Because . . . Well, night before last the Customs Officer went to Cape White to seize a shipment of licker. He was backed by men o' the Temp'rance Division. They knowed when it was t' be landed and who by. By yer friend, Dellie Watt Hines. The receivers of it was a-waitin' by the waterside and, sure enough, in come the *Bluebell's* boat, deep-laden. She'd scarce grounded when out jumped the Customs Officer from the trees and ordered everyone to halt in the name o' the law."

Dan listened, trying to hide surprise; Dellie Watt had made no mention of this encounter.

Sparrow continued, "The *Bluebell's* crew was taken aback; then they was all fer gettin' aboard ship. The others, they was all fer holdin' 'em, once they'd got their hands on the slippery buggers. In the dark the' was a few blows give an' took. Then first thing anybuddy knowed, young Ensign Swain was a-groanin' on the sand. With a knife in his ribs."

The skipper had been addressing the spile before him, the stem of his pipe, the harbor waters. Now his eyes darted to Dan's face.

Dan felt them pierce like . . . like a knife in the ribs. He licked his lips, suddenly dry. "I hope . . . I trust the young man was not seriously hurt."

"The doctor gives him a chance in a hundred," the other cut off grimly. "One thing, Ensign's blood ain't never been contamin-ated by alcohol, that poison of the Evil One." Sparrow nodded his head in qualified hopefulness.

"If it was dark, as you say, and a number of men milling around, how can you know who struck the blow?" Dan protested, ignoring Sparrow's comments.

"Here's how. The Cape Whiters, they'd thought it fun to diddle the Customs, but they hadn't counted on no sech thing as stabbin' a neighbor. So yestiddy they went in a body to the Magistrate,

279

ready to take their punishment. They swore they'd noan of them had a knife in their hands and that every man who'd been on the beach was there and accounted fer. All, that is, but Josiah. He's reckoned an ugly-tempered man, especially when under the influence, an' knowed t' have drawed a knife more'n once."

This was the man I hid under my roof, Dan told himself, ashamed.

"Some swore they'd see Josiah jump aboard the *Bluebell's* boat when it put off, water flyin'. After the fuddle at Cape White, Dellie Watt would hafta find another place for his a-bom-in-able cargo." The skipper didn't look at Dan as he said this, but he might as well have done so. "Barry wasn't aboard the *Bluebell* yestiddy morning when we searched her in Hines's Harbor. Lots of other things wasn't aboard either, Mr. Redmond, but no need t' tell ye about *them.*"

Sparrow had been rolling tobacco in his hands, he stuffed it into his pipe and scratched a match.

"Then last night the' was talk around. The's allus talk, t' be sure, but this come quite straight. About a man bein' landed at night on New Erin."

The match found the tamped tobacco and blue smoke rose. Dan recalled that Waitstill had been off the main yesterday. Someone had pumped him—without his realizing it; for Waitstill would never have betrayed Dan Redmond if the boy's mind matched his splendid body.

Word had spread swiftly. By now the whole shore must be buzzing against Dan Redmond. What was Sparrow Smith thinking? The *Beagle's* crew? Surely they couldn't believe he'd harbor a felon! Yet what were they to think if a man was known by the company he kept?

He saw now how far he had come and on what road.

Though he had meant to carry off today's encounter with his usual insouciance, he heard himself blurting, "Captain Smith, the man is not here."

An angry sliding of boots and clearing of throats sounded from the *Beagle's* deck and Sparrow turned to face him squarely. "I was swore in, Mr. Redmond, t' find and arrest Josiah."

"I've no wish to hinder you, Captain Smith. Believe me. The man was landed here, as my hired boy disclosed." He saw that he had guessed correctly the "talk's" source.

He hesitated. Although his partner's had no doubt laughed at him last night for a gullible fool, he couldn't betray them. He swallowed his anger, bilious-tasting at the back of his throat. "I was told the man was wanted as a witness against . . . men I know. I was merely to get him aboard an American. Captain Smith, had I guessed the truth . . . No matter what you think of some of the things I've done, you must know I wouldn't shelter a man who had knifed another!"

The captain said nothing. No sound came from the deck below. Dan went on quickly, "I hid him and no Yankee vessel made harbor. Then this morning before dawn I . . ." (he mustn't give the gossips thread for their looms lest they weave a fabric about little Adria that might entangle her good name forever) ". . . I found him wandering about the house."

"Lookin' fer a drink o' *water,* most like," a cynical voice tossed up from the *Beagle's* deck.

Dan ignored the interruption. *"This* is what matters to you, Captain Smith. Just at dawn I put Josiah Barry into a dory, gave him a sail and a water jug, and I pushed him off into the fog."

He shied from the memory of the figure cringing on the center thwart, for he'd been rougher than necessary, perhaps, but as he'd sent the dory rocking clear his anger had still been blazing. "Go," he'd said. "Go where you please, so long as it's out of my sight. Tell what you like. But if I ever catch your feet fouling New Erin again. I'll put you where you'll frighten no more children."

Sparrow's sharp eyes were watching him. "Perhaps," Dan said, "you sighted a dory—a new one, riding light, and freshly painted yellow."

The other shook his head. "No, we never."

Dan realized the other thought him lying—"yarnin'"—to throw them off the scent. He sickened at his old pride in outwitting Sparrow, in nonplusing him without recourse to actual falsehood.

Sparrow was speaking. "Man dear, if what ye say be true, ye've aided a crim-in-al to escape the law. True or not," he knocked

281

out his pipe as a sign that talking was over, "I'm duty bound t' search yer place."

He brought a folded paper from his wide coat pocket. "This here's a warrant, Mr. Redmond, fer me t' search boats, buildin's and house. If Josiah's here I mean t' rout him out and ye must take the consequences. Likewise if I find contraband anywhere-somever.

"Fer yer wife's sake I've never put foot inside the house door. I figgered you wouldn't force sech stuff into yer home ag'in yer wife's wishes, an' M'is Redmond is knowed far an' wide as a real good woman. The opinion is that she don't know what's goin' on."

"That's the truth of the matter," Dan replied earnestly. "She doesn't know. She is far from well. I dread what a search . . ."

"Man dear, ye should 'a' thought o' that before this late date," Sparrow reminded him. "Folks is riled up an' determined. Feelin' has been agrowin' ag'inst smugglin' and this fracas with Josiah has brung it to a head. If young Ensign dies . . . Aye-ah, I gotta look. Ye'll see I've brung plenty o' help, too."

He stepped to the stringer. "Come ashore, b'ys."

Half a dozen men scrambled up on the wharf. Some of their faces were faintly familiar to Dan, others completely strange. One or two grinned good-naturedly, but most of them were solemnly bent upon doing their duty.

They did it thoroughly, ransacking the warehouse, the fish stores, barrel shop, sail loft and icehouse, haymows, outbuildings. They borrowed lanterns and swung back the slanting outside doors of the new cellar. They inspected its walls and tried for loose stones so perseveringly that Dan suspected they had had word of a cellar hiding place. But they desisted at last and climbed into the sunlight again.

Then there was nothing left to search but the dwelling. Dan would have given New Erin itself for that stormy spring evening again and the right to say to Dellie Watt's jeering green eyes and his plausible tongue, "I have no place for your lawless cargo." Instead he must lead these men into Mercy's home.

Mercy and Serena were baking and both women looked up sharply as a group of strangers crossed before the window and the sound of voices approached the door.

Mercy's first thought was of a vessel gone down and a crew making the safety of New Erin. Her mind flew to the bread box, the cooky crock, the pantry shelves, gauging their contents and their spending power against hungry men. Almost she moved to set the teapot down, but was held back by something—perhaps her reluctancy to face even needy men this morning, with her unwieldy body and her leaden heart. She straightened the yoke of her apron and the folds that fell from it; they could not hide but they could soften the awkward lines of her figure. She moved to put the table between her and the opening door.

She saw Dan step ahead as the men moved into the kitchen, crowding back upon one another with much wiping of heavy boots, but pushed forward by those behind. In front was a wizened man whom Dan introduced as Captain Smith. At his name Mercy knew why these men were in her house.

The leader put out a work-distorted hand and murmured, "Pleased t' make yer acquaintance, Mi's Redmond." Mercy noted how his sharp chin and nose cut off his words.

"A fine morning on the water, Captain Smith." Mercy gave him a serene greeting, but Dan, seeing the effort in the bravely held figure, the blue-shadowed eyes and the face drawn by weariness and lost sleep, crossed to her and put his shoulder against hers.

Behind their captain the men looked at the floor, at the ceiling, anywhere but at the white-faced woman before them, until in relief they could fasten their eyes upon Sparrow as he spoke.

"Mi's Redmond, I'd give a heap if I didn't hafta do this day's work. Or, sence it must be done, if you didn't hafta know about it." He stopped and swallowed; the nose and chin barely escaped collision. "I've come t' search this house fer . . . fer smuggled spirits. And—and—sech. Man dear, Mi's Redmond, it's my *duty*. I gotta do it."

At this Serena, who had been eying the intruders much as a cat eyes a pack of strange dogs, tossed her head with an audible sniff and turned to the stove. Her opinion of such doings was expressed and punctuated by the banging of iron pots and pans, the vicious rattling of stove lids, and no listener missed her meaning though they strove to ignore it.

Dan felt Mercy sway, but she came swiftly upright and laid her hands along the edge of the table before her. She bowed her head slightly in Sparrow's direction, as if to ease his tortured embarrassment. "We all have hard duties to perform sometimes, Captain Smith. It won't interfere if we women go about getting dinner ready?"

There could be no hiding place in the clean, bare kitchen; the men turned up the boxed-in stairway to the open kitchen chamber with relief in every clumping footstep. Captain Smith spoke to Dan. "Mr. Redmond, I'd like ye to come with us t' see that noan o' my men don't touch aught they shouldn't." Dan left Mercy without meeting her eyes.

As the sounds of chests being dragged over the floor, bunks being thumped, floorboards lifted, came from overhead Mercy turned to Adria, who stood in a trance by the pan of soapy water and dirty cooking dishes. "Dry your hands, dear," Mercy told her, striving for an ordinary tone. "Run into Gramma Damie's room. Tell her some men are going through the house but there's no cause for her to fret. Stay and talk to her, so she won't be upset. Tie her cap and straighten her covers. Tell her I'll come to her as soon as I can."

The dining room offered as few possibilities as the kitchen and when Sparrow glanced at a closed door Mercy told him, "My mother is ill in that room. I assure you . . ."

"Now, Mi's Redmond, we ain't that cruel. To upset an old lady an' her sick abed!"

Then like a winter wind the men swept through the house; the middle room and the schoolroom above it, the spare rooms, the family bedrooms, music room and parlor, up stairs and down again, for there were no connecting doors between the upper stories of the three wings.

In the office they found Dan's wine closet and his personal

supply of wines and brandies—none of it bearing an excise stamp. They seized it gleefully; but Sparrow reminded them, "Not a drop in the bucket—an' not what I'm a-lookin' fer t' day."

Most rooms warranted the most cursory inspection, but Dan saw there was much tapping of walls and stamping on floorboards to locate "lost" spaces.

In the front wing's upper hall half the men went into the rooms on one side of the passage, half into the others. A cry came from the men who had entered Patrick's room and Sparrow was through the door in a flash. When Dan followed he saw the bed had been moved inside, the low door was blocked by a stooping searcher and the quilt provided for Josiah lay in a flung heap.

"Yes," Dan said, "that's where I hid Barry. You'll find nothing there, now."

Nevertheless, Sparrow bent through the small door to gauge the recess's dimensions. "I can see where he laid," he said as he withdrew his head, disappointed after the first hope of a discovery. "The marks is plain in the floor dust."

Adria's dainty room got only a glance and then the men were tramping down the front stairs. It did Dan's pride no good to see the admiring looks cast upon the broad stairway, the fine hall furnishings, the parlor's plush and gilt, the music room's piano. He was relieved to notice, however, that the men were all tiring of their fruitless search. They rummaged halfheartedly through the huge hall wardrobe, then stood awkward and embarrassed. As Sparrow moved towards the door Dan thought he read complete discouragement in the bowed legs under their baggy homespun.

But the little man paused in the doorway. He turned about and looked back up the stairs with their wine-red runner vivid against the white steps. He hesitated, his eyes screwed up in concentration, his mouth lost between nose and chin. His men stepped aside as he walked back into the hall with renewed determination.

He went straight to the shadowy angle formed by the floor and the stair-slope. He dropped to one knee and ran his hand

285

between baseboard and carpet's edge, then drew his breath in sharp. He folded the carpet back from the trap door. Two jubilant men clattered down into the abandoned cellar while the others crowded close above the opening. There followed scratching of matches, brief flickers, the sound of sullen boots ascending the stone steps.

Sparrow had found a hiding place, and Dan Redmond thanked his lucky stars for the uneasiness, the premonition, that had made him entreat Kiah's aid and move the contents of the old cellar.

Sparrow again paused in the open doorway, chagrined. "Well," he admitted, "I've found nawthin'. An' caused a heap o' heartache, I know. I mistrust you'm a-tellin' the truth as fur as Josiah's concerned; but most like I'll hafta come back."

Dan felt no triumph in the other's failure. It was insignificant beside his own. "Captain Smith," he said, "I've no hard feelings, but you'll excuse me if I don't see you to your boat today." He closed the door behind the departing searchers, then sat down heavily upon the bottom stair.

Mercy was still to be faced. *She'll never believe now that I meant to break away from the wretched smuggling. She'll know only that I've deceived her all these years. How can I tell her I put a drunken stabber into Patrick's room?* He sat a long time with his black head low in his hands.

Mercy had gone about her customary work, fighting off any pause that would allow memories and questions to rise. When dinnertime came she carried a tray to her mother. Captain Sam had gone to his wife's room when he came ashore from the *Didamia;* as Mercy neared the bedroom door his voice came to her, troubled but indistinct.

Her mother's words came clearer. ". . . and our names will be in *everybuddy's* mouth. I sh'l die o' shame an' never hold my head up again." Strangled sounds of Damie's weeping. Then, "Oh, Sam, take me away from here an' Dan Redmond's doin's. He means kindly to us, an' Mercy's the best o' dorters—but Sam! take me away."

"Where to, wife? Tell me where I can take you." Mercy had never thought to hear her father's voice so beaten, so piteous. "But don't fret, Damie. I'll see. I'll see what I can do."

Mercy stepped back unheard. She laid the tray upon the dining table and put her arm across her smarting eyes. *It's too much,* she grieved, *too much, that I haven't a home fit for my parents. Dan! Dan! To bring evil into our home.*

The man who had frightened Adria was tied up with Dan's lawlessness and, without conscious reasoning, she gave Dellie Watt and Hazelitt Morris their proper roles in the smuggling. Nausea threatened her while her heart ached and strained to cope with this added worry—this disgrace.

Later that afternoon the shocking pieces began to fall into a new pattern of life; the peace that follows a tremendous change and falsely promises this has been the ultimate break, eased her pain somewhat.

"Serena," she said, *"you* must have known. You must have noticed . . . things . . ."

Serena's eyes remained bleak, her tone flat. "I *could* 'a' knowed. But I thought it best fer you not t' suspicion an' if I didn't know, I wouldn't have ary thing t' blab."

Her thin lips closed on this rather baffling explanation, then reopened to admit, "When the' was muddy prints an' damp spots on the hall carpet of a mornin', I'd get 'em cleaned up quick, afore ye'd come acrost 'em. Yes, if I'd gone a-pokin', I *could* 'a' knowed. I won't deny I mistrusted."

How unseeing can mistaken loyalty keep one? Mercy wondered. *Did I willfully blind myself as Serena did?* She could recall no least suspicion. *Too trusting,* she accused herself. *Yet, if I couldn't trust my husband . . .* The despair of middle age is a dreary thing.

Now that I know, now that Dan will be heartrendingly penitent and humble, she thought wearily, *how am I to believe his protestations of regret? How honor a man who does such things?*

It was too much to think through now. Her bruised mind

refused to cope with the problems raised by the day's events, and onrushing time was to spare her the necessity of doing so.

Chapter 33

THE NEXT MORNING DAWNED BREATHLESS. A BRASSY SUN, STREAKED with verdigris, peered over the brow of Further Hill, then sulkily pulled the low overcast across its face. The sea lay like quicksilver; where the ledges broke its metallic surface it swirled about them heavily, with no gay splashes, no saucy leaps. Pilot Point loomed close and Narrah looked only a step away. Mainland sounds came strongly: wham-wham, a maul drove a fence post, clang-clang, a hammer shaped metal.

Uneasy swallows skimmed the grass; crows, foresightedly gorging, blackened the tide-line banks of rotting seaweed; gulls, pure white against purple-gray clouds, abandoned their accustomed coves and bars to swoop and swoon over Nigh Hill and Further, their raucous predictions grating upon the ear. Skipper curled himself into the darkest corner of the barn and slept. In all the long list of weather signs scarcely one that presaged a storm was missing.

The oppressive air sapped initiative and lowered spirits. Damie's ankle, paining abominably, made her irritable; the boys were, Serena vowed, possessed of the devil; and Waitstill in a black mood for no other imaginable reason than his customary responsiveness to the weather. Kiah went about his work, apparently unaffected; but Mercy glimpsed him halted midway to the barn, sniffing the rank air off the shore and scanning the four quadrants of the sky.

During the morning the quicksilver sea began to rise in long, slow mounds, still glitteringly metallic, though here and there a fine crest feathered whitely and subsided. When the mounds toppled upon the shore their rumble was hollow and menacing, and they worried the pebbles in ugly discontent.

The first puffs of wind, heavy and hot, brought no relief. However, they wafted closer a sail that had been hovering off the Cape, and this was recognized as the *Arthenese,* apparently heading for Redmond's Harbor. But near the point she veered off and lowered her boat, which came with swift glistening blades to the seaward shore, while a man in the stern beckoned with a swinging arm.

Will's long legs flew to meet him while Dan followed more leisurely. The boat backed in, the man in the stern passed something into Will's outstretched hand, then it pulled away strongly towards the waiting *Arthenese.* Will hastened to his father with the explanation of the boat's errand—the white oblong of a letter —in his hand.

"From Philip, Joe Amirault says. Captain d'Entremont can't tarry. He figures there's a gale behind all this." Will's gesture included the polished surges, the heavy air, the cloud streaks, the brassy smur to the westward. His handsome face was aglow with the excitement aroused by the coming storm.

At the moment Dan was not interested in the weather. He ripped the letter open, ran his eye across it and strode off eagerly to give Mercy its news. When he glanced back, before entering the house, the *Arthenese* was standing well out, homeward-bound ahead of the storm.

Dan led Mercy to a chair and laid the letter in her lap. Though neither of them had yet mentioned yesterday's search, all its implications stood between them, but through the barrier the bonds of family life, the ties of habit still held. "This will comfort you, my darling," he told her, his dark eyes humble and loving.

Philip had written from Boston:

Dear Mercy and Dan:

Tamsin is safe and well at her Aunt Molly's. I know with what fears and hopes you will open this letter so I write that first of all.

On my arrival I went at once to the waterfront, but the *Resolution* had not made port recently. On the second morning

I met Captain d'Entremont on Tea Wharf and he gave me great good news. This was, in short, that O'Shaughnessy Clark had got turned around in the fog and that he and Tamsin were aboard the *Arthenese* with Charlie's dory cast adrift before he discovered his mistake. He then put Tamsin in the small boat and hid himself among the deckload of barreled fish. Neither was found until the schooner was well outside the bay and it was too late to put back.

The captain gave Tamsin his cabin and sent Clark, as a stowaway, to earn his passage helping Cyriac, the cook. (It did me a world of good to hear that the galley smells made Clark violently ill.)

Clark confesses that the *Resolution* was bound for New York and not, as he had told Tamsin, to Boston where he had promised to have a second ceremony performed by a priest. Captain d'Entremont says, "Thank le bon Dieu for thick fog!" And I do thank Him.

I have secured a position as teacher and shall be staying in Boston, near Tamsin, for the present.

Wishing all on New Erin and Grannie's Head the Best the World can give, and More, I am,

Ever yours,
PHILIP.

P.S. Tamsin will be writing you fully. But Captain d'Entremont sails on the next tide and promises to drop this letter off at New Erin. May it set your minds at rest. P.

Mercy wept, great rolling tears of relief. She refolded the precious letter and smiled up at Dan through the tears. "I've been praying Philip would find her," she said simply.

Dan stroked her hair, too moved for speech.

When Mercy showed the letter to her mother, Damie cackled, "What did I tell ye? But when milady gits back home, I mean t' give her a piece o' my mind. Causin' all that upset—let alone the talk! Tsch! She might jest as well married Philip in the first goin' off."

Mercy's spirits lightened at the happy news of Tamsin, but the coming storm, recent stresses and impending events still pressed upon her. She dragged about, wan-faced and languid, drawing each breath with effort while perspiration dampened the heavy hair about her forehead. Serena, watching from the corner of her eye, muttered vicious denunciations of men and, to hide her worry, rattled dishes in a fine rinctum.

Mercy excused herself from dinner as being too tired and hot to eat; she would rest and have a cup of tea later. The terrible emptiness and strangeness that was Mercy's absence settled over the kitchen. Mercy did not come back. Instead, Serena, having slipped into the bedroom with a cup of tea, returned bleak-eyed and called Kiah aside.

Of their conversation the family heard only an impatient, "I *might* 'a' said October. The trouble is, Kiah Atwood, that *I* ain't the Lord."

Kiah spoke to Dan with a troubled air. "Serena here, she thinks I sh'd mebbe go fer the doctor."

When the two men stepped out they found the wind had freshened surprisingly and now held an insistent whine. Under it the long, leaden-sided swells had blackened and roughened.

Dan looked an apprehensive question.

"Oh, I figger I can make it, Mr. Redmond. Certainly. It's true I'd ruther have the new dory; but thyah, Josiah Barry's got *that*."

Dan's weary conscience stirred again.

"Not but what the sloop's an able boat, don't think she ain't," Kiah hastened to reassure him. "New calked an' tight as a cup."

As a sudden gust tumbled the harbor water viciously, Dan said, "Kiah, Mercy's *my* wife, my responsibility. I should be the one to go."

"That wouldn't make much sense, now would it?" Kiah asked reasonably. "T' leave Mi's Redmond a widder, mebbe, with young 'uns t' bring up alone.

"I ain't one t' brag—ye *must* give me that—but if any man can sail the *Katie* t' Barrin'ton t'day, I'm that man. Certainly."

291

He stepped down into the one-man sloop, and immediately his long awkward body became fluid strength. Pulling and pushing his boat along the spiles, he spoke matter-of-factly. "In a way I hate t' be aleavin' ye with a bad storm about t' break; but Cap'n Sam's faced many a blow an' Waits'l is able as ary man."

He looked up at Dan above him on the wharf and spoke with unwonted seriousness. "I'll make Barrin'ton afore night—if the Lord spares me. But when the doctor will git *here,* if this keeps up—well, that's another story." Kiah watched a black squall rip across the harbor, then finished what he had to say. "No matter what comes, Mercy will know I done my best fer her."

He bent then and Dan had the absurd feeling that he did so to hide something in his face. For the first time Dan wondered why Kiah, who so deeply loved the sea and the feel of a boat underfoot, should have contented himself all these years ashore on New Erin.

Meanwhile, in her bedroom, Mercy was preparing for her premature lyin-in. *It's so long since I've had a baby, this might almost be the first one.* Except, she thought wryly, gripping the bed's footboard until a knotting pain had passed, *except that I know what lies ahead.* She wiped the sweat from her face and tucked in a blanket.

When the wind struck the house a savage blow she went to the window overlooking the harbor mouth; by craning she could see a patch of the outer bay. It was frightening. *Kiah should never have set sail. He won't make Barrington before the heft of the wind strikes.* She recalled Kiah's unselfish devotion to her and hers from the first, but not yet would she let herself remember the black night when he had found her among the rocks.

It's useless to worry. We are all in God's hands. And His ways are good ways. Else we are no more than the flying blobs of curdled foam, dissolving in the wind. In the bosom of her dress was Philip's letter to prove that He cared for His own. Its arrival at this juncture was in itself a blessing. *If I am taken,* she thought, *I can go with my mind at rest about Tamsin.*

Mercy was too honest to deny to herself, whatever brave words she might find for Dan, that this accouchement was not normal. It reminded her of Adria's birth which had come near to costing both their lives. Dr. Whitehouse had arrived in time on that occasion, but it had been on a fine summer's day.

The storm increased with the dragging hours. Mercy walked the floor of her room or wandered to the windows of the deserted front wing, realizing, when her tortured body released her mind, that she had never seen this storm's equal.

Hill-like surges crossed the harbor mouth on their way to batter Grannie's Head and the steep end of Narrah. Not all ran past. Some, feeling their feet caught among the rocks off New Erin's point, swung in fury and roared down the harbor, smashing against the back of Long Wharf, sending their spray clear across the dock to stream down the wrinkled old face of the barrel shop and racing on to pound each miniature cape of the harbor shore. Sheltered Potato Point was a white welter.

Mercy knew a pang of fear at the thought of the high water, for the combination of storm and full moon inevitably meant disaster along the coast.

But before the high water, Mercy was caught in a tide of her own, an agonizing flood that bade fair to wash her away from this shore. Only Serena saved her from it. Serena's gnarled hands gripped her relaxing ones to pull her back; Serena's pale eyes held hers when she most wanted to drift with that tide.

In the kitchen, supper was dished up by a frightened Adria and eaten by the boys and Waitstill in an awkward silence. Captain Sam took his with his wife; Dan, after drinking a cup of tea without tasting it, pushed his chair back and went early to tend the lighthouse lamps.

When Serena did appear in the kitchen, she was unapproachable, as if for her the world held only herself, the enemy she had engaged and Mercy, for whom she fought. She told Adria briefly, "You'm most a woman growed; I'm dependin' on ye to keep the fire agoin' and the kittle full."

Waitstill, anxious to help, piled the woodbox and filled the coal hod. Then he asked for Dan's attention. "Mr. Redmond, ye know that flock o' sheep that's been tendin' on the southern p'int? Ain't they apt t' be washed away? I been a-thinkin' I could run 'em onto high land."

Returning from the lighthouse Dan had seen that, with three hours still to rise, the tide was already lipping the dike, was level with the planking of Short Wharf. "Why, yes," he said, "take Will and Charlie and run those sheep out of danger." Later he wondered how he could have given permission for them to leave the point; actually he had scarcely grasped what Waitstill proposed, for his mind had been with Mercy.

The three boys left with Skipper, huge and black, at their heels and Dan, closing shed doors against the night, paused to watch them fight their way over the hill behind the pond and disappear.

Soon after, Captain Sam decided, "Since Kiah's not here, I'll milk up while the boys are gone. Adria, you look in on your Grammie once in a while; the wind's beating right on her room."

He opened the door and Adria squeezed beside him, frightened and fascinated by the smoking seas.

"Grampy, where are all the vessels?" she asked. "In such a storm the harbor should be full; but there's only your *Didamia*."

Sam was grave. "The inshore fleets should be in home ports and fairly safe. The vessels on George's and Brown's, they've either anchored in hopes of riding it out, or they're running before it." His eyes went offshore. "It'll be breaking from bottom on the banks before this is over." His saddened voice conceded the storm and the outer banks their victims.

He turned to Adria more cheerfully. "Now run in, child, before the wind carries you away."

Through the window Adria watched him make his way towards the barn, twisting his body to form a windbreak for the three milk buckets over his arm, for the wind found their open mouths and filled them like sails to tug him off the boardwalk.

When Sam reached shelter in the barn doorway he paused to look across the harbor. Clouds pressed down upon the sea and mingled with the driven spray, rolling and wreathing and breaking like the waves beneath. However, the frenzied turmoil of the outer bay had not yet reached the harbor. There the wind was flattening the water with a heavy hand; blowing the tops off the seas that swung in around the point and slowing them with a vicious cross chop.

He set the pails carefully aside; stepped through the door and out again into the wind. Cows should be milked by lantern-light, but before darkness fell he must see how the *Didamia* fared. He and Kiah had planned to snug her down for the storm, but Mercy's need had pushed the schooner out of mind.

He made his way to the shore and stood watching the *Didamia* as she reeled, first to the gusty wind and then to the running seas. She looked pitifully forlorn, the sole vessel on the harbor's face, and left without a crew to fight her first battle with the elements. She was riding high, for the barreled herring and mackerel that would form the greater part of her cargo still lined Long Wharf. Captain Sam saw she was dragging a bit; she needed her second bower.

The boys had been aboard during the morning. They had rigged a knotted hawser to swing from the topsail yardarm and, white as a gull, first one naked body and then the other had arched outward, released its hold upon the rope and plummeted into the harbor; reappeared clambering over the stern to run forward again. No harm in that, he had conceded, watching; but he had thought, too, that long before he'd been the age of Will or Charlie his swinging aboard ship had been in dead earnest. The pit of his stomach had recalled suspensions over black water when he'd been certain the yardarm was bent upon thrusting him underwater—and leaving him there!

No, Mercy's boys hadn't been trained aboard a vessel; they might not have left things shipshape.

The *Didamia* lay not more than a hundred yards from the wharf end; the point was still holding back much of the swell; the island hills broke the fiercest squalls from the anchorage. The skiff was able, with a good man at the oars she'd do. *And,* he told himself with gentle mockery at his pride, *Sam Nicker-son's still a good man at the oars.*

It proved a longer row and a harder one than he had expected. *Could be you're getting old, Sam,* he told himself as he finally reached the lee of the schooner.

The *Didamia* was leaping nervously and shying from side to side, tossing her head against the hawser's clutch, straining to be free. Listening to the protest of new timbers, the lash of rope ends, the pounding of blocks, he thought, *A good thing I rowed out. A deal too much slatting and banging going on aboard.* From the foremast, just as he'd expected, a hawser swung with every pitch and roll of the schooner. It still had a loop for the boys' feet and higher up a knot to hold by.

He climbed aboard, paid the skiff off and made it fast. He moved forward, rubbing his feet along the boards to relish again the good feel of a leaping deck beneath him. Strange, though, how a short row tired him these days; he'd have to take a breathing spell. Then he'd make sure the hatches and scuttle were tight, and he'd drop the second anchor. The one now over seemed to have found holding ground for the moment, since he heard the snap of a tautening hawser, but it would need help when the tide rose and the mounting seas had their turn at the schooner.

He shouldn't be as dizzy as this, though the deck *was* tossing and slanting at such peculiar angles. He never used to be dizzy on shipboard. Come to think of it, he'd had a touch of vertigo ashore, too, this last while, ever since the *Didamia's* launching.

He thought back over that day and Nabby Nolan's curse. *All my life I've been one to laugh at witches and spells and such. I've put my trust in the Lord. And I still do. But Nabby, now. I don't know. I don't know.* His mind recoiled from memories of his burning home; instead he recalled the house as he had so often watched it, lingeringly, outward-bound, and with surging affection when the helm was for home.

Sad that a house like that, with all its memories of love and birth and death, of children's laughter and mother's tears, of warm beds and hearty meals—sad that these should lie under a heap of ashes. From little Adria, who loved to visit there, to

Gransir Will, who had ended his days under its roof, all the family, quick or dead, had suffered a diminution in its loss.

I haven't given a thought to Gansir Will for ages, Sam mused, *and yet I see him plain now, sitting in the sun, his long white hair falling over his coat collar, his hands folded upon his walking stick and his faded eyes always looking over the skyline. When I was but six or seven I asked him once if he saw anything 'way off there and he said yes, he saw Monomoy beach and Chatham harbor. That puzzled me, for I couldn't pick out a thing but ocean.* For a moment Captain Sam was again a baffled small boy. *When I asked Ma she said Gransir Will was using his mind's eye.*

And now, here I am using my mind's eye to look back, through time, upon my old home.

The *Didamia* returned him to the present by a violent plunge that flung a shower aft. *I must get for'rd, dizzy or not. Darkness is falling and Damie'll be fretting. Poor Damie. It thorns her to be tied abed by that ankle—and in another's home! As for me, I only ask that I'm not left to be a burden. Mercy has more than enough on her shoulders. Mercy. How is it going with her, poor girl?* He bowed his head in intercession for his daughter.

Standing in prayer on the deck of the straining vessel, with the roar of the wind and sea about him, Sam felt the anxieties of the last weeks drain from him; felt a resurgence of his old faith in the Great Plan and its fulfilment.

He put his hand on the mainmast's curve and felt it vibrate under the contact as might a high-strung horse; not to his touch, however, but to the wind in the rigging. The rising gale was shrilling aloft and howling about the lower spars. He thought again of the anchor and his schooner's peril.

But when he moved, the dull ache at his heart grew into an agonizing squeeze. For a few moments he clung to a stay and fought for breath before he dropped his hand and stepped forward. The heavy loop of the boys' swing cracked against his temple and he crumpled upon the clean deck. The first huge drops of rain fell like tears beside him.

Slanting rain-sheets and steaming drift drew a curtain between the shore and the beset *Didamia* as the fulling tide and mounting seas pushed the schooner back and again back. The anchor gave reluctantly, grabbing here and there until a swiping sea spun the vessel sidewise and tore loose its grip. Black night had fallen when the *Didamia* leapt to the first cruel stab of rocks beneath her; she was upon the outer rocks of Potato Point. Her new timbers splintered and snapped as breakers lifted and dropped her, lifted and dropped her, pounded her down, smashed her down, upon the obdurate granite.

As darkness settled Damie pulled herself up in bed and gazed through her window. The small frame limited her view to Clam Cove. But that was enough. "I never see sech a storm in all my remembering days," she said aloud and even above the rattling sash and the groans of the wind-tormented house her voice came back upon her ears strained and afraid.

"What's that passage from Jude?" she whispered. "Sam allus used t' say it, looking down from the kitchen windah when the surf was high. 'Raging waves of the sea, foaming out their own shame.' That was it. 'Foaming out their own shame.' "

Foaming out destruction, too! A monster, the sea. A devouring beast with a bottomless belly for ships and men. Ah, how she hated it. Hated and feared it. *Yes, I'm afeared this very minute,* she admitted and cowered down into bed again.

Where's Sam? Why don't he come t' comfort me? She thought of the long years when, with Sam at sea, every storm tore the very heart out of her breast; and of the blessed winter nights when her husband's big arm had encircled her as the wind howled.

She prayed, but the storm drowned her prayers. She wept weak tears that did not ease her worry. Yet why should she fret so, Sam was nowhere but out around the barn, or helping Dan and Kiah at some defence against the storm. She bemoaned her own helplessness. Finally she dozed when the wind would let her. Dozed and woke and dozed again, alone in her bed, in her shattered world that no longer held the loving heart behind the encircling arms.

Chapter 34

THE STORM PROVED TO BE A HURRICANE ESCAPED FROM TROPICAL bounds, a mad murderer that left a trail of battered coasts, of broken ships and drowned seamen from Cape Hatteras to Cape Race. Afterwards, when news of its toll seeped into Redmond's Harbor, Dan was appalled by its scope, but while it raged he felt its total fury converged upon New Erin.

The clock on the mantel said eight and the wind was hammering the house like a mighty, tireless fist when Captain Nickerson's continued absence finally broke through Dan's worry for Mercy in travail, for Kiah, who had sailed into the gale, for the boys beyond his help. He asked Adria, "Where did you say Grampy Sam went?"

Though her chin quivered, Adria's eyes—Ah, how like Mercy's gray gaze!—came to his straight. Dan thought, *She has Mercy's courage as well as her eyes,* while his daughter answered, "He took the milk buckets and went toward the barn."

"I'll look around," he told her. "I won't be gone long." Donning oilskins and sea boots, he put matches in an inner pocket and picked up an unlit lantern.

The wind tore the door from his hand and slammed it back against the outer wall as if to jerk it from its hinges. Rain drove across the kitchen and Adria sprang to shield the lamp lest flying drops break the chimney before her father could succeed in closing the door.

Dan struggled across the open spaces between outbuildings and gained the barn. Once inside the door, he lit his lantern and saw the milk buckets almost at his feet. Though he called and swung his lantern towards the black corners, there was no further sign of Captain Nickerson.

In the stable the cattle were dancing about and straining at their stanchions. Dan lifted the lantern level with the row of terrified eyes, sensing that the animals' distress was due to more than unrelieved udders. Something unusual in the sound of the stamping hooves caught his ear and, unbelieving, he hastened through the swinging door into the stable.

His lantern blinked back from the floor. Over the planking, climbing about the cattle's hocks, was a black line of water. Water? Then the sea must be breaking through the dike, swelling the pond to this unheard-of height. And the flood's peak not due for another hour!

A nervous heifer kicked frantically and fell on her side, her eyes rolling wildly as she struggled to be free of her stanchion bars. Panic swept the length of the stable.

Dan hung his lantern high, waded through the dirty water and threw back the bar of the outer door. It took his utmost effort to push the heavy door back between gusts. Then he released the terrified creatures one by one. Sliding and slipping, they poured out into the storm; he heard the wet ground sucking at their hooves as they turned the barn corner and were swallowed by the night. He hoped instinct would lead them to the safety of high ground. It did.

Dan stepped into the shallow water outside the stable door and the wind snatched the lantern from his hand. It flared briefly as it disappeared.

Somewhere behind the boiling clouds the full moon was rising and its gray diffusion showed him that a heaving flood had replaced the pond and pasture field. Where sheltered Clam Cove should lie he could detect the changing shapes of sluicing combers, the tearing white froth as seas rushed at each other and fell in mutual annihilation. He heard waves striking the shore in rolling thunder and recoiling with a rumbling suck of backwash. Along the outer reefs, seas exploded like a continuous salvo of mighty guns.

Dan turned from the scene's awful fascination and, because he could think of no other reasonable explanation, he told himself that Captain Nickerson must have gone to help Waitstill and the boys. This was a comforting thought, for they might well be in need of older counsel.

Back in the middle room he found the bedroom door still closed; Serena was not to be seen. In the kitchen he reassured Adria with the explanation by which he strove to calm his own uneasiness, "Likely Grampy Sam has the boys with him somewhere in a sheltered spot, until it's safe to start home."

Adria, close to the lamp whose flame flickered and bent to the draughts, was heavy-eyed but determined to fulfil Serena's trust in her.

"Lie down, dear," Dan told her. "Papa will keep the fire."

For a moment surprise washed sleep from her face. Serena declared Papa was the most useless man around a house that she ever did see, though Mama said it was because he had been brought up a gentleman. But *anybody* could put wood in a stove. And it *was* growing desperately hard to keep her eyes open.

Dan led her to the couch with tenderness; to Adria, so like her mother, he could implement some of the love and remorse he owed Mercy, and in this youngest daughter he had at last discovered an overlooked but precious treasure. He unfolded the quilt from the couch foot, tucked it about her and bent to kiss her forehead. Her childish arms came up strong and warm about his neck, her smooth face pressed his close for an instant; but Adria had none of Catherine's beguilement, none of Tamsin's merry, affectionate ways, she shyly turned away and lay still. Despite the outer pandemonium, she slept till morning.

On his way to the middle room Dan looked in at Damie's door to find her dozing with the lamp's unsteady flame picking out the defenselessness of her face.

How empty the middle room, and all the house! The sound of dripping water came from the office and Dan knew that every room, except this new and sheltered portion, would by now have its widening puddles on the floor, but he felt no urge to cope with those trivial manifestations of the storm.

He wished for a cheerful fire on the hearth, but an earlier

attempt at lighting one had meant blown-back smoke and ashes. As he glanced at the fireplace he saw that even the middle room had its puddle where rain had flowed down the chimney and seeped across the floor.

The hours dragged while Dan listened to the wind's wild beating and prying, its strangled cry in the chimney. To the heaviest gusts the house moved as if its feet had slipped and given ground in a mighty wrestling, but it immediately braced itself and strained in every timber to hold firm. The room, like the world outside, was filled with the sound of crashing seas and shrieking winds, yet above, or through, the tumult he caught an occasional cry or muffled groan from behind the closed door of Mercy's room.

So suddenly that his ears ached with the quietude came the storm's first lull. Dan again donned oilskins and struggled out into the night, and this time he turned towards the point.

The ragged clouds rode higher now; by the moon's brighter light he could see (now that the pressure of the wind was lifted) how the released seas and swollen tide ravaged the helpless island.

Out of the bay's chaos a monster sea rose and rose above the level of the land on which he stood. He held his breath and looked for something solid to grasp, for such a mass must overwhelm the point. But the glimmering ridge, the abysmal black trough, the white-fleeced flank, were bound down the harbor between the restricting shores of Narrah and New Erin. As it passed him the mass leaned forward, leaned and leaned then, all at once, toppled in a roaring avalanche of effulgent white that spread and raced on to disappear along the shaken shore. It was followed by another and another, endlessly.

Through the flying spray and clotted foam that whirled across the point, Dan glimpsed a ruby glimmer. *Ah! The brave little light tower stands.* Enheartened by its steadfastness, he turned back towards the wharves.

The lull was over. A mighty thrust of wind struck him; rain streamed swiftly after and blotted out the sliding hills of harbor water. But not again would wind and rain flatten the surges;

these now embodied the storm's full impetus and the tide's utmost force; no shallow seas from the bay, these billows came swinging in from the heaving Atlantic.

Bent almost double, Dan struggled into the wind, whose exultant howls again mingled with the roar of exploding water. He stumbled against the graded terrace and swung around towards the wharves and stores, but before he gained the inner end of the icehouse he was stopped short by a line of foam and swirling water.

The seas, he knew then, were breaking clean across the wharves. He caught the sound of battering logs and loose planks slapping. The old barrel shop must be gone, the rows of herring and mackerel barrels awaiting shipment must be washed away. He dared hope new and strongly built Long Wharf would hold, but no effort of his could affect its fate. Utter helplessness gave him a singular detachment from the ruin surrounding him.

He was scarcely back in the kitchen when Serena appeared, silent and haggard-faced. She filled a pitcher from the kettle and turned to leave, apparently unaware of Dan's imploring face; but at the door she paused. "Mi's Redmond seems t' be holdin' her own fer a time." Neither her tone nor her expression was encouraging. As a surge of wind struck, she said (as if she, too, felt the need of friendly words), "The poor house is takin' a cobbin' t'night, Mr. Redmond," and shook her head in commiseration at its plight.

Dan, grateful for a crumb of companionship, answered, "The whole island is badly pummeled, Serena." He pushed back any mention of the boys on the exposed southern shore. "If only the storm had struck on a neap tide. High water was due at nine, but at midnight when I was out the tide was still rising. As if it would never ebb."

Serena lifted the latch. "Pray that it don't. For my part, I dread the turn o' the tide this night." The door closed behind her.

It's as bad as that, then. Serena fears Mercy's soul may go out on the ebb. Dan dropped into a chair and laid his weary head upon the table. His lips repeated half-forgotten prayers.

The squalls lessened in intensity, the lulls lengthened, the rain no longer struck in horizontal sheets. Dan tended the kitchen fire and returned to the middle room. In spite of his anxiety, he dozed in his chair.

The southeasterly had worn a cloak of spray and foam-gobs, a veil of spindrift. Now came a naked wind out of the north. It hit like a giant's sledgehammer. The nearly empty icehouse collapsed then; Dan heard a vast tearing as the roof lifted.

At the time the sound lacked meaning, for simultaneously Serena opened the bedroom door and brought him to his feet. Gray dawn outlined her weary figure and blurred her features, though her face showed ravaged. Dan wiped his forehead of fear's cold drops.

"It's over. Mercy's alive but yer little girl was born dead." Serena put her hands upon the table and sagged briefly upon them. Looking up, she saw pity on Dan's face. "No call t' worry over me, now!" she said sharply, then drooped again. "But, Mr. Redmond, fer onct I'm swonked." She looked it.

Dan forgot her bleak tongue, her sour belittling of men which often rubbed him sore; he saw only a woman spent by her efforts to save a loved one—hers and his. He laid his hand on her narrow, bony shoulder, the first time he had ever done so. "Serena," he said, "I can't begin to tell you what it's meant to have you here tonight."

She straightened her shoulders, gave her red eyes a hasty swipe with an apron corner and was herself again. "I'm afeared things ain't jest as they should be with yer wife. Ye'd best come." She led him into Mercy's room, neither of them conscious of the quivering house or of the thunderous surf surrounding the island.

Mercy, emptied of pain, lay light and whitened as a tossed shell on some far, misty shore. She was faintly aware of Dan bending above her, of his tender hand holding hers. Or holding the hand of the figure upon the bed; she herself was floating above them both, remote, beyond need to respond to his imploring fingers.

"Mercy, my dear one," Dan's broken voice came up to her. "Don't slip away. Stay with me, beloved, stay." His stricken face would not let her seek the sweet rest that beckoned.

"Dan, dear, . . ." She tried to smile. Her hand went limp. Dan's chest contracted upon his stopped heart.

Serena leaned her cheek over the parted lips. She lifted a transfigured face. "Why, she's fell asleep! Natural-like."

Dan tiptoed away and a few minutes later stepped out into the blurred outlines of a still-beleaguered but dawn-lit world.

Chapter 35

DAN SHIVERED TO THE NORTHERLY'S KEEN EDGE, AFTER THE NIGHT'S sultriness, but he found that except in the strongest gusts he could now stand upright without difficulty. The hollow resonance of overfalls, the roar of confused waters came from the outer reefs where the ebb had dragged them, but the north wind had already curbed seas and tide; they would not repeat the night's excesses.

The gray light showed a desolated New Erin. A line of seaweed, broken shells and tangled driftwood marked where the rapacious flood had licked at the terrace before falling back to leave its flotsam across front yard and fields.

Directly before Dan the inner end of the icehouse stood with a corner of roof clinging raggedly to it, as a torn scalp might dangle over a forehead; the other three sides, now broken and buckled slabs, lay razed nearby.

It was when he had worked his way through the broken sections of fish flakes blocking the path and stood looking out across the dock that he grasped the full ruin wrought by coupled wind and sea. All that remained of Short Wharf was the inner blocking with rocks spewing out of broken logs. The barrel shop might never have been, but a few barrels rolled in the wash at tide-edge while others, with broken staves like snag teeth, lay spilling pickled fish over the greensward upon which they had been flung; but awash or aground, all were ruined. With its outer underpinning washed away, the fish store clung drunkenly to the shore, but a black line at shoulder height showed where the tide had found and spoiled the carefully dried and piled cod, ready for the Boston market.

Across the dock a similar line marked the warehouse on Long Wharf, but the wharf's outer end (battered and swept clean) had survived. Between warehouse and greensward, however, was a great gap lined by jagged timber ends and tumbled rocks through which the tide had manifestly raced. Dan's well for smuggled liquor was gone, taking its blocking and the barrels that had disguised it.

In the ebb-bared portion of the dock planks and wharf timbers lay tossed like a petulant giant's discarded jackstraws; the outer end was a heaving carpet of seawrack and broken boards.

Among the age- and water- darkened pieces gleamed bits of new wood and upon the harbor face were more of these, tossed and flung by the incoming seas; they puzzled Dan briefly. Then, among the swashing tangle off the wharf end he sighted what was unmistakably a vessel's hatch, a new one. *Some poor schooner,* Dan mused, saddened, *caught out in last night's . . . My God! The Didamia!*

He brought his eyes up to the harbor face but, so determined were they to reflect again the *Didamia* in her accustomed place, for a few seconds they refused to focus on the terrible emptiness. Then he saw a broken bow section on Potato Point and, awash, a long section of neatly treenailed hull. Dan knew then why Captain Nickerson had not returned to milk the cows. Knew so surely that when the time came he walked directly to the crumpled body with one arm flung among the storm-wilted stalks of the potato patch and with the timbers of the *Didamia* about it.

Now the knowledge that Captain Nickerson had not been

with his grandsons heightened Dan's anxiety for them. The boys should be on their way home; if they did not soon come he must go in search of them. Was there no end to the storm's havoc? "Not Will and Charlie," he moaned, and knew, by a thousand rushing memories, their place in his life and heart.

Fear hurried him, but when he turned the front wing he saw at the kitchen door three bedraggled boyish figures and a drooping Skipper. The sun could not have chosen a better moment to top Further Hill and pour its morning gold across fields and buildings.

In the kitchen Dan found Adria stirring the breakfast porridge. Her braids were tousled, her eyes heavy, but she was doing what she could for her menfolk. Dan was aware yet again of all Mercy had given him, of how much of her would abide with him in their children, even if she were taken.

The boys were subdued, stiff with wet and cold and matured by their encounter with the elemental world, with the starkly merciless storm.

"I thank God to see you safely home again, boys. I should never have let you go in such a storm. You must tell me about how you spent the night, but first of all, change into dry clothes and come get your breakfast."

At the door Charlie paused. "Papa," he said, his voice showing his dread, "is Mamma . . .? How is she? All night I was thinking about her."

"I knew you would be, son. She's not well, but Serena says she's resting until the doctor gets here."

Later all three boys sat down gratefully to bowls of porridge, bread and butter, wedges of pie set out by Adria. Now that they were back in the familiar kitchen they could belittle the night's discomforts and fears, and laugh a bit tremulously.

They had found a flock of some fifty sheep threatened by the rising tide and with Skipper's help had finally succeeded in driving or dragging the last of the frightened, stupid creatures to high land and safety. By then, seawalls were covered, swamps awash, and darkness had fallen so that they dared no attempt to reach the house; but finding a thicket of young spruce had huddled in its partial shelter through the long night of lashing wind and rain and seas that shook the island. With dawn's first faint light they had started for home.

"Did you know the dike was breached in two places?" Will asked, "and all the water out as if the sluice were raised?"

"I'm not surprised," his father replied and told the boys of the black water over the stable floor. "The pond may be empty now but at the full tide last night it was a lake that reached the foot of Nigh Hill."

"It was a horrid night, Mr. Redmond," Waitstill assured him with simple matter-of-factness. "With the foam-gobs a-flyin' and the wind comin' at us and the seas tearin' the island t' pieces."

It frightened Dan even now to think of the boys cut off from all help, and he praised their good sense that had made them endure the storm rather than attempt to win home over the flooded paths. "I couldn't leave and wouldn't have known where to look for you." Then hoping against hope, he asked, "Grampy Sam wasn't with you? You didn't see him?"

"No." Charlie's eyes were extraordinarily blue in his white face as they went to his father's. "No, we never saw Grampy Sam."

"I was afraid not." His voice told them more than his words. "I'd like to say, 'Go to bed and sleep,' but before high water I must have your help. The *Didamia* dragged her anchor during the storm; this morning she's nothing but broken bits along the shore."

The last color drained from his sons' faces. They knew what manner of task demanded their help.

Dan left the kitchen, thankfulness at his sons' and the faithful Waitstill's safety now overlaid with shrinking from what lay ahead. If Kiah could go beside him to search the shore! He looked across the bay, but although the northerly had moderated to little more than a high wind, a glance killed any hopes of Kiah's immediate return. *Return,* if he had ever made a landing.

Before he left the house he must inquire again how Mercy was faring. As he passed Damie's door he heard Serena making an embarrassed effort to sooth, and Damie's weary complaints after the night of fear. He knocked and Serena poked her head around the door. "Oh, it's you," she said flatly.

"Yes," Dan replied. "How is Mrs. Redmond?"

"She's a-restin'," and Dan knew by the finality with which Serena closed the door that she was retreating into her old abrupt ways to repudiate any emotion shared during the night's ordeal.

He left the house with the quiet boys. Outside the sun was brilliant, the air fresh and rain-washed, the ocean reaches sparkling. Up the bay the crested breakers were marching like an army with a thunderous measured tread, their proud white banners backward streaming. The north wind met each with a volley that slowed them perceptibly, but they curved forward, pressed on and flung themselves into foaming dissolution. Their beauty was superb but Dan knew what malevolence was at their core; he was sated with the sight and sound of breaking seas.

In contrast to the bay the harbor, though it was flecked with whitecaps, lay comparatively peaceful, escaping the brunt of the seas running past its mouth to batter Grannie's Head, and sheltered from the wind by the mainland hills and Narrah.

Over New Erin lay a strange light, or so Dan thought for an instant before he saw that all the vegetation, which yesterday was lush, now showed sere and brown; alders, bayberry and raspberry bushes, the clumps of blue flag, the reeds edging the swamps, the grass itself, all had been blighted and burned by the spray-laden blasts.

New angles along the outer edges of the copses he had nurtured so carefully showed outer trees uprooted and flung aslant those still erect. Only the huge granite blocks atop Further Hill kept their familiar outlines against the sky.

Dan was numbed now by the accumulating weight of changes. He began to wonder when he would wake and find again the sun across the placid harbor, the *Didamia* nodding at her reflection, the island resting after summer's fruition.

The boys said nothing as they saw for the first time the havoc at wharves and dock. Truly it was beyond words. They moved along the dockhead silently, their minds upon their grim errand, their eyes upon the wreckage lining Potato Point.

Dan turned to them. "Wait here, boys. I'll call you if I need you. It may be I'm mistaken . . ."

"No," Charlie interrupted positively. "Grampy Sam would go to his schooner."

Dan had scarcely left them when he heard Will's shout and saw his arm pointing down the harbor. A white slab of sail was tacking among the islets and ledges of the lower harbor. He hurried back to the dock.

"The *Katie!*" Charlie called.

Dan breathed, "Kiah with the doctor, thank God!"

Waitstill shook his head. "No, not the *Katie,* but a sloop o' her build."

They rigged a hasty walk of planks across the gap at the head of Long Wharf and were waiting at the wharf end when the sloop drew alongside. They saw Sparrow Smith at the tiller and Dr. Whitehouse huddled against the mast.

The physician was a rotund man who wore a pepper-and-salt beard that distinguished him from his clean-shaven or whiskered neighbors. He was given to cogitations in a mumbling half-tone and was quite at home in a community that cherished its eccentrics. When he stepped ashore, stiff from hours braced against the mast, Dan greeted him eagerly, "I hadn't dared expect you today, Doctor."

"Now, you know I've always said I'd go when a boat and crew would take me," he returned cheerfully, shaking his wet clothes into place like Skipper freeing himself from water.

"Kiah?" Dan asked. "He must have made Barrington safely, then?"

"Well, not altogether, not altogether. Seems he had to drive the sloop ashore 'bout two miles this side of Barrington. The *Katie* can be patched up. So could Kiah, so could Kiah. He broke two ribs and sprained his arm when she struck and he

310

jumped for shore. But he made it, he made it. I fixed him up. He wanted to bring me back but I didn't want him stove in a second time. I thought it might be a rough passage."

"*Might* be!" Dan ejaculated.

"Well, yes, 'twas just as I thought, just as I thought. We *did* bounce around some. Anyway, Sparrow came to Kiah with word he'd borrowed a sloop and figgered he could make it up the inner passage if I had a mind to come, so Kiah was content with that.

"Never made such a trip." The doctor shook his head and looked back wonderingly at the way he had come. "A rough passage," he repeated as if the words held new meaning for him. "Once when the Thrums gave us a bit of lee and I could make myself heard, I asked Sparrow why he had come. A doctor, well, you know a doctor . . ." His voice trailed off indistinctly. "Sparrow says Mrs. Redmond's a good woman and he feels some to blame. Some to blame, he says."

Sparrow had stepped ashore and he heard this last with embarrassment. He interrupted, "I see the *Didamia's* broke up. A blow t' Captain Sam."

Dan replied heavily, "I'm afraid Captain Nickerson was aboard when she went, or was lost rowing out to her."

Sparrow's eyes went swiftly over strewn wreckage to the main section of the high-tossed bow, and came back bleakly to Dan's face.

"I would be glad of your help as I search the shore, Captain Smith; it's a hard job for lads." Their eyes went to the grouped boys who were scanning the sloop.

"Aye-ah, be glad t' help."

The doctor, who had pursed his lips at Dan's words, now said soberly, "Cap'n Nickerson will be sadly missed along the shore; a stanch backstay to more than the Cove."

Then he rubbed his hands, picked up the black bag at his feet, said briskly, "Now about your wife, Mr. Redmond, your wife," and set off up the wharf, keeping his eyes upon the treacherous seaweeds bestrewing the planks. Dan told him what he could

311

of Mercy's condition and the bearded lips mumbled over the information.

Abruptly he changed the subject, "Mrs. Damie, now? How did that ankle get? Still abed? I'll look in on her before I leave. A woman after my own heart, Mrs. Damie. But Sam's going will hit her hard. Hit her hard." His voice trailed off again.

Dan left the doctor in the cluttered sickroom where Mercy lay still and white, frighteningly quiet, and went again to the shore.

He found Sparrow Smith gazing down into the gap at Long Wharf's head. The rising tide was pounding broken casks and broached kegs against the crumbling cribbing, and bottles bobbed amongst the conglomeration covering the waters of the dock. The fumes of spirits rose above all else. At last Sparrow had discovered the ingenious hiding place which had "diddled" him so long. He look up as Dan neared him, "Man dear," he said reproachfully, " 'twas a sin and a shame t' weaken a good wharf that way!"

"Yes, I see that now," Dan admitted. Then he added, "You have evidence aplenty before you, Captain Smith," and was surprised at how little he cared.

Sparrow rubbed his hooked nose vigorously, drew forth a bandanna and blew into it a tremendous blast. "This danged cold," he snuffled, and his pale eyes met Dan's innocently. "Can't smell nawthin'. Ain't been able to fer weeks—well, days, anyway. Can't see noan too good, neither; head all stuffed up, eyes running water." He cut off his barefaced lies with the familiar movement of nose and chin.

It was then Dan decided he would never understand these Nova Scotians.

Sparrow spread his thin lips, showing what stubs of teeth he possessed. "Meant t' tell ye, Cap'n John Kenney sighted jest sech a dory as ye described t' me. Off the Cape 'twas. I guess you was speaking truth after all, an' I misjudged ye. Looks like Josiah Barry might be aboard a Yankee b' now, and since young

312

Ensign's a-gettin' better—well, I guess they can have him, fer all o' me."

To this Dan gave unqualified agreement.

Sparrow's next words startled him. "They tell me that Haze-litt Morris has levanted; skipped out the night Josiah Barry was landed here. And left Dellie Watt holding the bag—so they say. You might know already, an' I don't want t' add t' yer worries," he broke off apologetically.

Dan pushed the disturbing news to the back of his mind for the time being.

They found Sam Nickerson's body in the wreckage of his *Didamia*. Dan brought a sail and with Sparrow's help wrapped the broken frame and covered the battered face. On one of the schooner's splintered hatches the men and boys carried into the front hall the empty and discarded shell of the man they had all loved.

They stepped out again into the sunshine and Charlie, looking over the strewn water towards Potato Point and the broken sections of the *Didamia's* hull, said almost in a whisper, "She never did wet her jib, did she? And she drowned the only man aboard. Just like Nabby Nolan said."

He turned guiltily at a sound from Waitstill. The witch's son awkwardly covered his stricken eyes in the crook of his arm and wept.

"Aw, Waits'l, I forgot about you. Nobody's blaming *you*," Charlie said remorsefully and laid his hand upon the crooked arm.

Dan said, "Let him cry, Charlie. He has lost a kind friend. Let's leave him alone, now."

To Damie, cowering in her bed, Dan's approaching feet were hushed and solemn. Damie knew that sound; it announced death. She knew what tidings were coming to her.

It was pitiful to see how a night and a morning had shrunk Damie. Dan took the trembling hand, workworn for love of her husband and his children; he thought that now it could do no

313

more for that husband, not even prepare his body for the grave. He gave her his news gently.

"Oh, I knowed. I knowed."

She moved her head and her lips found the words of the Psalmist, "all thy waves and thy billows are gone over me." But her spirit was still too stanch to be quenched completely by the flood. She clutched at Dan's hand. "Mercy," she said, "Mercy and her baby?"

"The baby was born dead," he told her. "And Dr. Whitehouse is with Mercy now." Then for the first time he gave the precious title to this little woman so different from his remembered mother. "I think she will be spared to us, Mother."

Weak tears formed under the wrinkled lids and ran down the grooved cheeks. Dan put her veined hand gently on the counterpane and left her for a time.

Whenever women of the district compared notes there were shared smiles for Dr. Whitehouse's sparse and unvarying bits of advice, as familiar as his raw-boned nag and the piled bearskins of his winter rig. He encouraged each laboring mother with, "Remember all things come to an end," and when time had proved this truth and released him, he would pause at the door of the confinement chamber and with a nod towards the new arrival adjure the midwife, "Keep it well wrapped. Remember, babies come from a warm country, a warm country."

Leaving Mercy's room, he paused with his hand upon the latch. This baby could not be swathed against the cold. His brown eyes lost for a moment their customary inward gazing, the lips above the graying beard were curved. "Serena," he said, "Mrs. Redmond owes you her life. You're a fine woman, a fine woman." He slid through the door and was gone.

"My lands!" Serena gasped, upset at this aberration from ritual. "It's true what people tell, then. Dr. Whitehouse *is* a-gettin' queer. Sayin' a thing like that t' *me!*"

When the doctor rejoined Dan and Sparrow at the wharf, the wind had moderated and the sea died down.

Sparrow turned to Dan. "We must take advantage of the ebb.

314

Be ye sure ye can make out with the boys? I can come back fer a day."

Dan thanked him warmly. "I wish I had words . . ." he went on.

"Man dear, what good is words?"

"What good, indeed. Except to tell you this. You need never come to New Erin as revenue man again. My smuggling days are done. Believe me. But I shall be proud to welcome you as a friend."

Sparrow beamed. "Ye'll be a-seein' me," he promised happily. "Now, Dr. Whitehouse, I can promise ye a smoother trip than what ye had a-comin'."

He hoisted the sail, swung his tiller and went racing down the harbor with his sail full and the ebb under his keel.

At the house Dan slipped into his wife's room. He stood looking down at Mercy as if for the first—or the last—time. Now that her features had lost the coarsening of pregnancy's last months, he saw restored the Mercy he had loved at sight. He saw, too, the gray in the heavy braids, the sharper features now bloodless and refined by suffering. He saw the blue veins at her temples, in the lids with the bronze lashes that veiled her eyes.

Mercy roused at his gaze, put a hand up feebly and asked, "Dan, the storm? Your boats, your wharves. Have you . . . lost much?"

"Nothing that matters, mavourneen."

Serena gave him a long stare and a grim nod of approval. *It took a hurricane and Death anigh to learn him, but Dan Redmond's gettin' some sense at last.*

Chapter 36

Over New Erin the October sun poured its memories of summer's richness, its threat of winter's bitterness. Though the air outside was mild, a small fire seethed and crumpled in the middle room fireplace, for Mercy, still weak, felt the need of warmth. Dan, across the hearth, was thinking that just to have her once more in her rocker before the fire made the room alive and rich. Mercy herself was achingly conscious of her empty arms, the arms that would never again hold a baby of their own. The children would soon be grown and gone, there would be only herself and Dan as there had been only they two at the start. This reminded her of her mother bereft of her mate after all the years and, giving swift thanks that she and Dan still had each other, she lifted her face to his.

It was a thin and colorless face but the large gray eyes were soft and clear. Her hands lay in her lap, strangely idle and pitifully thin, yet still bespeaking their intrinsic strength and capacity for service. Dan remembered their invigorating pulse against his own, their healing in sickness.

Mercy held one up ruefully, "So useless, Dan! But I shouldn't complain. The work gets done without my hands." She folded them resignedly. "Everyone has been good to us, Dan, in our trouble."

Dan agreed. Neighbors, for a time alienated by Dan's traffic in liquor, had rallied loyally. Perhaps they felt God's hand had been sufficiently heavy upon him and, remembering their own trespasses, had shown pity and understanding not apparent (or needed) during his prosperous days. In the home the boys and Adria had turned to with a will, outdoors Kiah and Waitstill had redoubled their efforts, while Damie . . .

"Your mother is a valorous soul, Mercy," Dan gave honest praise. "She does most of the cooking, propped up on one leg—claiming Serena has more to do than one pair of hands can 'cooper.' She scolds that the house is poorly laid out for women-folks and I can see she's right. I'd always planned, Mercy . . ."

"Oh, no, Dan," she begged him. "I wouldn't want a board or a nail changed. It's all so precious to me now, so filled with our life together. I used to think perhaps . . . But not now. And soon I can come to meals and save steps."

"No one begrudges caring for you, Mercy, after the years

when you spent yourself for us all. I suspect Serena revels in your dependence upon her. I was merely paying tribute to your indomitable mother."

Damie deserved tribute.

When the first realization of complete disaster had broken through Dan's numbness after the storm and his joy in Mercy's survival, he had thought sadly, *No Captain Nickerson to help me out of this mess.* Later, hoping to please Damie, he had voiced this regret.

She had shown the first signs of returning spirit. "Shame on yer whinin', Mr. Redmond. Ye've got Sam's dorter an' ye've got his grandchildren. They must 'a' heired some of his gumption. An' ye ain't the fust man t' be wiped out an' t' start afresh —even at fifty."

Cove talk had come to New Erin, dark talk of firing Nabby Nolan's house, of tar and feathers. Damie had declared to visiting neighbors, "Sam would never rest in his grave if harm was done on his account. He used t' claim that Nabby never had no chance t' be different from what she was an' wasn't all t' blame." She added with truth and dignity, "As fer her curses, the's no curse can hurt me now. If she could put me in my grave beside Sam, I'd thank her kindly."

When Mercy had proudly commended her for this attitude, Damie had replied, "Grouty an' sharp as I be by nature, I couldn't 'a' lived all those years with a man like yer pa without soakin' in some of his goodness." Then her face had crumpled. "But, Mercy! I pray the Lord t' take me soon. Without Sam I'm nawthin'. Nawthin'."

Dan's chief regret was that he had not been given time to prove his resolve to break away from the smuggling. He told Mercy now, "I meant to; I'd have found a way, Mercy, once you were strong enough to be left alone. It would have pleased Captain Nickerson to see me quit of it." He added in self-condemnation, "The consequence of that business brought you to Death's door and lost us a child."

"That's not for us to know. Remember Pa's belief that all

317

things work to fulfil a great and proper Plan. You may have brought some of your trouble on yourself, as you say; but, Dan, you can't be held responsible for the worst gale this shore remembers."

She asked sympathetically, "Just how bad are things with you? I know you've suffered heavy losses." Would he resent her interest? Rebuff her as he had done in the past?

Dan was eager to share everything with his wife again, but it was difficult to convey a picture of the general disruption and demolition. "The dike's smashed, the icehouse flattened," he began. "Those two things we must repair this fall if we are to hold the schooners' trade. All the summer's fish, barreled and dried, is lost. Short Wharf must be replaced from its bottom timbers up."

He paused and watched her face. "But there's more and worse news. Shall I wait until you are stronger?"

Mercy smiled at this masculine notion that she might rest and grow stronger with calamity awaiting disclosure. "Wouldn't you rather tell me, Dan?"

"I'd like to," he admitted. "I stayed with you this afternoon to talk while we were alone."

He seemed uncertain of how to begin. "Well, first of all—the *Bluebell* was lost in the gale."

Mercy's swift pity rose. "The crew? Captain Hines?"

"All lost. In the storm she tried to cross the bar into Hines's Harbor. No boat could get to her and she went to pieces almost at once."

"Poor souls!" Mercy felt her eyes filling for the lost men, the widows and orphans. She said softly, "I remember the look on Captain Hines's face as he patted Adria—that first night when all this trouble had its start—afterwards we decided she reminded him of his own girl."

"Every one says he was good to his daughter." This commandation was the utmost Dan could muster for Dellie Watt Hines, who had come to represent for him all the most ignoble in the repented partnership. He brought the conversation back to his own affairs. "The loss of the *Bluebell* was a blow to me,

318

as well. You see, I was half-owner of her as I was of the *Pride of Erin*."

"There'd be insurance on the *Bluebell*," Mercy suggested.

"There should have been but there wasn't. I'd paid Hazelitt my share but he pocketed it and so the *Bluebell* was a complete loss. A few days before the storm," he continued, "the *Pride of Erin* was seized with a contraband cargo. Captain Hines must have known but didn't tell me, when he was last in."

Mercy sounded puzzled. "Surely Hazelitt should bear most of these losses."

"He will bear none of them," Dan said savagely. "Two days before the storm Haze Morris skipped out to the States."

"Skipped out! Then Catherine . . . She'll be coming home to us?" Mercy's voice betrayed how eagerly she would welcome her daughter.

"No, Catherine went with him. They'll not be in want, Mercy," he continued bitterly, "for Hazelitt had turned everything possible into cash and has taken my share and Captain Hines's with him, leaving the debts. Captain Hines is beyond the law, and I am left to pay. I've been a fool, Mercy, and worse than fool, to trust a man I knew in my heart to be a scoundrel.

"How could Catherine have loved him, Mercy? It must have been only for his money. Now she has helped him run off with mine—for they say she aided his plans in every way. In spite of her beauty," Dan's voice nearly broke, "only her hair—my mother's hair, which came to her through me—only it is warm."

"Dan, my dear," Mercy sought to excuse Catherine, knowing her deflection had dealt Dan the deepest hurt of all. "She may not have known all. And her place is with her husband. But," she admitted, "Catherine *is* cold. I've long known it. And known the blame is mine. I marked her when I carried her under a stony heart. I've often thought a blemish on her perfect body would have been better than the one I left on her soul."

"You mean because of our old . . . misunderstanding," Dan grasped her meaning only after an effort. "Oh, no, Mercy!"

She sat with sad, firm lips and darkened eyes; she would never

319

feel free from the guilt of Catherine's deficiencies. "Yes, Dan. I did wrong to harbor a hurt and a grudge because you didn't balance the scales I had for you."

Dan would not agree. "Always, Mercy, your scales proved right. I fell short in my early pride and extravagance, my attempt to force your religion, and worst of all, in the smuggling. I knew it would lower me in your eyes—that your scale would show my loss of true value—or I'd never have hidden it so carefully from you."

He looked into her eyes and Mercy saw that his headstrong pride had been replaced by self-assessment and an even stronger humility. "It took a hurricane," he continued, "to reveal the weakness of what I'd been building, to show me that the enduring thing is your love for me, and mine for you."

He left his chair and came to kneel beside her. Mercy, turning his face up to hers, noticed the lines about the deep blue eyes, the gray among the black hair that curved away so endearingly from brow and ears.

"Do you remember the night your father brought me home?"

She smiled down at him tenderly. Remember!

"During the evening I wakened to hear him reading to his family. At first the words came from a long way and across troubled waters to me. Then the last ones reached me clearly. 'He bringeth them unto their desired haven.' Mercy, that's what you have always been for me, my port and refuge. No matter on what far voyages I left you, you were, and are, my 'desired haven.'"

Mercy had a swift picture of New Erin's harbor with the vessels riding out the storms, and she felt her love like deep and quiet waters. Dan was a stanch craft, if apt to pay off before the winds of ambition and pride. But a perfect ship that could weather any storm would need no port. *I never wished to be the star to steer by, the wind in the sail, the hand on the helm.*

She leaned and laid her lips against her husband's. "What more could I ask," she told him tenderly, "than to be my beloved's 'desired haven'?"

320